# EARNING
# ETERNITY

# EARNING ETERNITY

by

Josi S. Kilpack

BONNEVILLE BOOKS™
Springville, Utah

ISBN: 1-55517-473-6
e. 3

Published Bonneville Books

Distributed by:

Cover design by Lyle and Sheila Mortimer
Cover design © 2000 by Lyle Mortimer

Printed in the United States of America

Library of Congress Cataloging-in-Publication Data

Kilpack, Josi S.
  Earning eternity / by Josi S. Kilpack.
        p. cm.
   ISBN 1-55517-473-6 (pbk. : alk. paper)
1.  Separated people--Fiction. 2.  Mothers and sons--Fiction. 3.
Single mothers--Fiction.  I. Title.

  PS3561.I412E25 2003
  813'.6--dc21

                        2003012022

For everyone whose life didn't turn out
quite the way they planned.

To Lee,
my husband and best friend.

For his unfailing support
and confidence in me.

"Dream Baby Dream"

Thanks for the advice.

# CHAPTER ONE

"Hey, Robb, catch!"

Robb looked up just in time to lift a hand and catch the bottle that was flying toward his head. Giving his friend a triumphant look, he put the edge of the bottle cap on the end table to his right and slammed his fist against the bottle. The aluminum cap clattered along the varnished wood and fell silently to the carpeted floor as a slight mist rose from the glass rim. Robb raised the bottle to his lips and tipped his head back just enough to get a mouthful. Wiping off his lips, he burped slightly and drummed his fingers against the blue-gray label on the bottle. "Why don't you ever buy good beer?"

"It is good beer," Derrick protested as he plopped down into the recliner across the room from Robb.

"No, it's cheap beer; there's a difference."

"Almost two bucks a six-pack worth of difference."

Robb pointed the top of his bottle at him. "Quality costs money, my friend," he said.

Derrick took a swig from his own bottle and snorted, "Yeah, my money. You should be grateful I pay the extra to get you bottles instead of cans."

Robb shrugged and took another swig just as the door opened to admit the third roomie. Mark threw his keys on the counter and went immediately to the fridge. "Terri just pulled up," he said, looking at Robb as he popped the top off his own beer and poured it into a glass. "She's waiting for you in the car."

Robb smiled broadly, finished the last of his beer and put the bottle firmly down on the coffee table. "Well, boys, I can't leave the woman waiting."

Derrick shook his head. "I've said it before and I'll say it again, you are the luckiest man I have ever known."

"Me?" Robb said with exaggerated surprise before extending his hand in feigned humility. "You flatter me."

"Look at you," Derrick said with a hint of irritation. "You hardly ever work, you're sleeping with the most beautiful woman I have ever met, and when you get tired of all this you'll go back home to your wife and kid and start up right where you left off."

Robb's expression had darkened during Derrick's description of his life. Derrick was confused at the sudden change. "What?"

"You know he doesn't like you referring to his family back home," Mark said, his eyes slightly narrowed as he looked toward Robb. "Personally, I can't wait to see how Kim reacts when he finally does go back; it ought to be one hell of a reunion."

Robb stood up and visibly forced himself to offer a cool response. "Kim is waiting with bated breath for that day." He sauntered into the bathroom while the other two men exchanged looks of irritated amusement. Derrick had just moved to Evanston a few months before and he didn't know Robb as well as Mark did. Although Derrick had caught on to Robb's dislikes, he slipped up from time to time.

Mark and Robb had been friends for years. They came to Evanston for a week-long fishing trip that had somehow turned into new lives for both of them. They hadn't planned to stay, but once they were there they didn't talk about going home either. They crashed with some other friends for the first couple of weeks and met Derrick when they ran out of money and got hired on at a construction site. Derrick was new in town himself and the three of them rented an apartment a few weeks later. Back in Salt Lake, Robb had been an easy-going, fun-loving guy who was good for beer runs and Monday night football. Since coming to Wyoming, Mark had learned he wasn't nearly as much fun as a roommate. Mark wondered how Robb's wife, Kim, had ever put up with him— why anyone did.

"Four months may have changed her mind, Robb," Derrick called over his shoulder, apparently feeling some beer-induced bravery.

The toilet flushed in the back of the apartment, and Robb reappeared a few seconds later. "Not Kim's," he said confidently and raised his arms above his head like a football hero soaking up the admiration of his fans. "She loves me. What can I say?" He dropped his arms to his side and sat on a kitchen chair to put on his shoes. "Let me give you guys a little advice. Reform yourselves enough to find a nice Mormon girl, play by the rules long enough to get married in a temple and you've got it made. Even when you go back to enjoying life again, she'll be too *dedicated* to turn her back. She'll figure she's got a lifetime to help you find the Straight and Narrow and then you've got eternity to make up for lost time. You live your life on your terms, with a nice warm bed to come home to at night. It's the perfect situation. I highly recommend it."

Mark snorted with mild disgust and shook his head.

"Meanwhile you shack up with the town whore until—"

Robb suddenly sprang from his chair, darted across the room and pinned Mark against the kitchen cabinets. His dark brown eyes, that had just moments ago been dancing with amusement, were now burning with fury.

"I have told you before," he hissed, "never to call her that."

For an intense moment the two men exchanged heated looks, then Mark took a breath and pushed Robb away. They continued to spar with their eyes, while Derrick remained in his chair, lazily watching the show.

"That's what she is, Robb. You can fool yourself all you want, but waitresses can't live like she does."

Robb's look darkened even more and Mark swallowed. After several seconds, Mark chuckled tensely as he backed down. "But you'd know more than I would about it, wouldn't you?"

"Yes, I would," Robb said slowly and finally turned away. "If she were what you say she is, then I wouldn't be with her."

Mark kept silent, although he wanted very badly to tell Robb that Terri probably knew that. For whatever reason, she wanted him badly enough to let him have freely what other men paid for.

It was easy to see why Terri made him the exception. Robb had a physique that contrasted sharply with the lazy, beer-drinking, couch-potato life he lived. With broad shoulders, tapered waist, long legs and a head of dark, curly hair, he was what beer commercials were made of. With his looks, charisma and engaging smile, there was no doubt why he was so appealing.

As far as Mark knew, Robb had been faithful to his wife in Salt Lake City. In fact, before living in Wyoming, Robb hadn't seemed to notice the female attention he drew. But they weren't in Salt Lake anymore and Robb didn't have a wife to stumble home to now. Once Robb had given into Terri's deliberate seduction, he figured that what Kim didn't know wouldn't hurt her. But Mark wasn't so sure. In his own disconnected way he felt sorry for Kim.

Robb finished his preparation and turned to look at them both. "My life is my business; my women are my business. Neither of you are to bring them up again. Do you understand?"

Derrick nodded in casual agreement. Mark just turned and walked toward his bedroom.

"Do you understand me!" Robb bellowed at Mark's back.

Mark stopped, took a breath, and turned on his heel. "You know, Robb, you're wearing out your welcome awfully fast here.

We're tired of paying your way and letting you treat us like garbage."

Robb straightened and crossed his arms across his chest. "Really?" he drawled.

"Yeah, really," Mark echoed sarcastically. He hated how Robb could switch his emotions so quickly. Robb hadn't always been so volatile and Mark wondered if it was his guilty conscience that made him that way. Whatever the cause, it left Mark constantly feeling like he was on the brink of Robb's rage. "It was all fun and games for a while, but I think maybe it's time for you to go back home. See just how your wife feels about your whoring around and leave us alone."

The tension that followed his words hung in the air. Mark held his breath, knowing he had said too much and hoped he wouldn't have a black eye to show for it in the morning. "Maybe I'll do just that," Robb finally said, provoking a look of surprise in the other men. Then, looking between them, he continued, "This scene isn't nearly what it used to be. But don't forget who's the life of the party around here; you guys won't have any idea how to have fun once I'm gone."

The door slammed shut behind him and Mark shook his head. After a moment, he took a long drink of his beer, placed the glass on the table and sprawled out on the couch. "His idea of fun is hanging out at bars half the night, remaining unemployed and leeching off everybody else. And as far as the 'life of the party' goes, nearly every guy in town swears it's Terri."

# CHAPTER TWO

Kim turned the doorknob and slowly opened the door, hoping it wouldn't squeak and wake anyone. She shut it just as softly and leaned her back against it only a moment before stepping out of her shoes and turning the deadbolt. Allowing herself to collapse onto the sofa, she closed her eyes and took a deep breath. She was so tired. She had spent the last few nights cleaning out her home that she would soon be renting out. It was a miserable job of scrubbing toilets, vacuuming corners, filling nail-holes and making sure she didn't leave anything behind. She hated every minute of it, but she had renters moving in on Monday and she was running out of time to get it ready for them. Tonight she had finished; every detailed task was finally done. After plopping down on the couch, she stretched her legs, and basked in the feeling of completion. Despite her dislike of the chore, she couldn't deny that it had been good in some ways. Having the uninterrupted hours all to herself gave her time to reflect on what had brought her to this point. The realizations she came to were hard to face, but without the time alone she wondered if she'd ever have dared to look at things so closely. She had never liked solitude much, and since Robb had left she'd avoided it religiously as she fought against the self-inspection it invited. Now, she wondered if avoiding it this long had been a good thing. Perhaps she could have seen these things earlier if she had allowed herself to look this closely at the decisions she'd been making in her life.

After only another minute she peeled herself off the sofa and made her way to the staircase that lead to the bedrooms of her parents' home. She left the lights off and made her way carefully in the dark. The steps often held a child's treasure or two and she had no desire to fall down the stairs tonight.

"Second door on the left," she repeated a few times to herself. After almost a month, she was still getting used to the changes, but it didn't hurt to be reminded. At her house, the master bedroom was the first door on the right, just like it was here. However, the master bedroom in *this* house belonged to her parents and she was sure they wouldn't appreciate her walking in. The other two bedrooms on the top floor, one of which was hers, shared a Jack-

and-Jill bathroom. The co-op room allowed her to check on her son easily and tonight she lingered for a moment and watched him sleep. The innocence of childhood, she mused with a sigh. If only... She didn't finish the thought; it was useless anyway. She pulled his door shut and only then turned on the light in the bathroom.

After undressing quickly, she turned on the shower and adjusted the temperature of the water. Gingerly, she stepped inside the fiberglass tub and pulled the vinyl curtain shut behind her. The initial chill of water on her skin made her inhale sharply, reminding her of the reason she didn't prefer showers. The momentary shock of the spray of droplets had never been an experience she enjoyed. As the water pounded at her head she shampooed her hair and tried to remember the last time she had taken a bath. A real bath—one with bubbles, water that was too hot, and silence. She smiled at the fantasy, longing for it, yet at the same time she wondered if she was capable of that kind of relaxation anymore. It had been a very long time since she had indulged in anything, and she realized sadly that she seldom even thought about such things anymore. Even if she could find the time or the energy to pursue such pleasure, could she detach from her challenges long enough to enjoy them? Somehow, she doubted that she could.

Only a few minutes later, with a towel wrapped turban-style around her head, she removed the mascara smudges the shower had failed to wash away. The towel covered her shoulder length blonde hair that she hadn't even trimmed for over a year. Wispy bangs, that she cut herself, framed her oval face and, without the assistance of eyeliner and mascara, her blue eyes looked to her very dull and non-descript. The hot shower had pinked her cheeks and she wished she had that coloring all the time. She was quite fair— too fair in her opinion. There was little about her features that struck her as being remarkable, but she figured she was reasonably pretty. With the help of Revlon and Max Factor, no one pulled back in horror anyway. At just under five and a half feet tall and fifteen pounds heavier than she ought to be she figured she was average. Just plain average. Nothing special, nothing unique—just average. Plain and simple. She shrugged off the thoughts; they were pointless and a bit depressing. She had enough of that in her life right now.

The shower revived her a bit and since she felt up to it she decided to wash her face properly tonight. At age 29, she knew she couldn't ignore her skin much longer; thirty was just around the corner. Several months ago, she had purchased a skin care regimen that was supposed to last three months. Nine months later she still had at least half of the creams and toners left; she only ignored her skin two-thirds of the time now. She pulled open the top drawer next to the sink and found the pink and white containers mingled with a menagerie of make-up, styling products and bottles of mysterious content. The items had been unceremoniously dumped into the drawer when she moved in last month. She didn't use most of them, but she was too frugal to throw them away—just in case.

As she placed the bottles on the counter, she noticed something in the back of the drawer. Reaching in, she pulled out her husband's electric shaver and regarded it. Despite all the changes she had made in her life the last few months, Robb's things still surrounded her as if she fully expected him to come back and pick up right where they left off. After she examined the razor with something close to suspicion, she placed it on the edge of the sink and shuffled in the drawer some more. She found a bottle of cologne, some after-shave lotion, a stick of deodorant; symbols of the man she had once shared a life with. After further inspection she found his hair gel, a tube of Ben-Gay, even his toothbrush. As her movements quickened she felt her anger rise.

The house was rented, their furniture was now in a storage unit and all their mail came to her parents' home. Their son went to a new school, she had a new job Robb didn't even know about—and yet she waited. Despite her hurt, her humiliation and her anger, she had kept her husband's life together; his things right beside hers. She slammed the drawer shut and opened another, dismayed to find even more of Robb's things. She had packed his clothes and belongings weeks ago and they were with her own personal effects in her parents' garage. If Robb had showed up today, would she have hugged him and wept, grateful for his return? Would she gladly gather all these personal items to show him how she had waited? The thought disgusted and angered her more, especially since she realized that she would probably have done just that.

The third drawer that she opened brought her up short. She lifted out a stack of thin pink plastic cartridges held together by a rubber band. Snapping off the rubber band, she flipped open the lid of one container and stared at the little pink and green pills laid out in a circle. Along with all her husband's things she had kept the three-month supply of birth control pills given to her at her last doctor's appointment.

Shaken by the sight of the pills, her mind returned to the earlier scenario as she had imagined Robb coming home. Would she welcome him into her bed without hesitation? Live her life as if he'd never left? Again, she couldn't convince herself that she wouldn't, and the knowledge was painful as it revealed a part of herself that she would rather ignore. She popped out a little pink pill and stared at it for a moment. She hadn't taken the preventative for months, but it was waiting for Robb's return just as his personal effects were; just like she was. Impulsively, she tossed the pill into the toilet and the rest of the packages into the trash. In an instant she realized that she could not continue this way any longer. The thought had been playing in her head for some time, but now the reminders of him and the reminder of the attachment she still felt brought them completely to the surface. They could not be ignored anymore.

Looking up, she caught her reflection in the mirror and held her own gaze for a moment. She looked at herself in a new light, from another perspective and she didn't like the view very much. She'd been telling herself all these months, all these years, that she was strong and capable of handling whatever came her way. But she didn't see herself that way now. Today, she felt weak and stupid; like a needy woman so desperate for love she'd ignore the obvious. She wondered if that was how everyone else saw her and it made her feel very small. As she continued to stare at her reflection, however, a strange calm came over her for a moment and reminded her of something her dad had told her often in her life; "You are never as tall as when you're on your knees."

Beside her bed, she kneeled and offered a short but sincere prayer requesting help to become the strong, capable woman she wanted to be; she'd been trying to be that woman all by herself, without help from anyone else, but she could see now that she hadn't pulled it off. She couldn't do it alone any longer. Over the years, her prayers had become fewer and farther between; those that she did offer seemed to go nowhere. But despite the way they seemed to bounce back at her, she knew—well, at least she believed—that someone was up there. Maybe 'hoped' was a better word than believed. She had felt such little intervention from a higher power lately that she could only hope that He was listening this time.

She stayed on her knees for several minutes after the "Amen." Somehow, she didn't feel quite so alone. Was it possible that God had been listening tonight? That He did understand what was happening in her life after all? Every Sunday school lesson she had sat through in her life had tried to convince her that God was aware of her. Yet the experiences of the last few years had caused her to doubt it.

The feeling she was having at this moment seemed to prove the point that countless teachers had attempted to make. Then a thought came to her: perhaps she had forgotten God, instead of Him forgetting her. It was a humbling thought. Another certain thing was that Robb had been gone for over four months and for the first time since he left she didn't feel the frantic loneliness that existed even when she was surrounded by other people.

As she climbed gratefully into bed, she finally put a name to the feeling she simply could not talk herself out of. Peace she decided was close, and then it came to her as if someone had spoken the words, *"relief—now you can move forward."*

Was she ready for that? After so many years of doing everything she could think of to save him, and after failing every time, could she let go? She closed her eyes and after a few moments offered a very short but humble prayer in which she finally asked God to take over. This too was something she had learned from church yet had not thought of in a long time. Being made 'strong in the Lord,' submitting to and trusting His will. It wasn't easy, and it wasn't comfortable, but she finally understood that He was really the only one who could help at this point. She had done all she could. Someone else had to step in now.

As she finished her prayer, she realized how true that was. Perhaps there had been a time when she was responsible for Robb; a time when she could help him. But that time had passed. She had now turned Robb back to God and she felt as if an enormous burden had been removed.

It had been practicing the ultimate exercise in futility to try and solve Robb's problems. She absently twisted her wedding ring off and held it above her face, allowing it to catch the light of the street lamp that streamed through the window. She didn't feel quite ready to take it off just yet, and she put it back on her finger. Letting go is hard to do, she reminded herself. But she was getting started. At the very least, she wouldn't try to save him anymore—that was no longer her responsibility. The way she looked at her life and her future would be different now, because she wasn't going to base it around Robb anymore. She had a son who needed her energy, and that was where her heart needed to be. She didn't know where Robb was for sure, she didn't know what he was doing or even why he'd left; but she was done waiting for him to come back. The future was now; and he wasn't in it.

ↄ

At work the next day, Kim listened patiently to the woman on the other end of the phone line while she tapped her pen against the desktop. When the woman finished Kim spoke. "Okay, I'll be there within the hour, thank you...bye." Kim hung up the receiver and let her hand rest on the phone for only a moment before raising it back to her ear and dialing a number. Maddie walked into the office just before Kim's mom picked up on the other end of the line. Kim waved Maddie into a chair and signaled that she would just be a minute. Maddie followed Kim's orders, took a seat and listened to Kim's side of the conversation.

"Hi Mom...Yeah I'm okay, but Jack's sick...Well, he threw up in class and so I have to go get him. I was wondering if you were planning to be home this afternoon, otherwise I could..." she raised her eyes to the ceiling and mouthed a thank-you while Peggy, her mother, said she would tend him.

"Thanks, Mom, I don't know what I would do without your help...I'm leaving right now. Thanks." She hung up the phone and then smiled at Maddie who was leaning the chair against the wall, balancing it on the back two legs. "You know my Sunday school teachers always told us that we'd break the chairs by doing that."

"Did you believe them?" Maddie asked with a smile.

"No."

"Me neither." But she brought the chair back to the intended position anyway. "Jack's sick, huh?"

"Yes, again! It's the second time in a month I've had to pick him up early—thank goodness for my mother," Kim said as she stood up and gathered her things. "I'll be back by 1:00. Do you need anything?"

"Actually I do need something and you're just the gal help me with it." Maddie's exaggerated smile was indication enough that Kim wouldn't be thrilled with the assignment.

"It must not be about money then, if I'm the gal."

Maddie laughed, "Not money, my dear—something money can't buy."

It took Kim only a moment to figure out the insinuation and she laughed out loud, surprising them both. How long had it been since she had laughed like that? She cleared her throat. "I can't guarantee the love part, but I can probably find you a male counterpart for an evening; if that's what you mean."

"Oh, could you?" Maddie squeaked in feigned desperation. Maddie was several years younger than Kim but they had graduated from the Dietary and Nutrition program together last year and were lucky enough to find jobs with the same company. Despite being quite attractive, Maddie was still single at the age of 23. She'd had plenty of opportunity, but Maddie was the kind of woman who knew what she wanted; including the type of husband she would have one day. How Kim wished she had been so picky. In the past year, Kim had set Maddie up with two of her brothers.

Kim was the second of six children. Her only sister, who happened to be the oldest sibling, lived in Ohio with her husband and three daughters. Being somewhat of a tomboy as a kid, Kim had been closer to her four younger brothers, which worked out perfectly for Maddie.

"But remember," Kim added, "Glen got married in July and Chris is in California finishing up his internship. So how about Matt?" Kim walked around the desk, heading out of the office. Maddie got up quickly and followed her.

"I don't know. Matt and Maddie—kind of cheesy. How old is Sam again?"

"Nineteen, and that's 'Elder Shep'; he leaves on his mission next month. Besides you'll like Matt— he's not nearly as intellectual as Glen and Chris."

"Very funny."

"Yes, he is quite funny," Kim answered as if it were a question. "So, do I ask him out for you or can you not get past the name thing?"

"Go ahead and ask him," Maddie said with a sarcastic sigh, as if being really put out by the whole arrangement. "My brother just moved back here from Chicago and my parents are having a barbecue Friday night; they told me not to come alone. They are so desperate to get me married off that they're ready to exclude me from family parties."

"You are getting up there, Maddie," Kim teased. "I'll try to call Matt when I drop off Jack." She opened the outside door, waved quickly and hurried to her car.

♪

After getting Jackson settled, Kim shut the door to his room quietly and went in search of her mom. Peggy was in the kitchen mopping the linoleum with a vengeance. For as long as Kim could remember, her mother cleaned house as if the prophet would be dropping in at any minute. Not for the first time Kim wished she had inherited the same drive. Cooking and cleaning had never been her forte.

"You're hired," Kim said loudly, causing her mom to jump. She laughed as Peggy gave her a dirty look before resuming the task. Kim looked across the nearly-finished floor to the phone hanging on the wall. The cordless phone was also sitting abandoned on the far counter. The only other phone in the house was in her father's office in the basement, but she'd have to cross the kitchen floor to get to the staircase. "Uh, Mom, I need to call Matt, if I take off my shoes can I—"

Peggy cut her off and held the mop in front of her daughter, blocking the entryway. "No you may not, you don't wear shoes half the time anyway and your dirty feet will mar my floor."

"Mar?" Kim said giving her mother a questioning look.

"Yes, mar. And don't look at me like that," she smiled despite herself and went back to work.

"It's my dinosaur look; I only use it when you use words that haven't been used in common speech for at least twenty years. Besides," Kim said with a twinkle in her eye. "I only go barefoot indoors and you keep your floors spotless..." She let the sentence trail off in hopes to make her point a little more subtly.

"No," Peggy said with a forceful look. Kim shrugged—it had been worth a try. "Why do you need to call Matt?" Peggy added after a moment.

Kim leaned her shoulder against the doorframe trying to get comfortable. "Maddie needs a date Friday and I want to see if he has any plans."

"Matt and Maddie, huh? I don't think he'll go for it." Peggy finished the last spot of floor and pushed her short, brown hair back off her slightly sweaty face.

Kim looked at her mother in surprise. "That's just what she said; you guys are way too discriminating."

Peggy laughed and was about to respond when the phone rang. Kim snatched the opportunity and bounded across the floor, grabbing the handset of the wall phone on the second ring. Peggy gave her a dirty look but Kim pretended not to notice.

"Hello?" she said breathlessly with a smile. Peggy watched the lighthearted smile fade and felt a tug at her heart. It was rare for Kim to be so effortlessly cheerful these days and it saddened her to see it disappear so soon. She tuned into Kim's half of the conversation and disappointment turned to dread as she put the pieces together.

"Yes, I'll come...Uh, can you tell me what the charges are?" Kim closed her eyes and swallowed, turning so her mother couldn't see her face. For several seconds she was silent, then her eye's fluttered open again. "Yes, sorry, I'm still here...Uh, let me get a pen...Okay, go ahead." She scribbled an address on a piece of scratch paper.

"It will take me a couple of hours...all right. Thank you." She hung up the phone and put her forehead against the wall, then she turned to see her Mom's worried expression.

"What is it?" Peggy finally asked. "Is it Robb?" she added when Kim didn't answer.

Kim nodded and cleared her throat. "He was arrested this morning. He told them to call me but they were hoping he would sober up enough to call me himself," she shook her head in disgust and disbelief.

When it became apparent that Kim wasn't volunteering any more information, Peggy pushed by asking what he was arrested for. She was wondering whether Kim would answer when Kim looked up at her mother. "He shot someone."

# CHAPTER THREE

Thirty minutes later, Kim was on Interstate 80 heading up through Parley's Canyon on her way to Evanston, Wyoming. The initial shock had disappeared, allowing the bits and pieces of the phone call to filter through her mind. She put it all together as well as she could. Robb had been arrested for attempted murder. Her husband had his problems, that was sure, but she would never have guessed Robb was capable of violence. Then again, Robb continually surprised her. This was simply one more example of how grossly she misjudged him. Memories assailed her, and although she tried to focus on what lay ahead, wanting to prepare for it; the past would not be denied today.

Kim and Robb attended the same high school. He was a year older and they moved in different circles, but she knew very well who he was. Robb possessed a certain charisma that made him popular with nearly everyone. He was dynamic and 'larger than life,' the kind of guy everyone wanted to be around. He went to church but also skipped out on seminary and attended parties on the weekends. Like everyone else, Kim seemed to judge him differently; as if the rules didn't apply to him. Kim thought he was spirited and adventurous, years later she learned it was closer to stupid and rebellious. He did go on a mission, however, and that helped solidify the impression that he was just pushing the limits in high school. Robb's dad was on the high council then and Robb was the only son. Kim learned that, in regards to his mission, Robb had been told that he had a duty to fulfill to his family, if not to God. She had also learned that his dad had promised him a new car if he served a mission. Robb had received a brand new Pathfinder within days of his release. That situation seemed to illustrate Robb's life, although it had taken some time for Kim to realize it. Robb would do what was expected of him, so long as it worked in his favor somehow. But the integrity everyone assumed he had somewhere, didn't really exist.

After Kim graduated from high school, her family moved to East Sandy. But when Robb came home from his mission a mutual friend set him up with Kim. Kim was a junior at the University of Utah at the time and still lived with her parents. They dated almost a year before Robb proposed; Kim didn't hesitate in accepting him as the man with whom she'd spend forever. She was as moonstruck as everyone else seemed to be.

Ironically, one of the things she liked best about him was his approach to the gospel. He was so easygoing about it, not fanatical and preachy like most returned missionaries she'd dated. He said life was for living and it wasn't wrong to have a little fun. At the age of twenty, just tasting the fun parts of being an adult, being with someone who seemed to only see the good things in life seemed perfect.

Kim had always been active in the church, but she couldn't say she'd had divine revelation of exactly how the Gospel should be lived. Her parents lived the Gospel principles to the letter. Robb, on the other hand, seemed to bend the rules a little. He watched R rated movies now and then. He didn't feel it was any big deal: "It's all fake anyway," he would say, and she went along with it. He drank non-alcoholic beer because he liked the taste. Spiritual things were just never a concern, but he lived within the commandments and Kim couldn't find any concrete reason to object to his lifestyle. Even if he lacked the religious commitment of other men she had dated, he made up for it with his charm and easygoing nature. In almost every way, Robb was exactly the kind of guy she wanted in her life.

He asked her to marry him with a dozen roses and fake Champagne, after he popped the question she accepted, but added, "Only if it's in the temple."

Robb said, "Sure."

It didn't take long to realize how naive she had been. Being worthy to enter the temple seemed to be all that mattered, at least Kim thought so. But in the sealing room, surrounded by friends and family Kim realized that a temple marriage was bigger than she'd thought it was. It was that day that Kim received the first real spiritual experience of her life. She had felt the spirit before, confirmation of testimonies or doctrine, but nothing so personal; so real as this. By the time they kneeled across from one another at the altar, she finally understood everything she'd been taught about the sacred covenants she was making; *they* were making. At one point the sealer had looked at them and said, "I urge you to remember that love is not enough, and it will not solve all your problems. If you stay close to the Lord and keep the Light of Christ burning brightly in your hearts you will be given all you've been promised. But know that eternity is earned." Those words rang in her head that day and she made a commitment to make sure she earned the promise made. As time passed, those words began to haunt her. "Eternity is earned."

From that day on, she vowed to do better, to keep the details of her life in accordance with the teachings of Christ. Living the gospel now represented promises of forever and a stability on which to base their family. Her wedding day was indeed the greatest day of her life: she had embarked on a glorious relationship with Robb. Besides that, she had begun a journey towards the kind of testimony her parents had; something she longed for. Kim could only imagine the wonders and joy that the future held.

However, it didn't take long for reality to take over. Kim did her best to keep her end of the bargain, but she learned during that first year that many things were beyond her control. She and Robb were married now, they were one; but her own knowledge, *her* testimony could accomplish very little by itself. When their church time changed to 9 a.m. at the first of the year, Robb started sleeping in most Sundays. For awhile, he would come to sacrament meeting at 11:00, but by spring he didn't come at all.

When they celebrated their first wedding anniversary, Kim was four weeks pregnant. She hoped that starting a family would turn him in the right direction. When the college semester ended six weeks later, she had to go to work full time. Robb had a good job when they were married, but it hadn't lasted two months. He turned down the soccer scholarship he had to the University of Utah and decided to do construction work. It didn't seem to bother him that there was limited work available in the wintertime, or that since he didn't develop any specific skill, the jobs he got were only temporary. He would work for a few weeks, then be unemployed for a few more before finding a new job. It became clear that Kim would have to work at least for awhile until he became a little more stable. So she quit school, justifying it by admitting she had always planned to stay home with her children—she didn't need a degree. She believed that by the time the baby came, Robb would have a good steady job again; she was sure of it. But as soon as she was employed full-time he lost his job again, and she'd worked ever since.

When Jackson was born, Robb was unemployed. During Kim's six-week maternity leave she made a discouraging discovery. She had always assumed that Robb spent his time looking for a job, but she learned during her time at home that he didn't. He would get up about 10:00 and spend an hour reading the paper; sometimes he would set up an appointment for an interview for a job, but they never panned out. Kim came to suspect that he didn't really go to his interviews at all. Until that time, Kim had been very supportive of his struggles with keeping a job; now they began arguing over it on a regular basis. How could she not have noticed how lazy he was?

When Jackson was a month old, Kim needed to take him to the doctor. When she got into her car that day, she realized it was nearly out of gas; not wanting to lose time, she decided to take Robb's Pathfinder; he was, of course, still asleep and not planning to go anywhere. Kim loaded up the car seat, opened the back to put in the diaper bag, and her heart sank. The back was littered with beer cans. She stared at them for a long time before she removed the car seat and took her car after all.

Over the next week she tried to give Robb every opportunity to explain about the beer cans. She cleaned out his car, thinking he would know she knew and confront her. The Ensign had an article about a husband's alcoholism, so she read it to him. No response. One day when he left for an 'interview' she searched the house, and found a stash of various alcoholic beverages. Kim poured the contents down the sink and threw the bottles in the trash. Surely Robb would come to her when he noticed they were gone: nothing. Finally, feeling she had no other option, she confronted him directly.

"Robb, I know about your drinking."

"What drinking?" he said calmly, looking through the paper without even lifting his head.

"Robb, come on. I'm not stupid. I found cans in your Pathfinder. It's okay, we'll deal with it but—"

"Deal with what?"

"Your drinking!" she nearly shrieked.

"Kim, calm down," he patted her hand and looked her right in the eye. "I don't know what you're talking about."

Kim was stunned; she stared back at him and not only did she know he was lying, but he knew she knew. "Robb," she said slowly, panic rising in her chest, "I found the cans in your car."

Robb leaned back in his chair and folded his arms across his chest, staring at her. "There are no cans in my car."

"Well, not now! I took them out. But I saw them, Robb, and I found your stash in the house."

"My stash," he chuckled, as if she were a child.

"Yes," her voice no longer masked her anger, "I found it. I poured it down the sink."

Something flashed in Robb's eyes then, but he said nothing. Kim rambled on and on, but Robb just kept his patronizing stare locked with her almost-frantic eyes. She had never expected this. She was sure he would be angry, or repentant or... well, anything but this. He was lying; they both knew it and he didn't care. She finally stopped mid-sentence, and wiped at the tears in her eyes.

Robb stood and kissed her forehead. "Get some sleep, Honey. You've got to go back to work next week."

That was it. He never said another word about it. Kim tried to talk about it again but he only turned the facts around, making it sound like she was crazy. Eventually, she let it drop altogether. Kim told no one about their situation; she had never been more confused and humiliated. When she returned to work, she left Jackson at home with Robb—at least she didn't have to pay for child-care. She decided to be patient with him, that sooner or later he would change—he had to.

She had learned, during their marriage, how spoiled Robb was by his parents and she figured that it would just take some time for him to realize what life was really about. Every day he watched Jackson while Kim worked; unemployment didn't seem to bother him. But as time went by, the nights he handed off the baby to her and went out with the guys increased. On the nights he'd go out, he'd be back around midnight and crawl into bed beside her. More often than not she could smell the alcohol on his breath. On those nights, she pretended to be asleep, not wanting to confront him, and if he attempted to be 'amorous' she ignored him until he fell asleep. Now and then, he would come home sober and she would give herself to him freely, hoping he would put two and two together and realize how much better life was when he was sober. Maybe this would help him change. It didn't change anything.

When Jackson was almost three, she finally broke down and went to her bishop for advice. She was so frustrated, so disappointed. After four years she felt her efforts weren't getting her anywhere, and she needed advice. The advice she got was to continue honoring her covenants to him. She was reminded that we are all people with separate timelines and she needed to be patient and continue setting a good example. The counsel revived her and she recommitted herself. She wouldn't give up on him, he was her husband—in good times and bad. Another year passed and things hadn't gotten any better. Again she went to the bishop and he even spoke with Robb, but in the end his advice was the same: love him, hope he'll come around, and don't give up. She didn't give up but life didn't get better.

At times, she wondered if she were falling out of love with him, he hadn't lived up to any of her expectations, but was it fair to blame him for that? Perhaps her expectations were too high.

The next two years became routine and Kim finally decided that although she was attempting to remain supportive, she was also putting her life on hold. Jackson was almost five. After they decided they were ready to try for another baby, she also decided to go back to school. If she got pregnant right away she'd never finish her degree but she was tired of being stagnant. Robb had worked off-and-on enough that Kim's mom had been watching Jackson during the day for quite some time. Robb stayed with Jackson in the evenings when Kim went to school. Things seemed to be going well—at least not getting worse—and Kim was encouraged by that. Her expectations had become significantly lower.

Within a few months, Kim was pregnant and hopeful that perhaps this new addition to their family would help take them up a level, but she was also apprehensive. Was it selfishness that made her long for more children? Was it right to bring a baby into their relationship? As the pregnancy progressed, she wondered at her motives, worried about the life this baby would have, but she wanted more children. If the Lord gave them to her she would do her very best to give her children the life they deserved. But she was still plagued with worries. Then one day at work the questions stopped. When the cramping started she tried to call Robb but he wasn't home so she called her mom. Her doctor confirmed her suspicions, and a day or so later Kim miscarried. Robb was supportive in his own way, but Kim felt his sensitivity to be lacking. She got the distinct impression that Robb wasn't disappointed.

During the three-month waiting period the doctor had prescribed between pregnancies, Kim began to wonder if perhaps she had been hasty. During a discussion-turned-argument Robb admitted he didn't want more kids; he had agreed for her sake. It infuriated and depressed Kim incredibly to hear that. Their arguments increased and it became nearly impossible for them to have a civil conversation. Kim never stopped taking her birth control pills after the three months passed. Despite her own longing and disappointment, she refused to have a child with a man who didn't want it. When the intense pain of it began to subside, Kim began to see the true wisdom of her decision as Robb seemed to slide further downhill. Robb began to stay out later and later at night, and on

Kim's school nights his friends started hanging out at the house more often.

When she came home from school one night and found two guys passed out on the floor and a case of beer in the fridge, she was furious. She kicked them out and told Robb in no uncertain terms that there would be no drinking in her home, or around her son. An argument erupted that turned hot and Robb finally left to sleep it off at a friend's house.

Their relationship became almost one constant argument after that; Kim was so angry she couldn't make herself back off. If Robb was home, they were fighting. Poor Jackson would curl up in a chair and cover his ears until Robb slammed the door on his way out. The nights Robb came home sober became a thing of the past and Kim realized she either made love to a drunk man or denied him completely. In time it seemed to become the only relationship they had. One night Kim asked him if he was seeing someone—she had finally admitted to herself that she was naive to not consider the possibility. His look of shock and hurt answered the question before he spoke to reassure her that even though he had problems, infidelity was not one of them.

After that, things seemed to get better between them—at least a little bit. He seemed to be trying harder to show her that he was trustworthy. He didn't stop drinking, but he didn't pretend to stop either. She ignored the things she didn't approve of, and he accepted her ignorance. When he began leaving for a couple of days at a time, he would tell her that he was going camping or fishing with the guys and he would wait to come home until he was sober. Kim didn't like that and it started plenty of arguments but he did what he wanted to do and she came to accept it. Besides that, she had to admit that she was relieved that he wasn't hiding things from her.

At all costs, she avoided looking hard at the life she was living; it had fulfilled none of her expectations but to look at it too closely meant doing something about it and Kim felt completely incapable of doing so. Instead, she toughed it out, hoping and praying it would get better, focusing on the reasons behind the tribulations, waiting for things to change.

Then one weekend he didn't come home. The next night she waited and waited, but he never came and she knew this trip was different than the others. Had he left her for good? Was he dead? Somehow she knew neither was the case. It was yet one more phase of his deterioration—she was almost sure of it.

As hard as it was, she called Robb's parents after a full week had passed. They were surprised, shocked and pointedly cold towards her; it quickly became apparent that no one knew where he'd gone. He had never been close with his parents or his four sisters, so it didn't surprise her that they were all clueless. Kim had made a point of not knowing his friends and although she tried and tried to find something that would give her a lead, everything went nowhere. The friends she contacted didn't know where he was. Two weeks after his disappearance, Kim graduated and she received a letter in the mail a few days after that.

*Kim,*
*I need some time to think things through. Be patient with me, and don't give up. I'm yours forever, remember. I love you.*
*Robb*

Four months had passed since that letter. All together, she received three letters; all as vague and manipulative as the first. He never said where he was and always reminded her how badly he needed her. Since the envelopes were postmarked from Evanston, Wyoming, she tried directory assistance and called the police department there, but found nothing. She considered using a private investigator, but she was broke. As soon as she got back on her feet she intended to make some more attempts to locate him, but for now it was all she could do to keep her life together. Besides, what would she do if she did find him? Force him to come home? Tell him she was finished with this? She didn't know what to say or do, so she did nothing; hoping that the answers she sought would one day magically be found.

Robb's parents had contacted her on Jackson's birthday in June and taken him for a weekend sleep-over every month since then, but they remained very cool towards her. She suspected they blamed her for Robb's leaving, and it angered her. Having hidden everything all these years didn't make it any easier to make them understand, and after one failed attempt to explain the situation she dropped it all together. And as much as she would have liked to, she wouldn't keep Jackson from them. They may have scored a big zero in parenting their own son, but they were wonderful grandparents and Jackson deserved all the love he could get; especially now.

Time passed and she waited to hear more from Robb. Her brain screamed co-dependency, but she could not deny the feelings she still had for him. He was still her husband and it was hard for her to subtract that fact from the overall equation. Divorce was the obvious answer, but Kim just had this overwhelming feeling that it was too soon to make that decision and she refused to do anything until she could at least talk to him.

Kim had not told many people what she and Robb had been dealing with and the conditions under which Robb had left. But within a couple months, Kim had to admit she simply wasn't making it financially. Circumstances made secrets hard to keep. Robb had worked off and on doing odd temporary jobs the last year or so and they had purchased a small home in West Jordan in January. In the process, they had also managed to rack up a several thousand dollars in credit card bills and her student loans would come due now that Kim had graduated. Despite the increased income of her new job she couldn't make ends meet. It became apparent she would have to do something drastic; her decision was rent out the house they'd hadn't owned for even a year. She asked her parents if she could move back home with them and finally told them everything. They were sad, but not surprised. Kim hadn't been able to hide everything all these years.

In September Kim's brother Sam, who would be leaving on his mission soon, moved into the guest room in the basement so that Kim and Jackson could have the adjoining upstairs bedrooms. She started getting her house ready for renters and Consumer Credit Counseling helped her prepare a tight budget that would pay off the credit cards and student loans in just over a year. Moving home was humiliating and she hated the feeling of dependency, but she felt sure that if she let her pride make the decisions she would make an even bigger mess of things.

Kim resented having missed so much of Jackson's childhood while she tried to take over Robb's responsibilities. But Jackson was now an even greater source of joy for her. She was called to be Jackson's primary teacher—the first calling she had held in several years—and she loved being a part of his life in yet another way. She enrolled him in a fall soccer league and he liked his new school. Each time she was faced with a decision, she tried to think about how it would affect Jackson, and as she learned to follow that path, she almost always did the right thing. And, although she hated to admit it, she could see that Robb's absence from their lives seemed to be a benefit. Jackson had always been very shy and passive before, but now Kim marveled at how energetic and enthusiastic he was about life. There were several boys his age in the neighborhood who accepted him quickly into their group. When Jackson asked about his father Kim told him the truth: she didn't know where he was or when he was coming back. Jackson accepted it easily enough and Kim wished she could do the same.

Living with her parents seemed to be helping him a lot, and she knew it helped her, too. She didn't feel so alone anymore. Her own attendance at church had faltered over the years, yet in just a month of regular activity she could feel the difference. Being in a home where the spirit resided helped too. In fact she wondered why she ever let herself drift so far away from it in the first place.

Crossing the Wyoming border brought her back to the present and she realized the irony of the situation. Apparently the present crisis had helped her delve even deeper into the discoveries she'd begun making the night before. For years she had supported Robb's alcohol abuse and told herself that he would get better; he had only gotten worse. In the end everyone suffered. Now that she had finally decided not to be held back by Robb's choices, Robb had showed back up in her life. The words spoken just before their wedding ceremony echoed in her mind as she pulled into the Evanston police station: "Love is not enough...eternity is earned."

Kim sat in the waiting room for nearly an hour before finally being approached by a tall thin man. His youthful face contrasted with the aged expression in his eyes that seemed to say 'I've seen it all.' He introduced himself as Lieutenant Browning and led her past several crowded metal desks and into his office.

He invited her to sit down as he took a seat behind the large desk. The smile on his face looked uneasy and did nothing to alleviate the butterflies in Kim's stomach. "I may have been hasty in having you drive all the way up here, ma'am. It seems that as soon as your husband sobered up he didn't want to talk to you after all. I called you again but you had already left."

Kim tried to swallow her embarrassment that her own husband didn't want to see her and asked if Robb knew she was here now.

"Uh, yes he does; that's the reason you had to wait so long. We can't force him to see anyone but we tried to convince him to at least speak to you, since you had come all this way." Kim was speechless. Lt. Browning continued, "After we spoke to you, Mr. Larksley mentioned that you have been separated for a few months. If we had known we—"

"He said we were separated?" she asked, hoping she had heard wrong.

"Yes," he answered slowly. This whole experience was going from bad to worse for him. It was becoming quickly apparent that he had been given only bits and pieces of what to expect here. "When he was brought in he kept asking to speak with his wife. But he had used his one allowed phone call to call a friend. After a few hours I finally called you, which is not our usual policy." Browning left out the fact that Robb had cursed and said his wife was the last person in the world he wanted to see now. "Later, he told us about the separation."

"Well," she said calmly. "We've been on good terms despite . . . uh, everything." It sounded weak and stupid even to her. "I'll help him if I can."

Browning leaned forward on his elbows. "There isn't much anyone can do for him at this point, unless you have a really good attorney." He noticed her straighten a little, and knew it was an indication that she didn't. "The charges he is facing are very serious, Mrs. Larksley; he will be arraigned and formally charged tomorrow morning."

Kim took a deep breath and looked at the polished desk top that separated the two of them. "Can you tell me what happened; I was only told that he had shot someone."

"The man he shot was apparently a friend of his. Luckily he'll be okay; he took it in the leg. It missed the bone and artery. But your husband will still be charged with attempted murder."

"Can you tell me how this all happened?"

Browning quickly sat back in his chair; regarding her with speculation. "I'm not really at liberty to discuss the details with anyone until after he is formally charged."

Something in the slow and calculated way he answered her set off warning bells in her head. The way he avoided her eyes and the expression on his face also told her he was hiding something. There was something he didn't want her to know. What could be worse than shooting someone? She dwelled on that, and waited for him to reassure her in some way, but as the seconds ticked by his discomfort increased and she knew there was more. "And exactly what time will that be? I'll need to call my mother and ask her to watch my son while I wait." She smiled in a way that would tell him she wasn't giving up. She hadn't come all this way for nothing. She intended to leave with her questions answered.

Browning thought quickly about his choices. The first option was sticking to what he had just said and having her hear it the next morning with a few dozen spectators. Or he could tell her himself and let her deal with it privately. It didn't take him long to decide that she would rather find out now. He took a deep breath and leaned forward on his elbows again.

"He is still considered a suspect by law, but this situation is somewhat unique." He swallowed and hoped he could put this all together in a way that wouldn't be too difficult for her. "There were two police officers there when the shooting occurred and they each gave a complete report this morning. Therefore, many facts which would normally need a trial to straighten out are already known. I suspect that you are not aware of your husband's activities since your separation, but we have come to know him pretty well. Evanston is still a small town in many respects. We've brought him in a few times for public intoxication, but he sleeps it off, pays his fifty bucks and goes home. Last night we got a fairly routine call about some guys being rowdy at a bar. When our officers arrived it was apparent the situation was much more serious than we expected." He paused for a moment before continuing. "Your husband and some others had smashed up the bar before retiring to a nearby motel. The officers found your husband and the others in...the motel. When the officers attempted to bring them in, your husband produced a gun. In the chaos that followed, the other man in the motel took a bullet in the leg; the other two shots came within inches of the officers, one of the women was also nearly hit. Your husband is lucky the officers didn't return fire, they could see that he was very drunk and got the gun away from him before it came to that."

Kim's head swam; she couldn't seem to make sense of what she was hearing. One part in particular seemed to stick out. "Where did the women come from?" She already felt sick and wished she could make herself leave; the churning in her stomach was becoming more intense by the minute.

The lieutenant paused and stared at her with deep concentration. Kim held her breath, her eyes pleading with him to tell her the truth. After what seemed a long time, Lt. Browning swallowed and said, "The women had left the bar with your husband and his friend...they are prostitutes."

*Prostitutes!* she screamed in her mind. Robb was with a prostitute! Everything seemed to spin for a moment as the word sunk in. Lt. Browning was still speaking but she couldn't hear what he was saying. Her knuckles gripped the arms of the chair until they were white. Bursts of light exploded in her peripheral vision and she tasted the bile in her throat. This was too much! What kind of man went to prostitutes? In the next instant she realized she was going to throw up. Panicking, she put a hand over her mouth, hoping to stop the inevitable. Suddenly there was a waste basket thrust in front of her and she retched into it. After a few moments she was handed a tissue and she wiped at her mouth. It took a few minutes for everything to come back into focus. Lt. Browning was looking at her, concern mingled with fear showing in his expression. Kim knew she should feel humiliated but she didn't seem able to feel anything right now.

"Mrs. Larksley," Lt. Browning asked after a few more moments. "Are you going to be all right?"

"I'm sorry." Kim whispered, her throat still burning. "I...uh, just didn't expect..." She swallowed hard—what could she say to explain?

The phone rang, relieving them both. While Lt. Browning spoke on the phone, Kim tried to gather her thoughts. Just today she had been going over their life together, and had remembered how much she had gone through with Robb. She had always viewed his problems with pity. He seemed so innocent that she often treated him as she would a child who just hadn't learned his lessons yet. How dumb could she be? How could she have missed so much? It felt as though a part of her mind opened and she realized how much she had overlooked. She was reminded of the night she had told Robb of her fears of him being unfaithful. His words echoed back to her: "I would never hurt you like that." Yet how could she be so dense as to not realize there weren't many reasons for Robb to leave her as he had? After all, she let him drink whenever he wanted to; she didn't put many demands on him at home. He'd been able to do whatever he wanted, and still come home to a wife who tried hard to love him. A Sunday School lesson from long ago came back to her as if it had been taught yesterday: "One sin leads to another." Kim had never felt so stupid not to have realized that.

Lt. Browning hung up the phone and smiled at Kim weakly. It was obvious that he was miserable about this whole situation. He opened his mouth to speak, but Kim cut him off, feeling the need to finish this and get away. "I'm sorry, Lieutenant, I just had no idea." She paused for a moment, summoning every ounce of strength and dignity she could find, and continued, "So what exactly is he being charged with?"

"He'll be charged with public intoxication, destruction of property, two counts of assault, attempted murder and...soliciting prostitution."

The last two words hung in the air and Kim nodded slightly. "Well," Kim attempted to smile as she stood and put out a shaky hand. Lt. Browning shook her hand with slight reservation and stood also. "Thank you for telling me this now. I could have really embarrassed myself in that courtroom tomorrow. I...just...well...I never expected he could change so much. Could you do me a favor and not mention having told me all this?" Thus far she had been able to keep the tears back, but her vision blurred as she apologized again and quickly left the room.

⮵

"Are you sure you don't want to take the day off?" Peggy asked with concern the next morning. Kim had returned home late last night and although her eyes had been dry, it was obvious she had been crying. Her parents questioned her about it, but she told them bluntly that she wasn't ready to talk about it. They hadn't felt like they could argue with that.

"Mom, I can't afford to wallow. Besides, I want to stay busy." But her voice betrayed her longing to crawl back under the covers and stay there forever. "I packed Jack's lunch, he said he's feeling much better and he'll be ready in a minute." Kim busied herself by loading dishes into the dishwasher but paused to turn and look at her mom. "Please don't say anything to Jackson. I need to find out what is going to happen to Robb before I clue him in to everything."

"And how long will that be?" Peggy asked, resisting the impulse to add that Kim needed to stop letting Robb rule her decisions.

"I'm not sure. He's going before the judge this morning. I'll call the lieutenant at lunch; he'll have a better idea by then."

Peggy didn't answer. Kim finished the dishes as if Peggy weren't there and picked up her keys. She slung her purse over her shoulder and yelled up the stairs. "Jackson I'm leaving!"

"Okay, Mom," he called but he didn't come down.

"I'll see you after school," Kim yelled back—she really wished he would come down; she could use a hug, but she didn't want to make an issue out of it. "I love you."

"Love you, too," Jackson yelled just before she heard the door to the bathroom slam shut.

Kim looked back to her Mother and shrugged her shoulders. Peggy watched as Kim glanced up the stairs once more and headed out the door.

At the office, Kim was quiet and went about her work hoping no

27

one would bother her. Her mind was a constant whirl of thoughts. She needed to organize them, make sense of everything; but she couldn't seem to hold onto any one thought long enough to do so. Every time she tried to focus on a detail, another image would emerge and she'd try all over again.

Maddie popped her head in after lunch. "There you are. I was wondering if you had even shown up this morning; we had the planning meeting with the Hospital."

"I headed that up last quarter and Don said I could skip this time."

"Lucky you." Maddie looked at Kim for a few more seconds and added, "Are you okay?"

"Yeah, I'm fine," Kim said shortly; she had yet to meet Maddie's eyes.

"Liar," Maddie teased.

Kim refused to look up and pretended Maddie wasn't there at all. Maddie took a seat, not getting the hint.

"You didn't come back to work yesterday—what happened?"

Still Kim didn't look up, and again she was silent. She wasn't ready to get into this. Maddie was silent for a few more moments. "Kim, what's going on?"

Still she didn't speak. Maddie furrowed her brow, "Kim, I'm not leaving until you—"

Kim slammed down her pencil, making Maddie jump. "Look," she said angrily, fixing Maddie with a look that could kill. "I already missed half a day yesterday, and I don't have time to shoot the bull with you. If you need to say something, say it."

Maddie looked surprised and hurt; Kim had never spoken to her that way. She stood quickly and left the room without another word, leaving Kim alone just as she had requested. Kim dropped her head in her hands. What am I doing? she thought to herself. For several minutes she just sat there feeling miserable, knowing she should apologize and try to explain, but she couldn't summon the energy.

In an attempt to push the incident out of her mind, Kim pulled out a business card and dialed the number. She waited for Lt. Browning to pick up his phone and fought the temptation to hang up. Part of her never wanted to know what had happened at the hearing. When he answered she asked what had happened at Robb's arraignment. Browning didn't beat around the bush. He came right out and said it. "He was formally charged and is in the process of working out a plea bargain. That will take a few days, then the Judge will hand down the sentencing."

Kim was silent while she allowed herself to absorb the reality of what she had just heard. "So did he plead guilty?" she asked, unsure of what the exact process was.

"In essence, yes, they just haven't worked out the details. Most likely they'll drop everything but the assault and property damage in exchange for avoiding the time and expense of a trial."

She thanked him and hung up the phone, letting out a long breath. He was guilty, he said so himself; the last chance of this being a mistake was gone. Her husband, the father of her child, was going to prison. Her heart sank even further and she wiped furiously at her eyes telling herself that crying would solve nothing.

For the next week, Kim went about her life at home and work functioning by routine. Several times a day she would find herself staring into space, trying to make sense of everything, yet she never could. She avoided Maddie and tried hard not to be alone with either of her parents; she could tell they were all desperate to know what had happened, but were loath to ask. At work, she spent most of her time in her office, being sure to keep herself busy and detached from everyone. Sam was leaving on his mission soon, and she found him to be a 'soft place' for her right now. He let her help him with a lot of the last minute preparations, but didn't try to push for a heart to heart. When she wasn't helping Sam, she spent every second she could with Jackson, throwing around a baseball, playing soccer, going to his games and practices, doing homework—anything to stay occupied.

Each night after putting him to bed she would retire to her room, and try again to sort it all out. She felt like she had failed at everything. All she had wanted was a husband and kids; she had always tried to do what was right. Even if her testimony had been weak at times, she still had one. She was a good person, so why did this have to happen to her? What had gone wrong? She had the temple marriage, she had done her best to live the commandments. Yet here she was, twenty-nine years old and living with her parents. Her husband would be going to prison, and she was trying to raise her son—alone. Admittedly she was naive when she accepted Robb's proposal, but hadn't she done her best?

She talked to Lt. Browning again a few days after Robb's arraignment. Robb had pled guilty to the assault and property damage done to the bar, and all other charges were dropped. He was sentenced to 5 to 10 years in the Wyoming prison. Kim still hadn't heard a word from him.

Kim knew her family was worried, but that they were trying to be understanding. She wished she could keep it a secret forever, but she knew their patience would soon run out. Sam was leaving on his mission in a few days and Kim hoped she could wait until he was out of the house to tell her terrible secret. It seemed to her that her family understood that part; she was sure that was why the issue hadn't been pushed harder.

The day after Sam went into the Missionary Training Center, Kim came home from work and picked up the mail as usual. Absently thumbing through the stack as she walked into the house, she froze when she came to an envelope addressed to Jackson, forwarded to her parents' house and postmarked from Wyoming. For a moment she was bothered that Robb hadn't written to her, but it quickly turned to anger. How dare he do all of this to her and then write their son before he tries to explain himself to her. Sure that he was sending empty flattery meant to excuse his absence, Kim tore it open. The contents surprised and angered her all the more.

*Hey Buddy*

*Could you do me a favor and ask your mom to send me some money, I want to buy some magazines. I love you Jack, and I hope you'll come see me soon. I can have visitors on Mondays and Saturdays.*

*Dad*

Kim was furious. As if it was no big deal that he was in prison, as if it made no impact on their lives, he made no apology at all. He just asked for money. She crumpled up the letter and clenched it in her fist. What a wimp, she thought and stormed into the house.

Peggy looked up in surprise; she was paying bills at the kitchen counter. "Hi," she said.

Kim kicked the door shut behind her and threw the mail onto the entryway table without responding to her mother's greeting. The stack slid across the slick surface and tumbled to the floor on the other side. Kim cursed, louder than was necessary, and stooped down to pick it up. Peggy watched the drama from the kitchen.

Kim put the stack back on the table, keeping one item separate from the others. It was a rather bulky envelope postmarked in Wyoming and originally addressed to her home address, half of which was covered by a yellow printed sticker the post office had attached in order to accomplish getting it to her at her parents home.

Kim sat down at the kitchen table and simply stared at the envelope for a minute, uncertain whether she wanted to open it or not.

Finally, she tore a slit across the top. She pulled out a stack of papers and as she read one and then another her heart sank and her throat tightened. When she finished looking at the last sheet in her hand, Kim looked at her mother pleadingly and put her hands over her face. Peggy came over to the table and picked up the stack hesitantly. Her brow furrowed as she went through the items one by one.

There was a bill from an Instacare in Wyoming for $422, a bar tab for almost $200, an auto repair invoice of $1,557 and a Visa bill that had a balance of nearly $4,000. Besides those there were a few miscellaneous bills totaling another $200. Every single one was in the name of Kimberly Larksley.

"There's almost $7,000 of bills here," Peggy said as she pulled out a chair and sat down.

Kim looked at the stack Peggy put back on the table. "Did you notice they're all overdue?" she asked softly.

"Can these really be your responsibility?" Peggy asked.

"I don't know," Kim groaned, and waved towards the stack. "They all seem to think so."

"There's got to be something you can do about this."

"Any ideas?" Kim asked in a flat voice.

"Well, some of them have numbers you can call. How could he possibly get a credit card in your name?"

"It's my account; Robb doesn't have good enough credit to get one of his own. Consumer Credit told me to cancel it, I just never got around to it. I don't know how he got a new card; I cut up the one I had almost a year ago." Kim folded her arms on top of the table and dropped her head. "What am I going to do?"

Peggy straightened and reached across the table to touch Kim's arm. "Why don't I give your dad's attorney a call and ask him about it?"

Kim's head was still on her arms but she attempted to nod anyway. She heard Peggy go to the phone, rustle some pages and punch in a number. I can't believe this is happening, Kim thought to herself, as if I didn't have enough garbage to deal with. She could hear her mom on the phone but she wasn't listening. Why, she screamed inside. Why me? What did I do to deserve this? A sickening dread filled her as she tried to think of how on earth she would pay these bills. It was hard enough trying to sort out her life right now without Robb adding even more complications.

Kim wanted to rant and rave, but she couldn't muster up the energy. She felt too drained by all that had happened. Over and over she just kept asking herself what she was going to do. There was never an answer. After several minutes she heard her mom make the 'thank you' and 'goodbye' noises that indicated the phone conversation was over.

Peggy sat across the table from Kim. "Well," she started. "The bar tab and the sporting good store shouldn't be a problem. Robb would probably have had to sign your name illegally to get the credit, so all you need to do is write a letter explaining the situation and include your signature. The auto repair is a little trickier. You can try the letter thing with them but chances are they took a print of the credit card as insurance the bill would be paid. When they realize what's going on they will probably charge the card, if they haven't already. The two big ones are first, the insurance. Since you carry the policy, you are the responsible party and liable for the charges; if it isn't paid they can drop your coverage. The worst is this credit card. It's your responsibility to remove anyone who is no longer authorized to sign on your account, but he recommends that you call and see about it anyway." Peggy watched her daughter for a sign that she had even heard.

"Kim?" she said softly. Peggy reached across the table and lightly touched Kim's arm. "Penny for your thoughts?"

Kim stayed as she was, wondering if there was any way she could avoid discussing this with her mother. When she realized there wasn't, she finally lifted her head. "Mom, I have no way of paying any of this. I've already had to rent out my house, I'm trying to get my finances back under control, and now this. I don't know what else I can do? I just feel...totally lost."

"Your dad and I can help a little, dear."

Kim shook her head. "I didn't mean that, Mom, I...I just... " She paused as she felt the emotion rise in her throat. "Why is God doing this to me? Why is everything in my life going down hill? It seems the harder I try to do what is right the more things He throws at me. I don't have what it takes to handle this. I am at my breaking point and yet this..." she waved a hand towards the stack of bills. "This happens and I have no way to counter it. As if Robb hasn't caused me enough hardship and struggle, he has to heap this on me too." She fell silent.

"So who are you angry with? God or Robb?"

"Both."

"Now, Kim," her mother reprimanded, but Kim shook her head to stop the lecture about God's love that she knew was coming. Frankly she couldn't feel that right now.

"I know I'm not supposed to believe that God works this way, but I've also been taught that everything happens for a reason. So why is this happening? What possible reason is there to increase my debt when I am doing everything I can to decrease it, just like the prophet has said?" Her voice rose in pitch as anger flavored her argument. "I have tried for eight years to help my husband, to keep my marriage together, to be faithful, and teach my son about righteous living when his own father was living completely opposite to those values. I did what the Bishop said. I've tried to follow my heart, yet time and again I am crushed beneath things I have no control over. Where's the mercy in that? What's the point? What am I supposed to learn? That doing what's right doesn't pay off? That I shouldn't fight to keep my marriage together? That I shouldn't try to love my husband unconditionally? I've done those things and the only thing I'm convinced of is that if I had given up on all of this a long time ago Robb wouldn't have been able to hurt me this way. I've stuck it out; I've done what was 'right' and I'm the one that's suffering, over and over again. And just when I think it can't get worse, it does. Where is God's love in that?"

Peggy seemed to consider all that Kim said and when she spoke her voice was calm and soft. "Kim, God's ways are mysterious, but there is always a purpose; if only to make us stronger and to test our faith. I know you're hurting, and I know there doesn't seem to be much sense in what's happened in your life, but no matter what happens to you there are choices for you to make. Even now you can choose to be a victim or you can choose to find solutions, but being angry with God will get you nowhere—"

"I'm going nowhere anyway," Kim cut in angrily. "I have gotten one slam after another, with barely enough time in between to catch my breath. God isn't helping me, Mom; not a thing has happened in my favor for a very long time."

Peggy regarded Kim for a minute. "Then maybe He's trying to tell you something; what have you been doing that would necessitate His forcing understanding on you?"

Kim looked at her mother with confusion. "What's that supposed to mean?"

"When we ask for an answer to a dilemma in our life, God answers us with a confirmation or a stupor of thought, right?"

Kim nodded thoughtfully.

"So maybe these things are either confirming a direction you should go or showing you that you're going the wrong way."

"I don't understand," Kim said quietly.

"Is your goal to get back together with your husband, or to move on?"

Kim looked down at the table; she had no answer for that. "How am I supposed to know? I've tried to do what the Lord would want me to do for a very long time. I have tried to hold my marriage together no matter what, in hopes that one day Robb would come around. Even now after everything." She stopped thoughtfully for a moment and then met her mother's eye. "How do I know when it's okay to break those covenants?"

"Robb broke those covenants, Kim, not you; but to answer your question, I don't know when it's okay to end your marriage. I think you're the only one that can make that decision." Peggy watched Kim drop her eyes again and sighed. "Tell me what happened in Wyoming, Kim. What exactly happened there; if it was only the man he shot, I think you would talk to me, but since you haven't I can only guess there's more."

Kim just shook her head; she knew she needed to tell her family the truth, but now that it was time to do so she didn't feel ready.

"Can't you tell me?" Peggy asked after another moment of silence.

"I don't know," Kim admitted.

"You're a very private person, Kim, and I have tried to respect that." Peggy touched her daughter's hand as she continued. "But if you don't let some of this out, it will fester and poison you. Whatever the future holds, you must deal with this one way or another, and you must accept that what Robb has done is his weakness and no reflection of you."

Kim almost chuckled at the irony of her mother's words. Then the anger started radiating through her chest and she became angry again. Peggy was a good, sweet woman. Did she have any perception of the disgusting life Robb had chosen instead of being a husband and father? Then again maybe Peggy was right. Maybe getting this out would release her from some of her pain. Maybe her mom could tell her how she should prepare for the day she would have to tell her son that his father was in prison. Suddenly she wanted to share this pain, let her mother help her bear it. She'd kept it inside and that hadn't worked; maybe getting it out in the open would.

"Robb was arrested with a hooker, Mom." The words escaped before she could prepare herself and her body shuddered slightly when she said the words out loud. Peggy's eyes went wide and she simply stared at her daughter, dumfounded. "He trashed a bar, and was arrested in a motel room with a prostitute, where he shot another guy who was with another hooker." Her chin quivered and she looked back at the table. "The man I married and promised to honor and love forever chose a whore over me and his son." That final statement summed it all up. All her hurt and anger related to one powerful concept; choice. Robb made a choice. His choice disgusted her and made her question her personal worth as a woman, as a wife. At some point he had put his family, and all they had to offer him, on one side of the scale and a cheap, dirty thrill on the other. It was obvious which one had offered the greatest appeal. The tears coursed down her cheeks and her heart seemed to break all over again.

It took Peggy only another moment to overcome her shock and be at Kim's side. She pulled Kim to her shoulder and held her tightly as Kim finally gave in to the pain she had kept bound inside for all this time.

Peggy's chest tightened and she cried, too, as her daughter's sobs filled the room. A hooker, she said in her mind. No wonder Kim had avoided telling her, yet thank goodness she had finally let it out.

To say she was shocked was a supreme understatement. Peggy had never been particularly fond of Robb but she had never considered he would do something like that. When he and Kim were dating, Peggy had been very suspicious Robb's lack of religious tenacity, and his ability to convince others around him that it was all right. Unfortunately, a parent's opinions don't always carry enough weight. Trying to convince her daughter that she could do better went nowhere. Eventually, Peggy decided that supporting Kim's decision would be more effective than pushing her away by expressing negative opinions. As Kim's sobs turned to whimpering, Peggy prayed for guidance in offering some comfort.

Finally, Kim lifted her head and wiped her eyes, she was a bit embarrassed but certainly felt better; at least a little.

Peggy grasped her daughter by the shoulders and looked at her very seriously. "First of all, I want you to know that I am so sorry. But more than that, I want you to know this is not your fault. Robb did this, not you."

"Yeah right," Kim said shakily as she reigned in her emotions. "It's not my fault that my husband prefers the company of whores?" The word seemed to stick in her throat.

"No, it's not," Peggy said with conviction.

"That's easy for you to say, Mom. But put yourself in my place and tell me you wouldn't look at yourself in the mirror and wonder what it was that drove your husband to pay for sex. Tell me you wouldn't wonder if the extra pounds you put on didn't affect his decision. Tell me you wouldn't dissect every experience you shared, trying to determine where you had fallen short. Look me in the eye, Mom, and tell me that you wouldn't feel you were partly to blame." Her words were soft, but the meaning was harsh and undeniable.

Peggy didn't have anything to say to that. She simply looked at her daughter and reached up to wipe the fresh tears from Kim's cheeks. "I can't dispute that, Honey; all I can tell you is that," she paused for a moment, "we are told that by their fruits we shall know them. I see a beautiful woman who has given love and dedication and commitment to a man who has given very little. Robb is a weak man. He always has been. His decisions have taken away his freedom, but they haven't taken away yours. You are strong, Kim. You need to use your strength to overcome this."

"I don't know how, Mom," Kim said quietly. "It's been two weeks and I can barely get out of bed in the morning. I can't do anything without thinking about him and what he's done. I can't look at my son without wondering how I will ever be able to tell him this. And yet I can't let go of Robb either. I can't take off my wedding ring, I can't call an attorney. I'm stuck." Her voice shook.

"Have you prayed about this?" Peggy asked.

"I can't do that either," Kim whispered.

"If you don't ask, you can't receive an answer."

Just then Jackson came bounding through the door. "Hi, Mom," he said cheerfully as he passed them by and bounced down the stairs, followed by a small group of other kids. Peggy stood, "And if you need some motivation for finding the answer..." she let the question hang, but Kim understood.

# CHAPTER FOUR

Kim was already in the shower when she realized it was Saturday. Because of her mistake, she was the first one downstairs. Rather than giving in to her desire to go back to bed, she prepared a big breakfast of French toast, bacon, and orange juice and thoroughly enjoyed spending some time alone with her son before her parents got up. Jackson entertained her with stories about his friends and school. His second grade class was going on a field trip to a planetarium on Monday, and he couldn't wait. Kim smiled and marveled at the joy he could find in such simple things, and wondered how to learn that from him.

She felt so much lighter this morning, and was relieved when her mom came down and acted as if nothing out of the ordinary had happened the evening before. By 10:00 Jackson had left with Kim's dad to go pick out a fishing rod, and her mom had left to run some errands.

Left alone, her mind was drawn back to her thoughts of the night before, when she had decided she needed to go to the bishop. Although she was still unsure of what to do and what direction to move, she believed that if anyone could help her, Bishop Scott could. After dialing his number and listening to it ring a few times she realized she was probably supposed to call the executive secretary, not the bishop himself. She almost hung up; relieved that she could hang on to her secret a little longer, when the Bishop himself answered the phone.

"Hello," he said brightly, it sounded more like 'Yellow,' and Kim smiled. She had lived in this ward for a few years before her marriage, and she liked the people but hadn't developed any lasting relationships with anyone. But Bruce Scott had been the Gospel Doctrine Teacher and lived just one street over, so she was more familiar with him than with many other people in the ward.

"Hi, Bishop. This is Kim Larksley; I'm Todd and Peggy's daughter."

"I know who you are, Kim; how are things going?"

"Actually, I'm calling to see if I could can speak with you about... my situation. It wasn't until the phone started to ring that

I realized I probably should have called someone else to make an appointment. I can—"

"It's not a problem," he cut in. "Have you got time today?"

Kim was surprised and not at all sure she was ready to do this today, but she did have the time. "I do, but do you?" she asked. Bishops weren't well known for having a lot of extra time on their hands.

"Well, I'm on my way to the ward house right now. Why don't you meet me there in say a half an hour?"

"Uh, yeah. I can do that."

"See you then."

Kim hung up the phone with butterflies in her stomach, but refused to give in to her hesitation. Then she hurried upstairs to get ready.

Finally, after waiting in the hall for what felt like forever, Bishop Scott opened the door to his office and invited her inside. Bishop Scott was in his late fifties, and in excellent shape. When he wasn't attending to the needs of the ward, he coached football and track for a local junior college. Today he wore a plain white golf shirt and tan slacks. After a few minutes of small talk, the room was suddenly quiet. Kim continued to fidget with her coat, not quite meeting his eyes. After making sure it was all right with her to start the interview with prayer, he offered a short but humble request for the Spirit to guide them through the meeting. After saying "Amen" he began.

"I have to admit this is my least favorite part of these meetings, but go ahead, the floor is yours."

"I'm not here to confess anything really. I hope that makes you feel better." She gave him a weak smile and he wiped his forehead in feigned relief. "What I've come for is some advice: it's about my husband." The bishop nodded, so Kim continued, "I don't know what you know about us but I guess... you could say we are separated."

"You guess?"

"Well, not formally." She was at a loss of how to continue, but he solved her problem.

"Why don't you fill me in on your situation and then we'll see what we can do, okay?"

An hour later, Kim was wiping her eyes with a Kleenex and wishing she had used waterproof mascara. Bishop Scott was leaning one elbow on the desk and scratching his head with his other hand.

"Wow," was all he said, but he smiled. And Kim returned it with a weak smile of her own. "Who else knows about all this?"

"Just my mom—well, probably my dad too, by now, but that's it. I've become very good at keeping this stuff to myself."

"I can imagine it seems easier that way."

Kim nodded in agreement.

"So I assume that the question is, what do you do now."

"I know it sounds pathetic to say this, Bishop, but as sickened and hurt as I am, part of me still loves Robb; I think. I'm just at a loss to know what to do."

"Is there any chance that you can forgive him?"

"I *have* to forgive him," she said, acknowledging just one reason for her conflict. "I know I have to find a way to do that. But I don't know how and I don't know when."

"Maybe what I should have asked is if there is any chance of a reconciliation?"

"He hasn't even attempted to speak to me, he wrote to our son, but—"

"I'm not concerned with how he feels; I want to know how you feel."

"I feel sick," Kim said after a moment, not sure that was what Bishop Scott was asking.

"Besides that."

"I feel confused."

"About what?"

Kim sighed in frustration. "About everything. I'm confused about where I went wrong, and where he went wrong. I'm confused about why we ever got together in the first place. If we do get divorced, what was the point of us even being together? For all these years, I have felt that I loved him so much; that I would do anything for him. Yet in the last few weeks I've realized—I've wondered if I really love him at all anymore. Was I in love with the fantasy, the possibility more than the man?"

"So are you considering divorce?"

"That would seem the logical choice after what he did, but I still feel so...attached to him. How can I just pretend he's not a part of me anymore? And if I can forgive him, I mean *really* forgive him, then shouldn't I also remain as his wife too? But if I choose divorce, where does that leave Jackson? He'll be without a father—not just now, but forever. Is it fair for me to make this decision for both of us? After all these years, is it right for me to just turn my back on everything, even after what he did? Logic tells me yes, but logic isn't always right. And I just don't feel like I'm ready to make that decision."

Bishop Scott leaned back in his chair and rubbed his chin while he thought about everything she had said. He opened his mouth to speak but she hurried to continue.

"Everything just seems so complicated. I was very naive when I married Robb but I got wiser real fast. I was determined to make it work and keep the covenants I'd made. I don't take those promises lightly and I can't help wondering if it isn't up to me to help Robb with this. I've always thought that way before. I chose to marry him and I have to wonder if, because of that, I owe it to him to keep on trying. Don't get me wrong, I hate to imagine continuing my life this way, but maybe that's what I'm supposed to do."

"So you think there's a chance you can overcome this?"

"I don't know. I've fallen backward myself over the years, but I do believe that I can do anything the Lord wants me to do. I know that poor choices on my part are some reasons why I'm here, which is why I want to make sure I do it the Lord's way this time." Kim was surprised at her own words; she had never really even thought that to herself, but she knew it was true. In spite of her anger towards God, her faith hadn't wavered very much. If the Lord wanted her to see it through, she could do it; she just wished she didn't feel so nauseated by the thought of continuing as Robb's wife.

"I bet you wish you didn't feel so strongly about your covenants."

Kim laughed bitterly, glad for his candor. "It would be so easy to just walk away, especially when the very thought of seeing him again makes me ill."

He leaned forward on his elbows. "I'm sure you know that it's not in my power to make this decision for you." Kim nodded her understanding as he continued, "I can't tell you what to do, but I can help you to find your own answer; teach you how prepare yourself for it. I want to impress upon you the seriousness of this decision, but it sounds like you understand the weight of it. However, you need to understand the full scope of things. Robb will be excommunicated for this."

Kim startled, but she had already known that was a possibility. For some reason, having the bishop say it out loud made it much more real.

"That means that his temple blessings will be revoked, his

priesthood will be taken away and it will only be in his power to ever get those things back. He has made choices that brought him to this point and you need to make sure you don't decide to remain his wife because of some kind of penance you feel you owe him. You owe him nothing, Kim; whatever decision you make needs to be for your good. I'm not saying that you should get a divorce, that is your decision, but I want you to understand that your Father in Heaven loves you, and he wants you to make the decision that will give you happiness and joy again."

"I guess I understand that," she said softly.

"You guess?" the bishop repeated. He leaned forward and looked at her hard. "You deserve to *know*. So I advise you to go home and read your patriarchal blessing. I also want you to kneel in prayer morning and night. Read sections 131 and 132 in the Doctrine and Covenants; they teach about marriage and will increase your understanding. And last, but not least: when was your last visit to the temple?"

"Uh..." she was so intent on committing every bit of counsel to memory, that she had to stop and really concentrate. "I went with Sam when he received his endowments, but that was the first time in nearly three years. I'm afraid that it's yet one more area I haven't given my time to as I should. Robb returned only once since we were married and I didn't like to go alone."

"I am telling you to go alone. Fast before you go and listen carefully to the words of the session, feel what the temple has to offer you, and spend a good long time in the celestial room. I want to meet with you in two weeks. In the meantime I will also pray and think about this. When we meet again, we'll see how you're feeling and discuss what you've learned. How does that sound?"

Kim took a moment to gather her thoughts. "It sounds like a good plan."

"Good," Bishop Scott said as he stood. "It's a date then."

Kim sat in the parking lot for several minutes reviewing the bishop's counsel. She also tried to interpret her feelings. The Spirit had been so strong as the Bishop spoke to her. But she wasn't sure if its strength meant that she had become accustomed to not feeling the comfort of it, or because the Spirit was much more powerful than it had ever felt before. She didn't feel better about the situation, but she felt more capable of deciding on the solution. The bishop's words had given her new strength. She hadn't kept herself as close to the Spirit as she should have, now she'd been reminded that she was still entitled to guidance. But she had to seek it diligently; nothing in life was free.

She turned the key in the ignition and it only clicked. With a sigh she tried again. The battery had been undependable lately, but it hadn't ever not started before. She tried three more times and when it finally started she made a mental note to have her dad check it out. As she drove home the warmth faded, and as the weight of indecision returned, neither option seemed right. Divorcing Robb felt like quitting; giving up on the person she had promised to never abandon. Remaining married made her feel like an idiot. She had no reason to believe that her life with Robb would be any different than it had ever been. But how could she be sure? The choosing of which path to follow would be a painful process regardless of her choice, but she was at the crossroads, and it was time to seek answers.

Kim walked in the house and called out to see if anyone was home yet—apparently not, since no one answered. After setting her keys on the table she walked right to the phone and dialed the number before she chickened out. Just as she pulled into the driveway she had thought of something that had nothing to do with Robb, but everything to do with making things right concerning an entirely different relationship.

"Hello," said the voice on the phone.

"Hi, Maddie? This is Kim."

"Oh. Hi," she said cautiously. They had only exchanged the basics since Kim had freaked out on Maddie that day at work. Until now Kim hadn't been able to work up the energy to make amends, but now that she was becoming a little more proactive in her life, she knew she owed Maddie an apology and an explanation.

"Maddie, I'm so sorry," she said simply. "I was so rude and I feel very badly about it." Maddie didn't say anything, which was making it much harder, but Kim continued. "I found out what's been going on with Robb and I've had a tough time dealing with it. I know you don't owe me anything but I'd like to take you to dinner and try to make things right between us again."

"Well, I..."

Kim cut in before she could refuse, knowing exactly how to get her there. "I really need someone to talk to, and you've always been such a good listener." She knew it was wrong to manipulate her friend, but she also knew Maddie wouldn't refuse.

"Yeah, I can be there," Maddie finally answered cautiously. "Should I pick you up?"

"Uh, what if we met each other there?"

"Okay, where?"

"The Sizzler on State Street and Ninetieth South, is that okay? About 6:00."

"Alright, I'll see you there."

"Thanks, Maddie, I really appreciate this."

"No problem. See you later."

Kim smiled as she hung up the phone. Then she quickly picked it up again. One more call, she thought as it rang. Oh please—let this work.

With her mom watching Jackson, Kim was able to arrive at the restaurant a little early. When Maddie arrived, they ordered and sat down. Kim explained everything that had happened—well, almost everything, trying hard to make clear her reasons for backing away from everyone. Maddie didn't let her completely off the hook, however; she explained how hurt she had been and Kim was humbled by the understanding. After ten minutes the tension between them had been cleared away and Kim was warmed by relief that Maddie would forgive her.

"I spent so many years separating myself from people, trying to hide what was going on with Robb. I panicked this time and made a thorough mess of everything." She smiled across the table at her friend. "Maddie, I just can't remember ever having as good a friend as you."

"Hey, Kim," a tall, good-looking guy interrupted as he slid into the booth next to her. Maddie was a little startled, but smiled cautiously when he nodded a hello in her direction. Kim wanted to laugh; she couldn't have choreographed this better.

"Hi, Matt," she said brightly, punching him lightly in the shoulder. "Matt, this is my good friend Maddie. Maddie, this is Matt." She pretended not to notice their discomfort. They appraised each other a moment, until finally Maddie cleared her throat and broke the ice a little.

"Nice to meet you," Maddie said as she extended her hand across the table.

"Yeah, you too," Matt answered, stretching his own hand out while giving his sister a what-is-going-on look.

"Anyway," Kim drawled as she nudged Matt out of the booth to allow her through and then firmly pushed him back down. "I told Maddie awhile back that I would set you two up, but I didn't follow through," she said as she dug an envelope out of her purse and put it down in front of Matt. Maddie was red with embarrassment and tried hard to catch Kim's eye, which Kim discreetly avoided. "I ordered you steak and shrimp," she said to Matt. "And I got tickets to a movie." She glanced at her watch and added, "Have a good time." Then she hurried out before either one could stop her, hoping she wouldn't have more apologies to make tomorrow. It had seemed like a great idea when she'd put it all together, but now she worried that she'd acted too fast; maybe this should have waited until Maddie and herself were on firmer ground with one another. But as she got into the car she was smiling; it had been fun to be on the giving end for once. She hoped her instincts were good and that they would enjoy one another's company.

Late that night, she lay in bed unable to sleep. The light from the street lamp streamed through her window and she was reminded of a night not long ago when she had, for the first time, turned her troubles over to the Lord. Just as she had that night, she raised her hand above her head and allowed the diamond in her wedding ring to catch the light. She twisted the set off of her finger and stared at it for a moment. Finally, she rolled over and put the rings on the nightstand. Still on her side, she stared at them for what seemed to be a long time. She hadn't yet made her decision, but she was willing to admit that her marriage was on hold. With her husband in prison, she put her marriage on probation. She smiled sadly at the metaphor and rolled over to sleep.

ᴥ

"Kim!" Maddie said Monday morning, as she burst into Kim's office.

Kim sat up straight in her chair and cast her eyes down like a disobedient child; she'd been expecting this. "Okay, let me have it," she said.

"Why on earth," Maddie paused dramatically, "did you ever set me up with your other brothers?"

"What?" Kim said after a moment of shock.

Maddie laughed and sat down in one of the chairs across from the desk, leaning towards Kim, her eyes shining. "We had such a good time, Kim. Matt is wonderful."

"Really?" Kim said, sitting back in her chair, still a little stunned. When she had come up with the idea, she had hoped they'd have a good time, but she hadn't expected a reaction this positive.

"Matt is a great guy. He's so funny and smart and...Kim, he is so good-looking." Her eyes twinkled with excitement.

"Are you serious?" Kim questioned.

"Yes," Maddie laughed. In feigned exasperation she rolled her eyes as she picked up Kim's nail file from her 'pen can' and started repairing a snag. She looked up and coyly asked, "Did Matt call you?"

Kim was still staring and gave herself a mental shake. "Yes, he did," she said slowly.

"So, what did he say?"

"He left a message with my mom."

"And?"

"And he said to tell me 'Thanks a lot.'"

Maddie giggled, "Yeah, that's what he said he was going to do. He thought you'd take it the wrong way, I guess he was right."

Now Kim laughed—it was just like Matt to try and throw her off that way. "He's such a brat, Maddie. I should never have inflicted him on you."

"Oh, inflict me, please. He's great."

"I've always thought so. But since he's the only brother that didn't cut off my Barbie's hair, I could be biased."

"My only complaint is that your parents named him Matt. You have four brothers and I happen to fall in love with the one named Matt."

"Love? " Kim croaked after a slight pause. It had only been two days.

"I don't know, we'll see," Maddie then jumped up from her chair. "I've got to get back, I just wanted to thank you for the date. I'll keep you up to speed."

Kim was, again, stunned. "You do that," she said, more to herself than anyone else. Love, she repeated to herself. Then she shrugged it off; what were the chances?

# CHAPTER FIVE

Two weeks later, Kim was across the desk from the bishop again. She had felt better than usual since their meeting. Her mom made her talk about it some; her dad referred her to a few books he felt would help her make more sense of everything she was dealing with. But she still couldn't decide which direction to go. Sometimes she'd tell herself to just get it over with. Get a divorce. But something still held her back and she wasn't prepared to make such a big decision until she was absolutely sure it was the right one to make.

"So, how did it go?" Bishop Scott asked.

"Well I read the Doctrine and Covenants chapters and I understand why you recommended them to me. I don't remember ever pondering so deeply on the details of eternal marriage, but I have to admit I didn't really like what I read."

Bishop Scott raised his eyebrows, "Really?"

"I'm sure that for you it is very comforting, but it only leaves me more confused."

"How so?"

"I told you last time how serious I feel it is to toss my marriage covenants aside. After reading the section it only intensified my feelings that I am bound by those covenants. I know I *can* get a divorce, but will I be held accountable forever for breaking the promises I made? And where does it leave Jackson? Let's say that someday I remarry. And I have more children that are born in the covenant with my new husband; Jackson remains a spiritual bastard, you could say. Is it fair for me to reduce him to that if there is any chance that Robb and I can stay together? I know that Robb broke his covenants, but *he* isn't the one seeking a divorce; at least not as far as I know."

"You need to understand, Kim, that nothing is as 'cut and dried' as we mortals perceive it to be. We have an obnoxious habit of wanting to black-and-white everything. The plan of salvation is based on happiness—happiness dependent on our choices made in mortality. And as far as your hypothetical situation goes; in most circumstances, if a child is born in the covenant he cannot be sealed to someone else. But regardless of what happens between you and Robb, Jackson is sealed to *you*. And if you keep your end of the bargain, he will remain that way. It isn't the nice little package you would probably like, but just because Robb makes bad decisions doesn't mean you lose the son you two brought into this world. Robb might lose him, but you will not be punished for his transgressions."

"Oh," Kim said simply. "I didn't realize it worked that way."

"As far as your marriage covenants are concerned, you and Robb were not guaranteed anything more than a mortal connection unless you lived worthy of your temple blessings. Robb has obviously not fulfilled his end of the bargain and no matter how well you live your life, you cannot drag him with you to the celestial kingdom."

"I know that. But my concern in his regard is based on the possibility that he could come around. What if what he needs is for me to support him and help him, so that he can come back? Maybe that's what the Lord wants me to do."

The Bishop leaned back in his chair. "Have you determined that is what the Lord wants you to do?"

"No," Kim said in defeat. "I have prayed and prayed for an answer and I'm still utterly confused as to what is right. One minute I'm convinced that I need to give it one more chance, see if serving time in prison changes his heart. But at the same time I can't even think about Robb without a mental picture of...well, anyway, I can't get past what he's done." Kim looked down at her hands, willing the fresh tears to stay back. "I am so full of anger towards him, how can I even imagine remaining his wife? Yet I can't seem to take the steps necessary to remove him from my life either."

"Did you attend the temple?" Bishop Scott asked.

"Yes," she said, lifting her face to look at him again, "and I enjoyed it more than I ever have before. I listened really carefully to all that was said; it amazed me how much I have missed in the past."

"But it didn't help you form a conclusion?"

"Not really. I felt a great deal of peace there, but I left with the same lead weight in my heart."

"You know, Kim," the bishop said, leaning forward on his elbows, "many times the Spirit will only verify that what you are doing is right or wrong. So I think you need to decide which direction you feel best about and pursue it. Then continue to pray for confirmation. If you do that you'll know if it is right."

Kim felt the truth of his words and nodded. "Now my only problem is deciding which way to go."

"And that is hard to do. But remember that you will feel peace when you're on a righteous path; you will know you are doing the right thing."

Both were silent for a long time before Kim finally spoke. "Thank you Bishop. You've given me a lot to think about."

Bishop Scott stood as she rose to her feet. "One more thing. Did you read your patriarchal blessing?"

Kim had completely forgotten about that. "No, actually. I looked for it after our last meeting, but didn't find it. I think it's packed away in a box, and I forgot to look again."

"Read it," he said bluntly and then broke into a wide smile. "Same time, same place, in two weeks?"

"I'll be here."

Kim got home to find some mail addressed to her lying on the table along with a note telling her that Grandpa and Jackson had gone to Grandpa's office. She smiled; Jackson had great grandparents and she knew that their constant attention was a big part of his successful adjustment to all the changes in their lives.

"Oh, no," she muttered as she looked at one envelope in particular. It was the response to the strongly-worded letter she had sent to the credit card company. She had canceled the card and sent letters to the other debtors. To her relief, the letters of explanation to most of them had worked; although she felt badly that they had to take the financial loss. But she'd had to pay off the insurance bill. Now there was just the credit card to deal with; she held their response in her hands. Taking a deep breath, she sat down and tore open the envelope. It was a very official letter that reiterated what the customer service representative had told her over the phone. It stated that it was her responsibility to remove unauthorized signers from her account and that, although they were sorry for the situation, their policies were clearly stated in the original account agreement.

Kim dropped onto the couch and covered her face with her hands. As much as she wanted to, she couldn't cry; in fact she found herself wanting to laugh at the ridiculous nature of what was happening to her. Could it get any worse than this? And even though the answer was yes, she felt all right with things. Every day was a little easier than the last, and she believed that it would continue that way. The bishop had said she'd feel peace if she were on the right path, more than anything, she wanted that peace.

The ringing of the phone saved her from having to think any

more about the letter. Pulling herself off the couch, she hurried to the phone.

"Hello." Kim said, a little breathless.

"Hi, Honey. I'm so glad you're home." Peggy went on to ask Kim's help in picking up some things at Deseret Book that she needed for her Relief Society lesson the next day. An elderly sister in the ward had broken her hip and Peggy had been called to stay with her at the hospital until her daughter could get there. It might be late, she said and Kim agreed to run the errand.

Less than an hour later, Kim had completed the task and she got into her car, preparing for the drive home. She turned the key in the ignition; click. Not again! After four more tries and four more clicks she pressed her forehead to the steering wheel. She moaned and tried again... and again... and again. Finally, she gave up and went back into the store. Luckily they let her use the phone.

Kim dialed her parent's number. Please answer, Dad, she thought to herself, but after five rings the voice mail clicked on and she hung up. Matt lived in Provo and she couldn't think of anyone else to call except Maddie. A man answered.

"Hello?"

"Hi, is Maddie home?" Kim asked hopefully, a little confused. Who was this guy?

"Nope."

"Will she be home soon?"

"Nope."

"Well, thanks anyway," she replied with mild sarcasm. She hoped he didn't notice.

"Can I tell her you called?" he was suddenly so helpful.

"No," Kim said, distracted, while trying to think of whom else she could possibly call. "Uh, well yeah, actually just tell her Kim called but it won't matter later. I'll just call her back."

The voice on the other end was quiet; either he was writing down her message including the "uh's" and "well's" or he just wasn't listening. "Is everything okay?" he asked after a moment.

Kim wanted to ask why he would care but instead said, "My car won't start, but I'll just call somebody else. Thanks..." She really needed to get off the phone; maybe Matt wouldn't mind driving to Salt Lake; then again maybe he was in Salt Lake with Maddie. She tried to remember his cell phone number.

"Oh, you're Matt's sister."

"Yes, I am." Kim wondered again who this guy was, but only for a moment before returning her thoughts to her dilemma. Did the bus run on Saturday?

"This is Allen, Maddie's brother," he said as if she should know all about him.

"Oh, hi," Kim answered politely, remembering something Maddie had said about her brother moving here. What's he doing at her place without Maddie? Kim thought then thought again, I've got to get off this phone!

"Can I help?"

"What?" Kim said, wondering what he was talking about.

"Can I help with your car trouble?"

"Oh...um, that's okay, you don't need to—"

"I don't mind, I'm not doing anything—where are you?"

Kim was silent for a moment. "Are you sure?"

"You bet, it's not a problem—now where are you?"

"I'm at the Cottonwood Mall. I think the battery's dead. It's been giving me trouble, but I haven't gotten around to replacing it."

"Well, I'm not much of a car guy but tell me what kind of car you've got and I'll pick up a battery just in case. We'll see what we can do."

"You don't need to do that. If I could just get home, Matt or my dad could come later and—"

Allen cut her off. "Its no big deal—what part of the mall?"

Kim felt a little uncomfortable but realized she hadn't any other options. She explained where she was, and the type of car she drove. He said he would be there in about twenty minutes.

Almost exactly twenty minutes later, a beautiful black Camaro pulled up next to her. Whatever Kim had expected, it wasn't what stepped out of the sports car. The friendly smile and handsome face, that looked nothing like Maddie, couldn't distract her from the fact that Maddie's brother had no hair. Not only was he completely bald but he wore an earring to boot. How could Maddie never have told her about this guy?

"Are you Kim?" he said as he stretched out his hand.

Kim moved her gaze from the small silver hoop in his ear and put on a big smile, hoping it would hide the fact that she had been staring. She shook his hand, wincing a little because of his tight grip. "And you must be Allen."

"Yep," he said simply. Still smiling, he walked past her to the open hood of her car. Placing his hands on the front edge of the car, he assumed the all-male pose of studying-the-engine. Kim took in his overall appearance while he poked and peered under the hood.

Kim figured he must be about six foot two or so, since he looked a couple inches taller than Matt who was six-foot. But whereas Matt was somewhat slender, Allen had broad shoulders and the basic build of a barroom bouncer. He was dressed in casual khaki pants, and a darker beige sports coat over a plain white T-shirt. A little dressy for the weekend, she thought. Kim was wearing sweats and no make-up—the way people were *supposed* to dress on Saturdays. She was staring at his snakeskin cowboy boots when she realized he was talking to her.

"I'm sorry, I didn't hear what you asked me," she said with embarrassment—that was twice in sixty seconds that he had caught her staring at him.

Allen had to consciously stop himself from rolling his eyes. People's reactions to him were so obvious, and he was so tired of it. "I asked what kind of trouble you'd been having with the battery."

"For the last couple of weeks I've had trouble starting the car sometimes. I meant to have my dad look at it but like a million other things in my life, I put it off." Kim moved to stand by the car, and while they talked they looked into the engine as if suddenly one of them would understand exactly what was wrong.

"Well, the cables are tight. Why don't we hook it up to my car and you can try it one more time. It might be beyond charging though; we'll see."

Kim nodded and got into the driver's seat while he uncoiled the jumper cables he had brought with him. He fastened the little alligator clips to the appropriate spots and when he nodded she turned the key. Nothing happened—well, except the click. Allen nodded, disconnected the cables and went to work removing the old battery and installing the new one. When that was done he stood up, holding his now-soiled hands away from his clothing.

"You don't happen to have a rag do you?" he asked.

"Let me see," Kim hurried around to open the trunk. She searched and finally found a dirty T-shirt of Jackson's that she decided she could live without. Kim turned quickly and slammed directly into his chest.

"Oh, sorry," she said quickly, and stepped back in embarrassment. Kim looked up at him and was a little annoyed at the look on his face; he looked as if he found it very funny. She thought the look would go away but even after he took the shirt and cleaned up; it was still there. She was relieved when the car started easily. With the engine running, she thanked him and pulled out her checkbook.

"What do I owe you?" she asked, filling in the date and signature on a check.

"Nothing," Allen said as he opened the door to the Camaro.

"No, really. How much?"

"Don't worry about it," he leaned against the frame of the door and crossed his arms over his chest. There was still that smirk on his face.

Kim was getting annoyed. "That's very nice of you, but I would really rather pay for the battery myself."

Allen looked at her silently for a moment and then shrugged his shoulders. "If you like."

Kim smiled with relief. "How much?"

"Five bucks."

Kim took a deep breath; she really wasn't in the mood for this. "Five bucks?" she said, raising an eyebrow.

"Yep."

"Look, I really appreciate your help, but I am quite capable of paying for my own car repairs."

"Then you should have gone to a mechanic." He put one booted foot in the car, still with that blasted smirk and added, "It was nice to meet you, Kim. See you around." He then shut his door; started and revved the engine, and drove away, leaving Kim standing there with pen in hand.

Kim got back into her car feeling very annoyed. What an arrogant jerk, she thought. No wonder Maddie never talked about the guy—he was too obnoxious a subject for decent conversation. Then again, he had fixed her car, and she was very grateful for that. When she got home, Jackson was there, so although she had picked apart the experience, she quickly forgot all about it.

∽

Monday morning, Kim was sitting at her desk when Maddie came in.

"Good morning," Maddie said brightly.

Kim looked up and smiled. "Hey, how ya doing?"

"Never been better. So you met my brother?" she said as she plopped into a chair.

Kim noticed the slight apprehension in Maddie's eyes and wondered again why she had never heard about the man. "Yes I did. He helped me with my car, he is very, uh...nice."

"He is nice, so what else did you think?"

"He's...just nice." Kim didn't want to tell Maddie how odd her brother seemed or that she thought he looked like a pirate.

"He said you were weird."

Kim's head popped up so fast her eyes didn't focus for a moment. "I'm weird!" she snorted.

Maddie burst out laughing, and when she noticed Kim blushing she laughed even harder. Kim gave her a dirty look and went back to her paperwork, embarrassed at her response—after all, he was Maddie's brother.

Finally Maddie got hold of herself and wiped her eyes. "I'm sorry, Kim. When he told me he thought you were weird I just busted up. His whole shiny head turned as red as Rudolph's nose on Christmas Eve."

Kim just smiled, still feeling a little uncomfortable and not sure what to say.

Maddie continued. "I told him he had no room to talk."

Kim gave her another courtesy smile.

"Okay," Maddie stood up to leave, still smiling. "You don't want to talk about it. Fine."

"Wait," Kim said putting down her pen, suddenly not wanting to stop talking about him so soon. "Why didn't you tell me about Allen?"

"What's to tell?" Maddie said sarcastically.

"You have dated three of my four brothers and you don't even tell me about yours?"

Maddie sat back down. "I told you about him before, he just moved here from Chicago last month. He's been staying with my folks but since my grandma's moving in, there wasn't room in their condo anymore so he moved in with me for a few weeks until the loan on his house closes. He just moved in over the weekend."

"Isn't he married?" Kim asked, bits and pieces of past information finally registering in her brain.

"He was, but he got a divorce a couple of years ago."

"Oh," Kim said, then added, "It was very nice of him to help me out. In fact I need you to give him a check for me." She reached for her purse.

"Nope, he told me under no circumstances to accept any money from you."

Kim sighed in frustration. "Maddie, I'm really not comfortable with his paying for the battery."

"Well, get comfortable with it. Allen's very generous."

"I don't want his generosity. I find it ...offensive."

"Really? Why?" Maddie seemed genuinely surprised.

"Well...because..." Kim couldn't put it into words. "It's just not his responsibility."

Maddie leaned forward toward Kim. "Kim, drop it. He just does stuff like that. He won't let you pay him back."

Kim was still frustrated. "I think he's arrogant."

"He is; but he's a nice guy," Maddie said. Then, changing the subject, she added, "In fact I was going to ask you if you ever heard back about from that credit card Robb maxed out?"

The mention of Robb's name sent chills down Kim's back, but she tried to shake it off. Maddie surely noticed the reaction but was too polite to comment.

"They said it's my problem."

"Well, I was telling Allen about it." Kim gave her a *you-did-what* look. "Not everything," Maddie clarified, "just that your husband ran up a bill on your card and now you have to deal with it."

"You have no right to tell anyone what—"

"He's a shrink," Maddie interjected. "It's not like he was shocked to hear the story, besides I only told him because he's dealt with stuff like this and I thought he could help."

Kim was irritated but didn't reply.

"Look, you can be mad if you want, but Allen had some good ideas. If you want help with this, call him."

Kim couldn't deny she needed all the help she could get, but she still didn't like Maddie revealing her private life to her pirate brother. "Me?"

"Well, I don't know all the details, but he said you could call him if you want to. Here's his card." Maddie wasn't nearly as cheery as she had been when she came in and Kim reminded herself that Maddie was only trying to help. Kim picked up the business card, Dr. Allen L. Jackman, Family Psychiatrist. Kim chuckled, trying to picture Allen giving parents advice on how to raise their wayward children. He's a psychiatrist, Kim thought, and he thinks he can solve my credit card problems? Yeah, right.

By Saturday, everything had smoothed over again between Maddie and Kim. Despite her irritation, Kim had much more important things to worry about and she was learning how much she needed her friends and family. Having spent so many years keeping her troubles to herself, it was an incredible blessing to have people support her. Kim hadn't spent much time worrying about the credit card situation and, of course, hadn't called Allen—and didn't plan to.

The circus was in town and Kim's mom had bought tickets. Her parents, Kim, Jackson, Matt and Maddie were going to afternoon performance of "The Greatest Show on Earth." The morning sky was clear, but bitterly cold. The first frost of winter covered the ground and Kim was enjoying watching Jackson stomp through the crystallized grass while they waited for Matt and Maddie to arrive. Her parents were upstairs getting ready themselves. The ringing of the phone was an unwelcome interruption.

"Hello," she said cheerfully, stretching the cord as close to the window as possible so that she could still watch her son. After a brief pause, an automated voice told her she had a collect call from the Wyoming state prison. Would she accept the charges? Kim was momentarily stunned and unable to respond, but after a second or two agreed that she would accept the call. She heard a click and her heart started pounding even before Robb spoke.

"Kim?"

Just hearing him talk gave her butterflies and she couldn't speak.

"Uh, how are you?" Robb asked nervously.

"How do you think I am?" she replied bitterly, finally finding her tongue as the anger finally caught up with her.

"Probably better than I am."

How pathetic, Kim thought to herself. "I doubt that."

"You have no idea what it's like in here."

"And you have no idea what it's like for us over here, Robb."

"I know," Robb said forlornly. "I really messed up this time." He acts as if he forgot to take out the trash or something, she thought. He was searching for sympathy and Kim wasn't about to offer any. "I'm really sorry, Kim; I don't know how this happened."

"You don't know how *what* could happen?" She wondered how much he thought she knew, since he hadn't contacted her to tell her anything.

"Well, all this. They told me you came up here, and I should have called you sooner; but I didn't know what to say. It's so horrible here; I miss you guys so much."

"But you didn't miss us until you got locked up, did you? You really think that you can leave your family, and run around in a drunken stupor for months while your wife and son have to rent out their house and—"

"You rented out the house?" Robb said with genuine surprise.

"I couldn't make the payments on my own, Robb. We could barely pay when you were here; I had no way to meet the bills now that my student loans are due. Besides, you obviously know I'm living here, what did you think I had done with the house?"

"I can't believe you rented out our house," Robb said, sounding annoyed at her decision.

"You have no right to be angry with *me* about anything."

Robb's tone became light again. "Well, I guess we can kick out the renters when I'm released anyway."

"If I don't sell it by then."

Robb paused. "Kim, don't do anything drastic. I'll be out sooner than you think. I—"

"And you think that I'll be waiting?" Kim interrupted.

Robb was silent for so long Kim wondered if he was still there, finally he spoke. "Kim, I know I screwed up, but we can work it out. Being here has totally changed me, I understand so much more about us and how hard I made things. Please don't give up on me."

Part of Kim wanted to give in to the sweet talk, forget about everything that had happened, and believe every word he said. But another part of her, the part that had become strong since he left told her he hadn't earned her trust. She couldn't erase the mental picture of a motel room and a hooker. "Do you really expect me to forget everything that's happened in the last few months? Just forget about—"

"Look, I know I messed up," Robb said, the frustration rising in his voice. "But for heaven's sake, you're my wife and we have a son. Isn't it worth working on after all we've been through?"

"What we've been through!" Kim spat back. "Not we Robb— just me. What I have been through. I'm the one who has had to pick up the pieces over and over. I'm the one busting my hump trying to be the mom and the dad; I'm the one who's been betrayed here. I spent the last eight years of my life making excuses for you and doing everything in my power to help you. And now after leaving us for six months you call me from prison and expect me to—"

"I thought you loved me," Robb cut in.

"I pretended for years that you loved me, and then you left. The next thing I know, some guy gets shot because you're trying to shoot the cops who found you with a whore." How could he possibly expect her to just put that behind them?

"What?" Robb yelled into the phone. The absolute shock in his voice came through loud and clear.

Suddenly the pieces came together. He didn't know she knew about the prostitute! She'd forgotten about asking Lt. Browning not to tell Robb she knew, and then the prostitution charges had been dropped for the plea bargain, so it wasn't on his public record.

Lt. Browning had even said that he normally wouldn't tell her the circumstances. Robb had assumed she was ignorant and he was calling her to work things out; never planning to tell her. The intensity of her anger at that moment was incredible. "Do you want me to say it again? I'm getting pretty good at it!"

"Kim, you don't understand. I...I...it wasn't what it looked like. I didn't..." finally he just shut up.

"You were in a motel room with a hooker, and it wasn't what it looked like!?" Kim screamed into the phone. "There just aren't that many possibilities, Robb. I might be stupid, but I'm not an idiot."

Robb was silent for just a moment before he screamed back at her with an intensity she hadn't heard in him before. "Maybe you ought to think about what pushed me to that point, Kim. If you were such a perfect wife, why did your husband leave you? You're not some innocent bystander to this, Kim. Don't try to drop all of this on me. There is always cause and effect. Think about it." There was a click and the line went dead. Slowly, Kim hung up the phone and turned around to find her parents, Matt and Maddie standing in the doorway, staring at her. Her heart sank as she wondered how long they had been there; judging by the look on their faces it was long enough. Her parents knew what had happened, but although Matt and Maddie were aware of the charges against Robb, and that he'd been unfaithful, Kim hadn't told either of them that his infidelity was with a prostitute. She was so humiliated, her face burned with embarrassment. Rather than attempt to explain, she pushed past all of them and ran up to her room. Locking the door behind her, she slid to the floor and pulled her knees to her chest as the tears began coursing down her cheeks.

Ten minutes later, her mom knocked on the door. "We need to leave for the circus; are you still coming?" she asked hesitantly.

The circus. Kim groaned inwardly because Jackson was so looking forward to it. Kim had really wanted to go too, but she just couldn't go now. It seemed that all the progress she had made during the last few weeks disappeared the moment she heard Robb's voice. "I'm sorry, Mom, but I can't. Please tell Jackson I'm sorry and I'll make it up to him."

"Do you want to talk about this?"

"No," Kim choked. The last thing she wanted to do was talk about this.

"Okay, see ya later." The worry and disappointment in her voice tore at Kim but she was powerless to do anything about it.

As hurt as she was by Robb's words, they had affected her

perfectly. Throughout their entire marriage, she had tried to be the best wife she could be. And yet he had left her and chosen another woman over her. Was it really so far-fetched to think it had everything to do with her? Is it fair for me to give up on Robb, when it is possible that it's my fault as well as his? Kim wasn't ignorant enough to believe it was *all* her fault, but she couldn't ignore what he had said. "Think about it, Kim." She knew she would have to do just that: think about it. But was she capable of making her decision? Could she walk away any more easily today than she could have yesterday? She was definitely angrier today, but was that a good enough reason? Why must I be so weak? she asked herself. Why can't I acknowledge what kind of fruits he's shown me and make the decision to leave him behind?

She dropped her head into her hands and wished for the thousandth time that she were someone else, married to someone else. Admitting she was no closer to making her choice, she took the opportunity of being alone in her room to get on her knees and pray, even though it was one of the last things she wanted to do. "Please Father," she whispered, "help me. I feel so lost, help me to know which path is right for me."

# CHAPTER SIX

The next week passed without incident, but Kim had been unable to sort out her mixed feelings about her conversation with Robb. If anything, she felt more empty and alone than she ever had. It had been such a shock to hear Robb blame her. It only added to the self-blame she couldn't escape. To have Robb accuse her made it seem so much more believable. A thousand memories assailed her as she added up all the things she had done that could have driven Robb away. Yet even as she gathered the reasons together, she knew he was wrong. He had to be wrong. Didn't he?

It was also time for her to tell Robb's parents about his arrest. They had continued taking Jackson once a month, and she got the distinct impression that they were unaware of Robb's current address. Several times during the week she picked up the phone to call them, but she wasn't able to follow through. Finally, she took the easy way out and wrote them a brief note simply explaining that Robb had been arrested in Wyoming—how could they ignore that?

The heavy feeling in her chest wouldn't go away, and she wondered if she would ever feel at peace with herself. Even her prayers seemed hollow again. Before Robb's phone call, she had been feeling better, but she had crashed that day, and she couldn't seem to pick herself up again. Every day, she longed to stay in bed and hide from the world. Hide from everything. But she didn't; instead she forced herself to stay busy, remain involved in Jackson's life, and pretend she was all right.

It was fall now and she helped Peggy work on preparing the yard and garden for the coming snow. Jackson's need of a Ninja costume for Halloween sent Kim searching through boxes to find a few yards of black spandex she had purchased at a yard sale last spring. She found the fabric, but the search reminded her to look for her patriarchal blessing. She actually paused, not sure if she really wanted to find it. The realization surprised her. Why shouldn't she want to find it?

She sat down on the floor of the garage to better contemplate this. Who was the master of playing on people's weaknesses? Certainly not God. Only Satan would want her to remain stagnant like this. God would want her to find peace, find joy. She certainly wasn't finding that. So whose course of action was she following?

With new-found determination, she began looking through boxes. Since Robb's call, she hadn't opened her scriptures, or done much of what the bishop had counseled her to do. She had an appointment to see him this afternoon. Had she even been planning to go? She really hadn't thought about it at all. How could she be so blind to what she was allowing to happen? How could she give up so easily? As box after box was searched and put aside, Kim continued these thoughts while at the same time wondering when she had last read her blessing.

Finally, after nearly half an hour, she found it in her old Book of Mormon. The cracked, navy blue binding and faded gold lettering reminded Kim of her baptism day—the day she became a real member of the church. Sister Tate, her CTR teacher, had given her the blue book as a gift that day. Sitting back on her heels, she opened the book and inside the cover was a collection of childhood pictures—even a phone number for an old friend from junior high school. She remembered being a young girl and proudly taking the book to church with her. It was the only copy of the Book of Mormon she had ever read all the way through. In the middle of Alma, she found her blessing folded into fourths and tucked away for safe-keeping. Kim put the book aside while she finished straightening up the garage, and then took it inside.

Once again Kim was alone on Saturday. Jackson was at a friend's birthday party, while her parents were out of town visiting her dad's brother for the weekend. She took the cordless phone upstairs with her in case someone called. In her room, she kicked off her shoes and lay on the bed. Lightly fingering her blessing, she opened it up slowly. People said that a patriarchal blessing was amazing in that you could read it at different times in your life and find new insight and guidance that you hadn't understood before. Kim closed her eyes and offered a silent prayer asking for help in understanding what she needed to know. Then she focused on the first line and started to read.

Her eyes blurred with tears each time she was told of her Heavenly Father's love. She was also told that she had been sent to a good home, to parents who loved her and were committed to doing everything in their power to help her overcome her tribulations. The blessing told her that she had many spiritual gifts and she was filled with warmth and comfort as she read the admonitions to stay close to the church and to not give in to the powers of evil that would seek to separate her from the Spirit. One paragraph in particular held her attention and she reread it again and again. "You are reminded, Kimberly, that you are meant to have great happiness in this life, and although at times you will feel unable to obtain it, eternal gifts beyond your imagination will attest to your ability to know in what direction you are meant to go. Strength you have never known, exists in your spirit that will show unto you the path to follow."

Kim had read her blessing dozens of times and never been so affected by that phrase. At the same time, she read the paragraph concerning marriage and it made her wonder if this blessing was meant for her at all: "You will be taken to the temple of our Lord by someone who loves you and together you will build a family of love and righteousness." That didn't sound like her marriage. Wiping her tears away, she finished the blessing, feeling her Father in Heaven's love so strongly that she felt as if she were literally in his arms. Compared to the spiritual desolation she had felt during the week, this reminder of His love was astounding in its strength and clarity.

The sound of the phone ringing suddenly brought her back to the present. She let it ring twice before feeling composed enough to answer.

"Hello?"

"Hello, I'm calling for Kim," said the man on the other end of the line.

"This is Kim."

"Hi Kim, This is Allen—Maddie's brother."

"How are you," she said politely.

"I'm fine, thanks. I don't mean to bother you, but Maddie told me about the problem with your credit card and I think I can help."

Since you're a therapist and all, Kim thought sarcastically. Out loud, she said, "Maddie had mentioned that." And I didn't call you; take a hint!

"I know you didn't call," Allen said, reading her mind, "but I thought I'd give you the advice anyway; you can take it or leave it, but at least I'll get it off my chest."

"That's very thoughtful of you," Kim said, but they both knew she didn't mean it.

"Maddie said the card was in your name, with your husband as an authorized signer; is that right?"

"Yes." Maddie sure was specific.

"And it wasn't a joint card? He didn't sign the application?"

"No, just me."

"And after he left, he called and ordered a new card to be sent to his new address?"

"That's what I assume. I cut the card up several months before he left, but at some point he got a new one and changed the mailing address for the bill." She was embarrassed that he knew so much.

"Well," Allen said, sounding extremely satisfied with himself. "The only person who can legally order a new card is the person to which the card belongs. Even though your husband is an authorized signer, he has no holding on the account. To order a new card he would have had to either talk to a representative personally, and then it's their dumb fault, or he would have had to impersonate you, which is illegal. He couldn't have called from your home could he?"

"No. He was in Wyoming."

"Even better. They usually identify the state the call comes from, and since he was out-of-state, and you can prove you weren't in Wyoming, the problem is entirely theirs."

"You're kidding?" Kim said, afraid to believe it could be true.

"Nope, I counseled a kid once who did almost the same thing. I helped the parents straighten it out. Bottom line is, they can not issue a new card to anyone other than the cardholder; how he got past all their safeguards is beyond me. He must be a very smooth talker."

"Yes, he is. So can I just call them and work it out?"

"You betcha; most companies aren't open on Saturday though, so it'll probably have to wait till Monday morning."

Kim couldn't believe it. "This isn't dishonest, is it?"

"No. Like I said, it's their mistake; they should never have issued him a card. If you can afford to pay it, go ahead. I'm sure they'll increase your limit, but if you don't mind getting your card canceled, stick to your guns and you're off the hook."

"When I called before, they told me that it was my fault since I didn't remove him as an authorized signer."

"And if he had taken the card with him when he left that would be true, but he ordered a new one, which he can't do."

"I just can't believe it's so easy."

"Both parties have liability in a credit contract—this happens to be theirs."

Kim smiled. Wouldn't it be a relief if she could get this taken care of so easily? "I can't thank you enough; I really appreciate your call."

"No problem. Glad I could help."

Feeling relieved, Kim added happily, "Now I owe you another four thousand dollars in addition to the fifty I still owe you for the battery."

"The battery was only five bucks, remember?" Allen said lightly.

Kim smiled. "Oh yeah, so I guess I only owe you four thousand and five."

"Just pay me when it's convenient," he teased.

"Don't hold your breath."

Allen laughed. "If you say so."

"Well, anyway, thank you very much."

"You're welcome. Talk to you later."

"Okay, bye."

"Bye," Allen said and hung up the phone.

Kim couldn't believe it. She was tremendously relieved and couldn't wait to call that credit company on Monday. Please let him be right. She had already sent a payment, and it wasn't easy to fit into her tight budget. On top of that, her perceptions of Dr. Allen L. Jackman had changed somewhat. First he replaced her battery and now this. There weren't many people who would go out of their way. But then again, maybe he was just a busybody.

※

Two hours later, she was again sitting across from Bishop Scott. They had finished with the small talk and he had leaned back in his chair, which she had found was the sign that he was ready to listen. He didn't ask for her to start, he just smiled and lifted his eyebrows.

"It's been an interesting couple of weeks."

"How so?" The Bishop asked.

Kim related to him the phone conversation she had had with her husband. She explained how it made her feel, how it played so perfectly on her own fears concerning her part in this. Expressing her feelings out loud made it seem much more real and although she tried not to cry, the bishop finally had to hand her a tissue. Put into words, it sounded so much more clear. Robb was once again trying to manipulate her, make her take upon herself the responsibility for what he had done. It was so obvious to her now. The bishop asked her about her patriarchal blessing and she read him the passages that had stuck out to her.

The Bishop was smiling at her when she finished. "Those are some pretty powerful promises."

Kim looked up at him and felt a little switch in her head. *Promises.* The bishop had said that before, but it hadn't quite hit her until now. She thought about the part where her blessing had talked about temple marriage, and that she would raise a family of right-eousness with her husband; not despite him. None of the things she had read had guaranteed her anything; it was up to her whether or not those promises would be fulfilled. "Can I have those things if I stay married to Robb?"

"You tell me," Bishop Scott replied.

Kim's face fell a little; she had hoped he would answer the question for her. Even though things were clearer by the minute, she felt the way you feel when Christmas is almost over but there is still an unopened gift that you're sure is just what you wanted the very most. She hoped the bishop would be the end of her wondering and unwrap the last package for her and let her see that she had indeed gotten what she wished for.

"Kim, I am here to counsel you and help you find your answers but I can't tell you what to do. You are entitled to receive your own revelation; if you seek your answer through correct methods you will receive it." He paused for a minute, "Do you believe that?"

Kim wanted to say yes, but instead she told the truth. "I don't know. I want to, but I can't say I have ever had a 'revelation' about anything, I can't say that I would even recognize one if it came. I haven't developed the way I should have spiritually. In many ways I still feel like a kid, looking to other people to tell me what's true or not."

"Kim, you are a daughter of God, and you have been promised, just as every faithful member of the church has, that you can know." He leaned forward and looked at Kim until he caught and held her eyes. "You have had a lot of distractions to keep you below the spiritual level you think you should be at, but there is no set timeline. Everyone learns and grows at a different pace. Do you have a testimony of this Gospel?"

Kim stared at him and asked herself the question. The burning in her chest allowed her to answer him with conviction. "Yes, Bishop, I do. I know it's true; I truly do. But in some ways I feel that I've failed this church, that I haven't lived a life that entitles me to certain things."

"Kim, there is no reason God would want you to feel that way." Kim straightened and was reminded of her own realizations on that topic just that morning. "God blesses us with hope, and joy and peace. Not self-blame and fear. From what you have told me of your life, and from what I feel when we meet this way, I know that you are worthy to receive the gifts you have been promised. If you ask in faith and continue seeking earnestly for guidance, I testify to you that you will receive your answer."

Kim wiped the tears as her chest burned with the truth of what he had just said. She looked up at him. "Bishop, I don't think I can stay married to him. I haven't had any manifestation or bolt of lightening, but I just don't feel like I can remain his wife."

"But you're not sure?"

Kim shook her head and looked at the tissue in her hands. "No, I'm not sure."

"You need to be sure."

"I know."

He let her think about that for a minute before continuing. "Weren't you married in November?"

His question caused the butterflies to return to her stomach. She had been thinking of that very thing for the last two weeks. "Yes, our anniversary is November third. A week from Tuesday."

"Why don't you to attend the temple that day." Kim looked up, mildly surprised. "Wait to make this decision until you can go to the temple and pray there." Kim nodded slowly. Bishop Scott smiled back at her. "I want you to know that I truly admire your dedication, Kim. I've had people come in here that want a divorce for reasons that seem trivial when compared to what you have gone through. I am humbled by your faith and commitment. I know that the day will come when things will be better for you than you can imagine at this point."

⤍

At work Monday, Kim called the credit card company. After nearly an hour and talking to five different people, she was finally told she was not responsible to pay the bill.

She cheered out loud in her office and picked the phone back up. Kim was beside herself; she just couldn't believe it had worked. The first person she had spoken to confirmed that Robb had ordered the card two months after he left, but told her she was completely responsible for the charges anyway. Kim stood her ground and was transferred to the supervisor. The supervisor explained again that it was her fault, but Kim wouldn't accept that and asked for *his* supervisor. That supervisor sent Kim to the manager, who finally connected her with the junior financial officer of the corporation. Luckily, Kim still had the original agreement and read to him directly from the fine print. Despite the fact that he was not happy about it, the man finally admitted that they were liable. Kim was asked to submit her claim in writing and was promised a letter of absolution within thirty days, along with a reimbursement for the payment she had already made.

The phone rang three times before Maddie answered the line, "Madeline Jackman."

"Hey, want to go to lunch?" Kim asked cheerfully.

"You're sounding awfully chipper," Maddie said.

"I just made $4000," Kim gloated.

"Really?"

"Well, maybe I saved $4,000, but I feel like celebrating."

"When you say 'go to lunch', do you mean a restaurant or share yogurt at the park?"

Kim laughed. "That's up to you, you choose."

"Why is it up to me?" Maddie asked.

"Because if I didn't know you, Allen would never have told me what to do and I would be paying every dime of that credit card bill."

"Well," Maddie said with delight. "In that case I guess I earned it. But do me a favor and call Allen's voice mail, he was afraid he had ticked you off by his call."

Kim paused, not wanting to admit she'd rather not, but she supposed she owed him. "Okay. I'll call and you come to get me when you're ready."

"It's a date," Maddie laughed and hung up the phone.

Kim quickly dialed the number she found on Allen's card. After only one ring, she heard Allen's voice telling her to leave a message. Quickly she explained what had happened, thanked him and hung up.

"Ready to go?" Maddie said twenty minutes later.

"You bet." Kim said and grabbed her keys.

✢

Halloween night, Kim took Jackson and a couple of his friends door-to-door. Kids must have no perception of how cold it is out here, Kim thought, as she shifted from foot to foot. As a child she had loved this holiday too, but just like many things, it lost its thrill as an adult. Still, she couldn't deny she was looking forward to sampling his candy when they got home.

"Trick or Treat!" she heard them yell, again. And once again, following their announcement, she heard the feigned fright and interest in their costumes. It made her smile, but didn't take her mind off the terrible cold. They had been out for nearly two hours and Kim was sure she would never regain the feeling in her toes. Looking at her watch she was relieved that it was nearly 7:30.

"Only two more houses, Jack. We've got to be at Maddie's by 8:00."

"Do I have to go?" Jackson whined, looking up at her with puppy dog eyes.

"Yep. Uncle Matt will be there too; I promised them they'd get a good look at your costume."

"But Mo-om..."

"Or we could just stop now," Kim said giving her son the *it-isn't-working* smile that he knew well.

"Okay, two more houses," he said in defeat and then ran to catch up with his friends.

At exactly 7:55 Kim pulled up to the duplex Maddie rented. There were still a few groups of kids going door-to-door, but the cold had apparently sent most of the crowd home. Snow had yet to fall this season, but you wouldn't guess it with the current temperatures. Kim and Jackson went up to the door and knocked.

"Trick or Treat!" they yelled when the door opened.

For a second Kim thought she had gone to the wrong apartment, then she remembered and was embarrassed about the trick-or-treat bit they had yelled.

"Hi, Kim," Allen said as he lifted the patch covering his left eye. Kim had to clear her throat to cover the chuckle she was unable to suppress. Allen was dressed up as a pirate; complete with the bandanna, striped shirt, and vest—even knee-high black boots. How appropriate.

Allen squatted down to Jackson's height and stuck out his hand. "You must be Jackson. I'm Allen, Maddie's brother."

Jackson cautiously, but firmly, shook Allen's hand.

"Whoa, that's quite a handshake for a ballerina."

Jackson looked questioningly at his mother as if to say, "What is this guy talking about?"

Kim helped him out by explaining, "Actually, Allen, he's a Ninja, but I understand pirates aren't as smart as they like to think they are."

"Touché," Allen replied, looking up at Kim with a pleased smile before turning his attention back to Jackson. "I was just kidding, Jackson. Actually you have got the best costume I've seen all night."

"Thanks," Jackson said brightly; there's no better way to win a kid's affection than to compliment his Halloween costume. "Mom made it," he added as Allen stepped aside and showed them in.

"Really?" Allen said again looking at Kim. "Your mom is one talented lady."

Kim smiled sheepishly. Why did he make her so uncomfortable? He just had this way of looking at her that felt her feel that he knew all her deepest secrets. Thanks to Maddie he nearly did. In addition to that, it seemed that he still found her quite amusing. She didn't like it.

Jackson recaptured her attention when he yelled, "Holy cow! He's got a Playstation!"

"He has a Playstation," Kim corrected.

"Yeah, he has a Playstation!" he repeated with no lack of adulation. It took less than a second for Jackson to plant himself in front of the TV and start punching buttons on the controller. Kim didn't miss the fact that the screen was paused in the middle of a game. Jackson had not been excited to come, in the first place, but now she was sure he'd never want to leave. He'd already been asking for a Playstation for Christmas.

Allen smiled in her direction and shrugged his shoulders before walking over to where Jackson was enthralled even though nothing was moving on the screen. "Do you want to play?" he asked, exiting out of his game and starting up a new one.

"Yeah," Jackson bubbled. "This is so cool!"

Allen showed him how to play the game and finally gave the controls to Jackson, who was nearly out of his skin with excitement. With Jackson completely engrossed in his game, silence settled between Kim and Allen.

"So," Kim asked after an uncomfortable few seconds. "Where are Matt and Maddie?"

"Our folks were having a family Halloween party. Since it landed on a Saturday it was supposed to be an afternoon thing, but my twenty-three-year-old sister showing up with a man seemed to extend it."

Kim smiled, "I see. So why aren't you there?"

"She was nervous about your coming and no one being home. Since I already met and approved of Matt, I said my farewells so that she could stay and answer all the nosy questions."

"Oh," Kim said. Then thought to herself, I hope they hurry home.

"Have a seat," Allen said as he disappeared into the kitchen. "Want anything to drink?" he yelled back to her.

"Water would be fine, thank you," Kim said trying not to show her discomfort. What was her problem? What was it about him that made her so nervous and uncomfortable? Surely, he hadn't done anything to make her feel this way. It was probably because she felt guilty for the battery and $4,000 worth of credit counseling. Then for just a moment, she entertained the thought that perhaps she was attracted to him, but she dismissed the thought as quickly as it had come. Despite the fact that she was married, she had little faith in the male gender in general; the idea was preposterous.

Kim thanked him for the water as he handed her a glass and sat in the chair across from the couch where she was sitting. They were both silent for a minute, and Kim was a little annoyed when she caught his eye and once again he had that smirk on his face. She decided to call him on it this time.

"What's so funny?" she asked, trying to sound casual.

Allen shrugged and hid a smile by taking a drink of water. As the silence continued, Allen seemed to be really enjoying this exchange; apparently he was easily entertained. Finally he spoke. "You look very nice."

"It's Halloween, you're supposed to dress up," Kim said dryly.

Allen chuckled before responding, "Most people dress up in costumes."

"Who's to say this isn't my costume?" Kim added sarcastically. She wasn't dressed up at all, but she remembered that on the one occasion they had met she had been wearing her grubbies, no makeup and had her hair pulled back in a ponytail. At least tonight she was in somewhat flattering jeans, although they couldn't hide the extra ten pounds on her hips and backside. She was a little disappointed in herself when she realized how much she wished that they did. Her hair was done tonight and she had taken the time to put on a little make-up. She wondered what she looked like in his eyes and then shook the thought off all together.

"Interesting idea," Allen replied, liking the way her hair was slightly curled at the ends and hung around her shoulders as well as how her jeans fit in all the right places. He had always appreciated the figure of a woman, and he liked hers more than he wanted to admit. She wasn't as thin as she probably wanted to be, he was sure, but she had the look of a woman—one who had borne a child and looked softer for it. Allen looked away, annoyed at his own appraisal. He had yet to determine whether he even liked this woman, and didn't appreciate how disconcerting it was to be in her company. It was a feeling to which he was not accustomed.

Kim scolded herself for being so disagreeable; she just couldn't seem to relax. Deciding to be nicer, she changed the subject to every man's favorite topic: himself.

"So what kind of psychologist are you?" she asked politely, even though she knew the answer already.

"Family, mostly. Although I do some individual counseling as well. But I'm a *psychiatrist*, not a psychologist."

"What's the difference?" Kim asked with mild defensiveness. Big deal.

"Only five years of school and $60,000 in student loans," Allen answered quickly; then he shook his head. "Sorry, I don't mean to be obsessive, it's just one of those things that drive psychiatrists crazy. Most psychiatrists do heavy stuff, not family counseling, so it's common for people to assume I'm not one."

Kim furrowed her brow. "So why spend the extra $60,000 and five years if you don't need to?"

"I was planning to become a researcher on things like personality disorders and post-traumatic stress syndrome when I went to school, never really planning to practice. But I still had to do an internship and during that time I got introduced to family counseling and found a bit of a niche, you could say. So I explored the field a little more and decided it was where I really wanted to be."

"You like it then?" Kim asked finding his answer very interesting. He had worked very hard for something he really wanted, then found it wasn't all he wanted it to be, found something better and moved on, despite the reasons not to. Could she do the same in her life?

"I do," Allen said. "And you work with Maddie?"

"Yeah, we finished our degrees together and were able to find jobs at the same company."

"What do you do there? Maddie just tells me she counts calories."

Kim laughed, feeling the tension dissipate a little bit. "Well that's close. The company we work for is a group of dietitians that monitor and adjust menus for hospitals, day care centers, nursing homes and places that have state-regulated dietary needs."

"Wow. That's a mouthful… no pun intended."

Kim laughed at the joke. "So where do you work?" she asked.

"A friend of mine, that I went to school with, wanted to open his own family counseling practice. He asked me if I'd be interested in going in on it together, so here I am."

"And you moved from Chicago?" Kim prodded.

"Yeah, last month. I'd been there for years; it's a good change, I suppose."

"I can imagine it would be hard to leave, but at least you have family here."

"That is nice, but I'm used to being on my own and it's kind of hard to have people poking around."

"Poking around?" Kim asked, raising an eyebrow.

Allen chuckled. "I'm just not used to having my family know my business."

His comments made Kim curious and she became more forward in her questions. "They didn't know your business in Chicago?"

"Not much of it," Allen said as he squirmed in his chair. "I moved out on my own right after my mission, and put myself through school. Then I got married and we moved to Chicago. I used to talk to my folks every month or so, but it was up to me how much they knew."

"You sound like you have so much to hide," Kim pointed out.

"Nope, just the opposite. I have very little to hide," Allen added distractedly. Just then the front door flew open and Cinderella bounded in, escorted by her own Prince Charming.

"Kim," Maddie said, out of breath as she collapsed next to Kim on the couch, her hoop skirt bouncing around them both. "I'm so sorry. I had no idea that Matt would cause such a stir."

Kim caught the look that passed between the two of them and tried to ignore the envy she felt. Watching their relationship up close, it showed her all that Robb and she had missed in theirs.

"That's okay," Kim said with a smile. "Allen's a pretty good conversationalist," she added with a smile in his direction. She wished they would have waited another minute or two; her discomfort had passed and she found herself curious about the last comment he had made about having very little to hide. Did he mean he had very little in his life, or nothing worth hiding? Kim could relate to both options.

Allen stood up and stretched his arms over his head. "Well, I'll leave you guys. I told Mom I'd help her clean up—I'd better be on my way." He grabbed a black leather coat out of the hall closet and pretended to tip his imaginary hat in the ladies' direction. "Nice talkin' with you, Kim. I'll probably be home late Maddie, but I've got my key." Kim remembered something just as he opened the door and hopped up, not wanting to shout, but she may as well have—everyone was watching her.

"Uh, Allen. I forgot to thank you for the credit card thing."

"No you didn't, I got your message," he said with a smile as he shrugged his broad shoulders into the sleeves of his coat.

"I mean in person." Why was it suddenly so hard to talk to him again? "Uh, well thanks, I don't know what I would have done otherwise."

For a moment they just looked at each other. Kim felt uncomfortable and looked away, but finally he spoke.

"No problem," he said with a smile. "I'll see you later." And he was gone. Kim stood there for a second, wondering about the look she had seen on his face. She felt as though she should have gotten more out of it than she did. Realizing Matt and Maddie were watching her, she finally returned to the couch. She tried hard to be animated and get a conversation going in order to mask the thoughts in her head.

Kim and Jackson stayed until nearly ten—he never moved away from the TV. Finally feeling worn out herself, Kim turned off the game and handed Jackson his coat. Jackson protested but Kim ignored it and said their good-byes.

"Hey, Kim, can I catch a ride with you?" Matt asked just as she was leaving. Kim raised an eyebrow. Matt lived with some friends in Provo and he had his own car which was currently parked out front, so she couldn't imagine why he wanted to ride home with her. "I'm going to church with Maddie tomorrow and I'd like to leave my car here. She can pick me up at the house."

"Sure," she said, wondering about his true motives. His explanation seemed a little strange. Ushering Jackson to the car, she let them say their good-byes in private.

After a minute or so, Matt slid into the passenger seat. "Thanks, Sis, I appreciate the ride."

"Not a problem," Kim answered, as she backed out of the driveway.

After a few more moments Matt broke the silence. "Don't you want to know why I'm going to Mom and Dad's tonight?" he asked, making it obvious that he wanted her to know.

"Only if you want to tell me," she said coolly. For some reason she had an uneasy feeling about this; she really didn't want to hear whatever he wanted to tell her.

"I need to talk to Dad," Matt said, very content with himself.

"Oh," was all Kim said as she checked her blind spot and changed lanes.

"I need to ask him something."

"Really?" Kim replied distractedly, hoping to convince him she wasn't interested.

"Something a guy in my situation needs to ask his dad about,"

Matt baited further; he was staring directly at her, but she pretended not to notice.

"Hmm."

"Kim, what's your problem?" Matt asked with annoyance after a few moments.

"What do you mean?" Kim asked. Her heart was pounding and she didn't know why.

Matt looked at her hard for a minute then simply said, "I'm going to ask Maddie to marry me."

Kim swallowed—that's why she was feeling so weird. "You've only known her a month, Matt," she said, trying to sound calm.

"So?" Matt asked stubbornly, folding his arms across his chest.

"So..." Kim drawled. "You can't base a lifetime commitment on a one month relationship."

"Why not?" he asked with annoyance.

"Because you don't even know her, Matt."

"Okay," he said slowly, then looked at her again, "but you've known her for years. Is there any reason why you think she isn't the one for me?"

"I'm not saying she isn't *the one*," Kim clarified, "I just think you need to have known *the one* longer than a month to know she's *the one*."

"And if I told you that I did know, that there wasn't a doubt in my mind that she is the one, what would you say then?"

Kim didn't know what to say for a moment, and glanced in the rearview mirror to assure herself that Jackson was asleep; he was. Then she pulled over to the side of the road and stopped the car. She turned to face Matt and looked him directly in the eyes. "Matt, I want to say first that I am very happy for you." Tears came to her eyes as she continued, "Then I want to make sure you are absolutely certain. I can tell you from experience that there is nothing worse than a bad marriage. Whomever you marry will be a part of your life forever. Don't rush this, Matt. If Maddie is the one, then you have forever to be with her. Don't throw away this time to get to know one another well, you'll not lose anything by taking the time to be sure."

They stared at each other in silence until Matt spoke. "Just because Robb wasn't the right one for you doesn't mean that Maddie isn't mine."

"I didn't say Robb wasn't the right one for me," Kim said calmly, trying not to take offense at what Matt had said. Matt looked a little confused. "Matt, I am in the process of trying to determine what to do about my marriage." She stopped for a breath.

"But I thought you were getting a divorce? I mean, after what he did, how could you even consider staying married to such a creep?"

"I made covenants with the Lord to be committed to Robb forever. What he has done is atrocious and don't think for a minute I feel it is anything less than disgusting, degrading and nauseating. But I promised myself to him; I also made promises to the Lord. Now I have to make a monumentous decision about whether I keep that promise and continue to try to make it work or I break that promise and get a divorce."

Matt looked like he was about to speak, but she put up her hand to stop him. "Matt, my point is this: I thought Robb was the man I would spend forever with, and unfortunately I'm still not completely convinced he isn't. But I can honestly say I don't know that he is, and I never really did."

"Then why did you marry him?"

"Because I was in love," she leaned toward him and added with emphasis. "Matt, I loved him and I thought that was enough; it isn't. Loving Maddie isn't enough either. Make sure you know that she is 'the one'. Not just that you love her, that you have a lot in common, but that she's the one the Lord wants you to share forever with."

They were both silent for another minute, lost in their individual thoughts. Then Kim wiped her eyes and pulled back onto the road. They didn't speak the rest of the way home, and Kim prayed he would reflect deeply on what she had said. In a way, she felt guilty for destroying the *everything-is-perfect* thrill Matt was feeling; but life had taught her a harsh lesson, and she hoped that Matt could learn from her mistake. When they pulled into the driveway, Matt opened his door, but Kim stopped him before he got out.

"Matt, please don't get me wrong. Maddie is one of the best people I have ever known. I can think of nothing better than you two getting married and having a beautiful life together; I just want you to be able to look at her across the altar in the temple and know without a doubt that she is your soul mate."

Matt smiled at his sister. "I'll make sure—I promise."

He got out of the car and Kim watched him enter the house. Then she dropped her head to rest on the steering wheel. Since Jackson was asleep in the backseat, she allowed herself to review all that she and the Bishop had gone over during the proceeding weeks and all that this conversation with Matt had brought up. Tuesday would be her ninth wedding anniversary. If only she'd had the insight to see in Robb what she had been too blind to see before their wedding day. Jackson stirred in the backseat and new warmth filled her chest as tears once again filled her eyes. Without Robb there would be no Jackson said a voice in her head and suddenly she knew that whether or not she was meant to spend forever with Robb, she was definitely meant to spend it with Jackson. Without Robb, she would not have her son. Part of the immense pain she had been carrying for so long dissolved with that realization and she felt lighter. The Lord had a specific plan for her life and Kim felt hope—hope that one day, just as the Bishop had promised, she would find the happiness she had always longed for.

# CHAPTER SEVEN

Monday night Kim got very little sleep. She was anxious about attending the temple and she tossed and turned until finally rolling out of bed at the unthinkable time of 4:00 a.m. She wasn't sure why she was so nervous, but assumed that she would find out before the day was over. Her Dad had told her that the Jordan River Temple opened for sessions at 5:00 a.m. on Tuesday and since she couldn't sleep anyway, she might as well go now. The streets were dark and nearly empty, but the parking lot was nearly half-full. It surprised her that so many people would be there this early in the morning.

At times during the session she was so overcome with emotion that the attendant handed her tissues. Maybe another time it wouldn't have affected her so much, but nine years ago today she had married Robb and truly expected to spend eternity with him. Now here she was at the temple before the sun had even come up, and Robb was in prison, probably lifting weights with his new 'friends'. It was an interesting twist on the 'happily ever after' she had imagined on her wedding day.

Throughout the session, she kept asking herself what God would want her to do. It was a scary question because, until lately, she truly felt that God would always want her to work harder to keep the family together. Perhaps this was the key to the difficulty of her struggle; there had never been a divorce in her family. She had heard of a few high-school friends who had gotten divorced and there were a few divorced women whom she worked with, but she didn't intimately know anyone that had experienced a divorce. To her divorce just seemed wrong; some kind of weakness. She had always wanted to be strong and up until today she had understood 'strength' as enduring the disappointments of her marriage. Even after Robb left them, after the hooker, and the phone call, she kept coming back to the fact that she felt divorce was always the wrong thing to do: it was giving up when you promised not to. But did God want her to be miserable? And could she really hope that Robb would ever change? Would she want him even if he did?

With those questions swarming within her, she continued to ask herself what God would want her to do; her mind seemed to clear and her perception change. It seemed possible that divorce could be the right choice. Over and over again, that thought pierced her consciousness to the point where she could think of little else. She had wanted to do this the right way; that's why she had gone to the bishop; that's why she had spent so much time thinking and praying. She did not want to make a decision she would regret. Now she was putting her faith to the ultimate test. As the session continued, she discovered that she did have the strength to make this decision and that she would know for sure if this was right. Up until now she hadn't really believed she could do it—now she knew that she could.

After the session Kim was in the celestial room, enjoying the peace that isn't found outside the temple walls, as she contemplated what she had discovered. She was seated away from the main body of people, with her head resting on the back of the chair and her eyes closed. The hushed conversations increased, indicating that another session had finished. Continuing her meditation, she noted that someone slid into the chair next to her; the session must have been full if there were no other chairs available. Without opening her eyes, she bowed her head and with her hands clasped she offered a prayer of gratitude for all that she had been given in her life.

It was humbling to realize she had ignored those blessings lately and she vowed to make sure that despite her challenges, she would never forget the good parts of her life. One by one, she cited specific blessings; then, just as she'd been taught to do as a child, Kim poured out her heart to her Father in Heaven, asking once again for his help. Tears slid down her cheeks, dropping into her lap as she explained every detail of her frustrations as well as her fears. The peace she felt was so wonderful that she remained where she was, searching for more things to include in her prayer so as not to lose the peace too soon. Ever since her last meeting with the bishop she had noticed a difference in herself, a feeling of confidence that a conclusion was close and that she would be ready when it came. When she read her scriptures or prayed, she would remind herself of the fact that she could receive direction from God. She could have anything as long as she had faith that it was possible. Her fears had been fading, and now she pleaded wholeheartedly to the Lord to help her find the resolution; she was tired of being in limbo. And He was answering. At this very moment she could feel the changes. She had absolute faith and knowledge that she could do this.

The increased strength she had felt during the session seemed to grow, until she was all but free of her doubts. She felt confident in her feelings that to continue as Robb's wife was not the right thing for her to do. There wasn't a definite decision yet; she didn't know for sure, but she was getting closer. She felt that one way or another, this would be okay. Another chunk seemed to melt away from the rock she had been carrying around in her stomach and she felt the lightness and freedom of being very close to making her decision.

Kim ended her prayer when she had repeated herself a few more times. She raised her head, wiping at her tears with a damp, crumpled tissue. She had completely forgotten about the person who had sat down next to her until he held out a tissue.

"Thank you," she whispered with embarrassment, then startled when she glanced up at her benefactor.

"Are you okay?" Allen asked with concern.

Kim was stunned; she couldn't believe that, of all people, Allen Jackman was here.

Allen smiled at her surprise, and leaned toward her in order to keep the conversation hushed. "Yes, I do have a recommend," he whispered.

Kim's blush betrayed that he had guessed her thoughts correctly. Giving herself a mental shake, she smiled, hoping it looked sincere. "I'm just surprised to see you."

"To see *me* or to see me *here*?"

It was impossible to pretend she hadn't thought both. Shaking her head and smiling slightly she determined to tell the truth. Quietly she replied, "Both."

Allen nodded and gave her a feigned look of consternation. "Is it the hair?"

"The lack of actually, as well as the hole in your ear," she bantered lightly.

Allen fingered his ear lobe and smiled at the remark as he looked around the room for a moment. "Remind me to tell you my reasons for this someday," he said looking at his watch. "I've actually got to be going, but I wanted to make sure you were all right; that was a marathon prayer."

Kim was touched by the sincerity in his voice and gave him a grateful smile. "I'm fine; just trying to conquer my Goliath."

"Aren't we all," Allen said with a nod before falling silent. They sat that way for a moment, Allen looking down at his hands in his lap and Kim watching him with quick glances. Finally, he looked at her again and his bright blue eyes had just a hint of sadness, making her wonder what he had been thinking of just then. "Maybe someday you can tell me what your Goliath is."

"I think you can probably guess," Kim replied; he seemed to know everything about her anyway.

Allen smiled and paused again, his eyes locked on her in a gaze she couldn't break away from. "It's not as easy as it looks, is it?"

Kim just looked at him, not wanting to assume he knew her struggles, but feeling very strongly that he did. Lightly she asked, "You mean getting up at four a.m.?"

"That too," he said seriously and stared at her for another powerful moment before standing up to go. "Well, I've got a client at nine. I'll see you later."

"It was good seeing you," Kim said quickly, surprised that she said it at all and even more surprised that she meant it.

"Yeah, you too."

She watched him leave and wondered why she desired him to stay a little longer. Although she tried to overlook the connection, she couldn't ignore the fact that after praying for help she had opened her eyes to see Allen. And however short-lived it had been, he had made her forget how unhappy she was.

Kim returned home from work that night not nearly as tired as she expected to be. All day she had felt light and at peace. The only exceptions were when she was reminded of Robb, but even those moments weren't accompanied by the stab of pain they usually brought. Luckily, she was getting better at not thinking about him, and had to admit she'd had a very good day—the best one in a long time. After work, she helped her mom with dinner and corrected Jackson's homework. Jackson had been chosen to be Squanto in the second-grade Thanksgiving play, and she helped him memorize his first few lines before reading him a story and putting him to bed. Returning to the kitchen, she sat at the table and yawned, stretching her arms above her head for emphasis. Despite her fatigue she was reluctant to end the day just yet.

"I think it's finally catching up with me," she said to her mom who was finishing up the dishes. She watched Peggy stop and then turn. Apprehensive about the worried look on her mother's face, Kim watched as Peggy reached into the pocket of her house dress and pulled out a letter.

"This came for you today, Kim; I thought you'd rather read it after Jackson was in bed." She reached across the table and handed the envelope to Kim. "It's from Robb," she added.

A heavy dread settled in as she took the letter from her mom. Trying to remain upbeat she said, "Must be an anniversary card."

Peggy just smiled and went back to her dishes. Kim stayed at the table for several seconds, staring at the envelope. Then, deciding to get it over with, she stood and climbed the stairs to her room. She placed the envelope on the bed and watched it as she slowly undressed, taking great care to hang her clothes just right and straighten the room. The envelope seemed to glare at her so she turned her back on it as she pulled a T-shirt over her head and stepped into her flannel pajama bottoms. Her heart was pounding as she came to the bed and picked up the small, white envelope. Closing her eyes she offered a brief prayer and when she opened them again, she had the distinct feeling that all her wondering and searching was nearly over. Would this letter be one that would soften her heart towards him or convince her that she couldn't continue as Mrs. Robert Larksley? She sat on the bed and folded her legs beneath her before taking a deep breath, ripping the envelope open, and removing a single sheet of notebook paper.

Ten minutes later she was lying on the bed staring at the ceiling. Her heart rate had calmed and her breathing was steady as she forced herself to blink back the tears and finally sit up. The written word was a powerful weapon and Robb had used it well. His letter had told her exactly what he had been doing for the last few months. Without apology he had laid out the lifestyle he had chosen over the life he had with them. There were no regrets; just raw and coarse facts that showed aspects of her husband she had never seen before. They had cut like a razor blade. Mingled with them were stabbing accusations of her failures toward him, of her inability to care for him properly, of her forcing him away. It was staggering that he could hurt her like this.

There was one thing for certain though; despite the blame he heaped on her and his attempts to further manipulate and hurt her; Kim's decision was made. She would not remain married to him. There was immense relief in having decided and in feeling certain that her decision was correct. She was also grateful for the ability she had been blessed with to see through his insults toward her. She had picked herself to pieces over her marriage during these last few months, and she knew she had her faults, but the things Robb had said were not true. She was not responsible for his choices—she never had been.

Resolving to contact an attorney in the morning, she folded the letter and put it in her faded Book of Mormon next to her patriarchal blessing—just in case she needed a reminder later on. Then she knelt next to the bed and asked for confirmation that her decision to seek a divorce was the right one. The feeling that encircled her was beyond anything she could have ever imagined, even greater than the feelings of the temple this morning. With a power she had never experienced, she knew that her choice was the right one. For several minutes she stayed where she was, relishing the peace; trying hard to imprint it on her mind.

Aching knees finally brought her to her feet, and she felt the freedom of knowing where she was going. It was similar to the feeling she had felt some time ago when she had, for the first time, turned the future over to her Father in Heaven, only more powerful. Finally she was free! Free to really prepare a life for her and her son. Free to dissolve her marriage to Robb, knowing that she would not be held accountable for her covenants being broken. She had kept her end of the bargain. Robb had made his decision and now she could finally make hers.

Friday morning she was finally able to meet with her attorney. Eric Johnson was a good friend of her sister Cindy's husband. Just as she had hoped, Eric was very nice and even though at times it was uncomfortable to dissect and explain her life, she appreciated his thoroughness. After taking notes about the details of the case, they discussed the settlement Kim should seek.

This was all so new to her that she hadn't really thought about the settlement so she willingly followed Eric's advice. He proposed that she ask for everything after explaining that she was easily entitled to it all. Between Robb's intermittent work history, the abandonment of his family, and his criminal record, he was entitled to nothing. At first she was hesitant, but as she thought back to the letter that was still fresh in her mind she agreed and they drew up the papers. The other problem was custody. Obviously, Robb was in no position for visitation rights now, but when he was released it would be an entirely different situation. Kim struggled over the decision and finally decided to simply include a provision of custody assessment after Robb's release. Until then, Robb was to have no contact with Jackson except by letter, which he was to understand Kim would read first. The only thing Robb would keep when this was settled was his ten-year-old Pathfinder—wherever that was.

Eric finished his notes and flipped the pages back to the beginning. He smiled warmly at Kim and said, "Well, that does it for now. I'll file papers early next week. With his being in prison, this should go through quickly. I know you're probably in a hurry for this to be taken care of, but I would suggest that we take enough time to not miss anything. Is that all right with you?"

"I would like that very much. I'd rather take my time than have to fix anything later," Kim said as she stood. "Thank you, I really appreciate your help."

"No problem. I'll contact you when I've got papers for you to sign."

Kim said good-bye and went out to her car. She sat in her car for several minutes before going back to work. She had hoped to feel great elation at having started the process, but she didn't. Even after everything Robb had done, and despite her certainty that she was doing the right thing, she felt badly and wondered if she would ever feel good about the decisions she knew she had to make.

Kim was thrilled to be sent home early that day due to management meetings that didn't involve her, but quickly changed her mind when Robb's mom pulled up in front of her parents' home. It was their weekend to have Jackson and suddenly she wished she had stayed at work. Quickly, she called Jackson at a neighbor's house and told him to come home—fast. Robb's parents would pick Jackson up on Friday and drop him back off to Kim Sunday morning before church. She had only seen them a few times since Robb left. Dorothy, Robb's mom, had always been particularly negative toward Kim in that she was much more blatant with her disapproval than the rest of Robb's family. Kim took a deep breath as Dorothy came up the walk and steeled herself for a scene she knew would not be pretty.

"Hi, Dorothy," Kim said with reserve as she opened the door. Apparently Dorothy was surprised to see her at home. Judging from the look on the older woman's face she was no more happy to see Kim than Kim was to see her.

"Hello," Dorothy said with a tight smile.

"Jackson's on his way home from a friend's house; he'll be here in just a minute. Can I get you anything?" Kim asked politely as Dorothy took a seat.

"No thank you," Dorothy said stiffly as she adjusted her wide bottom into the chair and pushed a lock of black dyed hair off her forehead.

Kim wasn't sure if it was better to stay, or to go. She knew which option she would rather take, but she also knew she needed to tell Dorothy about the divorce sometime. She knew she should face the situation like an adult by not putting off until tomorrow what she could do today.

"Maybe it's good that I am home today," Kim began, her heart pounding. "I need to let you and Tom know that I...I've spoken to a lawyer. I started the process for a divorce today."

Dorothy's eyes went wide and she sprang to her feet with amazing speed, startling Kim. "What!" she screamed.

Kim knew she would be upset, but Dorothy's reaction stunned her. "I...Uh..."

Dorothy cut her off. "You are filing for divorce from *my* son?" she shrieked.

"Dorothy, you know what I have been dealing with these last few months," Kim said with forced calmness.

"Of what *you* have been dealing with," she glared at Kim as she spat out the words. "What about us? Have you any idea the torment we have had to deal with? And now that you two finally try to work things out you're throwing everything away?"

Throwing *what* away, Kim thought; there was nothing worth keeping. Out loud she said, "Dorothy, I understand this is upsetting for you, and I don't know what you think the last eight years have been like for me, but—"

"This is all about you, isn't it," Dorothy cut in. "Robb needs support now more than ever and you are turning your back on him!" Tears welled up in her eyes. "You'll ruin his life, Kim. You can't take away everything when he's already lost so much. You can't take away Jackson—you can't. All these years that he's struggled and tried his very best with you belittling and insulting his efforts, and now you-""

Kim was taken completely off guard by the accusations being hurled at her. Coming to her feet, and wishing she were just a few inches taller, she responded loudly, "Is that what he told you? That I am responsible for his unemployment, drinking, and laziness? I have done everything in my power to help him, Dorothy. I've supported us financially. *I've* been the one that takes Jack to church. *I've* put up with all Robb's problems and you are blaming me because I'm not willing to do it any more? You need to let go of your fantasy and face up to the facts: Robb is a spoiled, manipulative man who left his family and is finally getting what he deserves." Her chest heaved as she stared into the furious eyes of her mother-in-law.

"I should have known you would—"

"Yes, you should have known," Kim spat back. "You should have known that your son has had a very serious drinking problem for nearly six years. You should have known that he abandoned Jackson and I long before actually he left. You should have known he has no testimony of the gospel—but you don't know that because you are too blind to see him as he really is. He is not a perfect man, Dorothy. And whatever he has told you about me is his way of making excuses for the fact that he doesn't have what it takes to be a husband or a father."

Dorothy stared at her, her eyes narrowing in fury. Kim returned her look with one just as intense. "I refuse to listen to this," Dorothy finally said. "I will wait for Jackson in the car." And with that, she stomped out the door.

Kim took a minute to control her breathing and then went into action. She had to hurry before she chickened out. Kim's dad had a copy machine in his office downstairs and she grabbed her Book of Mormon before racing to the basement. Jackson walked in just as she got back upstairs.

"Jackson, grab your bag and then I've got a note for you to give to Grandma, okay?"

"Okay," Jackson yelled as he bounded up to his room.

By the time he returned, Kim had a sealed envelope ready to go. She thought about writing something like 'read it and weep' or 'so there!' on the back but she resisted. It would be enough as it was.

She gave Jackson a hug and kiss and then handed him the envelope. "Just give this to Grandma for me, all right?"

"She's outside in the car, how come you don't give it to her?"

Kim smiled. "Trust me, I'd better not."

Jackson shrugged, "Okay. See you later, Mom." Kim watched him get into the car, and wondered if she had done the right thing. Too late now, she decided, and went back to her dad's office to be sure nothing was left behind.

Kim expected to hear from Robb's parents at any time, and spent an anxious weekend waiting for their phone call. Several times, she berated herself for doing this to them but each time she was reminded that they had to face facts and that she could never convince them otherwise. To her surprise, she heard nothing until Sunday morning when they dropped Jackson off before church. This time Tom, Robb's dad, brought Jackson home and walked him to the door. Attempting to make herself scarce because she was unsure how to act, Kim was in her room, listening as Peggy answered the door.

"Hello, Tom," she heard her mom say. "Thanks for bringing Jack home."

"No problem," Tom said in a strained voice. Clearing his throat he continued, "Is Kim here?"

"Uh, yes. She's upstairs. Come on in, I'll go get her."

"Thank you," Kim heard him say as Peggy came upstairs. Kim clenched her eyes shut and took a breath.

"Kim," Peggy whispered after knocking. Kim opened the door and met her mother's anxious face.

"It's okay, Mom. I heard." Kim slipped past her and forced herself to walk calmly.

Entering the living room just as Jackson scurried past her and bounded up the stairs with a wave, she gave Tom a tight smile. "Hello."

Tom looked even more uncomfortable than she felt. "Can I talk to you?" he said.

"Sure, we can use my dad's office," she offered. She had butterflies in her stomach as she tried and failed to read his expression.

"I would rather speak in my car, if that would be all right."

"That's fine," Kim said and followed him out.

Once in the car, Tom was silent for what seemed to be a long time. Finally he whispered, "Kim, is there any possible reason for us to believe that that letter was written by anyone other than my son?"

Kim could hear the pain in his voice, and momentarily wished she could tell him something other than the truth, but she couldn't. "Robb sent it to me earlier this week."

Tom raised a hand to his face as if to rub his eyes, but when his shoulders started shaking she knew that he was crying. She didn't know what to do; what comfort she could possibly offer. She just sat there, waiting for him to speak again. Tears came to her own eyes as she listened to her husband's father sob. For a moment she imagined what it would be like to know about Jackson the things that this man had just learned about his son and her heart sank a little deeper. Robb was their baby; the only son in a family that saw him as being almost godly. Tom had served on the stake's high council for seven years before being called to be a bishop; he'd been released just two years ago. Having his only son be a righteous man was a very big deal and wouldn't be a dream easy to let go of.

After a few minutes, Tom seemed to get hold of himself and wiped at his eyes with the back of his sleeve.

"I'm sorry, Tom," was all she could say, and she meant it. She was very sorry for Tom and Dorothy. She wondered if Robb would ever fully realize how many people he had hurt. "I didn't know how else to make you understand."

Tom shook his head. "It's us who owe you an apology," he said with obvious difficulty. "I just can't believe it," he added and covered his mouth with his hand.

Kim swallowed the lump in her throat and looked at her hands clasped in her lap. "I should have told you about the drinking a long time ago, but ..." she let it hang, knowing she couldn't adequately explain herself.

Tom just nodded his understanding. After a moment he asked, "Do you have an address for him?"

"Yes, shall I go get it for you?"

Tom nodded, and Kim let herself out of the car. When she returned she could see that Tom had been crying again. After handing him the scrap of paper, Kim said goodbye. Tom couldn't speak. She was backing out of the car when Tom grabbed her hand. Looking from her hand to his face, she knew without his speaking that he was truly sorry and that he was feeling nearly as deep a pain as she was. Fresh tears spilled down his cheeks as he squeezed her hand.

"Will you let us continue to see Jack?" he choked out, desperation in his eyes.

"Of course," Kim said; she had never thought otherwise.

Tom tried to smile. "Thank you," he whispered and dropped her hand.

Kim shut the door and hurried back to the house.

Peggy was fixing Jackson's tie when Kim came back inside the house. "Is everything all right?" Peggy asked.

"It will be," Kim said heading for the stairs, relieved that it was over. "It will be."

That night after the bedtime routine, Kim sat on the edge of Jackson's bed and began explaining to her son his father's situation. She told Jackson about Robb going to jail, that he would be there for a long time and that when he got out he wouldn't live with them anymore. She explained to him about divorce, that she and his dad would not be married when Robb got out. Jackson asked a few questions which Kim answered carefully, not wanting to tell him too much or too little. He told her about a friend at school whose parents didn't live together and she said that was what divorce was. The discussed it for almost twenty minutes and Kim was relieved that Jackson seemed to understand and accept the situation.

"Will you marry someone else?" he asked when she finished.

Kim smiled sadly. "Maybe some day, but not for a very long time I think." At the present time, she couldn't imagine wanting to remarry.

"If you marry someone else will he be my new dad?"

"He would be your step-dad; your dad will always be your dad. Nothing will ever change that."

Jackson looked at her for a while. "Will you be happy now?"

"You don't think I'm happy?" Kim asked with surprise. He didn't answer, but he shook his head.

Kim paused for a moment considering the full extent of his question. "No, Jackson, I haven't been happy; but I'm feeling better now."

Jackson smiled. "Good, my teacher says everyone should be happy. That's why we choose the right."

Kim chuckled at his innocent logic. "I'm doing my best to choose the right, so I guess I should be happy now, huh?"

"That's what my teacher says," Jackson said with authority. Kim smiled and leaned down to kiss him on the forehead.

"I love you, Jackson," she whispered and wanted to say a hundred more things. She wanted to tell him how sorry she was that he couldn't have the normal family she always wished for him. She wanted to explain to him how hard it would be when he got old enough to realize what his father had done. She wished there was some way to protect him from the hardships ahead of them, but he wouldn't understand and so for now she had to have faith that when the time came he could handle those issues. A small pair of arms reached around her neck and she pulled her son close, not even trying to keep the tears back. For almost a minute she held him, rocking gently, overcome with the preciousness of the child God had given her. "I love you too, Mom," he whispered.

# CHAPTER EIGHT

The holidays seemed to grab everyone by the hand and run full speed. The snows came in and the shovels came out. Jackson made a wonderful, if not pale and skinny, Squanto in his class play and Kim enjoyed sharing a Thanksgiving dinner, comprised of foods starting with each letter of the alphabet, with him and his class-mates afterward. She signed the divorce papers a few days before the holiday weekend and before Kim knew it Thanksgiving Day arrived. The last two Thanksgivings had been miserable for her due to Robb's insistence of visiting friends for a 'Turkey Bowl' party and her insistence that they spend the holiday together as a family. She looked forward to spending this one on her terms for a change. More than anything she wanted to truly enjoy the spirit of the season with her family. Any fears of discomfort at having everyone know about the pending divorce were soon dissipated by the easy manner in which everyone treated her.

Her family had a tradition of baking a pie for each adult at dinner. Whatever wasn't eaten that day was finished off for break-fast the next morning; this year they set a new record with sixteen pies. After the turkey, everyone rested for an hour or so; and then it was pie time.

Maddie arrived just as the first pie was cut. "Hello," Kim called from the kitchen when she entered.

"Hi," Maddie answered, her eyes wide as she took in the display of pastry. "I don't think I've ever seen so many pies."

"Get used to it," Matt cut in as he came up behind Maddie and wrapped his arms around her waist, making her giggle. Kim was still surprised that things had worked so well for the two of them. She hadn't had any idea it would end up like this when she set up that silly first date. She had only done it to make herself feel better.

Kim smiled and continued cutting. "So how are things?" Kim asked after their hello kiss was over.

"Great," Maddie said as she planted herself on a stool and took a fingerful of blueberry filling. Matt started laying out plates and silverware and soon everyone was making introductions and welcoming Maddie between forkfuls. Before Kim knew it, and in what seemed to be no time at all, only two-pies-worth of miscellaneous pieces were left. Even after so many Thanksgivings it still amazed her that people could eat so much. Kim herself had inhaled at least five pieces and was reminded of how sick a person could feel when they got this full.

"Mom," she said when Peggy entered the kitchen to dump more plates into the sink. "Next year why don't we skip the turkey?"

"Good idea," Peggy laughed. She then placed a hand on Kim's shoulder, "You've been in here all afternoon—why don't you go lay down for a minute."

"I think I'd better," Kim said gratefully and was heading up the stairs when someone called her name. Turning, she saw Maddie coming toward her.

"Hey, can I talk to you for a minute?"

"Sure, I was just on my way to my room. Come on." She waddled to the room and dropped on the bed groaning. "Remind me not to do this next year," she moaned as she closed her eyes and put a hand on her stomach.

Maddie smiled nervously and shut the door behind her. "Kim, I need to ask you a big favor."

"Okay," Kim replied cautiously as she opened one eye, suspicious because of Maddie's tone.

"You're not going to like it," Maddie said, wringing her hands. All of the sudden Maddie jumped on the bed, making Kim worry that she might throw up. "Sorry," Maddie said, evidently realizing the same thing.

"I'm all right. What do you need?"

"Did I already mention you wouldn't like it?"

"Yes."

"Oh. Well then, here's the deal," she paused, took a breath and then began quickly. "Allen has this weekend workshop coming up and he asked me to go with him, which was fine, so I said yes. But then Matt asked me out for the same night and I...I think he's going to propose."

"Really?" Kim said, momentarily forgetting about her physical discomfort as she propped herself up on an elbow. Matt hadn't said another word about it to Kim after their conversation almost a month ago.

"I found a receipt for a ring in his glove box and yesterday, while I had his cell phone, this limo guy called him to confirm a reservation. Matt doesn't think I know."

"I see," Kim said slowly. She was about to chastise Maddie for being such a snoop but then Maddie started talking again.

"And I was wondering if you would go with Allen—he already paid and has to have somebody go with him to be his partner."

Kim just blinked. "Maddie, I can't just—"

"Kim, you don't understand," Maddie cut in desperately. "Allen has paid like $1,000 and he'll lose every penny if he doesn't go and he can't go alone."

"Why not?" Kim said in a near-whining voice.

If possible, Maddie looked even more uncomfortable. "It's a relationship conference, for couples."

Kim blinked at her again. "And you want me to go with Allen?" Kim couldn't believe Maddie was asking this of her.

"Oh, Kim, please. See, it's this conference that is only offered every three months nationwide. They only allow one therapist from the state they chose to hold the conference in and it's in Logan this time. It is like the highest rated of its kind. Allen was extremely lucky to get this spot and probably won't ever get the chance again. I can't ruin this for him."

"Maddie, I'm married; I can't go to a couples conference with some guy," Kim pointed out.

"He is there for observation purposes only. You won't have to do anything."

"Except spend a weekend with some man I barely know!"

"Kim, please." Maddie begged. "You are my only hope. I already tried my sisters but Amy's pregnant again and really sick and Jeri's husband is having surgery on his knee that Friday."

Kim groaned and closed her eyes. "What do I have to do?" she said in defeat. She knew she couldn't say no, but wondered how she could possibly say yes; and she did feel that she owed Allen something for the help he'd given her. This was nuts.

"You just have to attend a couple of classes with him. Then there are some classes for women only that they won't allow the men to go to. He needs you to take notes in them."

"Do you promise me that nothing weird will happen?"

"Kim, he was going to take his sister. And he specifically requested two rooms. I swear there is nothing to worry about."

Kim closed her eyes again. "When is it?" she finally groaned.

"Two weeks from tomorrow. Is that a yes?" Maddie squeaked.

"Yes," Kim replied just before having the wind squeezed out of her by Maddie's bear hug.

"Oh, thank you so much, Kim. I owe you big time."

Kim laughed, pushing Maddie away. "You bet you do."

# CHAPTER NINE

The following Tuesday, Kim got a call from her attorney. Robb was contesting the divorce. He was insisting that he and Kim needed to meet in person before he would sign anything. Kim refused. "Tell him that I have to work every day and that I have a son to raise. I can't just drive to Wyoming because he wants to talk over things that should have been discussed months ago."

"Is that your formal response?" her attorney asked.

Sensing his reluctance, she asked, "Do you think I should go?" She certainly didn't want to; she was tired of playing Robb's games.

"I think it's worth consideration. Keep in mind that Robb has nothing better to do than pursue this. It isn't any big deal for him to make this difficult and drag it on for months. He's in a corner and he knows it, but he can still make this hard on you. Refusing the simple things could just make him get more creative."

"He's in prison. How creative can he get?" Kim asked in frustration.

"He has free legal representation and nothing else to do with his time; the possibilities are plentiful."

Kim sighed and wanted to hit something, "I assume he wants me to go to Evanston, then?"

"He can't go anywhere else."

Clenching her fists she wished she could scream. The last thing she wanted right now was to see her husband, but Eric had a point. "Okay," she said in defeat. "When?"

That Saturday morning she was on her way to Wyoming. Eric was with her which irritated her all the more since she had to pay him by the hour to play this little game. They spoke of very little, other than what she could expect. They would meet with Robb and his attorney for thirty minutes, Kim would stick to her guns and then they would leave. It all sounded very simple, but Kim was nervous. It had been six months since she had seen Robb and a whole lot had happened since then. What would it be like? What did he hope to accomplish?

Too soon, they pulled up outside the prison and Kim followed Eric through the routine of checking in. Being in the building gave her the creeps—her husband lived here! They were eventually led to a small room which contained some chairs and one long table. Robb was already there when they entered but Kim refused to meet his eyes. She sat across the table from him, next to her attorney and they all remained silent for a moment.

"You look great, Kim," Robb said. Kim clenched her teeth as she glanced up at him. His curly brown hair was overgrown and wild-looking, but his brown eyes were just as soft and pitiful as she remembered them. He was all smiles and sympathy. She wanted to slap him.

Eric cleared his throat and addressed his comments to Robb's attorney. "Since your client called this meeting you may as well get us started; as I told you before, we only have thirty minutes."

Robb's attorney, a wiry little man with a bad toupee and thick-rimmed glassed, nodded. "We would like to propose that we put this divorce on hold..." Kim sat there listening as he rattled on and on about the problems with such hasty actions. He explained that because of good behavior, Robb would likely be out on parole in only two years and that 'his client' was very sorry and would like to pursue the opportunity to make restitution to his family. For almost five minutes, Kim listened to the list of pathetic reasons, and through it all her anger continued to rise. Did Robb really think she was going to go for this? Had he forgotten about all the things that had brought them to this point? Had he forgotten the lovely letter he had sent her just a month ago that pointed out what a terrible wife she was in the first place? Had she really been so weak and insipid that he could imagine she would just smile and agree to wait for him? Two years! Several times she wanted to interrupt and tell them both to stop wasting their time but she had promised Eric she would listen. So, she held her peace while she boiled inside. Finally they stopped, and she looked up to see their satisfied smiles as they looked at her expectantly. She glared back at them, insulted that either of them could even imagine she would consider such a ridiculous suggestion.

"We didn't come here to discuss options," Eric said bluntly. "We came to discuss the details of the divorce settlement. My client has no interest in continuing her marriage, the papers you were served should have made that perfectly clear, so unless you have specific problems with the terms of this divorcement you're just wasting your time and our money."

"Your client is angry," Robb's attorney replied. "And rightfully so. But does her anger justify breaking up a family, leaving her son without a father—"

"We are not a family!" Kim suddenly interrupted. She looked directly at Robb, indignation thick in her voice. "We never were. Your client abandoned us after years of neglect and alcoholism. He has never—NEVER given us any regard and now you want me to put the rest of my life on hold in hopes that he'll change? I've already wasted too much time waiting for that and I have no desire to spend another day of my life waiting for the impossible."

Robb's smile was gone and he glared back at her, the muscles in his jaw flexing.

Directing her comments directly at him, she added, "I did everything I could for nine years to help you take responsibility for your life, Robb; you made your choices—we refuse to suffer with you any longer. We are getting on with our lives."

"I'm sorry about that letter, Kim, about everything; but you have to understand that—"

"No, Robb!" she snapped as she leaned across the table towards him. "You have to understand. This is it. I'm done. It's over. There is nothing you can say that will change it. I'm glad you're sorry, but that isn't enough. Nothing can change my mind."

Everyone was silent until Robb's attorney opened his mouth to speak, but Robb beat him to it. "Does Jackson know about this? Does he want a life without me, have you considered his feeling in this at all?"

"Have I considered his feelings?" Kim shot back bitterly, almost laughing at the absurdity of the question. "Have you? Have you even once wondered about how your life has affected his? How it's affected all of us? I'm tired of it, Robb. I'm tired of trying to save you from yourself. And yes, Jackson does know about this and he understands. I suggest you take what we offered the first time and hope he'll want something to do with you when you're released. I have the option of fighting for custody which would stop you from ever seeing him again and I won't hesitate to fight for it if you insist on making this more difficult than it already is."

Her heart was thumping in her chest and her cheeks burned, but she relished the fact that for once in their endless bouts of arguing she was able to express her true feelings.

"Kim, I didn't know she was a prostitute, I—"

"I don't care," she said very loud and very slow. "You are not listening to me. I won't be here when you get out, Robb. You made your choice, and you should have known that it would eventually lead to this. I don't care anymore. I don't care about you or your life. You must accept that."

Robb was silent; then he narrowed his eyes. "You're making a big mistake, Kim."

"Are you threatening me?" she asked angrily. He didn't answer. "You deserve what you've got, but Jackson and I deserve a whole lot more than you can ever give us." Then she said the magic words that had been so long in coming. "I want a divorce; I will not be your wife any more."

Eric stood and Kim stood with him. "I think my client has made her point," Eric said. "From now on we will consider only negotiations in writing. No more visits, no personal letters, and no phone calls. If Mr. Larksley has anything to say he can speak through his attorney." They turned to go.

"Wait," Robb called and they turned to look at him once more. He simply stared at Kim and she stared back with equal intensity, wondering how she stayed with him for so long. "You are making a big mistake," he repeated.

"No, Robb, I'm just not going to clean up after your mistakes anymore." They held each other's gaze for another moment until Kim turned and walked through the door that Eric was holding open for her.

Once they were in the car, she shook her head, "I can't believe that's my husband; he's like a stranger, yet he's the same." She turned to look at Eric. "Does that make sense?"

Eric turned the key in the engine and nodded. "It all comes down to perception. When you look at him as a father and husband you see the parts that support that theory. But when you look at him as a bum, you see other parts you missed before." He looked over at her and smiled. "I've seen it a thousand times." He smiled to soften the possibly insulting nature of what he had said and turned his attention to driving. "You were great in there. Normally, people don't get an opportunity to get their point across so well, but I wasn't going to object if his attorney didn't."

Kim couldn't help but smile. "It felt great," she admitted. "We've had our share of arguments, but for the first time I was finally able to say what I wanted to."

Eric nodded and she stared out the window feeling slightly guilty for feeling so good about their exchange. Their previous arguments either ended with him slamming doors or her crying— most of the time both. This time she had been strong, honest and unmovable; she had taken control and not lost it. She liked thinking of herself that way. She liked it a lot.

Monday morning Eric called her at work to tell her that Robb's attorney was requesting a stipend.

"A what?"

"Robb seems to think he deserves a monthly allowance—at least until the divorce is settled. His claim is that since you're renting out the house you're receiving income that is jointly his and he wants some of it."

"Why on earth does he need money?" Kim asked angrily; Robb just didn't quit.

"Cigarettes and magazines is about all he has access to."

Kim paused thoughtfully. "Tell his attorney to have Robb sell his car—it's the only thing that's rightfully his; the rent is paying his child support."

"I'll give him a call right now," Eric said and hung up. Kim took a deep breath in an attempt to calm herself; then she got an idea. Pulling open her desk drawer, she fished around until she found the business card she was after. She dialed the phone number and listened to the ringing of the other end.

"Yes, I'd like to speak with Lt. Browning," she said when the phone was answered. A minute later she was taken off hold.

"Browning."

"Hi, this is Kim Larksley. You probably don't remember me but I'm the woman that threw up in your trashcan a couple of months ago."

"Oh, yes. How could I forget," he said with a chuckle.

Kim smiled. "I want to ask you a favor."

"I can't promise anything till I know what it is."

"I know. I need to send something to my husband, Robb, but I'm pretty sure the prison won't deliver it. I can promise you it isn't anything bad, but I want to know, if I Fed Ex it to you, will you see that he gets it?"

"Well, that depends on what it is," he said suspiciously.

"I'll just send it to you. If you have a problem with it, just send it back C.O.D—how's that?"

"I guess that's okay. You don't want to just tell me?" Lt. Browning asked.

"If I did you'd tell me not to waste my time, but once you get it you'll see my point."

"Well, send me your mystery package and I'll let you know how it goes."

"Thanks, Lieutenant. I really appreciate it."

"No problem," he said and hung up.

When Browning received the overnight package he opened it

and out dropped a regular white letter-sized envelope, but with something three dimensional inside. Curious, he opened the envelope and dropped the items into the palm of his hand. He chuckled and looked around to see if anyone was watching him; he didn't know how he would explain this to someone who was looking on. Pocketing the items, he grabbed his coat and told the dispatcher he was going to the prison.

Nearly an hour later he was led to a small gray room with a table and two chairs. Robb was led in a minute later, wearing handcuffs. Browning was surprised to see such a good-looking guy. Despite how badly he needed a hair cut and the day or two worth of beard on his chin, Robb Larksley still possessed a certain James Bond look. His eyes, however, ruined the image: they were hard and cold. He sat down, staring at Browning the entire time. Browning waved the guard out and returned Robb's look. For a time, they tried to stare each other down; finally, Robb looked away.

"I have something for you," Browning said.

"Oh yeah," Robb replied sarcastically.

"It's from your wife," Browning said blandly.

"Really?" Robb said as he sat forward in anticipation. "Did she finally send me some money?"

"Nope," Browning said and pulled his hand out of his pocket, depositing the items in the middle of the table. For a moment Robb stared at them.

"Kim's rings?" he asked as if he weren't sure.

"Looks like it," Browning said, delighted at the look on Robb's face. "She probably didn't realize you'll just trade them for smokes, but then again maybe she did. Maybe their value is low enough in her mind that she didn't care. Either way, I guess you get the message."

Robb's eyes snapped with fury. "Who the hell are you?" he hissed as he looked up at the taller man.

"Maybe I'm the guy taking your place; restoring her faith in men," Browning said with a gloating smile.

"Like hell you are," Robb spat. "She'll never..." he stopped himself.

"What?" Browning prodded with amusement. "Leave you?" Robb looked away and Browning chuckled as he walked toward the door. Nodding toward the rings on the table he added, "I would assume she's past that now." He looked down on the other man. "You're an idiot, Mr. Larksley. If nothing else, I hope being here will teach you that."

# CHAPTER TEN

Browning had updated her on the ring presentation and Kim was well satisfied with Robb's reaction. Eric heard nothing more from Robb's attorney and Kim felt confident she had made her point. With any luck she would have no more problems with Robb. With him out of the way, at least for now, Kim found herself obsessed with the weekend which was quickly approaching. It seemed she barely went an hour without worrying about it. She had talked to her mom and although Peggy agreed it was a little strange, she was sure it would be all right. Kim even asked Bishop Scott what he thought about it when she spoke to him about the progress she had made towards the divorce. He surprised her by saying it might be just what she needed.

"But, Bishop, my divorce isn't even final yet and it's a relationship conference. I'll be there with a man. Don't you think that is highly inappropriate?"

"I think it will be beneficial for you to learn about good relationships between men and women; this is a great opportunity. If this man you're going with is an honorable priesthood holder, you have nothing to worry about. It's not like you'll be sharing a room."

The bishop's words came back to haunt her when she and Allen reached the hotel. They had driven toward Logan, being polite to one another but not talking much. Allen seemed as uncomfortable with the situation as she was. Finally, Allen broke the ice by explaining to her what to expect.

"They separate the day into several classes. I believe that although a few will be together, most are separated into men's and women's classes. I just need you to take notes and then fill me in afterwards."

"Sounds easy enough," Kim said. The farther from the city they got the more relaxed she became. Despite the odd circumstances, it was so nice to get away. "This is really beautiful," Kim said as they entered Wellsville Canyon, also called Sardine Canyon, that led from Brigham City to Logan. There had been new snow recently and the trees were heavy with unshed drifts, while expansive valleys stretched forever, covered in a canvas of pure white snow. The sky was overcast but bright and she longed to step out of the car and fill her lungs with the crisp mountain air. "I hope it isn't too much of an inconvenience for you to have me along."

"Quite the contrary," Allen said. "They are very strict about not letting men attend or even record the women's classes and vice versa. Without you, I'll never receive the insight into a woman's mind that I so desperately need."

Kim laughed and glanced quickly at her weekend companion. "Lose the earring. There's some insight for you."

Allen chuckled, but didn't explain.

Kim watched him for a moment, worried she might have offended him, but when he said nothing she felt a wave of courage and pushed a little harder "You said you'd tell me the story about that someday, you know."

"I did, didn't I," Allen said.

"Yep, so go ahead—I'd love to know what drives a grown man who attends the temple at five a.m. to pierce his ear."

"It's not nearly as interesting as you probably expect," he said with a smile, casting a quick glance in her direction. "There is a kid who I counseled with in Chicago who was having some problems with his parents. One of his biggest struggles was in his school attendance, so we made a deal: for every week he attended class without absences, I would wear an earring for a month."

"You're kidding?" Kim snickered.

"Nope. Unfortunately, I underestimated him and ended up with an 18 month earring sentence before his counseling ended. I had done it as an incentive for him, but he took it as a challenge."

Kim laughed and shook her head. "I can't believe you would do that."

"It worked. He'll graduate this June. Having an adult get down to his level helped him realize that we weren't all out to get him."

"After you left Chicago why didn't you just take it out?"

Allen shrugged, "I promised."

Kim's estimation of the man rose a little bit at that. "Well, good for you. How much longer do you have?"

"I can take it out on February 10. Then I'm going to mail it back to him as an early graduation present."

Kim looked quickly at his shaved head. "Was the hair another deal?"

"Nope," Allen said with a smile. "I started going bald in high school. I hated it. After my mission, I shaved it off for good and decided I prefer it that way; since then it's become all the rage to have a shaved head—lucky me."

"You are a very interesting person, Allen," Kim said with a smile, shaking her head again.

"Oh, yeah?" he asked brightly.

"Oh, yeah," Kim repeated with a nod just as they pulled into the parking lot.

Allen carried in most of the bags, leaving only one for Kim. The parking lot was almost full and they had to park quite a ways away from the building. The snow was deep and there were several patches of ice, which kept them at a slow pace, concentrating on their feet. Once inside, Kim had a chance to look around and was impressed at the décor. She had expected a formal-but-basic hotel, not the comfortable and inviting lodge she found herself in. It was decorated as if it were a family cabin, with weathered pine paneled walls, antique furniture and hand-stitched quilts hanging on the walls. There was a fire blazing in the fireplace and several leather couches arranged around the room. The perfect setting for a romantic weekend, she thought somewhat sadly before pushing the thought from her mind. Everything about this place communicated comfort and relaxation; Kim felt herself loosen up just being here. It even smelled rustic, she thought, taking in the woodsy, dry pine scent.

The check-in counter was around a corner and Allen had passed her up while she was taking it all in. She turned the corner in time to hear the end of the conversation between Allen and the apologizing desk clerk.

"You mean to tell me you have no empty rooms?" Allen quipped, obviously very close to losing his temper.

The clerk was punching buttons and scanning the computer monitor in front of her. "We are booked solid all weekend, sir; if you had specified two rooms—"

"I did specify," Allen said sharply, then added, "Get me your manager." It was then that he saw Kim. He looked at her quickly before being informed that the manager would meet with him in his office. Without meeting Kim's eye again, he walked around the desk and went out of sight. It didn't take a rocket scientist to figure out what Allen was upset about, and Kim moaned inwardly. There were no separate rooms after all. There was no way she could stay in a room with a man that wasn't her husband. She felt sick and cursed Maddie for making her agree to do this in the first place.

Allen came back out, ignoring the clerk as she tried again to apologize. Taking Kim's arm, he guided her to an empty corner.

"They messed up my reservation," he whispered without

meeting her eyes. "I specifically requested two rooms, but they gave me a double room instead."

Kim didn't know what to say, so she remained silent. Allen's anger and disappointment were obvious. When she didn't answer, he added, deflated, "I'll bring the car around." Then he went out the door.

Kim watched the door shut behind him before making up her mind and running after him. Allen was stomping through the parked cars and didn't hear her when she called after him, although several other people did and turned to look at her. Breaking into a jog-walk she finally caught up with him and reached out to grab his arm just as he slipped on the ice and went down, causing her to topple over the top of him. Kim squealed as she tried to get her footing, but to no avail. They landed in a heap. After the initial shock, came the moans.

Kim groaned as she lifted her head only to find she had practically landed in his lap. Blushing with embarrassment, she quickly got to her feet and tried to avoid his eyes by brushing at her pants.

"Are you okay?" he asked after standing up himself.

"Yeah, are you?"

"I smacked my elbow, but I'm all right," he said rubbing the aforementioned area and then chuckled under his breath.

Kim's eyes narrowed. "What's so funny?" she asked.

"Nothing," he said without conviction. "Grace."

"Fine," she said indignantly. "Never mind then." With her nose in the air, she spun on her heel heading back to the hotel.

She didn't get two feet before Allen caught her arm. "Never mind what?" he asked.

Kim didn't know exactly how to answer now. He had ruined the moment for her.

"You came out here for a reason," Allen said, loosening his grip but not letting go. "What was it?"

Kim melted at the glimmer of hope in his eye. Unfortunately, he had now got her in a temper and she didn't like the way things had turned around. "I was going to tell you that it would be okay."

"What would be okay?" Allen asked carefully.

"You did say the room had two beds, right?"

Allen scooped her up into a hug that lifted her off the ground. "Oh thanks, Kim," he said squeezing her tightly. He set her down and, still holding her by the shoulders, looked her in the eyes. "Are you sure?" he questioned. "I don't want you to feel like you have to do this."

Kim was a little taken aback by his reaction—as if she could back out now. But she was able to smile as she asked, "Can you stay without me?"

Allen paused a minute, but told the truth when he said, "No."

"Would Maddie have shared the room with you if she had been here?"

"Not gladly, but yes she would have shared a room with me."

"Then I think I can handle it."

"I really appreciate this, Kim."

"I know," she said and wiggled out of his grip. She was suddenly uncomfortable that being close to him was so comfortable. They walked back to the hotel and asked for the keys to their room.

The room was large and decorated like the lobby. There were, in fact, two beds, also a sofa across from the fireplace, a small table with two chairs and a large rustic armoire. Allen offered Kim the bed closest to the bathroom and set about unpacking. After several minutes Kim asked, "So now what?"

Allen looked up at her and then at the clock on the wall. "We have about 30 minutes until the welcome speech and orientation dinner."

That didn't sound too bad, Kim thought. "And then?" she prodded.

"Then we separate for the 'I am' classes."

"I am?" Kim questioned raising an eyebrow.

Allen shut the last drawer and sat on his bed. "The philosophy is that you need to discover who you are before discovering who your spouse is," he answered as he took off his boots and stretched out on the bed. Kim made a point not to look at his prostrate form. It made her stomach flutter in a most disconcerting way.

That makes sense, Kim thought, as she tucked her now-empty suitcase under the bed. She looked over at Allen and was about to ask more about it, but he was asleep—just like that. Turning her back to him she sat at the small table and decided to do her scripture study. She opened her blue Book of Mormon and put her blessing and Robb's letter aside—she used them as a bookmark now. Ever since finding the book, she had used it on a daily basis, enjoying how familiar it felt. Allen snored and she rolled her eyes; that's great. Not only does she have to sleep in the same room as the man, but he snores. Could it get any better than this?

The dinner was excellent and Kim felt more relaxed after hearing the orientation. The woman who directed the conference, Liz, explained that the conference was designed to teach skills that ensure the lifelong communication and fulfillment necessary for a successful and rewarding marriage. Kim couldn't help feeling a little excited about what lay ahead. She reminded herself that she was a day late and a dollar short, but at the very least, maybe she'd learn where she went wrong.

They split for class, and Kim took a seat at the back of the room. Liz taught the class and began by explaining that being a wife and mother is like being a jug of milk, providing nourishment and strength to her family. The milk is given but has to be replenished; furthermore, any milk not given will spoil if neglected. Liz explained that although a good amount of the milk is replenished by the very people we give it to, much of the milk is self-produced. Just as a mother's breast milk, it cannot be produced by anyone or anything else. All the women were asked to list the things that they felt filled their jug. Everything had to be something not connected to husbands or children. Kim hadn't planned to participate until she caught Liz's eye and Liz motioned to the paper, giving her thumbs up sign. Giving a mental shrug, Kim decided she might as well join in and started her list. After five minutes Kim had written only two things: bubble baths and chocolate—pathetic. Her embarrassment increased as Liz randomly called on some women and asked how many they had listed. The first woman sheepishly said five, and the room chuckled as if that was ridiculous. One woman had seventeen!

"The goal, ladies, is that by the end of this conference you can add at least five more," Liz said cheerfully. Kim carefully put her paper back into the folder she had been given before anyone could see it. If she was supposed to feel optimistic at this point, she was failing. No one had to remind her that she had no hobbies and was terribly dull. She remembered it well enough on her own.

The class continued for another three hours although it didn't seem nearly that long. Kim felt herself near tears several times as Liz itemized numerous self-depreciating things we do to ourselves. She told a story about a woman married to an alcoholic for 20 years before realizing she was giving away her entire life to a man who didn't even care about his own. Kim's experience wasn't quite as drastic, but she got the point and felt even more frustrated with herself for being so blind for so long. The class was dismissed at 10:00, after each woman was given a number. Liz then met personally with each one for a few minutes before they were dismissed.

Kim was number 11 of 28 and when she entered the little office she didn't bother to take a seat.

"I'm just observing with Dr. Jackman," she said, expecting to excuse herself from the interview.

Liz smiled and waved her towards a seat. "Yes, he pointed you out to me when we broke for class." She smiled and asked, "What do you think so far?"

"Uh, it's very good," Kim said then added lightly. "I should have come years ago."

Liz raised her eyebrows. "Are you married?" she asked.

"Well, I'm actually in the middle of a divorce," Kim said, wishing she could leave. She still hadn't sat down. Liz brushed over the strange arrangement by asking to see Kim's list. "Oh, that's okay," Kim said nervously, clutching her folder to her chest.

"The couples here have paid a lot of money to get this information; you may as well take full advantage of the opportunity."

"All the more reason for me not to waste your time."

Liz smiled her understanding and said, "Don't make me waste their time and money fighting you; sit." Kim sat. Liz took the paper Kim offered and read both items before looking up at Kim. Kim gave her a weak smile. "Tell you what," Liz said as she put the paper back into the folder. "Breakfast is at 8:00 tomorrow; meet me here at 7:30 and we'll talk."

"You really don't need to do that, I know you—"

Liz cut her off by putting up a hand, "7:30."

Kim was embarrassed and opened her mouth to voice another protest, but Liz only put up her hand again and repeated "7:30."

Kim nodded and left, feeling uncomfortable but knowing there was nothing she could do about it. Allen wasn't there when she entered their room and she felt her stomach twinge when she looked at the two beds again. Reminding herself that it couldn't be helped, she grabbed her makeup bag and pajamas before locking herself in the bathroom. Taking her time, she removed her makeup, actually did her skin-care routine for the first time in weeks, and folded her clothes. She hesitated when she held up her pajamas and felt her face heat up as she realized Allen would get a good look at her oversized Winnie-the-Pooh T-shirt and plaid flannel pants. Had she known he would see her this way, she would have brought something a little more flattering. Then again, she wasn't out to impress anyone...was she?

Kim unlocked the door and entered the room. Allen was sitting on his bed, his back to her.

"Hello," she said lightly, trying to hide her discomfort.

"Hi," Allen said tonelessly, and when Kim looked over at him, he held a folded piece of paper over his head.

That looks like a letter, Kim thought curiously and took a step closer. My letter! She bounded across the room, jumped on the bed and snatched the paper out of his hand. Her heart was thumping. My letter, she thought again, Robb's nasty letter! She crushed it against her chest and felt her face burn. Allen's back was still toward her when she looked up at him again. Did he read it? she thought with alarm.

Allen twisted around so he was facing her, guilt written all over his face. "Kim, I'm sorry. I—"

"You read this?" she croaked.

"I didn't know it was yours; I was straightening the table and thought it was garbage, but I saw the writing and flipped it open," he admitted.

Kim was in shock, "And you read it?"

"Only the first few lines," Allen said apologetically. "Once I realized what it was, I stopped."

Three lines were plenty, Kim thought as she jumped off the bed, glaring at him. She wanted to say a thousand insulting things but couldn't speak. Instead she ran back to the bathroom and slammed the door.

Allen let out a deep breath. He felt terrible. He had told the truth when he said it was an accident and he had told the truth about only reading a few lines. What was that about the truth setting you free? He was sure they would have both been better off if he had just put it back on the table and never said a word. Even though he'd read very little, he could understand her humiliation. Poor Kim. From his own experience, he knew how difficult it was to try to start your life all over again, and from the things he had gathered in those few sentences her soon-to-be-ex wasn't making it any easier for her. What should he do now? His mind was blank. Not only did he hate her being upset, he also needed to know what they had gone over in the women's class. And... he really needed to use that bathroom.

After giving her a few minutes, Allen knocked lightly on the door. "Kim?" he asked. No answer. "Do you want to talk about this?"

"No, I don't want to talk about it," she said bluntly.

Allen sighed and decided he had better not ask if he could use the bathroom. Remembering there was one in the lobby he decided maybe she needed some space anyway.

Kim heard him leave and felt badly, despite her anger; he had paid for the room, after all. She opened the letter and read the opening sentences again. Closing her eyes she shook her head. Of all the humiliating things she had experienced during the last few months, this topped everything. Why had she kept that letter anyway? And of all people to have read it—Allen, he didn't know her well enough to believe it wasn't true. Her chest burned with humiliation.

She was sitting on the bathroom floor with her back against the door and her knees pulled up to her chest. She couldn't really be mad at him though; she believed it had been an accident and she had to give him credit for admitting it. Had the situation been reversed, she couldn't guarantee that she would have stopped reading after the first few lines. But her rationalizations didn't make her feel any better. He would look at her differently now. The things Robb said were so cutting and she had no doubt that even the most fair-minded person would wonder whether or not it was true. How could she face him now that he knew these things? She wiped at a hot tear on her cheek and scolded herself again for keeping the letter. How could she be so foolish?

Another ten minutes passed before Kim got herself off the floor and went back into the room, determining that she had to deal with this like an adult. There had been too many things in her life she had refused to face—she had to start facing her challenges head on. Allen hadn't returned and she hoped he wasn't going to stay away all night. She waited for a few minutes and then was just about to turn off the lights when the key turned in the door and Allen entered.

He didn't smile and just looked at her, as if hoping for a sign of encouragement and forgiveness. Kim gave him a weak smile and looked down before heading for her bed while Allen entered the room and threw his key on the table.

"I am sorry, Kim."

"I know."

Allen waited for her to say more. "I hate that I've made this even more uncomfortable."

Kim looked up. "It's not your fault, I should have burned it a long time ago." Allen said nothing. "I assume you're going to tell me I should talk about it, vent and all that, huh?"

"That's completely up to you," he said, sitting on the edge of his bed and removing his boots. "But I won't charge you."

Kim managed a smile. "I don't know how you can stand listening to people's problems," she said, unsure of whether she hated the idea of talking to him or longed to have someone listen.

Allen looked up and returned her smile with a sincere one of his own. "It has its drawbacks, but it makes my problems seem minor." She smiled weakly and looked away from the intensity of his gaze. "I've also found there's no better way to get to know someone than to start at the bottom and work your way up."

A little thrill rushed through her as she considered the meaning of those words. Did he want to get to know her? Did she want him to?

"Huh," Kim said noncommittally. "I'll think about it."

Allen watched her pull back the covers of her bed and tuck her feet underneath them. She piled the pillows behind her back and tucked her hair behind her ears before opening her Book of Mormon. The little details seemed so normal and yet so interesting to him. He watched how she licked her finger and turned the page. She didn't seem to notice he was watching her and finally he forced himself to stop and went into the bathroom to change. He spent far too much time getting changed and finally just swallowed his pride and emerged dressed in a camouflage T-shirt and thermal pants. He caught her watching before she looked away and tried to hide her smile.

"I know, I know," he said, "I look like something out of 'One Flew Over The Cuckoo's Nest."

Kim just smiled and shut the book as if she hadn't really noticed. "Tomorrow starts early, I guess."

Allen nodded. "Can I turn off the lights then?"

"I guess you'd better."

He flipped the switch and the room went black. Kim stayed propped up and listened to the sound of his feet cross the floor. The sheets rustled and little bursts of blue static momentarily flickered as he pulled back the blankets and got into his bed. Her heart was pounding for reasons she couldn't quite determine, but she waited, absorbing the sounds of him adjusting himself for sleep.

"How much did you read?" she asked quietly. Until she said the words she hadn't decided whether she wanted to talk about this or not; apparently some part of her wanted to.

"I stopped at the second F-word."

Kim nodded to herself in the darkness—at least he stopped there, she thought. "It's hard to believe that it was my husband who wrote that letter. I lived with him for eight years and never had a clue he was capable of this. Then again, in hindsight I see that I should have picked up on some of it. Somehow it seems like I should have known things would turn out this way."

Allen was silent and Kim wondered if he would start spouting Freud or something. When he did speak it was soft and personal. "I've wondered the same thing about my own marriage. I looked at my wife one day and wondered if I could do it all over again, would I? It was almost a year before I could admit to myself that the answer was no. And then I had to ask myself why we got married in the first place. We were married for ten years and we've been divorced almost two and I still haven't been able to answer that question."

Kim was silent, focusing on how sad this was, for both of them. Suddenly she realized that of all the people in her life, Allen was one of the few who had been through something similar to her own tragedy. That thought made her feel both at ease and a little uneasy. Clearing her throat, she asked, "Why did you get a divorce? If you don't mind my asking."

Allen smiled into the darkness and looked towards her although it was too dark to see anything. "I don't think anyone other than my mother has ever asked me what our reasons were, I think people just assume one of us was a psycho weirdo and they don't want to learn it was me." He was silent. Then, as if hoping to get out of answering, he asked, "You sure you want to hear this?"

"The only people I get to talk to either have never been married, or they're married now. I can't help but feel that, although they're sympathetic, they really don't understand what it's like."

"Okay then," Allen paused to take a breath. "Janet and I were married in college. I told you before that I left home right after my mission; I went to school at Berkley and that's where we met. She was a fashion merchandising major and I was pre-med. We dated about a year and married as soon as she graduated. I finished up at Berkley and then we went to Chicago, where I had been accepted into medical school. Janet got a great job and when I finished school I thought we would start a family. We had talked about it off and on, but never felt the need to hurry; especially due to how incredibly busy I was in school and she was in taking care of us financially. That plan completely backfired. By the time I was ready, Janet had decided that children weren't a part of her future. For the next few years I tried to support her but I hoped she would change her mind. She didn't. She had been promoted and worked nearly sixty hours a week; she told me she would never give up her career. Eventually, I had to admit to myself that the future I wanted wasn't the same as hers. We separated for a little while and when it became apparent that things were not going to change, we finally divorced."

"Is Janet a member of the church?" Kim asked, she thought he had married in the temple but his story wasn't fitting together like she thought.

"Yep. She was born in California but moved to Provo when she was a kid. Don't get me wrong—she is a good person, and she's active in the church. But she comes from a pretty dysfunctional background, most of which she refused to tell me about. I think that twisted her impressions of parenthood. Her career is very important to her. If we'd had kids right away, I think we could have kept it together, but we waited too long. By the time I was ready, she had made up her mind—but her career wasn't enough for me."

"You sound so matter-of-fact about it."

"I've spent a lot of time on my knees. First, I asked for Janet's heart to change, and then I asked for mine to change. But eventually I knew that I was meant to be a father. Janet and I are still on good terms, although we haven't spoken for awhile. But she's not my forever gal." Allen paused before continuing, "Unfortunately, as strong as my witness was, it's hard to find much comfort in it sometimes."

"I can relate to that," Kim said thoughtfully as she remembered all the lonely moments when she wished Robb was with her. Just to be held again, kissed hello; she hadn't imagined she would ever have missed it as much as she did. And yet missing those things bothered her too.

They were both silent, lost in their own thoughts, until Allen spoke. "Sometimes I wonder if it's better to live without children, or to grow old alone."

Kim thought about that for a minute and was saddened by the thought. She was also reminded that with or without Robb, she would never be alone because she would always have Jackson. "Don't give up," she said quietly. "If you feel that strongly that you are meant to have a family, you'll get it. I don't know what I would do without my son; there's pleasure in children that I don't think can be found anywhere else."

"I really envy that, Kim. You're a lucky woman."

"In that way, I am."

They both lapsed into silence for a moment until Allen spoke again. "I'll be thirty-six years old this year; I can't help but worry that I'm running out of time."

The vulnerability of his comment made her smile in the darkness and she searched for some kind of encouragement. "You're a man, you've got no real timeline you have to fit it into," she said with just a hint of bitterness she hadn't expected. Then she hurried to cover it up. "Abraham was ninety-something wasn't he?"

Allen smiled at her comment. "Abraham also had two wives; I don't even have one." Kim chuckled and he continued. "I'll never give up, but the only women I meet nowadays either have messed-up kids or they're crazy themselves."

Kim laughed before replying, "Gee, thanks."

"Or crazy husbands—I forgot about that one," Allen teased.

"Almost-ex-husband," Kim corrected.

"Sorry. Crazy, almost-ex-husband."

Kim smiled and was silent, wondering if having a crazy almost-ex-husband made her as uninviting as the other women he met. Then she rolled her eyes—what was she thinking?

After a few minutes Kim thought he had fallen asleep, both relieved and concerned that the conversation was over, when he spoke again.

"Good night, Kim," Allen said softly.

"Good night," she added and wished there were some way of knowing what he was thinking about now.

Kim settled down in her bed and pulled the blankets to her chin. Both of them lay awake for a long time that night, ignorant of each other's ponderings, trying to make sense of their own feelings. They each wondered why they should be so affected by such a normal conversation, yet as they replayed it in their minds they were each sure there was something poignant they had somehow overlooked.

# CHAPTER ELEVEN

The morning routine was interesting. During showers, shaving, brushing teeth, and getting dressed, there were plenty of uncomfortable moments. Although every bit of it was part of a normal routine, every exercise seemed intimate. Allen watched out of the corner of his eye while Kim applied her make-up, and enjoyed the transformation until she stuck her tongue out at him and he left the bathroom with a smile. She found it interesting that he brushed his teeth for nearly five minutes and was revolted by the fact that in the end, his entire hand was covered with toothpaste suds. Allen watched her twist in front of the mirror and nearly told her that she looked great in her black slacks and v-necked cardigan. However, he held back, embarrassed that he noticed with appreciation the way both items of clothing fit the curves of her figure. And it was on the tip of Kim's tongue to suggest that he wear the navy blue sweater, to emphasize his eyes, but she stopped herself just in time. They didn't say much other than the necessities, and they tried hard not to watch one another, but it couldn't be helped and it was hard to resist. Kim was relieved when she finally left the room to meet with Liz, and as she made her way down the hall she forced herself to turn her thoughts to what lie ahead.

"Good morning," Liz said brightly when Kim shyly entered the room.

"Good morning," Kim replied, wishing she didn't feel so nervous.

"Take a seat," Liz said and cleared the small table of the papers she had been working on. Folding her arms and resting them on top of the table she began. "Is this meeting okay with you, Kim?"

"I just don't want to waste your time," Kim said honestly.

Liz smiled. "Yeah, you said that yesterday. You don't have to discuss anything with me if you don't want to, but I sense that you could use some help in sorting things out."

Kim couldn't deny that was true and made the conscious choice to take advantage of this opportunity. "I need all the help I can get," she said with a smile, feeling herself relax due to Liz's calm and concerned attitude.

"Good. Now get your list out again and let's go over this."

Half an hour later Kim emerged feeling as if a whole new world had just opened up for her. First, Kim had described her marriage and divorce briefly. Liz had then painstakingly pointed out several of Kim's greatest strengths that doubled as her greatest weaknesses. Liz gave her some insight into specific difficulties that Kim had a tendency to repeat. When Kim felt she had been supporting Robb and providing unconditional love she had in fact been allowing him to manipulate and use her. More often than not, she provided the excuses for Robb's behavior before he did and therefore removed the responsibility from him. Some of what Liz said Kim felt she had been discovering on her own, but having another person put it into words and point out exactly how not to continue the pattern seemed to lighten the burden. Liz reminded her that although Kim may have reacted badly to Robb's problems, she did not cause them and needed to absolve herself of the guilt she felt.

Liz also reiterated the need for Kim to find ways of rejuvenating herself without depending on others, suggesting that Kim concentrate on things she used to enjoy doing that she had been unable to pursue due to the efforts her marriage required of her. When Kim told her how embarrassed she had been yesterday to have so few of such activities, Liz reminded her that the other women at this conference were not like her, in that most of them had fulfilling marriages that they and their spouses wanted to improve. They both decided this was an excellent opportunity for Kim and that she should make a point of absorbing everything she could in order to find perspective in her own marriage. Kim laughed when Liz told her, "Don't look at it as a failed marriage, rather a practice one."

Completely forgetting the earlier discomfort of the morning, Kim slid into her seat next to Allen and eagerly told him most of Liz's analysis. Allen agreed completely with the advice she had been given and added only that he felt Kim should actively engage in learning how to enjoy her life. She smiled contentedly and returned to her meal feeling lighter than she had in a very long time. When breakfast was finished, Liz and her husband Greg introduced the day's events. They would meet together for about an hour, split, and then come back together for an evening joint class.

"Now," Greg began after instructing everyone to relax, stretch and concentrate on his voice. "We would like everyone to close your eyes; don't be embarrassed. Now with eyes closed, take deep breaths and focus on yourself. Think about your appearance, your health, your job." He paused for nearly a minute. "Now focus on your strengths, go through them one by one." He paused for thirty seconds and continued. "Now bring to your mind your fears, the things in the future that scare you. With several in your mind, focus on the one thing you fear the most—what frightens you more than anything else. Feel it, repeat it in your mind. Take all the time you need until you know what this greatest fear is." He paused again. "Now, in a few moments you will be told to open your eyes and at that time you will write the fear on a piece of paper. You will not want to write it. You won't want to put it into words, but keep in mind it is necessary, and no one will hurt you with it. Do not allow your partner to see it. Tuck it into your folder and we will dismiss. Concentrate on that fear. Good. Now open your eyes and write."

Kim and Allen both opened their eyes and like the rest of the class, paused. To write it down was scary; it made Kim feel very vulnerable, but Greg reassured everyone that it would be okay. Finally she wrote it down quickly and tucked it into the folder. Kim and Allen exchanged a look and a smile before she went to her class; she hadn't seen him write anything yet.

Almost ten minutes passed before all the women were accounted for. Once everyone was seated Liz began. "Okay, ladies, this is the best class of the weekend. We are going to spend the next four hours talking about sex; what it is and what it isn't." A few giggles could be heard in the room. Kim sunk down in her chair; the last thing she wanted or needed was a four-hour discussion about sex. Meanwhile, Liz continued. "Women and men are as different when it comes to sex as with sports. Women would rather miss the game but know the score, whereas men care about every play as they watch a game. With sex it's the other way around: Men want the score, women want the plays." Kim wanted to disappear. "Now I'm the first to admit to that being far from a perfect analogy. In fact it points out the biggest mistake we all make concerning our sex lives. We stereotype everything: us, our husbands, and our methods. The first thing you need to understand is that your sex life is not your neighbor's, your sister's, your friend's; it is yours and your husband's and that is it. The second thing that you must believe is that our goal is to help you and your husband enjoy the game as well as the score. So I'll give you a minute to get out some paper, 'cause believe me, you'll want to take some good notes on this one."

They took lunch in class and at 1:30 finally dismissed. Liz had explained that while the women were learning all about their men, the men were learning all the nitty gritty of sex from a woman's point of view. How on earth could she face Allen after this? In the beginning of the discussion all Kim could think about was that Allen would be reading her notes; finally she had to completely block him from her mind and force herself to simply pay attention. Liz had talked about things Kim had never considered important, and when Liz opened it up to questions, Kim felt sure she would never stop blushing. The discussion was not all about sex; much of it was about the effect a good sex life had on a relationship. But every bit of it pertained to sex in one way or another and Kim didn't know what she would ever do with all she had learned. When the class ended, Kim stayed in her chair, dreading seeing Allen again. Maddie would pay for this, she decided, as she finally stood up and left.

Spotting Allen up front, Kim swallowed and made her way to the seat beside him. He didn't even look up when she sat down and she could feel the tension between them. Nearly five minutes passed without their acknowledging each other's presence. The other couples were winking and snuggling towards one another; both Kim and Allen were stiff and up-tight.

Finally, Allen leaned towards her and whispered, "It's not just for making babies anymore, is it?"

All the bottled tension made Kim unable to keep herself from laughing out loud, which did nothing to lessen her embarrassment. Boy, she felt foolish. Finally, after what seemed like forever, Greg stood up in front of the group.

"Don't worry everybody, you'll get plenty of time to go over all this information later." Everyone else chuckled; Kim and Allen spontaneously looked at their shoes. Greg then kicked off the communications class. Between him and Liz they explained gender differences in communication. Women, they said, enjoy knowing details, men don't appreciate the details so much. Men like to solve problems whereas women want to be listened too. After pointing out several gender deficiencies, they explained how to adjust. How to get your needs met and meet the needs of your partner.

After taking a dinner break, Greg and Liz taught about stress management and healthy ways of expressing anger. They explained that women need to back off and allow their man time to put his thoughts together rather than push for conclusions. Men needed to understand how difficult it is for women to spend a lot of time waiting to solve the problems between them. Kim found it very interesting and liked that she could see her own faults more clearly. She made a mental note to ask Allen for a copy of the notes she was taking. The fact that all this information drew the attention away from the earlier class made her feel much more relaxed. She and Allen were able to discuss the information during the break without the earlier tension. With any luck they could pretend the sex class never happened.

By 10:00 Kim was feeling the fatigue caused by only a few hours of sleep the night before and was relieved when Liz announced they had only one more short exercise and then they would dismiss for the night. Liz asked everyone to arrange the chairs around the walls of the room and then sit on the floor.

"Now I want each of you to sit with your legs crossed and turn your bodies so that your knees touch the knees of your partner." Everyone scooted around; Allen and Kim stayed put. Greg was suddenly there and told them nicely that if they didn't want to participate they would need to leave. Kim thought that was a great idea, but Allen simply twisted around, crossed his legs and smiled at her. She hesitated only a moment and then inched forward so their knees touched—she couldn't believe she was doing this.

"With your knees touching, take both of your partner's hands in your own." Allen and Kim exchanged looks, but complied. "Now lean forward so that your foreheads are touching as well, you don't need to be looking in each other's eyes." Allen and Kim were even more hesitant with this one but Greg started making his way toward them, so they did it. Kim was keenly aware of Allen's closeness and hoped he didn't notice the way her pulse-rate had increased.

"Close your eyes," Liz said slowly as soft music filled the room. "Relax. Take deep, cleansing breaths. Focus on the warmth of your hands. Concentrate on your breathing, keep it steady. Imagine a large bowl balancing on your head. The bowl is full of water." Kim's breathing was even, but no matter how hard she tried she was couldn't ignore the warmth of Allen's hands around hers. "The bowl is full of warm, clear water and it is balancing on your head. Imagine the bowl disappearing. As the water falls over you, you feel your body relaxing. Your eyes soften, your neck and throat relax. Your shoulders. Your back. The tension of the day is washed away with the water. Your abdominal muscles, your legs. You are relaxed." She paused and then continued. "Now focus on your partner's breathing." Kim swallowed and when she inhaled she filled her lungs with the scent of him, a slight pine and musk that seemed to replace the relaxation she had begun to feel with a whole new kind of tension. Liz continued, "Take steady breaths. In and out, in and out. In your mind, go back to this morning's combined class. You wrote your greatest fear on a piece of paper." Kim felt

Allen tense and she impulsively squeezed his hand to convey her understanding. "Bring that fear to your mind, remembering that you are safe. Now take a deep breath, exhale. Focus on your partner. Their breathing, their hands." Kim couldn't do anything else and she nearly groaned with the escalating tension. I'm married, she reminded herself, this is so wrong! "Focus on their fears." Allen tensed again and Kim gripped his hand again, this time his own grip tightened on hers and her breath caught momentarily in her throat. "In your mind, picture what could be their fear. Try to feel it. Listen and feel. Continue to breathe. Focus on what you feel is their greatest fear. In a moment you will open your eyes. You will remain in this position. When I tell you to do so the women will say aloud what they feel is their partner's greatest fear. And then the men will do the same. Continue your breathing. Open your eyes. After the men have given their answer you are dismissed. Keep in mind that it is not the primary goal to get it right. Whatever answer is given is good; whatever it may be conveys your true beliefs about your partner's fears. Tomorrow we will discuss it in depth. Women, it's your turn."

Kim's heart was pumping and she was a little dismayed to realize how moist her hands were—had Allen noticed? She could hear hushed whispers around the room and at least one couple had finished and were leaving. This was so personal, how could she do this? Although she was tempted to pull her hands away and leave, she finally forced herself to get past her hesitation and took a deep breath. "You're afraid you'll never have the family you've always wanted." Once again Allen tensed and she felt his breathing stop momentarily.

Consciously, Allen willed himself to at least appear relaxed. He didn't know why he was having such a hard time with this. He had participated in this sort of thing many times, why was this so different? Yet even as he thought it, he knew the answer. It was different because it was Kim, and there was something about her that affected him as no one else ever had. Pushing the thoughts away, he focused on the fact that it was his turn. Calming his breathing again he whispered back. "You are afraid that no one will ever love you."

It was Kim's turn to tense up—she hadn't expected that. Immediately, she dropped his hands and pulled her face far enough back so that she could look at him. He returned her nervous expression with one of his own. They held each other's gaze for what seemed to be a long time until Kim finally looked away, not sure what she felt or what to say. She felt angry at his guess, but wasn't sure why.

"Hey guys, it's time to go," Liz interrupted before politely walking away. The room was empty. Allen got to his feet and extended a hand toward her; she regarded it with apprehension before finally taking it. Allen gently pulled her to her feet. This time when she looked into his eyes she seemed to see in them a depth she hadn't seen before, as though if she tried hard enough she could read his thoughts. Feeling strangely transparent herself, she dropped his hand and looked away. Without speaking, they gathered their things and went to their room. Throughout the entire bedtime routine they didn't speak. The lights went off and they lay in their separate beds, both staring into the dark, the air thick with unspoken thoughts and confusing emotions. It wasn't necessarily uncomfortable, just strange and very powerful. To speak meant taking the chance of breaking this feeling; both were hesitant to do so.

After several minutes Allen spoke, unable to resist. "Was I right?"

Kim blinked in the dark, relieved that he had broken the silence first and glad that her odd anger had changed to curiosity. "You were very close," she said, surprised at her sudden eagerness to tell him. What had happened to the heavy reluctance that was here just a moment ago?

"How close?" Allen prodded.

"The exact thing I had written was 'I'm afraid I will never be able to love again'."

Allen was quiet for a moment. "That isn't very close," he said simply.

"Actually, I think it's basically the same thing. Only that until you said it I didn't realize I meant it that way." She was thoughtful for a moment and then continued, "I loved Robb so much, and look where that got me. I still love him; as hard as it is to admit it, I do. But he has hurt me so much that I have to wonder if he ever really loved me the way I loved him. That's incredibly painful for me. And I worry that I'll never get over this. What if I stay this scared forever?"

"Why are you scared?"

Kim sighed, almost wishing he wasn't so easy to talk to. But he was, and after all that she had absorbed over the last two days, it was impossible for her not to talk about it. "I remember being a teenager and being told that loving someone was a frightening thing because they could hurt you worse than anyone. I proved that to be true. To love someone again means accepting those same possibilities; I don't know that I'll ever be able to do it. In the same thought if I can't fall in love, then I can't experience the incredible love I see between some people; my heart aches for that."

"Kim, I deal with a lot of people that feel very similar to you, and I have seen very few with as much insight as you have. It hasn't been that long ago that your marriage crashed and burned and you're doing very well."

"It feels like a lead weight in my stomach most of the time, and I look at my future and it seems impossible to believe I could ever feel differently."

"I can understand that, but when I find myself feeling that way I think back to the times when I was first married and everything was good and I couldn't imagine feeling differently than I did then. Life is full of changes, I think it's as much a blessing as it is a curse; things always change."

Kim thought on that for a moment and smiled. She liked the hope his words inspired and decided to tuck that away for future reference.

Changing the subject, Kim asked, "So how close was my guess?"

"Closer than mine. I wrote down that I was afraid I would never have the joy my parents share. They have a great marriage and wonderful kids; if I do say so myself. When Janet informed me that she didn't want children I realized that I had always wanted my parents' life and my chances had just been extinguished."

"I'd been married almost a year when I realized the same thing. I thought my parents were always too churchy and strict. Then Robb started slipping farther and farther away from the church and I wondered if I would ever have even a part of what they have."

"Don't you hate it, finding out that your stodgy, boring parents were right all along?"

Kim laughed, "Even worse, I hate knowing that I was completely wrong about feeling so much smarter than them."

Another silence ensued until once again Allen broke it. "So what do you think about the weekend so far?"

"It's been good, I've learned a lot of..." just as she said it she remembered the afternoon 'sex talk' and she wished they had never started this conversation.

Meanwhile Allen was chuckling, correctly interpreting her

sudden silence. "Don't worry, I won't make you tell me; I just need your notes."

Even the notes would embarrass her, but it was better than having to repeat it out loud. "You can have them!" Kim said with fervor. "I certainly don't have any use for them."

Allen almost said, "don't be so sure," but luckily caught himself in time, glad she couldn't see his face. Why shouldn't he give her a little encouragement? He opened his mouth to say it again but the words didn't come. Somehow it seemed very inappropriate. Instead he cleared his throat and said "I really appreciate your doing this for me, Kim. I know it wasn't convenient and I want you to know how grateful I am for your help."

A wave of warmth washed over her at his compliment and for just a moment she wished that she had met a man like this 10 years ago. Who knew what the possibilities could have been? "It's been really good for me, Allen, I'm glad I came."

I'm glad you did too, Allen thought to himself and immediately chastised himself—where was his head? "Well, good. I'll see you in the morning," he said and rolled onto his side turning his back in her direction, as if by doing so her presence wouldn't be so obvious. It didn't work.

"Goodnight," Kim answered and rolled onto her side, but facing him. She could just make out his lumpy silhouette in the darkness and sighed. So many thoughts and conflicting emotions were racing through her and she couldn't make sense of any of them. Despite the fact that she would rather not feel this way, she really enjoyed talking to Allen. Something about him made her feel safe, even when she was expected to feel uncomfortable with him. What if there was a chance? She thought to herself and then immediately tried to push it from her mind. She was married! It would be some time before her divorce was finalized and she couldn't guess how long it would take after that to really trust a man again. Yet, here she was allowing herself to fantasize about a future with another man? I'm going to make myself crazy, Kim decided and rolled over so her back was toward him. Even though she had just told him that she was glad she came, she now berated herself for coming; it was completely inappropriate for her to be here. She had more than her share of things to worry about, she didn't need or want this too. At the same time, she admitted that if she had it to do all over, she'd do nothing differently.

Allen snored again, and between his rumblings and her own thoughts Kim, again, got very little sleep. The morning routine was much the same as Saturday's, except that there was surprisingly less tension. Kim got a kick out of watching Allen shave his head and was dismayed to realize how much she enjoyed being physically close to him. Even after the discussion she'd had with herself the night before, she couldn't seem to help it. Allen laughed at something she said that she hadn't meant to be funny, and she reveled in it. How was it that he could make her feel so good and so scared at the same time? The scared part finally took over and she made the excuse that she had to meet with Liz before breakfast. Once out of the room, she scolded herself again: what was she doing? And what did she think it would lead to?

The thoughts frightened her and she hurried her pace; if she could, she wanted to talk to Liz about this. She knew she would never see Liz again so Kim felt it would be safe, and she really needed some advice. Her life seemed to have changed in the last 48 hours. She needed to talk to someone because she couldn't understand this by herself.

Kim found Liz in the hallway and stood about five feet away while Liz finished up the conversation she was having with one of the other couples. As she waited, she nearly convinced herself that she was making too big a deal of this. Allen was a nice guy, one of the nicest she had ever had the opportunity to spend time with since her marriage. Being so unaccustomed to attention of any kind, she was probably placing ridiculous expectations upon mere pleasantries. If Allen had any idea she was feeling this way, he would just laugh and write her off as being as crazy as the rest of the women he met.

"Good morning," Liz said, effectively interrupting Kim's thoughts. "Can I help you with something?"

Kim smiled nervously and had to make a split-second decision. Did she push this all aside? Or risk making a fool of herself over something that most likely was simply the twisted imagination of a love-deprived heart? Liz smiled expectantly and Kim made up her mind: she would take the risk and hope for a little enlightenment whether she would need it or not. "Actually, yes, if you have a few minutes. I could use some advice."

"You bet," Liz said and took Kim's arm. All meals were served in a conference room set up with dozens of "tables for two" complete with name cards for each couple on their appointed table. Liz steered Kim to the table she shared with Greg and invited her to sit. She smiled at Kim and folded her hands across the table. "So what's up?"

Kim took a deep breath and proceeded to lay out all her conflicting feelings and thoughts. Liz listened patiently, prodding for clarification now and then, until Kim finished with, "I feel like some freak; I'm still married and I'm in the middle of the most difficult circumstance I could have ever imagined. Yet Allen has this effect on me that I don't understand."

"Or that you don't want to understand," Liz added. Kim shrugged, reluctant to accept that possibility, but she said nothing. "So, Kim, what exactly do you want from me?"

Kim felt belittled by her question; she assumed that she would lay it all out and Liz would put it all together in a nice little package that Kim could look at and say "yeah, that's exactly what I needed." "Well, I don't know..." Kim said and then said out loud exactly what she wanted Liz to say. "I guess I want to hear that I'm insane and shouldn't feel this way."

"Is that really what you want?" Liz prodded.

"Yes," Kim said with resolution. Please tell me that, she begged silently. Tell me I'm a nut and I'm not Allen's type, he would never look at me the way I'm looking at him. Tell me that and I'll repeat it like a rosary.

"Well, you're not insane," Liz said and watched Kim slump a little bit. "You have been through an incredible amount of stress and conflict lately and I know that it makes you feel as if you will never get away from it. Reality is that you will; and you will be so much stronger because of it. The feelings you have are difficult to make sense of, but they aren't bad. You may be in the middle of a divorce, and your dreams may seem to have been dashed, but that doesn't mean you can't feel attraction; or that you can't attract, for that matter." Kim knit her brow, what did that mean? "You're still a woman, Kim—a person—and whether it's Allen or someone else, the biggest mistake you could make would be to write these feelings off completely. You could miss a wonderful opportunity. Now there is a chance that this can be the 'rebound' effect and for that reason I would advise you to be careful—don't trifle with him."

Kim straightened at the statement. "Oh no, I don't mean to insinuate that Allen...that there is...I mean there isn't." She stopped at the look on Liz's face. "What?" she asked, confused.

"Oh please," Liz laughed. "You haven't been paying enough attention." Kim looked surprised and unless Liz was mistaken, a little frightened. "But that's none of my business so let's leave that alone. But..." She reached across the table and touched Kim's hand, "Life is a funny thing, Kim, don't try to pretend to know what's around the next corner, just drive carefully."

Kim nodded, afraid to acknowledge to herself even a little of what she had just heard. After a few more moments Liz stood and patted Kim on the shoulder.

Shortly after Kim had left their room that morning, Allen followed. He found Greg in the lobby and they sat to discuss some questions Allen had. A few minutes into the conversation, Allen looked up and saw Liz and Kim sitting at a table in the conference room across the hall. He unconsciously paused for a minute and then shook his thoughts away from it and continued speaking with Greg. Several times, he found himself looking up at Kim again and missing whatever Greg was saying. On one of his peeks, he saw Liz stand and leave Kim at the table. Kim put her elbows on the table and dropped her head in her hands. She looked troubled and Allen's brow furrowed as he wondered if it was something he had done. When he looked away from her, he realized Greg wasn't speaking any longer. Allen turned his full attention back to the conversation he was supposed to be having, only to find Greg smiling.

"What was that?" Allen asked in an attempt to pick up where Greg had left off. "My mind wandered."

Greg chuckled. "You've barely heard a word I've said ever since you realized that door was open."

"Sorry," Allen was caught and he wasn't sure of what to say.

"So what's the deal with you two anyway?" Greg asked as he lifted his Styrofoam coffee cup to his lips, his eyes dancing.

"Kim?" Allen asked, as if he didn't know. Greg gave him a 'yes dummy' nod and so Allen continued. "She just came to take the notes for the women's class, she's a friend of my sister," Allen said simply and averted his eyes.

"Aren't you guys sharing a room?"

Allen actually blushed. "Well, yeah but that was by accident."

"Thank goodness for accidents," Greg said with a laugh as he placed his cup on the coffee table between them.

"It's really not like that. I asked for two rooms and I got two beds instead."

"Lucky you."

"Look Greg, I really don't appreciate..." He stopped when Greg laughed loudly and clapped him on the knee.

"I'm just giving you a hard time," Greg admitted. "Liz told me the situation, I just couldn't resist." Allen only nodded and wiped at a spot on his boot. He was not enjoying himself.

"You could do worse, ya know."

"You have no idea how far away that is from reality. Kim's just beginning a divorce from a nasty husband. She isn't even pointed in that direction."

"Then what's she talking to Liz about?"

"She's got a lot of baggage to unpack and probably just needs someone to help her out."

"You're a psychiatrist, why wouldn't she go to you for help with that?"

"You'd have to ask her that question," Allen said without feeling.

"Maybe I will," Greg said, but when he saw Allen's quick look of mild panic he laughed. "Just kidding. I'll give you some advice though. Don't blow it off, there is potential here if nothing else."

"Amen," Liz said loudly behind Allen's head causing him to jump. How long had she been there? Allen wondered. Liz and Greg laughed together over the joke before excusing themselves.

"You can take my seat," Greg teased just before they walked away. "It's a better angle."

Allen tried to hide his annoyance with a smile but it didn't work. Frustration bubbled inside him at the encounter. What was he supposed to make of all this? He was the first to admit that there was something special about Kim, but he hadn't even tried to figure out what it was. Attraction? Probably; she was an attractive woman. But even if she weren't in the middle of a divorce and afraid of relationships in general, what could she see in him? This move back to Salt Lake had, at least, been partly for the purpose of increasing the single LDS women pool, but he learned soon that it wasn't that easy. He looked like a punk compared to most LDS guys. And he knew, maybe better than anyone, that even the thought of considering a relationship, especially with him, was the farthest thing from Kim's mind. Yet he couldn't deny that he liked her company. As he remembered the few exchanges they had shared, he smiled, enjoying the sensation that thoughts of her seemed to create for him. As soon as he noticed what he was doing, he shook it off and groaned in frustration. He should never have agreed to let Kim take Maddie's place. Yet even as the thoughts darted through his brain, he couldn't seem to take his eyes off her. She sat at the table for several minutes and finally, when other couples started getting ready for breakfast, she stood and looked around. Immediately she caught Allen's gaze and smiled slightly, but she didn't look away. Allen stared back and wished he could pull his eyes away; they showed too much. Finally, she broke the spell and motioned towards their table before heading for it.

The rest of the conference was very tense. Nothing should have been different now. They should have been able to continue with the light exchanges they had shared that morning. But it was different and neither one knew how to react to it. They exchanged few words and were relieved when they split for one last gender specific course. Allen couldn't keep his mind off his earlier thoughts whereas Kim buried herself in taking good notes and wondered why he was so tense. Closing ceremonies were at 2:00 and they were on their way home by 3:00. Together in the car, they kept the conversation light and comfortable, they were each relieved and also disappointed that the conference was over. One thing was certain: they both hoped that everything would be just as it had been—or did they?

"Didn't you say Jackson's grandparents lived in South Salt Lake?" Allen asked as the buildings of downtown Salt Lake appeared outside the car windows.

"Yeah, 13th East and about 27th South."

"Well, that's on our way home, why don't we just pick Jackson up?"

"Oh, I don't know," she said nervously. Her soon to be ex-in-laws might not appreciate her showing up with a man.

"It's up to you, but it would save you some time."

Kim thought about it for a minute; Robb's parents would not take it well. Then again he'd be out in the car and she would run up to the door. With any luck they wouldn't even see Allen. It was a tempting offer. The hour she'd save herself meant more sleep, and Kim was in great need of that. She'd already spent nine years catering to that family in one form or another; she had no desire to continue the pattern. Sitting up a little straighter, she gave Allen a grateful smile. "Actually, that's a good idea, if you're sure you don't mind."

"Not a bit," Allen said.

Within a few minutes they pulled up in front of the house and Allen stayed in the car while Kim ran up to the door.

Tom answered the door. "Hi, Kim," he said and ushered her inside. "Jackson's getting together the last of his things; he'll be ready in a minute."

Kim smiled, wishing she could make herself feel more comfortable. "How did everything go?" she asked.

"Great," Tom said nervously. "We had a wonderful time." He

paused and then continued, "Uh, Dorothy and I were wondering if Jackson could spend some of the holidays with us this year."

"Sure," Kim said, trying to sound more comfortable with the idea than she felt. Jackson would enjoy spending part of Christmas day with her grandparents. "What do you have in mind?" she asked, suppressing the unbidden thought that sometimes she wished they were as far away from Jackson as Robb was. She was ashamed to admit it, but she didn't like to share her son—even a little.

"Well, we were planning to head down to Arizona and visit Sheryl; we want to take Jackson with us—he hasn't seen his cousins in a long time."

Arizona! Kim tried to hide her reaction. She didn't like this idea at all but she tried to remain diplomatic. "When are you going?"

"We want to leave on the twenty-sixth and plan to come home on the 2nd of January," Tom answered sheepishly.

"That's a week!" Kim said too loudly with too much surprise.

"I know it seems like a long time, and if you're not comfortable with it we...well, I'll understand, but the whole family is getting together and we would really like to take him with us."

The whole family minus your son, Kim thought bitterly. She turned her back to him and took the opportunity to try and digest the whole thing. "I don't know, Tom, he's never been away from me that long."

"Just think about it...please," Tom said, sounding defeated. "Dorothy is having a really hard time with this whole situation and I think it would go a long way toward her healing to know that our relationship with Jackson isn't hindered by this. So please...just...think about it."

Kim considered this and wondered if they had ever thought about her healing, but she said nothing. Just then, Jackson bounded into the room and Tom helped him put on his coat. Kim watched the scene sadly, touched by the bond the two had with each other and wondered how it was that Robb was never this close to his son. Tom gave Jackson one last hug before whispering to Kim, "We haven't said anything to him, let us know."

"I will," Kim promised and followed Jackson out the door, glad to know they hadn't spoken to him first and that they were respecting her authority.

Kim opened the door of Allen's Camaro and Jackson jumped in the back seat. "Hey, I remember you!" he said cheerfully as he poked his head around the seat.

"I'd hope so," Allen laughed. "It's only been a couple months."

"Is this your car?"

"Yep," Allen said as Kim slid into the passenger seat.

"It's like Batman's car," Jackson said knowingly as he bounced back and forth from one bucket seat to another.

"It doesn't go nearly as fast though."

"My mom got a ticket because she drove too fast." Jackson said innocently, still inspecting the car's interior.

"Jackson!" Kim scolded, then shook her head. Allen laughed and glanced in his rearview mirror as he pulled back onto the street.

"She did! It was in the summer when we were coming back from the lake," Jackson continued with a nod. "She told me I should never do that when I learn how to drive."

"That's enough, Jackson," Kim said, though her tone was light.

Allen patted her leg impulsively. "I won't judge you too harshly," he said playfully.

Kim stared at the spot his hand had touched on her thigh and wondered how it was she could still feel the warmth when his hand hadn't lingered more than a moment. Clearing her throat, she changed the subject. "So what did you do with Grandma and Grandpa this weekend, Jack?"

Jackson launched into a detailed description of his adventures, most of which centered around their black lab named Ping. The two adults listened quietly, commenting only when appropriate, enjoying his innocence and enthusiasm. When he finally finished and involved himself with looking at a road map Allen had left on the floor, Allen looked over at Kim. "I think you might be in trouble," he said.

Kim looked up at him with surprise, "Why?"

"Just after you went inside, a woman parted the drapes upstairs and stared at me until you came out again; she didn't look particularly happy to see me there."

Kim groaned: Dorothy. Kim had told them when she dropped Jackson off that she was going out of town for the weekend. She could well imagine what Dorothy was thinking. So much for the luck she had hoped for. Her stomach tightened slightly, which irritated her even more than Dorothy's probable assumptions. Why should she care what they think? "Oh well," she said out loud. "I need to not care."

"But you do."

She sighed and looked out her window thoughtfully. "Yeah, I do. But it can't be helped."

Allen looked over at her sympathetically, wishing they were back in a hotel room where the darkness made it easier to talk about these things. He understood her reluctance to share such personal feelings, but he longed to hear them. "You're doing a good job, Kim."

Kim looked over at him, startled, and knit her brow; Allen caught the look. "You are. You're raising your boy alone, making all the necessary sacrifices to insure a better future than your past has been and trying to get along with your husband's family. It's not an easy thing to do."

Kim simply stared at him for a moment, more affected by his praise than she was willing to admit. As she looked at him, he looked back at her and the corners of his mouth pulled into a smile that made his eyes sparkle, and sent a warm shiver down her spine. "Uh, thanks," she finally said, and forced herself to look away from those eyes.

"You're welcome."

The rest of the drive was quiet, although Kim noted it wasn't one of those uncomfortable silences where you search for some-thing—anything—to say. Rather, it was a silence that made her feel perfectly content, as if their thoughts were enhanced by the silence, rather than strained by it. Kim continued to stare out the window, afraid to look over at him again, and tried to remind herself of what she had nearly convinced herself earlier that day: That Allen's effect on her simply stemmed from the fact that she hadn't been around "nice" guys for so long. But somehow it didn't work now. Instead, the reminder made her feel rather empty inside. Just as she had felt when she tried to convince herself, in the past, that Robb simply needed time to become a responsible husband and father. The feeling had seemed to tell her then, that she was being over-opti-mistic about her husband; now it seemed to reprimand her for being too pessimistic about Allen. Perhaps she was wrong to dismiss him so easily, yet how on earth could she do anything else? He was kind and compassionate, attractive and good, but had he really done anything that communicated more than those basics? There had been little things; touches, looks—but how could she be sure they were anything more than just that; touches and looks? Liz's words echoed back to her: "Don't pretend to know what's around the corner, but drive carefully." She had never been able to guess what was around the next bend so far in her life, and it would be silly to think she could do any better at that now, but she would definitely drive carefully. If the feelings she had felt were not hers alone it would have to be up to Allen to let her know—he had more to lose. She resolved to do nothing other than be his friend. There was really nothing more that she could do anyway. She had a divorce to settle, a child to raise, a career to focus on and a future to prepare. There was no time for pursuing a romance. For some reason, the thought depressed her.

Allen pulled his car into Maddie's driveway and Kim breathed a sigh of relief. It seemed that as long as he was around he was all she could think about, and because of what she had just determined, that was a disconcerting thing. Kim began transferring her things into her own car, until Allen took the bags wordlessly from her hands. She stayed where she was and watched him for a few moments, finally shaking herself out of her trance and ushering Jackson to the car. When he was buckled in, she went around to her door, annoyed at her reluctance to leave, and found Allen waiting there. She smiled weakly. Was it her imagination that he returned a smile equally filled with conflict and disappointment? She looked down quickly, deciding not to analyze her feelings; Allen opened her door. She looked up impulsively as she asked herself if Robb had ever opened a door for her? And when she smiled gratefully at Allen, she knew the answer was no; chivalry had never been Robb's strong point. She was just about to slide into the driver's seat when she suddenly turned toward Allen, reminded of an excuse to lengthen this moment just a little. "May I ask you a question?" she asked.

"You just did," he answered with a smile and crossed his arms along the top of the car door that separated them.

Kim smiled, loving the way his words melted the tension away. "Another one?"

"You just did again."

"Never mind," she said with mock frustration, and attempted to sit; but Allen touched her arm to stop her; just as she somehow knew he would.

"Sorry," he laughed, and then added, "go ahead."

"Robb's parents want to take Jackson to Arizona for the week after Christmas. Do you think I should let him go?" Why he would have any impact on her decision she couldn't fathom. Then again, he was a family therapist: that's it, she determined quickly. She had asked because he was a psychiatrist and he would understand the psychological impact of such a decision. Thank goodness for rationalization.

"What's in Arizona?" Allen asked.

"Robb's sister. Apparently his entire family is meeting down there for the Holidays and they would really Jackson to be with them."

"But you don't want him to go?"

"No, I don't."

"Why?"

Kim thought for a moment, it wasn't hard to come up with an answer. "I've never gotten along with them very well, and they're taking the divorce kind of hard."

"Are you afraid they might use Jackson to get back at you?"

"No!" Kim said quickly. "Not at all, it's just..." she bit her lip and searched for the right words. "I don't like sending him away with people who don't like me; it doesn't seem right, somehow. Boy, that sounds really petty, doesn't it?"

Allen smiled. "Not at all. To let him go means you're entrusting them to parent him and you don't seem to have a lot of faith in them in that capacity. Besides that, they're angry and that anger is directed at you—common divorce complication. How are they with Jackson?"

"They are great with him, I really have no worries in that department. But...well, Jackson and I haven't ever been apart for that long before."

Allen nodded his understanding. "You're the mom; it's your decision and if you decide not to let him go they would have to respect that. But I think it must be hard for your husband's parents to feel separated from their grandson. If you think about it, I think you'll see that their fears are warranted. In a divorce, the mother usually gets custody and it becomes her discretion where and when the grandparents get visitation. In this situation it's worse because Dad isn't going to be bringing Jackson around to see them. So maybe showing them that you do trust them, and that you are in support of their relationship with Jackson, will help them see you as a friend rather than the enemy. But, it is still *your* decision and you should follow your instincts—no matter what they think."

Kim nodded slowly and looked up at him gratefully. "That's a good point. Thanks." With that, she got behind the wheel and gave him one last look before she pulled away.

Allen watched her car until it turned a corner and disappeared from view. "You are an idiot," he told himself after it disappeared, trying to ignore how alone he suddenly felt. After a few minutes, he picked up his bags and went into the house, afraid to speculate too much on the effect this weekend was having on him.

The following Wednesday, after much thought, Kim called Robb's parents and left a message on their answering machine to tell them that Jackson could go with them to Arizona and to let her know what time they would pick him up. The more she had thought about it the more she felt that Allen was right. She needed to make sure that they knew she wasn't going to keep Jackson away from them. She had asked Jackson about it the night before and he was very excited to see his cousins; it had been a long time. So, despite her misgivings and dislike about being separated from her son she made the decision to let go—just a little. Following Allen's advice she made sure to focus on her instincts and realized it wasn't Dorothy and Tom that made her feel uneasy. She just hated to send her little boy away; she would have to get over it.

For the first few days after the conference, Kim couldn't seem to get Allen out of her mind—no matter how hard she tried. It was a bit irritating, but she couldn't deny how much she enjoyed having someone so nice to think about. While he was not around, it was easy to talk herself out of the feelings she'd had, and she was almost convinced that she was simply caught up in the whirlwind of emotions the conference had stirred up.

Yet, even with those justifications fresh in her mind, she often found herself dissecting the conversations they'd shared, relishing the compliments he had given her and dwelling on the feelings these memories evoked. What was the harm? It had been so long since she'd felt anything as pleasant as this. It couldn't be that bad to draw a little enjoyment from the encounters they had shared. It was all innocent, no one would get hurt, and it helped ease the dull ache of loneliness she was experiencing these last few months. She had no expectations—what were the chances? If something were to happen, it would be too perfect, too convenient; something out of a story book, not real life. Her best friend's brother, an attractive man who liked her son, shared her heartache of a marriage-gone-bad and had the same goals for the future. How perfect it could be only cemented the fact that she knew it was impossible: life didn't work that way. Then Allen called and all her convincing went right down the sink.

The phone rang as she was finishing up some paperwork Friday afternoon. "Kim Larksley," she said in her best professional tone.

"Kim. Hi, it's Allen."

"Oh, Hi. How ya doin?" Kim drawled cheerfully; that familiar wave of warmth was back.

"I'm good. How are you?"

"I'm okay," she answered knowing that the days since that conference had been the most enjoyable she'd had in a very long time.

"And how is Jackson?"

Her smiled widened even more. "Jackson is doing great. I decided to let him go to Arizona and he's very excited."

"Well, good, I'm sure he'll have a great time. When does he go?"

"The day after Christmas. I don't know what I'm going to do without him here."

"You can help me move," Allen said boldly.

"That sounds like fun," Kim said sarcastically but she felt a little tremble in her belly because of his invitation. "I figured you were going to live with Maddie forever."

Allen laughed. "Yeah, I wondered if that would happen too, but I'm scheduled to close on my home loan the 23rd of December. Now that you need a diversion, you're the perfect person to help me move that next week."

"Lucky me," Kim said dryly. "Is that why you called me?" Please say no, please say no.

"Nope. Actually a client of mine gave me some free ski passes and I want to know if Jackson would like to go."

"Oh," Kim said lightly after a moment.

Allen chuckled. "It's an adult and child combined pass, so it's up to him who he takes, I guess."

"I see, and if he chooses me then you don't go?" Kim asked.

"Not exactly; if he chooses you I'll take the adult-only pass."

Kim shook her head; she could barely keep up with this guy. "And if he chooses you?"

"Then you take the other pass."

Kim beamed. "Ah, so what you really want to know is if Jackson and I will go skiing with you?"

"If you put it that way."

This sounds like a date, Kim thought to herself, and the realization made her thoughtful. She hadn't yet considered how to deal with dating. Her discomfort signaled that perhaps she should make some things clear. She tapped her pencil absently on the top of her desk when she spoke. "How long did it take your divorce to be final?"

Allen hesitated for a few moments and she hoped it was because he got the point. "Once we filed the actual papers, it took a few months. Why?"

"I was just curious," Kim replied. Then she added, "When is

this free-ski-pass day again?"

"Saturday—well, I guess that's tomorrow."

She had made herself clear: it wasn't a date, just friends going skiing. "We haven't got anything else going on; I think it sounds great."

"Make sure you ask Jackson," he reminded. And since he had gotten her point earlier he added, "If he doesn't want to go, I'm afraid the deal is off."

Kim smiled, "I'll tell him."

"Let me know," Allen said.

Kim hung up after telling him she would call him tonight. Then she pushed all the other thoughts out of her head and simply enjoyed the moment, and all the tantalizing aspects of it. She hadn't been skiing since high school, which was almost like never having skied. And it had been a long time since she'd looked forward to spending time with a man—even her husband. As much as she tried to tell herself it wasn't a date, suspicions wouldn't be denied. The thoughts returned and she worried if this were an appropriate thing to do. The more she pondered on it, the more she suspected it wasn't, but should she really decline the invitation? The idea of turning down this opportunity to be with him seemed very disappointing, even if she was married. Robb made his decision, she had made hers. It was merely a formality that they were still married at all. Didn't she have a right to enjoy herself?

Later that day, Maddie came by and showed Kim her engagement ring. Maddie had been sent out of town to fix some menu problems at a hospital facing a huge fine if they didn't comply with dietary regulations by a specific date, and so Kim hadn't gotten to hear about how things turned out. Maddie told her all about the proposal; everything had gone perfectly, except that because Maddie had been called out of town, they hadn't had a chance to speak with either set of parents. Maddie asked if Kim would be home when they came to tell her folks; they were a little nervous about the reaction to such a quick engagement. Kim agreed to be there and knew her parents would be thrilled. There were still nagging doubts in her mind, but she knew she had to have faith in Maddie and Matt. She was the first to admit she was a cynic about love these days, but for all intents and purposes the two of them seemed very good for one another. She had said her piece almost two months before; it was now completely up to them.

# CHAPTER TWELVE

That night, Matt and Maddie dropped in and sat Kim's parents down to break the happy news. Peggy hopped right up and hugged them both the moment they got the words out. They couldn't have been more supportive and Kim smiled at the relief on Matt's and Maddie's faces. She also compared it to when she and Robb had announced their engagement; her parents hadn't been nearly so thrilled, although they *had* been supportive. If only she had known then what she knew now. She shook off the memory and turned her attention back to the wedding plans being laid out. Peggy's enthusiasm eased everyone's minds considerably. They soon left to see Maddie's folks. Matt had spoken to her parents a week or so before, but they hadn't made the official announcement yet. Kim wished them well and watched them walk out to the car. Matt opened the car door for Maddie and she gave him a fierce hug that lasted several moments.

Kim couldn't hear the words they exchanged when Matt pulled away, but she could feel the love that radiated between them and felt a tug at her own heart, a deep longing for that in her life. There had been a time, in the early days of her own marriage, when she'd felt she had everything every woman expected. But the fantasy hadn't lasted long, and she silently prayed for one more chance to find it.

While Kim had waited for Matt and Maddie's announcement she hadn't given in to dwelling on Allen, but now she felt the return of her concerns. After she finished helping her Mom with the dishes, and Jackson with his homework, she sat down at the counter and cleared her throat. "Mom, may I ask you something?"

Peggy looked up from where she was scrubbing the sink and smiled, "Of course you can."

"Allen called me at work today and invited Jack and me to go skiing tomorrow; what do you think?"

Peggy was silent for a minute before answering. "I'm not sure what to think; but if it's just for fun I don't see a problem." She paused thoughtfully before continuing, "But if it's a date, then I don't think it's a good idea."

"What's the difference between a date and just having fun?"

Peggy put down the sponge before she answered, "How do you feel about Allen?"

"We're just friends." And it was the truth: they were just friends.

"Then go," Peggy said simply.

Just like that, Kim thought to herself. Maybe she was making too much of this. If her own mother didn't see anything wrong, it must be okay. If only the uneasy feeling in her stomach would go away. Peggy returned to straightening the kitchen while Kim continued arguing with herself. "And if I do have feelings for him?" she finally admitted timidly.

"You are still a married woman, Kim."

"But my husband has broken our marital vows and I'm getting a divorce."

"That's true, but you didn't make a promise just to Robb; you made it to God and yourself. Despite Robb's decisions you are still accountable for your own actions."

"So I can't go skiing with a man because I'm still married?" Kim said with mild irritation, not necessarily at her mother, just at how well her mom could express the concept.

"You can do whatever you want, Kim. All I'm saying is that until your divorce is final you have certain commitments to keep; no matter how lightly Robb took them."

Kim was frustrated and discouraged, although she'd expected her mother to say just what she'd said. "When I asked you about going to that weekend relationship conference you thought it was a great idea, but now skiing, with my son along, is inappropriate?"

Peggy looked at her daughter and tried to organize her words so that Kim wouldn't storm off. "Kim, the conference sounded like it would be good for you. I didn't enter your feelings for Allen into that equation. Now your feelings seem to be a major consideration. Until you're divorced from Robb, you are married in the eyes of the law as well as in the eyes of God. Do you really want to overlook something like this?"

Peggy had hit the nail on the head and Kim couldn't deny it. If Kim felt anything toward Allen then she not only had no right to explore her feelings, but she had an obligation to not pursue them. Being obligated to avoid Allen actually brought tears to her eyes. "But I want to go skiing with him, Mom. I reeeeallly want to go," she whispered, well aware of how childish her response sounded.

When she finally looked up because Peggy hadn't answered, it surprised her to see her mother smiling, "And I am thrilled that you do, but there will still be snow when you're single."

"But I want to go tomorrow," she whined.

Now Peggy actually laughed out loud and patted Kim's hand. Kim looked up in confusion: what was so funny about her disappointment? "Kim, the fact that you have found a man you want to be with, and who, from what I have heard, is kind and wonderful, makes me very happy. And the fact that he has asked you out, and therefore must see in you all the things Robb took for granted, thrills me all the more. But it doesn't change your situation." Kim understood and wiped quickly at her eyes. Peggy stepped closer to her daughter and placed a reassuring hand on her arm. "Kim, I can't tell you how painful it is to watch you suffer the way you do. If it were my prerogative I would tell you to go with him tomorrow and kiss Robb off completely. Unfortunately, it isn't my decision and it really isn't yours. You committed to your marriage a long time ago and it isn't over yet."

Kim simply nodded this time and Peggy squeezed her arm in understanding. "I've always hated how good you are at saying what I don't want to hear, Mom."

Peggy just smiled and Kim left to go upstairs, taking the cordless phone with her. Jackson was watching a movie until bedtime so she went straight to her room and shut the door. Once again, she lay on her bed and stared at the ceiling. The disappointment was keen, but so was the confirmation that Peggy was right. Darn it anyway. She picked up the phone and called Maddie's number.

Allen answered, since Maddie was still at her parents' house.

"Hi, Allen. It's Kim," she said allowing herself to enjoy the thrill of hearing his voice again.

"Well hi," he drawled, and she was sure she could hear him smile.

Kim took a breath and plunged ahead. "I'm calling to let you know that I won't be able to go tomorrow. I'm sorry."

They were both silent for a while before he spoke, "I guess that goes for Jackson too, huh?"

Kim hadn't thought of that, but why should Jackson miss out? Jackson wasn't married. "Well, actually, if you're still interested in taking him I'm sure he'd love to go."

"I'd love to take him."

"I think I'd better tell him first thing in the morning; he'll never sleep otherwise. He'll be thrilled."

"Good." Allen said before pausing thoughtfully. "May I ask why you aren't able to come?"

Kim wasn't sure how to answer that. After the conference, she had promised herself not to make any moves, not push for anything. Then, too, she would be a fool to lie to him. "To be honest, Allen, until my divorce is final I don't think it would be appropriate."

"Because of me?" he asked.

"Yes, because of you," Kim answered nervously. She felt she was quickly becoming very transparent and wasn't sure if it was a good thing. She desperately wanted to make him understand that she did want to go, but the right words wouldn't come. Taking a deep breath she plunged ahead anyway, deciding that if Allen didn't have these same feelings she had, at least she would save herself from future embarrassments. "Allen, I have really enjoyed spending time with you, but until I'm officially divorced it isn't good for us to be together."

There was a long pause during which Kim couldn't even breathe. Would he laugh at her and hang up the phone or simply try to soothe her feelings and save her from the looming embarrassment? "And after it's official?"

Kim inhaled gratefully, and a happy grin spread across her face as her heart flip-flopped joyously. He wants to be with me! "That's entirely up to you. I'm the first to admit I'm no great catch."

"I think you're a little hard on yourself," he said. Then he was silent for a minute. "When is it supposed to be official?"

"Hopefully in February. But Robb's fighting me on it so it could take longer."

"Hmm," Allen said thoughtfully. "Well, then I'd like to ask you out."

"I thought I just explained—"

"I'd like to ask you out for March first, how about 7:00?"

Kim laughed, "What should I wear?"

"Uh, I'll get back to you on that."

"Well, then I accept," Kim said with a chuckle. Then feeling bold she added, "With the provision that if this divorce drags out...I can get a rain check?"

"You bet."

"It's a date then." After a few more moments of delicious silence Kim asked quietly "Are you sure you know what you're getting into here?"

"No. Do you?"

Good point, Kim thought to herself. "Until then I guess I won't be seeing you."

"And I guess you won't be helping me move then will you?"

"Actually that was my real motivation for this whole thing. I hate moving."

Allen chuckled but then the conversation turned serious again. "Can I call?"

"Can I?" Kim answered quickly, trying to ignore how junior high-ish this all sounded.

"Anytime...and Kim..."

Kim swallowed at the sudden intimacy she felt in his voice. "Yeah?"

"It's been a long time since I have enjoyed a woman's company as much as I enjoy yours."

Kim was sure her heart would burst; she wasn't used to hearing such things. And to have the words coming from Allen sent her spirit soaring. Her tongue as well as her heart was running away from her. "And I never expected to enjoy anyone's company as much as I've enjoyed yours."

Another long silence ensued and Kim had no doubt that their feelings were on the same level now. Finally she broke in, "What time should I have Jackson ready to go in the morning?"

"Is eight o'clock too early?"

"Not at all."

"Well then, I'll see you in the morning."

Kim said goodbye and hung up the phone. I can't believe that just happened, she thought, and searched her mind for someone she could share it with. This was just too much to keep inside. Instantly, Maddie came to mind but Kim shook her head. The fact that Allen was Maddie's brother complicated matters substantially. For the first time in their entire friendship, Kim had something positive to share and yet telling Maddie did not seem appropriate. The last thing Allen needed was pressure from his baby sister: two brother-sister combinations were strange enough already. "I'll just have to keep it to myself," Kim decided and smiled secretly. "Don't pretend to know what's around the corner," she repeated in her mind and then looked up. "But don't worry, I'll drive carefully."

# CHAPTER THIRTEEN

Kim sent Jackson out the door with Allen the next morning and wished she was going with them more than ever. Allen caught her eye and winked, awakening Kim's butterflies again as she watched them drive away. She wondered if March would ever come. She turned away from the window with a sigh. "What?" she asked her mom when she saw the look on Peggy's face.

Peggy smiled and folded her arms as she leaned against the door frame. "Oh, nothing," she said lightly. But when Kim tried to walk past her she put out an arm, bringing Kim up short. "Isn't it strange that it's Saturday morning and yet you look like you're ready for a night on the town."

Kim blushed and tried to push her mom's arm away, but Peggy kept it firmly in place. "Call your lawyer, Kim."

Kim's brow furrowed. Had the phone rang? She hadn't heard it, and it was barely 8:00 on a Saturday morning.

"If I'm reading you correctly, and if the look I saw on Allen's face is any indication, you'd better tell that attorney of yours to step on it."

*ॐ*

Monday, Kim went to lunch with Maddie. "What are we celebrating?" Maddie asked after they ordered.

"Do we have to be celebrating to go out to lunch?"

"For you, yes," Maddie said bluntly. "You're the queen of brown-bag lunch breaks."

Kim gave her a dirty look. "We're celebrating your engagement—I assume everything went well with your parents on Friday?"

Maddie nodded, "Everything went great; by the time we left, Mom was already making phone calls and Dad was clapping Matt on the back."

"That's great," Kim said with complete sincerity; she was so happy for them. Was she happier for them than she had been on Friday? "So what's the date?"

"February 16th. It's the Monday of a short week at school for Matt—some professor's conference or something. He's going to work it out to take off an additional week of school so we can have a two-week honeymoon."

"Two weeks!" Kim exclaimed. "Robb and I went to Vegas for the weekend on our honeymoon."

"Then that was your first mistake," Maddie teased. "Besides your parents offered to give us two weeks in Jackson Hole—all expenses paid."

"What on earth are you going to do in Jackson Hole for two weeks?" Kim said then quickly put up a hand and added, "Don't answer that."

Maddie laughed, and didn't answer the question. Instead she continued sharing their wedding plans. "We're getting married in the Salt Lake Temple, in fact I just called this morning and our time is 1:00."

The waitress brought their plates and set them down. After she left, they busied themselves with preparing their meals before continuing.

"That's great, Maddie," Kim said, resisting the urge to tell all about her and Robb's wedding day; after all that had happened since then, even the good parts of her marriage were tainted.

"Yeah, we are really excited," Maddie said between bites, then paused with her fork in mid-air. "So, are you going to tell me or what?"

"Tell you what?" Kim asked with genuine surprise.

"Why my brother was doing a 'touchdown' dance when Matt and I came home on Friday night?"

"He was doing what?" Kim asked expectantly, unable to suppress her smile.

Maddie eyed her suspiciously "He wouldn't say anything, but your parents' number was the last one on the caller ID."

"Well, we talked," Kim said innocently.

"About what?"

"Things," Kim said distractedly, suddenly absorbed in her Fettuccini Alfredo.

"What kind of things?"

Kim realized she couldn't keep this from Maddie indefinitely, but she hesitated. How would Maddie take this? Looking up, she regarded Maddie for a moment and finally said, "Allen asked me out."

Maddie's eyes nearly bugged out of her head. "He what?"

"He asked me out."

"On a date?"

"No," Kim said sarcastically, then rolled her eyes, "of course on a date."

"When?" Maddie squealed, completely forgetting her meal.

"When we spoke on the phone Friday."

"I got that part, I mean when are you going out."

"March first."

Maddie scrunched her brow. "March first? That's three months away."

"My divorce won't be final till sometime in February."

Maddie's eyes suddenly lit up with amusement. "Oh my gosh! I can't believe this. I'm engaged to your brother and you're dating mine."

"We're not dating—"

"Yet!" Maddie cut in and laughed again. "This is so awesome."

"You don't think it's weird?"

Maddie shook her head, "It's great! You guys will be so good for each other. I can't believe I didn't think of it myself!"

"It's just a date, and it's not for three months. By then he'll probably have thought better of it and called it off all together."

"Don't count on it," Maddie beamed and spent the rest of their lunch break pointing out all the wonderful things about Allen; Kim listened intently and loved every minute of it. Sharing was definitely better than keeping the secret to herself. She couldn't ever remember being so happy. Robb seemed a lifetime ago.

❦

Any worries that their phone calls would be uncomfortable were quickly put to rest. Allen called her Wednesday and they talked about the mundane details of life that were incredibly interesting now. Kim relished learning about his work, and more about his family; even though she knew plenty about them already from Maddie, it was different hearing it from Allen. Allen told her that he would be traveling back to Chicago for Christmas in order to pick up some furniture from a storage unit there. He would rent a U-haul and drive back on Christmas day so as not to cut into his work week. Kim felt a strange sadness at knowing he would be away on Christmas even though she reminded herself that she wouldn't get to see him anyway, she knew she'd miss him just the same. When she got off the phone, she reflected on her feelings and couldn't deny that there was something…something unidentifiable that seemed to draw her to him and unless she was gravely mistaken he was drawn to her too. She had heard stories about people who felt an instant bond to the person they knew they should be with, but having not felt that way about her own husband, it was easy to discount the phenomenon. This feeling she had when she thought about Allen seemed to testify of the possibility that destiny does exist. It was still nearly impossible to believe that she could really have this in her life. It hadn't been so long ago that she had determined she could never love again, and yet here she was falling for a man she knew very little about. It was so strange, and yet so strangely perfect.

The night before Allen was supposed to fly to Chicago, Kim called him. They spoke for nearly an hour about work, Christmas, his trip. Kim loved hearing about his plans and suppressed her own longing to be part of them. As simple as it was, it seemed like an adventure and she fantasized about how much fun it would be to just go somewhere—do whatever she wanted for a few days. It was pathetically attractive. Finally, Allen yawned and she realized she had kept him talking too long. They said their good-byes and Allen promised to call her when he got home on the 27th. Jackson was leaving with Robb's parents on the 26th and she was apprehensive about being without him for an entire week. It was Christmas and she needed to catch the spirit, but it wasn't easy—the holiday seemed bleak.

❧

Allen stomped snow off his boots on the porch and quickly rang the doorbell before stuffing his hands back into his pockets. He had forgotten how blasted cold Chicago was in December. Utah had its share of cold weather, but it just didn't compare to this and it served as one more reminder that he had made the right choice in leaving this place. He was just about to ring the bell again when the door flew open.

"Oh Allen, you made it!" announced a somewhat stout little woman. She smiled broadly and tucked a lock of chestnut hair behind her ear before standing to the side of the doorway.

"Finally!" he said with a smile as he pulled open the storm door and stepped inside. The warmth of the home made him want to collapse on the spot, but he resisted. Manners.

Candy shut the door behind him and rubbed her arms to compensate for the chilly gust of wind that had followed him in. "Kurt just ran out to get me some walnuts, but he'll be back in a minute; he is so excited to see you."

Allen smiled his understanding—he had looked forward to this visit and the opportunity to catch up with both of them—it was the bright spot in this obnoxious trip. Kurt had been Allen's closest friend in Chicago. They had met in the Elders' Quorum of the ward Allen and Janet had moved into when they purchased their home over eight years ago. Kurt and Allen's lives couldn't have been more different, but they had many things in common and were almost like brothers. Allen and Janet had been in the ward for almost six years before they got divorced and although Allen had moved into an apartment, he had remained in the ward boundaries. That caused further complications. Despite his and Janet's acceptance of their situation, several ward members were highly critical and Allen got more than his share of insulting advice and calls to repentance. If it hadn't been for Kurt, Allen was sure he would have become inactive. There had been no other time in Allen's life when his testimony had been so challenged. He gained a whole new understanding of the commandment to not judge others. Through every offensive encounter, Kurt continually reminded Allen of the reasons he had made the decision in the first place, and further cemented Allen's knowledge that he had done the right thing. Allen seriously wondered how he could have made it through the experience without the support of Kurt and Candy. They often invited him over for Sunday dinner, and watching their family bustle and grow was just the continuing motivation he had needed. They had five children, and if Allen wasn't mistaken, Candy looked to be expecting their sixth. When Allen had called and asked if he could borrow their couch for a night, Kurt had been thrilled to have a chance to visit.

Until this moment in their home, Allen hadn't realized just how much he had missed them. He shrugged out of his coat and gloves and hung them on the row of hooks beside the door, many of which were already draped with brightly colored coats, scarves and backpacks. "Where are the kids?" he asked.

"Angie took them sledding; she just got her drivers license, ya know. I figure I've got a few months when she'll do anything to get behind the wheel and I'm taking full advantage of it."

Allen laughed. "Tricks of the trade."

"And I'll use any tricks I can." She returned to the kitchen and started peeling potatoes. Allen pondered for a moment what kitchen concoction could possibly require potatoes and walnuts, but quickly realized she was probably working on two different things. That was another thing he missed: Candy's incredible cooking. "So tell me about Salt Lake," she said after a moment.

"It's not as cold as it is here," he said, entering the kitchen and rolling up his sleeves. There was a pile of dishes calling his name.

"Is anywhere colder than here?"

"Nowhere I've ever been," Allen said with a chuckle and turned on the hot water. Kurt returned in a few minutes and the three of them caught up on the gossip of the ward, Allen's new office and tidbits of family info. Allen told them about Maddie's wedding, but was somehow reluctant to discuss Kim. What do you say about the woman you care very much about when she's still married and refuses to see you; yet you think of her throughout each day and can't remember feeling like this before in your life? It was hard to explain so he didn't try. The kids came home soon and after much cajoling, Kurt and Allen went outside and helped them build a snowman. Watching Kurt with his children had always been bitter-sweet for Allen, but today for some reason, it was particularly poignant and particularly painful.

Dinner was wonderful, as always, and afterwards they sang carols around the tree. Allen remembered their tradition of reen-acting the birth of Christ every Christmas Eve and he drew the part of the Innkeeper. Good—very little speaking. If the drama was supposed to be serious, it didn't work; if it was supposed to be a hilarious catastrophe, they pulled it off to perfection. Candy admitted that every year she hoped they didn't offend the heavens. Allen didn't know how to answer that, but he figured they couldn't be judged too harshly. After the play, the kids went eagerly to bed and Allen assisted with the setting-out of gifts. It was nearly eleven when they finally collapsed on the couch with mugs of hot choco-late in hand.

"I really appreciate your letting me intrude on your holiday," Allen said after a few moments of twinkling silence.

"We said you were always welcome—there were no provisions in the invitation," Kurt said as he twisted around on the couch so he could lay his head on what remained of Candy's lap due to her protruding belly. She mussed up his hair and he turned his head to kiss her stomach. The scene made Allen smile sadly and he stared into his mug in hopes that the pain would go away faster if he didn't watch the two of them. At dinner, Kurt had informed him that Candy was, in fact, pregnant; five months and it was another girl. That would give them four girls and two boys. Allen was truly happy for them, but he said a silent prayer to someday have at least a part of what they had.

Allen was thinking of something to say when there was a knock at the door. Kurt looked up at Candy but she just shrugged. Allen moved to get up, but Kurt motioned for him to stay put. They all wondered who on earth would drop in at eleven-thirty on Christmas Eve—probably a neighbor with a late plate of fudge who had seen their lights on. With Kurt gone, Allen asked Candy about the pregnancy; she told him how things were going and was just getting to the names she and Kurt were fighting about when she looked up at the doorway and struggled to her feet.

"Janet!" she said and cast a surprised look toward Allen, who craned his neck to see if he had heard right. Janet stood slightly in front of Kurt and Allen quickly got to his feet, setting his mug on the end table as he did so. He hadn't seen or even spoken to his ex-wife in more than a year and a half—not since she had sold their house and moved out of the ward.

"Uh, hi Janet," he fumbled, wondering how on earth she knew he was here, and why she would care enough to come see him late Christmas Eve.

Janet simply stared back at him and guessed his thoughts. "Candy mentioned your coming to Dora, and she told me you'd be here tonight."

Dora was another member of the ward who worked in Janet's office. The explanation made sense enough; he hadn't tried to hide his visit. But he still didn't understand what motivation Janet could have in tracking him down. He was searching for words when she explained, "I really need to talk to you."

Kurt and Candy both looked at Allen for a moment; then Candy spoke up, "We've got to get to bed anyway." She took Kurt's hand as she walked out of the room, saying, "Nice to see you again, Janet."

Janet didn't even respond; her focus was on Allen and he was irritated by her rudeness. She had often been that way, self-centered and above conforming to the small social graces if they didn't serve her purpose. The question of why she was here in the first place continued to baffle him. For a few moments, he stared at her, waiting for her to explain her sudden appearance. He considered mentioning how well she looked or that it was good to see her, but there was a look in her eye that told him she was here for something specific.

"So what's going on?" he finally asked evenly. Her lip started to tremble when he spoke and her eyes became moist, but it wasn't until she covered her face with her hands and her shoulders shuddered that he realized she was crying. In shock, he watched her slump to the floor. He couldn't believe this; he had never seen her cry. When the initial disbelief passed, he hurried over to her and knelt beside her on the floor, wondering what could possibly make her act like this. Her long black hair cascaded over her shaking shoulders. Hesitantly, he reached out and touched her arm. At his touch, she threw her arms around his neck and buried her head in his chest, nearly knocking him off balance. Allen awkwardly patted her back and searched his mind for any possible reason she could have for such behavior. Throughout their marriage, Janet had shown great restraint for displaying emotions of nearly any kind, thus he was at a loss as to how to handle it now. After another minute or so, he finally put a hand under her chin and tilted her tear streaked face toward his.

"Janet, what's wrong?"

She seemed to be in such pain it shocked him further and her chin started to quiver again. "Janet," he whispered again and tenderly brushed a stray lock of hair from her forehead.

"Allen," she said and her face crumpled again. "I'm pregnant."

If her earlier behavior had shocked him, this information left him completely numb and it took several seconds for him to respond. "What?" he finally whispered—he couldn't possibly have heard her correctly.

"I'm pregnant," she repeated. Allen let go of her and stood up as instant anger flamed in his chest. How many years had he longed to hear those words from her? How many times had he prayed them? Yet they never came. The words of their final argument on the subject echoed back to him: 'I will never have a baby, Allen—not yours, not anyone's, so if you can't be satisfied with me then leave—it will never happen. Never.' His eyes hardened at the memory and he turned away from the pathetic scene in front of him. He was sick to his stomach and sick at heart. Staring at the Christmas lights, he tried to swallow his anger. "Obviously it has nothing to do with me, Janet. So why are you here?"

"I got married, Allen," she whispered and raised herself off the floor to a standing position.

Allen clenched his jaw—another surprise—yet she still didn't answer his question. His anger got the best of him and he spun around. "Then go home to him." Was she trying to rub it in? To punish him somehow?

Janet shook her head. "You don't understand," she stammered. "He left me."

Allen's heart softened a little, but he still couldn't see his part in this situation. Janet stood and wiped her eyes before taking a step towards him; he narrowed his eyes suspiciously and took a step backward. She stopped and blinked her large blue eyes in an attempt to hold back the tears. "I'm so scared, Allen." He merely stared back at her. "I don't know what to do. When I told him about the baby he was furious—the next day he was gone; we hadn't planned on this; we weren't ready." She waited for him to say something but he just looked away. When he looked back she was right in front of him. He was startled and took a quick breath in. She reached a hand to his face and, although his entire mind and soul screamed at him to move away, he didn't. Her hand brushed his cheek and he tried to ignore the intimacy in her touch. Her face moved towards his and he simply stared at her, his mind reeling and his senses keen. When her lips touched his, he didn't feel the tenderness he had expected; he felt nothing. Although he didn't push her away, he didn't respond. She pulled back momentarily, obviously confused at his lack of response, but immediately wrapped her arms around his neck and lifted her face again. This time Allen had the sense to move, but her lips caught the corner of his mouth and the warmth of her kiss awakened a dull ache in his stomach. When she tried again he didn't resist; he couldn't seem to help it. Without thinking about it, his hand came to rest on the small of her back and she tightened her embrace. The kiss deepened and continued for nearly a minute before Allen's conscience finally overrode his physical response and he pulled away.

"What are you doing?" he asked after taking a few more seconds to gather his senses.

Janet glanced down at the floor between them and then looked up, the tears coming easily, now that she realized she needed them again. "I don't know what to do, Allen. I'm so scared."

"And what does that have to do with me?" he asked angrily.

"This is what you always wanted: a family for us."

"I wanted *our* family, not someone else's, and you didn't want that, Janet—you still don't."

She tried to smile. "Yes, I do," she said, but her words were hollow. "Things are different now—I'm different."

Allen shook his head and stepped further away. "Go home, Janet."

Her eyes narrowed and her innocent victim role disappeared. "You really don't care, do you?" she asked bitterly. "All that we had means nothing to you now. I need help, I can't do this alone— you know I can't."

"Then you should have been more careful," he shot back. "You were always very careful when we were married."

"That's not fair, Allen."

"What's not fair, Janet? You come back now because you suddenly have something I want, which you would never give me; that's what isn't fair. Go home." His tone was severe.

"Oh Allen, please," she begged, switching back to her earlier desperation tactics. "Please give us a chance; I was unfair to you and I'm so sorry. But things are different now. I've changed." She put a hand to her chest and stepped towards him again. "I need you."

Allen simply stared back at her. This was too much for him to absorb all at once. He had known for a long time that he still cared for Janet. There were times when he wished he was still with her, but such feelings weren't enough and the moments of wanting her had been fading lately. Especially since he met Kim. Looking into her eyes at this moment, he could see that she knew exactly how he felt and it angered him that she would use it against him. Janet was inches away from him again and she looked deeply into his eyes. "Please, Allen. Think about it; you and me again. We could have this child together. No more wondering about our future… no more nights alone." She looked up at him with what he recognized as her seductive look. Yet just as he remembered; her eyes reflected no passion. After a moment, she planted a sweet kiss on his cheek. "Isn't that better than what we have now?" Allen didn't answer and after a few more moments she turned to leave.

Allen stood rooted in place; as much as he would have liked to, he was unable to discount the temptation of her offer. Janet stopped at the doorway and looked back at him. "Tell Candy I'm sorry to have interrupted their evening." And she slipped out of the room. When he heard the front door shut he was finally able to move and he sank into the nearest seat. He swallowed hard as he went over what Janet had just told him and he tried to make sense of it. He was the first to admit that he and Janet had not had the greatest of marriages, but he had felt that the reasons were mainly her lack of affection, her overzealous self interest and her refusal to become a mother. Tonight, two of those things had changed and he didn't know how the pieces fit back together now. After a few minutes, he looked up to see Kurt standing in the doorway with a look of concern on his face.

Allen just shook his head in disbelief to communicate that he had no way of explaining what had just happened. Kurt came in and sat down. When Allen looked up again, Kurt nodded, "I have always believed strongly in eavesdropping."

Allen looked back down, unable to respond to the humor. "Did you know she had remarried?"

"Yes," Kurt admitted. "I should have told you, but I didn't quite see the point. After awhile I just assumed you knew. It's been almost a year, I think."

"Who's the guy?" The guy who got my ex-wife pregnant and abandoned her—the whole thing made him sick.

"All I know is that she met him in her new ward—he wasn't very active. I never met him but I heard he was kind of a jerk—apparently I heard right."

Allen nodded slowly. "I guess you heard her...offer."

"I also didn't hear you reject it."

"It's ludicrous," Allen spat. "She really believes I should just step in and raise some other man's kid."

"Is it so far fetched?" Kurt asked and Allen's head snapped up. "I mean you two were together a long time, and if what drove you apart isn't there anymore, then is it so hard to imagine trying again?"

"I can't believe you're saying this. You're the one who continually reminded me why I got a divorce in the first place."

"Allen," Kurt began and leaned towards him. "I'm not saying I thought you were wrong, and I don't pretend to know what's right for you to do now. But do you really think that I don't see the hunger in your eyes when you look at my family?" Allen looked away. "Or the longing in your voice when you ask about them? I may know better than anyone how desperately you have wanted a family—it is why you got a divorce in the first place. It's been two years and you haven't so much as mentioned another woman to me; maybe you're being too hasty in rejecting Janet's offer."

His words brought Kim to mind, and he longed to be able to see her, touch her; somehow be reminded of the hopes he had with her. But even as he thought it, he realized they really had nothing more than hope. He knew very little about her; he had never even kissed her. Was she even a real option? Was he being foolish to write this off? "It seems so impossible," he said out loud, and even he wasn't sure whether he was talking about Kim or Janet.

Kurt stood and looked sympathetically at his friend. "And I'm not trying to tell you that it isn't, I just don't think you should let your pride make the decision for you. Family is everything, Allen—nothing compares with it...and there aren't infinite chances waiting for any of us."

Allen got very little sleep that night as he tried in vain to make sense of everything. By morning, the only decision he had reached was that he couldn't sit around and do nothing. He had arranged to leave for Salt Lake on Christmas morning, so he pushed his plans back a day. He and Janet met at her apartment and she fixed them a simple holiday meal of ham and cheese sandwiches; eerily reminiscent of the many empty holidays they had shared in the past. After only an hour, he left; no closer to his decision than he had been when he arrived, but feeling more sympathetic toward her situation and more confused about his own.

Janet told him about Craig; how they met just a year ago when she moved and she'd been so lonely that she hadn't seen his faults. She gave Allen the overview of their relationship; one thing they had both agreed on was that neither of them wanted or expected children. When Janet found out she was pregnant in November, Craig hightailed it out of there and she hadn't heard from him since. Allen could sense that she was trying hard to convince him of how much she had changed, but it seemed fake to him and he had little doubt that if they were to try again this "new" Janet wouldn't last long. As he left she had kissed him again, but once again it was lifeless.

Getting into his car, the kiss still fresh on his mouth and in his mind, he remembered how the very sound of Kim's voice on the phone could make his heart beat faster and his worries fade away. Yet they had shared so little. How could he guess what the future really held for them? There was no answer. He wished he could call Kim and discuss the whole matter, but it would be completely out of place. She was in no position to make promises to him. Their future was hopeful, but unknown. Oh Kim, he thought to himself, why does our timing have to be so wrong? Is someone trying to tell us something and we just aren't listening? Was Kim the answer to his prayers, or was she simply an obstacle that could keep him from his real destiny?

He didn't return to Kurt's house until late, having spent the day driving around contemplating this new twist in his life. When he did return to Kurt's house, he was relieved that he and Candy avoided the subject. But as he watched their family interact, he realized that this was what he could be turning down. Just the night before, he had prayed again for just a part of what Kurt had. Now, Janet had offered it to him. Could he walk away from this? Could this be his last chance?

# CHAPTER FOURTEEN

Kim was sure things couldn't be worse. Christmas Day was nice, but far too long. Her parents gave Jackson more gifts than she did, and her dependence on them was depressing. All of her frustrations with her current situation seemed to pile up and she was in a foul mood all day. Knowing that Robb's parents were coming to pick Jackson up early the next morning didn't help and made her even more irritable. A whole week without her son, could she stand it? Cousins were everywhere all day long and as much as Kim wanted some snuggle time with her son it just wasn't to be.

She finally pulled him away from his new toys at 9:30, but he was so wound up and hyper that he wouldn't sit still and she ended up storming out of his room in frustration. Then she collapsed onto her own bed and tried not to cry. I should never have agreed to let him go, she decided, and if she could have, she would have called off his trip all together.

Morning came and Jackson bounded out the door with hardly a glance back at her. How would she make it through the week? She hadn't ever felt so lonely. Throughout the day, Kim found herself looking forward to Allen's call the next day, and although she chastised herself for making such a big deal out of it, it was the only bright spot she saw in an otherwise long and dismal week. Over and over, she reminded herself they were just friends and to not start piling expectations on top of that. She went back to work and looked forward to the phone call he had promised. But Allen didn't call Friday, the 27th. He didn't call the next day either and on Sunday when she simply couldn't wait any longer. She called him, half-hoping he wouldn't answer, although she had no idea why that would help.

"Hello."

The sound of his voice made her heart sink: he was home. She felt so foolish; she should have waited. "Uh, hi," she stammered after a moment.

Allen grimaced; he had been meaning to call but kept putting it off for reasons he still didn't fully understand. "I'm sorry I didn't call, Kim. I just got home; things took longer than I thought."

His words should have lifted her spirits, but his tone concerned her. "That's okay, I just wanted to make sure everything was all right," she said weakly; she was sure she had "desperate" written all over her. When Allen didn't answer right away, she added softly, "Allen, are you okay?"

"Yeah. Yeah, I'm okay," he said. But his distraction was obvious.

"Are you sure?"

"I said I'm okay!" Allen said shortly.

"Fine," she snapped back and hung up the phone, embarrassed and hurt. Now she felt worse than ever. He was always so level and easy going; what she had done wrong? Had things changed so much in these few days? The phone rang before she could figure it out.

"It's me. Don't hang up."

Kim didn't hang up, but she didn't speak either; what should she say? Once Allen realized she wasn't going to hang up on him, he took a deep breath. "I'm sorry. I didn't mean to take it out on you."

"Take what out on me?" she asked cautiously; she was glad he had called back, but he sounded strange.

"Some things happened in Chicago," Allen said simply and seemed reluctant to continue.

"What?"

He took another breath and had to make an instantaneous decision. Here goes everything. "Janet's pregnant."

Janet-Janet-Janet; Kim searched her brain for the connection. Ooh, the ex-wife. The implications that this could have on Allen hit her hard and she swallowed. "Oh."

"I didn't know she had remarried," Allen said when she didn't say anything more. "Apparently it was about a year ago, and now she's having his baby." The bitterness in his voice was thicker than either of them would have liked it to be. "Oh, Allen. I'm sorry."

"I don't know why it should be such a big deal, we've been divorced for two years. If she wants kids now; well, that's up to her. Right?"

He was searching for some help; Kim didn't have a problem offering her own opinions on this. "It's a big deal because she told you in no uncertain terms she had no interest in motherhood. I can only imagine how hard this must be to know that now she's starting a family with someone else."

"There really isn't anyone else."

"What?" Kim asked cautiously. What was that supposed to mean?

"Apparently the guy left her and wants nothing to do with the baby when it's born."

"Whoa," Kim said for lack of anything better coming to mind, poor Janet. Maybe she wasn't the only one with misery in marriage.

"It gets even better than that," Allen said. "I spent Christmas Eve at a friend's place, knowing nothing about any of this, and then suddenly Janet's at the door bawling. She's not due until June but she went on and on about how she was all alone." A cold dread filled Kim and she thought she knew now where this was headed. "She wants to make another go of it."

Kim swallowed, why did she have to be right about this one. "What did you say?" she asked, but Allen didn't answer and she thought she might be sick. Yet, despite her own feelings, she could imagine how this felt to Allen. Her thoughts went back to the night at the hotel when he had told her all about his marriage. He hadn't said anything about how he felt towards Janet now, only that he couldn't stay with her if there was no hope of ever having a family. As hard as it was, she tried to keep her voice level as she said, "It's what you always wanted, Allen."

Still he didn't say anything. For nearly a minute they sat in silence and Kim's heart sank even farther. Maybe he said yes, and she didn't know if she could bear that. She knew as well as he did that they had no commitments to each other.

"I told her I wasn't interested."

"Why?" Kim asked, her spirits lifted a little.

"She told me for years she would never have my children, so I left and now she gets married again, gets pregnant, loses the husband and comes running back to me. I'm not stupid enough to think it's me that she really wants—it's a daddy. A daddy for another man's child. Yet she knows how enticing that is to me. I'm thirty-six years old. I'm not getting any younger and here's this opportunity. It is what I've always wanted. But not this way."

She didn't want to, but she had to say it. "Allen, why did you get a divorce?"

"You know the answer to that," Allen said quietly.

Kim wanted to cry. "Apparently that's changed now, hasn't it. Janet's changed."

"I don't know that she has. Besides the baby issues we had, I realized a lot of other things about Janet that I didn't like. I think I always saw them, and once things started falling apart I didn't ignore them anymore. She is very selfish, immature, and self-serving; she can be cold and insensitive too. It was almost as if once I realized she would never become a mother, all hopes that those things would improve disappeared. I realized that I was simply subjecting myself to unhappiness; and it wasn't worth the price any more."

"But now she is going to be a mother," Kim said, wanting to slap herself. Why couldn't she just rip the woman to shreds and tell Allen what a manipulative beast she was and that he'd be a fool to even consider going back to her. Then too, why couldn't Kim promise him that she would give him all the beautiful babies he had ever dreamed about and promise him a full, happy life? The answer to either question was the same: she was in no position to plan his future.

"Yeah," Allen said thoughtfully. "Now she is going to a mother."

"And that could change everything." Mental slap again.

"And it could change nothing."

"And it could change everything," Kim repeated.

"You said that already. You sound like you think I ought to move right in," Allen said with just a hint of the disappointment he felt at her support of Janet.

"I'm in no position to tell you what to do, either way." Don't be a fool, her brain screamed. "I would just hate to see you make a decision that you'd regret. I understand how angry you must feel about the whole thing, but five years from now that might not even matter to you; you'd have a family."

"And live happily ever after?"

"Maybe, maybe not." NOT.

"I just don't think I could do it. I don't want to do it. But…"

"But it's a baby."

There was another pause, then Allen spoke again. "If things were to change this dramatically with Robb, would you be able to put things back together?"

"Things are different between Robb and me," Kim said with a chill in her voice.

"What's so different about it?"

"He cheated on me, abandoned us, and is a miserable manipulative person; you and Janet parted as friends—that's very different."

Allen was silent for a few moments, "I'm pretty certain that this is not my destiny."

Kim closed her eyes wishing there were more finality in his voice. "Is 'pretty certain', certain enough?"

Allen ignored the question and continued divulging more information. "She requested a job transfer to come back here; her Mom lives in Ogden now...and it looks like she'll get the job."

It took a moment for Kim to process this new information. "She'll be living here...in Salt Lake?"

"Probably."

"When will she move out here? If she does, I mean."

"It would most likely be within the next few months."

Kim swallowed the growing lump in her throat. She wanted so badly to talk about the two of them; Allen and Kim, together. Give him some hope. But she knew too well that she didn't have much more to offer him than Janet did. Allen had loved Janet once before, and probably still did. When it came right down to it, he barely knew Kim. Janet probably made enough money that she didn't have to live with her parents, either. What right did Kim have to put herself above Janet? "Well, you've got quite a decision to make now, don't you." That ache that Allen had been helping to ease lately was deeper and more intense than it had ever been.

"I already told you, I turned down the offer," Allen said, but the conviction Kim was looking for wasn't as strong as she would have liked.

"I hope you don't think I would stand in your way." As soon as she said it, she wished she hadn't. She had meant to say he shouldn't make his decision just because of her. Or maybe she meant to say that she wouldn't stop him, or heck maybe she should have said that she saw distinct relationship possibilities in their future that would greatly increased his potential happiness; she should have just kept her mouth shut.

But it had been said, and Allen thought he understood where she was coming from. He had made no commitment to Kim other than the silly date in March; maybe she was kindly trying to give him permission to go fly a kite. Then again, she had called him. He groaned inwardly; damn, but life was complicated. Here he had thought the worst was over and now this. There was no way he could seriously consider going back to Janet. Was there? "I guess I'd better go," Allen finally said quietly.

"Yeah, me too," Kim lied.

Once off the phone, Allen put his head in his hands and moaned. What did he want? What did he really want? He had loved Janet once and they had planned a life together; it had devastated him when that fell apart. Now, here it was laid out in front of him again. Everything he had dreamed of was right on his doorstep. Janet was a good person, he had never denied that; but she turned out to be so different from what he had expected. What if she was to get better? What if she could be that sweet girl he thought he had married? Then again, what if she was exactly the same as she had been when he left? What if they just repeated their old marriage and lost all over again? When would he figure out his mistake? Five years? Ten?

Despite how vehemently he disagreed with Janet's feelings about parenthood, Allen understood some of the reasons she had decided not to have children. Janet had grown up with an unstable mother. Janet had always refused to talk about the details of her childhood. Allen knew there was more to her past, but she had been unwilling to tell him anything more than the basics. He believed that she was afraid to be a mother—afraid she would repeat her own mother's pattern. That possibility left Allen with a whole new concern. Was Janet capable of raising a child on her own?

And then there was Kim. If Kim had told him to walk away, he would have. There was just something about her; something he couldn't quite put into words. Had he ever felt that with Janet? He couldn't remember; he didn't think so. Even the things he had shared with Janet these last few days didn't cause the feelings that this phone call with Kim summoned up. He didn't think he had ever felt like this. But then, Kim had been so non-committal on the phone. Previously, he had sensed that she shared his feelings, but he didn't know for sure. What did she want? Should he just call her back and ask exactly what she thought? Was he a fool to look to her for the future he wanted, or was he a fool to waste his time considering anything else?

He barely knew Kim; then again he didn't like a lot of what he knew about Janet. "Why now?" he asked of no one in particular. Why not six months from now? For some reason he was sure that in six months he could make a better decision. In six months, Kim's divorce would be final, they would have at least explored their feelings for one another and he would have a much better idea of where he stood with her.

I am going to make myself neurotic, he decided. He should never have gone to Chicago. If he had stayed home, none of this would have happened. Janet had found out he was in town and she was desperate. *Desperate*—the word suddenly struck him like a ton of bricks. He had just gone over all his jumbled thoughts and it came down to the fact that Janet was desperate. Not desperate for him. Not desperate for anyone in particular. Just desperate—and scared. He suddenly felt very sorry for her. She didn't want a baby, yet she had no choice. He, however, still did.

Finally, he got on his knees and prayed. He felt so drained that he just kept repeating the same things over and over. He wanted to do what is right, he wanted a family, he wanted Janet to be happy, and he wanted to be happy too. But he didn't think that Janet was the ticket to his happiness; not anymore. He had been praying for days, but had yet to feel an answer. Now he had made a decision and he asked if it was right. Was it right to leave this struggle to Janet? It was a hard question to ask. In a very real sense, he wanted to help her with this. Kneeling amid piles and boxes in his new home he felt the spirit of peace and calm fill his entire being. With it came a tangible peace that the decisions he had made two years ago were the right ones; they were still the right ones. Janet was no longer meant for him. He stayed on his knees until the feeling faded, longing for it to stay and wishing he felt it more often.

Allen had always felt a unique closeness to the Spirit. Maybe that's why he could listen to the sometimes horrific details of other people's lives and not feel violated himself as many of his colleagues admitted they felt. Since he was a child, he had a testimony of the gospel. It just never occurred to him that it couldn't be true. People he had explained that to, as a youth, told him that one day he would question it; but he hadn't. Even with the struggles he had faced in the church during his divorce he had never wondered if the church was true, only if he could stand going anymore. And despite all the loneliness and fear that followed, he had felt the Spirit beside him and he never felt forgotten. But he also knew that he often took the gift for granted and didn't seek out the true confirmation of the Spirit as often as he ought to. He resolved to do better from now on. He got off his knees feeling much better, still tense but secure in the fact that everything would work out right if he continued to follow his heart.

Throughout the next few days he busied himself with unpacking and reassuring himself that his decision was the right one. Each time he questioned it, he was reminded that this was right. Several times he thought about calling Kim, but he was still unsure how to interpret their last conversation. Despite how hard he tried, he couldn't come to a conclusion concerning her feelings and it frustrated him.

Tuesday at lunch, his private line rang. In his office, most calls were sent through the front receptionist but the therapists also had a private line for personal calls. He usually let his voice mail answer them, but since he was only doing some routine paperwork he picked up the receiver. "This is Dr. Jackman," he said.

"You are the most idiotic, blind and stupid man I have ever known."

Allen blinked and after overcoming his initial shock asked in a calm, very therapeutic tone, "May I ask who's speaking please?"

"It's your sister you dolt, jerk, fool-of-a-man, incompetent jerk, idiotic..."

"You're repeating yourself, Maddie."

"Well then, double on that one!"

"May I ask why I get the colorful titles all of the sudden?" Allen asked with a fair amount of intrigue.

"Why do you think?" She paused and took a breath before continuing, "I can not believe that you would even consider; for one minute going back to that...that...uh."

"What? Your potty mouth failing you all of the sudden?"

"Don't be such a—"

"Name-calling isn't your style, Maddie. Now if you could just calm down we can talk about this like adults and perhaps figure out some things."

"Are you really thinking about going back to Janet?" Her calmness was a stark contrast to her earlier rage.

"Bad news travels fast," Allen commented. He wasn't sure whether he approved of Kim talking about his personal problems.

"Not by Kim's choice. I just knew there was something wrong—I've been bugging her all day. At first I thought it was just Jackson's being gone, but it seemed like more than that. Finally I got it out of her, and I have to say I am shocked that you would think about it for even a second."

"What did Kim say about it?" he asked almost eagerly.

"She tried to shrug it off as your decision, but I know her better than that. Something has come alive in her the last couple of weeks, Allen, and you killed it."

Allen rolled his eyes. She should have been a drama major; or a politician. "I think Kim's upset about Jackson," he offered half-heartedly.

"Hello!" Maddie said, exasperated. "Did you hear what I just said? It's not about Jackson. It's about you." Allen tingled a little at hearing that. But he didn't answer; he knew Maddie would take over again. "Tell me what's going on," Maddie demanded when he didn't respond. Allen sighed and filled her in on the details. She waited patiently until he finished. "And you're going to do it?"

"No, I'm not. But I'd be lying if I said it hasn't occupied my mind a lot."

"So you were considering it?" The disgust in her voice irritated Allen even more.

"Maddie, you have no idea what my life is like. Janet's offer, no matter the demographics, is exactly what I've wanted—what I wanted with her for a long time. I can't just write that off, without even wondering if this could be the answer to years of prayer."

"But you divorced her. It makes no sense to go back after all of that."

"Yeah, well it doesn't make sense because it isn't *your* life, Maddie. You've got Matt and thank heaven things are different for you."

"I'll admit that it is different, but you've got...uh."

"Exactly my point, Maddie," Allen said, his frustration growing. "It's easy for you to look in from the outside and plan a merry little future for me, but there is nothing certain here. I really like Kim, I think she is a great person. But that doesn't change the fact that she is in the middle of a very difficult time in her life. I have very little indication that leads me to believe anything will come of the friendship we share. I would like to think so, but the timing is complex. She is still married. She also has a lot of healing to do. I don't know that she feels capable of any sort of relationship—with me or anyone. So before you start criticizing me for considering an option that would offer me my greatest desire, look at it from my point of view. It's not cut and dried the way you would like it to be."

Maddie was silent for a moment, but only in order to put her own opinions together. "I don't think you're seeing the big picture here because you're scared. You are both scared. You both have had lame marriages that hurt you and so you sit there and deny the feelings you have. You would like to believe that no one knows how you operate. But you're not that difficult to figure out, Allen. I know how badly you want a family. And I know how you feel about Kim. I can feel it when you talk about her. On top of that, I know how Kim feels about you; I feel that too and I think you are both being vastly immature about this whole thing. Pretending you don't feel the way you do doesn't change your feelings."

Allen had chills and was reminded of the strange way Maddie 'knew' things sometimes. He could remember being helped by

Maddie's insights several times. It was a bit of a family joke that if you wanted to know the answer to a quandary in your life, ask Maddie. More often than not, she could at least point you in the right direction. "There is something between the two of you that is powerful. You're both trying to deny it, but that's only going to complicate things more."

"Things are about as complicated as they can be right now."

"Right, so accept how you feel and get on with it."

"She is still married, Maddie," Allen reminded her with frustration.

"I know that!" she retorted with exasperation. "I'm not telling you to do anything inappropriate, just stop fooling yourself. And when March first comes around you'll be ready."

"Ready for what?"

"Ready to get on with your life."

"Janet's offering me that opportunity right now," Allen replied, prodding for a little more insight.

"SHE IS NOT THE ONE!" Maddie yelled, causing Allen to pull the phone away from his ear.

"And Kim is?" Allen asked. Maddie didn't respond and he repeated "And Kim is the one?" He said it lightly, but he wanted very much to hear her opinion.

Maddie replied lightly, "I've used my powers enough for one day."

Allen rolled his eyes; sometimes she scared him. "And have you told Kim all this?"

"Yep."

"You did?" Now Allen was embarrassed.

"Yes, I did. But she got the gentle version. She isn't nearly as pig-headed as you are."

"I feel sufficiently humbled now that you have used nearly every derogatory name I know to describe me."

"In humility comes redemption, Allen."

Allen blew that off. "What did Kim say?"

"I'm not telling you."

"It doesn't do me any good then does it," Allen grumbled, he thought she would at least give him something to work with.

"I told her you were calling her tonight and you two could discuss it."

"Maddie!"

"Well, you are. I've just given you the topic of discussion."

He had actually been planning to call Kim, but he certainly

hadn't told Maddie that. She was really freaky. "Well, thanks a lot," Allen said dryly.

"You're welcome," Maddie retorted cheerfully. "I've got to go; bye."

Allen's stomach was in knots; he hated this. What was he supposed to do now? He had to call Kim, there was no doubt about that. How embarrassing.

"Dr. Jackman, your one o'clock appointment is here," the receptionist chirped into the speaker. Thank goodness, he thought. Now he could block it out for a little while at least.

Kim returned from work wondering if she should ever tell Maddie anything again. It seemed that every time she did, it complicated things. Maddie had informed her of the basics of her conversation with Allen, and Kim was humiliated, although she couldn't deny her relief to know that Allen wasn't going to accept Janet's offer. The entire situation made her relationship with Allen seem much more fragile. No longer the comfortable friendship she had planned on for the next few months. It made her realize that there were more timetables to consider than just her own. Somehow, she had to find a balance between keeping her covenants and not taking Allen for granted. The problem was that she had no idea how she was supposed to do that.

She walked in the door with her mind so full of these thoughts Peggy's greeting caught her off guard.

"What was that, Mom? I wasn't paying attention."

"I said your lawyer called; he left a number for you to call him back—he just missed you at the office." She handed Kim a slip of paper.

Kim's stomach sank. What now? They had set up an appointment for the fifteenth of January to sign all the final papers to present to the judge. Eric didn't think they would have to appear because Robb was unable to do so and Kim had such a good case. His final words, the last time they met, had been, "No news is good news and I'll only contact you if we run into trouble."

Now he was calling her. Assuming that Robb must have come up with some kind of argument infuriated her. She walked directly to the phone and punched in the number.

As Eric explained the latest development, her anger increased. Apparently, Robb was still smarting over her refusal to send him a monthly allowance and had requested an itemized list of all her expenses. She was now required to itemize every bill, debt and payment she made. She had to report the amount owing on loans and the balance in their bank account as well as the balance in her own savings account which she had kept open after they married.

"And what is the point of my doing all this?" she asked with forced evenness.

"My guess is that Robb wants to show that you can afford to send him some money until the divorce is finalized."

"I don't have any money! I'm living with my parents, for heaven's sake, and I'm putting every dime I earn on my debts so that I can have a life again. This is ridiculous."

"But it's perfectly legal."

"The divorce will be final in just over a month anyway, so what's the point."

"First of all this situation will extend our time line at least another month." Kim groaned but let him continue. "They've given us two weeks to make up the report. Then they have two more weeks to review it before we can proceed with any settlement. Secondly; what does he have to lose? He's shown that he doesn't want this divorce and he has found another way to drag it out."

"And so I get to play along. Again."

"I'm afraid so," Eric said apologetically. "I'm sorry, Kim, the system isn't always fair."

"Isn't there anything we can do about this?"

"Well, that depends."

"On what?"

"On what risks you're willing to take. We can stipulate that they push this through quickly, say in half the time. But we run the risk of upsetting them and issuing more of a challenge than anything else; or you can simply agree to pay him an allowance until things are finalized and hope that shuts him up. And of course we can fight it, but that will take even more time."

Kim thought about the options and wanted to drive up to Evanston and strangle her husband for making everything so hard. The least he could do now was back off and let her get on with her life. "I'm not giving him money, Eric. And I don't care how mad it makes him; I'm not going to extend this for any longer than is absolutely necessary. I will have this report for you by Thursday with the stipulation that they have ten days to review it; that's it."

"Your husband is trying to make a point and I don't think this is the best way to counter it."

"I've got a point to make too!" she shot back angrily and then paused to calm herself down. "I'm sorry, Eric. I don't mean to take it out on you, but Robb has got to realize that he can't boss me around anymore. I'm not going to play by his rules. I don't have to and I won't. Somehow, he has got to understand that I am serious about getting on with my life without him. I can't hope to show him that if I pussyfoot around the issue and give in to him every time he pushes me. Do you understand that?"

"Yes, Kim, I do; but I just want to warn you that—"

"You did warn me, Eric, and I appreciate it but this is my choice. I'll have it by Thursday, then they get ten days—that's it."

Eric hesitated for a moment. "All right. If I have your figures by Thursday I'll get an official report sent out on Friday. As long as they don't come up with anything else, it will move the settlement back only a couple of weeks."

"Mid-February?" Kim asked.

"Around then."

"Okay, I'll see you on Thursday."

She turned off the phone and let out a loud breath before turning to go up the stairs. This was just what she needed, one more problem to deal with. As she passed Jackson's room the anger receded and she was struck with a wave of emotion. She hurried to her room, shut the door, covered her face with her hands and let the tears come. Why was her happiness such a threat to Robb? Why couldn't he leave her alone? The ringing of the phone she had placed on her bed caught her attention; thinking it was Eric again she pushed the button and put it to her ear.

If he's going to try to convince me of another route, so help me... "Hello!" she said briskly, sniffling slightly and wiping at her eyes while preparing herself to stand her ground. She had been telling herself for weeks that she had to force herself to be stronger; she had been liking the change in herself but it still seemed easier to not fight so much.

"Kim?"

She was brought up short by the voice. "Allen?" she asked. She had completely forgotten about his call.

"Did I call at a bad time?" he asked cautiously.

"No. I'm sorry, I thought you were my attorney."

Allen paused. "Tell me what he did so I'm sure not to do it too."

Kim smiled weakly and felt herself relax despite what lay between them. It was so nice to be able to talk to someone who could understand, even a little. "It's not his fault, he's just the messenger; Robb's getting creative again."

"How creative?"

She sat on the bed and kicked off her shoes. "Creative enough to keep me married for another few weeks." It just came out; she didn't plan to say it that way and it embarrassed her slightly to be so upfront, but then again that is probably just what she needed to be. She was so tired of hiding things but what bothered her the most was that Robb was once again keeping her from getting on with her life.

"You don't sound very happy about that."

"I'm furious about it!" Kim said, realizing that this wasn't the reason he had called but being unable to stop the train of thoughts that were chugging through her mind. "I've finally realized that the reason we stayed married for so long was because it worked out better for him. I paid the bills, he did as he pleased. He left to party it up for a few months because that's what he wanted to do and all the time that he's whoring...sorry, that he's gone, he actually believes that when he comes home we'll pick up right where we left off. Now it suddenly isn't in his best interest to get a divorce and so he's fighting me without any regard to what I want—again. He asked for an allowance and I refused. So now I have to itemize every dollar I spend each month, find out how much I owe on our loans and try to justify why I can't support his nicotine habit."

"Discovery," Allen interjected.

"What?"

"It's called a discovery, it's pretty common."

"Maybe so, but in this case it's ridiculous. I don't have any money to give him and even though he's a bum and he's in prison, I'm the one who has to dig up this information. I also get to pay more attorney fees and continue living in limbo while I try to convince everyone that I don't owe him a dime, even if I had a dime to give him."

"You're really mad about this," Allen said.

Kim sighed, was she not obvious enough about that already? "Yes, I am really mad about this."

"So what are you going to do?"

"My attorney thinks I should either submit the forms and wait patiently or pay him. I told him to cut the 'waiting' time in half, even if it upsets them, tell them I'm not paying anything and get on with it."

"Good for you," Allen said triumphantly. "Show Robb you're not going to be pushed around."

"My attorney thinks it's a bad idea," Kim said cautiously, feeling her own reservations increase.

"Ah, what does he know."

Kim smiled. "At ninety bucks an hour I hope he knows something, but I can't expect him to know everything; right?"

"Right. Sometimes we just have to do what we feel is right despite what other people think." His words caused both of them to pause and reflect on why Allen had called in the first place. Allen cleared his throat and continued. "When Janet showed up that night in Chicago, the friend I was staying with thought I should consider her offer more seriously than I wanted to." Kim hated the guy already. "And so I spent some time with Janet, listened to her situation, tried to force myself to consider the opportunity, but it just didn't feel right. I stressed about it for days, not wanting to be too prideful, but not wanting to be a fool either. When I talked to you that night it irritated me that you would be so supportive of her."

"I wasn't trying to be supportive of her, I just—"

"Let me finish," Allen interrupted, and Kim went obediently quiet. "But I realized that you were only trying to emphasize that I needed to do what was best for me." Kim's brow furrowed—is that what she had done? "And when I got off the phone and thought about it again I realized that Janet isn't right for me. There are too many things she doesn't complete for me, and it would be foolish for me to try to find happiness with her again. I do care about Janet, Kim. I really feel badly for her situation; it's going to be incredibly hard for her. But I don't love her anymore—not that way at least—and she can't change that. For whatever reason, we had a season to be together, but it's over now and our destinies are no longer connected." Kim didn't know what to say, but her eyes became moist again and her heart swelled in her chest as the reality of his words lifted her spirits. "Being with Janet taught me something else too," he added.

"And what was that?" Kim whispered after a long thoughtful silence.

"That just hearing your voice does something inside me that she could never do."

Kim smiled and wished she had a pen to write down those words. "And what are you implying?"

"I don't know," Allen said softly.

"You want to know what I think?" Kim asked finding courage in his words. Then without letting him answer, she added. "I think Janet was a fool to let you go."

"Oh yeah?" he prodded, and she could hear the smile in his voice.

"If I'd had a husband like you...I'd have never let you get away."

They were both silent and Kim worried that perhaps she had said too much; perhaps she had already upset the balance of her objectives and set them up to backfire. The blatantly brave woman she was becoming was awfully scary sometimes.

"I'm looking forward to March first," Allen finally said.

A smile spread across Kim's face. "So am I. More than ever."

Kim spent the next two evenings sifting through bills and invoices in order to compile her list accurately. On Thursday she finished up, making several phone calls to verify payoff amounts and then faxed the information to Eric, glad to be rid of it. She marked her calendar for ten days and began her countdown.

Jackson returned from Arizona Wednesday night and that put her mind to rest as well. He'd had a great time, and she was grateful for that, but she resolved she would never do it again; her heart couldn't handle it. She waited until Sunday night to call Allen and they spent some more time talking and getting to know each other better. Allen informed her that he had called Janet, just to make things clear, and that although she hadn't taken it well, he hadn't changed his mind. Kim was relieved, yet frustrated that March first seemed to be getting farther and farther away.

The following Friday, Kim got a call at work and once again the stitches of life began to slip out.

"They want a copy of your statements, rental agreement and paychecks," Eric said over the phone.

"What?" Kim asked with frustration. "They don't believe me?"

"Apparently not, and they are also claiming that you rented out the house without Robb's permission and since his name is on the mortgage you owe him a portion of the rent you have received."

"The rent on that house doesn't even cover the mortgage I pay every month; they can see that on the documents you already sent them."

"That's not the point. Legally, you did not have Robb's permission to rent it so they are simply asking for his half of the rent in exchange for not pressing charges."

"Pressing charges, against me?" Kim asked in shock.

"Technically you breached a legal contract."

"He abandoned us, I didn't know where he was!"

"And because of that you'll probably win, but you'll also have to pay the attorney fees to take it to court, and it will delay the divorce settlement indefinitely."

Kim dropped her head into her free hand and pushed a hand through her hair as she gripped the phone tighter. "I don't believe he can do this."

"They have offered a compromise."

Kim groaned, "Do I want to hear this?"

Eric didn't answer her question directly. "They'll drop everything if you'll agree to withdraw the divorce until Robb's released."

Kim's head snapped up. "Are you serious?" she breathed.

"Unfortunately, yes. In fact Robb will allow you to sell the house and he'll withdraw his petition for an allowance if you'll agree to wait."

"I can't wait any longer," she said distractedly, Allen suddenly coming to mind, frustration nearly overwhelming her. "What can I do?"

"I think our best option is for you to appear before a judge and show him that Robb's expectations are ridiculous and unfair. You made the visit to Evanston just like he requested, you submitted your financial statements and have basically done everything to show your cooperation with them. I think if we show that to a judge, he'll overturn Robb's grievances and hopefully grant you the divorce despite Robb's contest."

"It sounds too easy," Kim said suspiciously.

"It won't be easy," he clarified. "It will require character references for both of you, a detailed description of your marriage as well as Robb's abandonment. Job histories, police reports, possible psychological profiles on you, him and Jackson, and after all that there is a still a chance the judge won't approve it and we'll be right back where we started. Meanwhile we'll have to find some way to appease Robb—probably agree to the allowance to give us some time. It will require a lot more legal work than this divorce. I'll cut my time where I can but court fees alone will be a definite strain."

Kim let out a long breath and tried to gather her thoughts. "Can I think about this?"

"Of course. We have until next Friday to submit the statements I mentioned earlier if we keep going as we are right now, but if you decide to take this to court I'll need to petition for a court date soon."

"When do you think we would get in?"

"If we're lucky, we'll get a date in late March, but that's fairly optimistic."

Kim wanted to scream and cry and laugh all at the same time; this was insane. But she just sat there frozen by the defeat she felt.

"Give me the weekend to decide. I'll call you on Monday."

"Alright, and Kim?"

"Yeah."

"For what it's worth, I'm sorry."

Kim smiled weakly. "Thanks, I do appreciate all your work on this."

By the time Kim got home she was completely spent, emotionally and physically. Jackson was sleeping over at a friend's house and she wished he were home, if only to keep her mind off the decisions that were oppressing her. It was too much all at once. Tomorrow, she told herself. Tomorrow she would figure it out—tonight she needed a break. Her parents asked what was bothering her, but she couldn't bear to explain it and they accepted that. She considered calling Allen, but they had unofficially set up Wednesdays and Sundays for their phone dates. The more they got to know each other the more difficult it became to pretend they were just friends—they needed to limit their contact. Instead she tried to watch TV, but it held no interest for her and when Maddie called to see if she wanted to come over and help address wedding invitations she readily agreed. What would have seemed a tedious task that morning became a welcome reprieve from her thoughts tonight.

She pulled on a pair of jeans and a hip-length white shirt that buttoned up the front. She twisted her hair up into a casual bun and put on a swipe of lipstick. As an afterthought, she outlined her lips with a lip-liner and smiled at the way the color enhanced her subtle features. Maddie had commented just the other day how nice Kim was looking and although she had never considered herself a great beauty, she had come to find a measure of satisfaction in at least the attempt to look a little better; if only for herself. Grabbing her car keys and a box of Wheat Thins for a snack, she headed out the door, refusing to put together Allen's presence in her life and her new interest in her appearance.

Turning up the radio helped her escape her thoughts as she tapped out the beat on the steering wheel. She turned Maddie's corner and slowed down. Allen's Camaro was parked in front of Maddie's apartment, shining in the streetlight as she pulled to a stop beside it. As she stared at the car, she felt certain she should leave—she had already decided not to see him. Because of the new intimacy that had entered their conversations she felt sure that she being with him would complicate matters even more. She leaned her head against the back of the seat and closed her eyes for a moment. Do I leave and kick myself for missing the opportunity or do I give in to my desires and enjoy myself?

She opened her eyes into the glare of approaching headlights and quickly pulled into Maddie's driveway. Hesitating for only another moment, she turned off the car and got out. She was doing nothing inappropriate; she was addressing invitations and her friend's brother happened to be there. She entered without knocking and her eyes were drawn immediately to his. He gave her a guilty smile and shrugged as if to say "I couldn't resist" and she couldn't help but smile back, well aware of the way her pulse quickened and her spirits lifted when she was near him. Maddie rushed over and apologized, but Kim told her that planned repentance was of the devil. Maddie hung her head guiltily, unable to hide her satisfied grin.

Despite her decision to stay, Kim was determined to be careful and for that reason sat across the table from Allen instead of next to him. But then she had to wonder at her wisdom when she realized that she would now see his deep blue eyes, attractive face, broad shoulders...every time she looked up. After the first ten minutes she knew she had made a terrible mistake.

For nearly three hours they painstakingly hand-wrote addresses on hundreds of small cream-colored envelopes, and Kim determined that when she got married she would have her invitations professionally addressed. The thought made her smile. When had she started planning another wedding for herself?

"Penny for your thoughts?" Allen said.

Kim looked up in surprise, unaware that he had been watching her so closely and placed the last invitation on top of the stack. Somehow she hadn't noticed when Matt and Maddie had left the room "Where'd they go?" she asked

Allen nodded towards the kitchen just as Kim heard a giggle from that direction. "You look great tonight, Kim," Allen said quietly.

"And I didn't even know you would be here," she countered lightly, yet she savored the compliment like a fine chocolate.

A slow smile crept across his face and he leaned forward. "I can only imagine what's in store when you're given adequate preparation time."

Kim smiled, but his reference to their future date reminded her of the conversation with Eric that afternoon and her smile faltered. Allen's brow furrowed as her face darkened. "What?"

"I talked to my attorney today."

"Am I to assume from your expression that he didn't bring good news?"

Kim looked up at him, sure that her eyes adequately reflected her dismay. "Robb's threatening to sue me for renting out our house without his consent unless I agree to wait for his release from prison before continuing with the divorce."

Allen laced his fingers together and rested them on his smooth head as he leaned back in the chair, attempting to absorb the information he had just heard. "Can he do that?"

"He probably wouldn't win the lawsuit since he abandoned us and left me with little choice, but it would take months for it to go to trial. One way or another I stay married." She looked at him sadly; here he was so close to her but out of her reach. "My attorney said we could take my case before a judge and petition for a divorce based on Robb's abandonment, criminal record and ridiculous terms, but it will be extensive and expensive."

"How long would it take?" Allen asked thoughtfully.

"He said late March would be optimistic."

Allen let out a breath and rubbed his chin for a moment. "But we have a date on March first!" he said with feigned lightness.

Kim smiled. "I thought of trying to explain that to him, but I didn't think it would help much."

"Is this still about that allowance Robb wants?"

"Yes. Well, maybe," Kim said with a shake of her head. "Eric mentioned once that Robb isn't as interested in these petty details as he is in making his point. I think his point is that he really doesn't want this divorce and he'll simply do anything to prevent it. I don't know that paying the allowance would help him make his point. It's funny that for years he didn't seem to care that he was married at all, except that I made his life as a bum much easier. Yet now that I want out, he refuses."

"He's lost control," Allen said thoughtfully and when Kim looked up at him in confusion he added. "He always had control of you, in one way or another; he was dependent on you but you were co-dependent on him and he knew it. You've finally broken free; he's finally paying for his crimes and he can't stand it. I think your strength makes him feel weak and so he'll do anything he can to force you to do things his way."

Kim blinked, it made so much sense when he put it all together. "So what do I do?"

"Fight," Allen said bluntly and leaned forward again, reaching his hand across the table and gently stroking her arm. "Show him how strong you are and have faith that what you're doing is right."

"You make it seem so easy," she said glancing down at his hand that was now resting on hers. She turned the palm of her hand up and he laced his fingers through hers. A shiver ran down her spine. When she looked up at him the desire in his eyes made her breath catch in her throat.

"Would it be easier to let him have his way?" he asked searchingly.

"No," Kim whispered, looking deep into his eyes as she tried to ignore the ache in her stomach that his touch had ignited. "This waiting is the hardest thing I've ever done."

Just then Matt came around the corner and Allen quickly pulled his hand away. Matt looked between the two of them, turned back around and left, whispering something to Maddie that they couldn't hear.

Kim cleared her throat and stood. "I'd better go," she said as a means to escape, but Allen stood with her.

"I'll walk you out," he said. She thought of protesting but instead she just turned and left, well aware of him following only a few steps behind. When she reached her car she turned to face him and felt the increased intimacy of the darkness, like moonlight on a lake, reflecting itself tenfold. Allen seemed to feel it too. He raised his hand to her face, keeping it just a breath away from actually touching her until, unable to resist, she leaned into it, inhaling deeply as the warmth of his skin caressed her face and eased her heart.

She closed her eyes to savor the moment, aching to press for more, and then emitted a little squeak of surprise when his lips were pressed against her cheek. His other hand came up so that his hands cradled her face. She feared that opening her eyes would make it too real so she kept them closed. She could almost believe that this was one of her fantasies brought to life by her own longings. Never in her life had she wanted something so badly as she wanted his touch to continue. As his lips made their way to her ear and his hands gently slid down her neck to rest upon her shoulders she felt certain her willpower could not hold her back from responding. How she wanted to reach her arms around his back and pull him closer! But her arms remained obediently at her sides. She couldn't respond—wouldn't respond—and sensing her struggle, Allen gently placed one last kiss on her temple and wrapped his arms loosely around her back, resting his chin on the top of her head.

"How much is it going to cost?"

It took a moment for Kim to block out the physical effect he had on her in order to shift gears. "I haven't any idea, but I'm guessing it will be a lot. That's the biggest reason I've considered—"

"Don't consider it," Allen broke in, almost harshly.

"I can barely afford the fees I already have, but I guess I can get a payment plan or something. I'll pay him for one hour a month for the rest of my life."

They lapsed into another silence until finally Allen dropped his arms and stepped back. "I don't think we should see each other again," he whispered and she merely nodded and quickly got into the car while her senses were still intact. It was far too dangerous to be together.

# CHAPTER FIFTEEN

Monday morning Kim began the process of preparing her case for the judge. This time she made sure her attorney agreed that it was the best course of action. He did, and so they began by filing a formal complaint against Robb and his attorney for unethical conduct—a silly attempt to buy some time.

Matt and Maddie's wedding was soon only three weeks away and Kim was so busy helping with last-minute preparations that she had barely any time at all to think about Robb. But on the rare occasion that he did intrude into her thoughts, she felt just a prickle of trepidation; he had accepted their grievance too easily. Eric had expected some kind of counterattack, but Robb's side of the battle had gone strangely silent and although she tried to feel confident about it, she felt a bit nervous instead, and remained on guard.

The phone calls continued between Allen and herself and every time she hung up the phone she was reminded of his embrace, the feel of his body holding her and the warmth of his mouth against her skin. It was a fantasy that made her feel devilish, but a little sexy as well, and she longed for the day when she would finally be free to explore these feelings.

Jackson was fitted for a tux just a week before the wedding, and Kim felt sure her heart would burst when she saw him in it for the first time. On an impulse, she had his picture taken in the tuxedo and when the photo was done, she hung an eight-by-ten on her bedroom wall. His soft brown eyes were so full of life and joy she smiled every time she looked at it.

One night, a few days before the big event, Jackson started asking questions about marriage, temples, why he couldn't go inside and yet she could. Kim explained as well as she could about the sacred nature of temples, how you had to be a grown-up to understand the things that happen there and you had to show that you could make good choices before you went inside. She explained about the promises grown-ups made there and that some of the things were kept secret because people who weren't Mormon wouldn't understand them.

"Being married in the temple means that even after Matt and Maddie die they will still be married, and when they have kids their family will still be together after they die too."

Jackson looked down at his covers and Kim thought she knew what he was about to ask next. "What if they get divorced?"

Kim swallowed. "Well, if they get divorced they won't be married anymore—on earth or in heaven."

"What about their kids, if they can't be a family anymore who will the kids be with in heaven?"

Kim took a few moments to put her words together carefully, and she prayed that Jackson could understand. "Jack, we don't know everything about heaven, or how things will be when we get there. But God has told us that if we live righteously and do the things he asks us to do that we will be happy in heaven. I know I would never be happy in heaven without you and so even though your dad and I aren't married, you and I will be together forever anyway."

Jackson looked up at her then and smiled. "I think you're right," he said with a grin. "When the angels talk to me they say you'll always be my mom, no matter what."

The innocent statement caught Kim off guard and after a moments hesitation she asked, "Angels talk to you?"

"Sometimes."

She'd never heard anyone say anything like this before, and it bothered her to hear it from her son. "When do angels talk to you?"

"In my dreams," he said as if it were the most natural thing in the world.

"Angels talk to you in your dreams?" she repeated slowly.

Jackson nodded, but he looked concerned with his Mom's reaction. "They say that Jesus loves me and you love me too."

"What else do they say?"

"Just what I said, that you'll be my mom forever."

A slow, cold premonition spread through Kim's chest as she digested this information. Why would Jackson be having dreams like this? "And I know where people go when they die," Jackson said and Kim's eyes jumped back to his face. "They stay on earth, just like real people. They help people that are dead learn about Jesus and they help people that are alive do things they want to do."

"Like what?" Kim whispered.

"I don't know," Jackson said, a little deflated. Then he smiled, "But everyone's happy when they die."

Kim nodded slowly. Was he being prepared for something? Her pulse quickened and she swallowed in an attempt to decrease her anxiety. Putting her hand on his head she spoke thoughtfully to him. "If I ever die, Jackson," she said quietly, "I hope you will always remember how much I love you, and because you and I have lived good lives you will always be my boy. Do you understand that?"

Jackson nodded, a look of discomfort on his face. Kim forced a smile and kissed him on the forehead before standing up. She turned off the light and had almost shut the door when she paused. "If you have any more dreams about angels, tell me—okay?"

"Okay," he said and she shut the door softly. She thought about what Jackson had said, and although it bothered her, she didn't feel the anxiety she would expect if it were really something she should worry about.

After saying her prayers and crawling into bed, she reviewed what he had said and felt an odd calming sensation. If Jackson were really being visited by angels, then it had to be for good. Messengers from God wouldn't come to a seven-year old boy for anything else. Lehi's dream was a focal point of the Restored Gospel of Christ, and Joseph's interpretation of the Pharaoh's dream had saved a nation. If Jackson needed dreams to help him understand a difficult concept then she should be grateful; and she should be at peace. Once more she reflected on how hard it was to explain how the sealing powers applied to their situation and she was glad that Jackson had some help in making sense of it all. Maybe his extra knowledge could help her understand it better too.

She and Allen saw each other for the first time in weeks at the wedding breakfast where Maddie had contrived to seat them together, away from the watchful eyes of their parents. Over chicken a la king, wild rice and cheesecake they experienced powerful emotions without a single touch—both well aware of the dangers of any physical contact. It hadn't taken this long for Kim to realize it but as she looked across the table, she knew in her heart that she was desperately in love with this man. And when he smiled at her, and winked, she felt sure she wasn't alone. She was sure that she should be frightened, shocked and scared because she was feeling this way, but she wasn't. She was thrilled, excited and filled by the joy of it. Never could she have imagined this for herself—especially right now, so soon after having her heart broken.

The temple ceremony was beautiful, and Kim's chest tightened as she remembered her wedding day, what a farce it seemed to have been. And then she looked around the room and caught Allen's eye and in that instant she felt the sadness of the past fade away and all she could see was the glory of the future shining brightly in front of her. She smiled then, and Allen smiled back: a shared destiny, just beyond their reach.

They were both in the receiving line throughout the wedding reception and although they exchanged enough smiles and looks to get some looks of interest from their families, they had very few opportunities to talk, which was probably for the best.

Jackson fell asleep on a row of chairs after the bride and groom had left. The last of the guests were trickling out when she reached down to pick him up. A tuxedo-clad pair of arms stretched in front of her; she startled slightly, but then stepped aside. Allen hoisted Jackson into his arms and Kim felt a lump in her throat at the sight of the two of them. Dressed identically, Jackson snuggled to Allen's chest as if he belonged there. She was strangely jealous of them both.

"Lead the way," Allen said and she walked ahead as he followed her to the car. After opening the back door for him, Kim stepped aside as Allen laid Jackson in the backseat and fumbled to fasten a seat belt around his waist as best he could.

He stood up and put his hands in his pockets as he rocked back on his heels, looking at her fondly. "Some day huh?" he finally said.

She took just one step devilishly closer, so that their frosted breath mixed together between them. "Do you mean this was some-day, or someday?" she whispered and a knowing smile lit Allen's face as he interpreted her meaning.

"Both," he said bluntly before they lapsed into a chilly silence. The cold air was numbing, but they were both reluctant to let the mere freezing temperatures shorten this rare opportunity to stand face to face.

"I like the no-earring look," she commented and he lifted a hand to rub his now-naked lobe. He had told her a week or so earlier that his sentence was over and he had mailed the small silver hoop back to its rightful owner.

"And I'm glad to be rid of it," he chuckled.

Kim paused for a moment and then looked at him with narrowed eyes. "My attorney said he's been receiving anonymous payments on my account."

Allen lifted his eyebrows as if surprised to hear it. "Really? How odd."

"So you wouldn't know anything about it then?"

"I think attorneys are incredibly expensive."

Kim wished she weren't smiling. "You didn't answer my question. Are you paying my bills? Because I don't think you should, it isn't—"

"If someone were paying *my* attorney fees I don't think I would be complaining."

"If someone were paying your attorney fees, who had no business paying your attorney fees, I think you should let that person know that it isn't their responsibility."

"It is my responsibility."

"No, it isn't."

"Yes," he said bluntly. "It is."

Kim was about to protest again but Allen stepped very close to her and smiled at the sharp intake of her breath. He ran a finger down her arm and put his mouth very close to her ear. "Have you any idea how much I want to kiss you right now?"

Kim closed her eyes and swallowed. He had no idea how much she wanted him to. "You know," Kim said shakily, willing her heart to stop pounding so hard. "I've watched you kiss lots of married women today."

Allen smiled and bent his head to kiss the curve of her shoulder. "Really?" he whispered and her entire body seemed to sizzle.

"Uh-huh. Your mother . . ." he planted a kiss on her cheek. "Grandma . . ." he kissed her eyebrow and let his lips linger sensuously. "Your sisters . . ." his lips moved to her forehead. "And it makes me wonder—what's one more married woman when you've been kissing so many."

She raised her eyes to meet his then and her lips parted slightly as she watched his face descend toward her. What have I done? She asked herself. But then his lips met hers and her arms wrapped around his neck without a moment's hesitation. His hands gripped her shoulders and then ran down her back until they rested on her hips. Kim doubted she had ever been so aroused and as the kiss deepened she felt sure she could never let go. It felt so good. It felt so right.

Someone honked a horn and they suddenly broke apart. The headlights were glaring and then the car slowly pulled up beside them. Kim's dad rolled down the driver's side window and they both looked guiltily at their shoes. "Do you need a ride somewhere, Allen?" he asked evenly, almost sweetly. From the passenger seat Kim's mother waved at them both.

"Uh," he stammered while straightening up and looking at her. "Actually yes." Kim furrowed her brow and watched as he walked over to the back door of her parents' car. Peggy looked startled,

Todd smiled. "I'll call you tomorrow, Kim," Allen said and she nodded slightly. He got into the car and pulled the door shut before the car drove away.

Kim lifted a hand to her lips and smiled to herself. She should not have done that, but it had felt so good. Not just physically, but on an even higher plane. It felt so right—could that be possible? Kissing Allen had been everything she had fantasized it to be. The memory of his kiss, of the desire and passion that fueled it, made her tingle with warmth again. But now that he was gone the cold air was numbing and she hurried into her car. What on earth Allen was talking about with her folks?

It was almost an hour before Kim's parents got home; a very long sixty minutes. When they walked in, she anxiously ran down the stairs.

"What took you guys so long?" she demanded to know.

"Have we been gone long?" Peggy returned innocently.

"It took me five minutes to get home."

Peggy and Todd exchanged a look. Todd cleared his throat. "I think Allen is a very good man."

"I agree," Peggy said with a nod. "Isn't it interesting that some of the worst struggles in life happen to those who seem to deserve it the least."

Kim's brow furrowed. "You mean Allen?" What had he told them?

Both of her parents looked at her for a moment, then Todd nodded his head. "Him, too."

Kim straightened and then Peggy came and gave her a hug. "Don't get upset, Kim," she said and then pulled back, her hands still on Kim's shoulders. "We explained some things to Allen, and then he explained some things to us." She brushed Kim's hair behind her shoulder and then looked up and met her eyes. "We approve of him completely. He is the kind of man we have always wanted for you."

Kim's eyebrows went up. Had Allen declared himself or something? Had he asked permission to propose to her when she wasn't even divorced yet?

"But stay away from him," Todd broke in. "You have no business being with that man for awhile."

"I . . . I have stayed away from him," Kim reminded them weakly. She wished she didn't feel like a fifteen-year-old kid begging her parents to allow her to date.

"Do better."

"Okay."

Peggy patted her cheek and Todd gave her a shoulder hug before they passed by and went up the stairs. Kim stood rooted in place for another moment or so, wishing she had been there to hear what Allen had said. Then a smile spread across her face as she realized that she didn't have very long to wait. What was one more month when Forever was just ahead of them?

# CHAPTER SIXTEEN

Lieutenant Browning hurried through the last security gate and pounded his fist on the front counter to get the front guard's attention.

"Can I help you?" the guard asked in a patronizing tone.

"I need my cell phone," he said brusquely; he didn't have time to waste.

"Lieutenant . . ."

"Browning," he cut in. She went into the back office and reappeared with his phone.

"You know you're not allowed to use this within the prison, right."

"Yes, I know," he replied curtly and grabbed the phone as he ran out to the parking lot. His day planner was on the passenger seat of his car and he quickly thumbed through it. For a minute he panicked, thinking that he'd lost it, but luckily the card he needed was there. When he received the call at his office that another detective had some information linked to Robb Larksley he had gone through the existing file and found Kim Larksley's business card— just in case. It was good that he had thought to bring it with him: every minute counted now.

He quickly punched in the number, silently praying that she was at her desk.

"Kim Larksley."

"Mrs. Larksley, this is Lt. Browning in Wyoming."

She paused for a minute, obviously not expecting to hear from him again. "Oh, Hello," she finally said cautiously.

"Are you alone?"

After a momentary pause she answered nervously. "Yes, is there something wrong?"

"I just left a friend of your husband's, here at the prison; he gave me some information. Mr. Larksley has an arrangement with someone to harm you, and I need to give you some instructions." It took a minute for the words to sink in; when they did, Kim's chest tightened and she had difficulty breathing. "You can't go home; you need to find someplace that your husband has no knowledge of and go there." He waited for her to speak; when she didn't, he asked, "Did you hear me?"

"Uh, I don't understand," Kim said in a shaky voice.

"Leave work now!" he nearly yelled into the phone. "Your husband has hired someone to kill you. You need to leave."

Her hands started shaking and she clutched the phone with both hands. "He doesn't know where I work, he left before I got this—"

"Mrs. Larksley you are in danger. Leave work—don't go home. Do you understand what I am saying to you?"

"What about my son?" This wasn't making any sense to her.

Browning groaned—he'd forgotten about the son. "Leave work and pick him up. Then go somewhere safe—away from the city if possible. The man he hired was released from this prison yesterday and if he hasn't found you yet he will soon. I know you're afraid, but you don't have time to think this through right now. Do what I say and be sure no one is following you. We're contacting the police department in your area but there isn't much they can do for you until we know exactly who and what we're dealing with. If you can go to a safe place just for a few days it will give us time to update your local authorities and work out some kind of protection for you. Right now your best protection is to not be found. Find a way to call me Friday and I will give you an update."

"Okay," Kim said numbly as she finally overcame her shock and started cleaning up her desk in preparation to leave.

"Do you have someone who can help you? You can't go home for any reason."

*Allen*, Kim thought immediately. Matt and Maddie were on their honeymoon and her parents had left Sunday night for a week's vacation to the Oregon coast to unwind after the wedding. There wasn't any one else she could think of. "Yes, I do. What about my job?"

"If you can transfer me to your supervisor I'll explain."

"I can do that," Kim said distractedly as she tried to organize her thoughts.

"Good. Now get going and don't tell anyone where you'll be if you can help it. Call me Friday."

"Okay," she said as she punched the buttons that would transfer him. As soon as her line was clear she pulled out Allen's card and called his office.

"Doctors Reynold and Jackman," said the chirpy voice of the receptionist.

"Yes, I need to speak with Dr. Jackman."

"I'm sorry, Dr. Jackman is with a patient right now; can I take a message?"

"This is an emergency—I have to talk to him now!" Kim demanded.

The receptionist paused. "Are you a patient?" she asked with obvious annoyance.

"Yes, I am; I have to speak to him," Kim lied.

"Your name?"

"None of your business—get him for me!" Kim yelled. Without another word the line clicked and for a moment Kim thought she had hung up the phone, but then Allen spoke.

"This is Dr. Jackman," he said cautiously.

"Allen, it's Kim," she said shakily and the relief she felt at talking to him quickly brought on the tears. "I need some help."

"What's wrong?" Allen said with concern.

"Robb's hired someone to . . . to find me and Jackson. A lieutenant called me from Wyoming and said I have to go away somewhere. I'm sorry I called you…at work, but I don't know what to do. I'm supposed to find someone to help me and everyone is gone except you."

It took Allen a moment to absorb the information, but then he kicked into high gear. "It's okay, Kim. What do you need?"

"I . . . I need to find someplace to go. And I need someone to go to my house and get me and Jackson some things for a few days."

"I can do that. My parents have a cabin in Kamas—you can go there. Uh, should I pick up Jackson for you?"

"I'm okay to do that, I think," she said, finally getting control of herself.

"Okay. Go to my place. The back door is open and I'll meet you guys there with your stuff. Then we can head up to the cabin. I'll get my afternoon appointments taken care of and meet you there as soon as possible."

"I'm sorry to make this your problem, Allen." Her voice was shaking and she closed her eyes in an attempt to keep control of herself.

"It's not a problem. Get a pen and I'll give you my address."

Kim did as he told her and scribbled the address on a post-it note. Jackson's school was twenty minutes away; but it felt much farther. Every few seconds, Kim glanced in the rear view mirror to be sure she wasn't being followed. This is crazy, she thought to herself. How did this happen? Tears threatened again but she knew she had to remain calm, for Jackson's sake at least.

Jackson was excited to be checked out of school early and his teacher gave Kim brief details about what he could work on while they were 'out of town.' By 1:30 they were safely at Allen's house and all they had to do was wait.

A few minutes after 3:00 Allen walked in bearing bags of clothing and Kim was embarrassed to realize that he had rummaged through her underwear drawer. Calm as always, Allen ushered them out the door and Kim followed him in her car as they drove out of the city and up Parley's canyon. It took over an hour to get to the cabin and yet her heart was still thumping. She didn't relax until the door was shut and locked behind them.

"Wow, this is so cool!" Jackson exclaimed as he looked around. The cabin was basically a big square room with a kitchen on one end, a fireplace on the other and a table and couch in between. A ladder was built-in on one wall and led to a loft half the size of the main room. There was an enclosed corner on the main floor that housed a toilet and mirror—that was the extent of the amenities.

"This is a great place," Kim said in admiration.

"It was a lot of fun when I was a kid, but I haven't been here in years," Allen said as he looked around in admiration as well. "I'm glad I could find it. There isn't any food kept up here though, so I'll run into town; you okay here?"

"Yeah, we'll be fine," Kim said in a less-than-convincing voice. She rubbed her arms in an attempt to warm up a little. February wasn't the best month to take to the hills. Before she knew it and before he thought twice about it, Allen walked to her and gathered her up in a tight embrace. She wrapped her arms tightly around his neck and thought she might melt, the sensation was so intense. She concentrated hard on absorbing the feel of his body so close to hers. It was so good to be held, she wished it wouldn't end. For nearly a minute they stood that way, lost in the experience. Finally, Allen pulled back and looked into her eyes. "Are you sure you're alright?" he asked, his voice thick with concern and probably some other emotions as well.

"I promise," Kim said, smiling up at him. She felt much better.

Allen pulled back, catching her hands for a moment before letting them go. He winked and left her there, watching the door close behind him.

❧

Lt. Browning slammed the phone down again and ran his fingers through his hair. "I can't believe this is happening," he groaned. It seemed everything concerning Robert Larksley was jinxed from the start. Never had he made so many stupid mistakes on one case.

After speaking to Mrs. Larksley on the phone, he had driven back to his office making several calls on the way. When he walked in, the clerk informed him that he had an urgent message to call Detective Peart. Peart was the detective that had clued him in on the Larksley developments. The informant involved was Mr. Larksley's cell mate who, after nearly a month of sitting on the information, finally decided to speak up in hope of chopping a few months off his own sentence. He told them that Robb was infuriated when he received word that his wife wanted a divorce. Robb had obsessed with the situation and said several times that he would never let her get a divorce, yet Mrs. Larksley had persevered, unswayed by his attempts to stop the process. Then Larksley met Luke.

Luke Adams was a small-time gangster with a big mouth. He was finishing up his sentence of three years for assault and drug trafficking. Good behavior meant nothing to Luke and he was one of the few first-time offenders who had served his entire sentence. Browning had never met the guy, but apparently he was a loose cannon with a short fuse.

Robb had met Luke a few weeks ago, just after being informed that his wife was going over his head to petition a judge for the divorce. Together they laid a plan. Robb wanted to convince his wife to stop divorce proceedings. He felt sure that a little fear would work in his favor. Once Luke was released, he would find Kim and 'persuade' her to drop everything.

Luke was released Tuesday morning; their informant waited a day and then asked to speak to someone. That's where Peart and Browning came in. Browning sat through only the first few minutes of the meeting before he'd stormed out to call Mrs. Larksley. Detective Peart had already informed him that Luke had not shown up to the first meeting with his parole officer that morning. Informing Mrs. Larksley immediately seemed like the obvious approach; now he knew he had made a terrible mistake leaving when he did.

After Browning had left the room the informant had given some more very important information. Larksley suspected his wife was seeing a man and had told Luke to watch for a guy: a bald guy in a black car.

Browning knew nothing about Mrs. Larksley's personal life and didn't care to know, but he had instructed her to have someone else pick up her things and if she were seeing someone; he could be the person she would turn to for help.

Mrs. Larksley had already left work and no one answered the phone at her house; he had told her what to do and she was apparently following his instructions perfectly. Her supervisor had given him all the emergency numbers located in her personnel file, but no one answered at any of them. It was now nearly eight p.m.; he had been re-calling all the numbers for nearly six hours. Browning had no way of contacting her and she wouldn't be calling him for two more days. He could only hope that the worst didn't happen.

Allen returned with some basic groceries and together he and Kim made a simple dinner of mac and cheese. They had Twinkies for dessert and were enjoying each other's company so much they almost forgot why they were there. There was no TV, so after dinner they sat in front of the fire and Allen and Kim took turns reading through a stack of children's books to Jackson. They read all the books, except the 'baby books' Jackson found insulting, when Allen glanced at his watch and announced it was nearly 9:00.

Jackson was sitting on Kim's lap—a rare event—and craned his neck around to look at her. "Mom, are we going to sleep here?" he asked. Kim and Allen exchanged looks; she hadn't told him.

"Yes we are, for a couple days anyway," she said giving him a squeeze she hoped was reassuring.

"How come?" he asked.

She took a deep breath and decided she had to tell him the truth. "Your Dad is really mad at me and a friend of his wants to find us, but I don't want him to; so we're taking a vacation." She knew how stupid it sounded, but she also knew that it wouldn't do any good to give him details he wouldn't understand.

Jackson accepted it easily enough. "Is Allen staying with us?"

Kim looked at Allen for the answer to that; they hadn't discussed it, and until this moment she hadn't considered Allen leaving them alone. Looking at Kim, he answered Jackson's question. "I have to go to work tomorrow, at least for a little while, but other than that I plan to stick around. That is, if it's okay with your mom."

"That's fine with his mom," Kim said holding his eyes with her own. Her personal flock of butterflies returned to her stomach and she smiled shyly before pushing Jackson to his feet. "Well, buddy, we'd better get ourselves to bed. Go get your stuff; we'll sleep in the loft," she said and watched him scurry around to comply.

Halfway up the ladder, he looked back at her. "I can get in my pajamas myself, Mom."

"Okay. Tell me when you're ready for me to tuck you in," she called back, but he had already disappeared. She turned around and found Allen watching her.

"What?" she asked self-consciously after a moment.

"You're a great mom, ya know."

Kim blushed at the compliment. "I don't know about that," she plopped down on the couch. Allen was sitting in a rocking chair across from her, gently moving back and forth.

"He's a wonderful kid."

"Do you know I don't remember much about him as a baby? Most of my energy was focused on Robb and making him happy." Kim shook her head as if she couldn't believe it. "Without realizing it, I neglected my little boy. When I should have been reading him stories and taking him on walks, I was worried about my husband, waiting for him to come home, or fighting with him about something. I missed so very much," she said sadly. "And now that things are different I'm amazed that I could have ever allowed it to happen. Sometimes I look at him and I feel like he could slip away from me if I don't hold on tight enough."

Allen said nothing, he just looked at her with warmth and understanding that surprised her. She could feel his longing and she wanted to tell him that someday he'd have a child to love, and then would know just how she felt. But as she looked into his eyes she realized her words were unnecessary; they could both feel it. Against his better judgement, Allen left his spot in the chair and slid next to Kim on the couch. Against her better judgement, she snuggled up to him and took a deep breath, imprinting his scent in her brain. From this moment on, anything even slightly romantic would be associated with this smell. Feeling the tingle of arousal, she told herself she should go now; she stayed right where she was. Several minutes passed without a word, both of them staring into the flames of the dwindling fire, keenly aware of each other. The way her hair tickled his chin, the feel of his heartbeat against her cheek. The tingle intensified as Allen stroked her hair and tightened his arm around her shoulder. She became acutely aware of his warm breath on the back of her neck. She wanted him to kiss her so badly it was painful. She knew she had to leave when she began telling herself that the Lord would understand, that He would overlook it. After all she had been through, after all Robb had done, she deserved a little pleasure and Allen did too. They wouldn't get carried away, they knew better than that. Would one more little kiss, maybe two, really make a big difference in relation to eternity? She wanted to convince herself of it; she wanted to be able to justify it; but she couldn't. Even at this moment in time she couldn't deny the commitments she had with God no matter what. The kiss after the wedding had been too much already, she couldn't risk giving in again. With obvious ambivalence she finally forced herself away from him and off the couch. The look on his face, and the desire in his eyes were easy to read and she took a step back hoping the distance would help.

"My mom reminded me once that I've made covenants with God as well as with Robb," she whispered in a lame attempt to explain why she couldn't stay.

Allen smiled his understanding. "She reminded me of that too, and someday I will be able to appreciate your tenacity at doing what's right."

Kim smiled and gave his hand a squeeze before she turned and made her way up the ladder. Jackson was asleep on the far bed. He had managed to get undressed, but the pajama part just didn't happen. Memories of all the times she had found him like this made her smile. Ever since he was very young, as he would be playing somewhere, he would suddenly become silent. She would go to check on him and find him sleeping. Knowing he wouldn't wake up; she wrestled his limp body into his pajamas and laid him on one of the full-sized beds. She gazed at him then. The dim firelight reflecting off the cabin walls illuminated his face and hair in flickering warmth. Her throat tightened as she thought of the latest card his father had dealt them and she wondered how on earth she could ever help him understand what Robb had done, or tried to do. It broke her heart to think of the pain and confusion he would have someday.

Rather than sleeping in the other bed, she felt the need to keep him close to her so she curled up behind him, holding him tightly. Tears came to her eyes as she felt her son in her arms. She smiled to think that if he were awake he would never allow her to hold him this way. She thought of what he had told her about the angels talking to him and she prayed silently that they wouldn't leave him yet. He muttered something in his sleep and she smiled, pulling him closer to her. *Thank you,* she prayed silently, *thank you so much for giving him to me.* She hugged him tighter and whispered, "I love you, Jack."

# CHAPTER SEVENTEEN

The sounds of someone rummaging around in the kitchen awakened Kim the next morning and she felt a moment of panic before she remembered where she was and that it must be Allen downstairs. Jackson was splayed out on the bed, no longer snuggled against her, and so she quietly made her way to the ladder and climbed down.

"Good morning," Allen said as he pulled the milk out of the fridge.

"Good morning," she answered back and made her way to the 'water closet'. One look in the mirror made her groan. Mascara was smudged all around her eyes and her hair was a mess. She hadn't taken the time to change into her pajamas and looked frumpy in the wrinkled shirt and slacks she'd been wearing the day before. Reality hurts, she decided after a moment of lamentation and then spent a few minutes repairing herself before going in search of clean clothes. Allen had made pretty good decisions about her clothes but had forgotten her make-up bag. So much for wooing him with my beauty, she thought to herself and tucked her hair behind her ears before fluffing her bangs and wishing it made more of a difference in her appearance.

By the time she emerged, Jackson and Allen were sitting at the table eating cereal. Allen was reading the cereal box.

"What does fort-if-eyed mean?" Jackson interrupted as he shoved a large spoonful of cereal into his mouth.

"It means they put extra vitamins in that you can't taste."

"Dats a goo idea."

"Don't talk with your mouth full," Kim admonished while bringing the milk back to the table.

"Thorry," Jackson said, mouth still full. Kim gave him a *that's-not-funny* look and he swallowed. "Sorry, Mom."

Allen chuckled to himself and when Kim turned the same look onto him, he was sufficiently humbled and focused on eating his cereal without another sound. Jackson entertained everyone with a monologue about his great dreams until Allen stood and put his dishes into the sink. "Well, I would love to stay up here with you guys today, but I have appointments I couldn't change."

JOSI S. KILPACK

"I'm sorry, Allen, you don't have to make so many arrange-ments. I'm sure we'll be fine," Kim said, but her voice betrayed her anxiety at being left alone in the mountains.

"It's not a problem, but I don't like the idea of you guys being up here by yourselves. My receptionist will try to get tomorrow cleared, so hopefully I'll be back up here this afternoon and can stay for the weekend."

"That would be great!" Kim said with a little too much enthu-siasm and relief. Allen smiled and Kim continued, "Are you going to tell your folks what's going on?"

"Not yet. I'll just let them know I'm staying at the cabin. They'll probably give me some chores to do. What about your folks? Don't they come home in the next few days?"

"Not 'til Sunday. I should probably leave them a note or some-thing."

"I'll stop by and leave a note telling them that you'll call on Monday if you want me to," Allen offered as he shrugged into his jacket and slipped on his trademark cowboy boots.

"That would be great. Could you also grab my make-up bag? It's in the bathroom upstairs next to—"

"Ah, we're roughing it. You don't need make-up."

"No shower is roughing it. No make-up is down right primi-tive."

"Alright, I'll get it," Allen chuckled and stood up to stomp his feet into his boots. He grabbed his keys off the counter and as he was passing behind Jackson he ruffled his hair. Then he leaned into Kim and for a moment she thought—hoped—that he was going to kiss her. Instead he stopped just inches away and smiled. "Gotcha," he said and gave her a chaste kiss on the forehead. Kim tried to think of a saucy retort but the door shut before she could think of anything.

Jackson found some old board games under one of the beds and they spent the morning playing a rousing game of Monopoly. Impressed that Jackson caught on so fast, she tried to teach him how to play Rook, but it was a little too much for him and they settled on Sorry instead. After lunch, Jackson wanted to play outside but Kim was uneasy about going out and told him they would have to wait for Allen. They continued to entertain themselves, but as the after-noon dragged slowly by, Kim became more and more uneasy. She kept the curtains closed and the doors locked, but still jumped at the slightest sound. Several times, she peeked out the windows to make sure there was nothing unusual outside—not that she had any idea what was normal up here. Over and over she tried to assure herself that everything was fine, but the fluttering in her chest wouldn't go away. At 4:00 she started dinner and Jackson fell asleep on the couch; Kim prayed Allen would return soon.

Kim nearly screamed when the doorknob turned but was able to catch herself. The knock that followed only increased her fear and with her heart racing she approached the door cautiously. Swallowing the panic she felt she looked out the peephole and let out a sigh of relief. Her hands were shaking as she undid the deadbolt and opened the door to let Allen in.

Once inside, Allen noticed the look on her face. "What's the matter?" he asked as he put down the bags he had brought up and hung up his coat on a peg by the door. Kim immediately shut and relocked the door behind him.

"Oh, I don't know." She felt so silly to be on edge like this. "I think things are just getting to me."

"I can imagine," Allen sympathized, "but I'm sure everything will be fine; the cops just need some time to find our lunatic."

"Yeah, I know. I mean, we've done everything we're supposed to do; right?" Kim nearly pleaded. She had never been threatened like this, so she assumed it must be normal to feel the way she did. She was so scared. Having Allen back made her feel much better, but she still felt inexplicably vulnerable and frightened.

"Right," Allen reassured her with a nod and looked around. "It's freezing in here. Didn't you keep the fire going?"

"Well, the wood was outside and I...uh, didn't want to go out." Kim answered, looking down at the winter coat she'd been wearing all day. Her lack of courage made her feel very foolish.

Allen shook his head as if to say 'women!' "I'll just grab a few logs and we'll get it going again."

He went out the side door where the huge pile of firewood was kept and the door bounced shut behind him. Every fall, his father bought a few cords of wood and brought it up to the cabin in his old truck. During the winter the pile had fallen apart a little bit and Allen spent a few minutes restacking it. That finally done, he started loading up his arms when a movement caught his eye. His heart started thumping and he paused for only a split-second before purposely dropping the wood he was holding. Slowly, he crouched down to pick it up again while his eyes darted around trying to determine exactly what he had seen. In hopes of masking his perusal, he started whistling. There was another cabin a few yards to the left and he fixed his gaze at the large space under the porch.

That was the area where he thought he had seen something. After a few moments, something moved again and he felt his neck prickle. If he hadn't been watching so closely, he would have missed it entirely. An animal would have darted for the trees—only a person that didn't want to be seen would have the need to hide. He finished collecting his wood and went calmly back into the cabin. As soon as the door was shut, he dropped the wood and moved quickly towards the kitchen table.

"Kim," he yelled causing her to jump. "Wake up Jackson!"

Kim just stared at him with wide eyes. "Someone's outside; get Jackson now!" As he was barking out the order, he fumbled around under the edge of the table and pulled out a shotgun his dad had always kept there.

"Allen!" Kim nearly screamed when she saw the gun.

"I'm not going to hurt anyone," he reassured her brusquely. "Now put on his shoes." Kim finally went into action and he peeked between the curtains as he dug his keys out of his pocket.

The keys landed near where Kim was fumbling with a disoriented Jackson, trying to get his shoes tied and she looked questioningly at Allen. "I'm going to get his attention while you take my car. Drive into town and go to the sheriff's office. I'll be right behind you in your car."

"I can take my own car; just come with us we'll—"

Allen fixed her with a hard look. "Kim, do what I said." Hopefully, he had been followed from the city today, but he had no real way of knowing how long the 'company' had been hanging around. He wouldn't take the risk of letting her use her car for fear it had been tampered with. His car had a security system, so it would be safe. To get to town, they would have to drive by that cabin with the porch and he knew that if he didn't provide some distraction, the possibilities were frightening. As he peeked out the window, he could just make out what looked like the shape of a small truck hidden a little way down the road, behind a cluster of aspens. Taking a deep breath, he blinked slowly; he couldn't believe this was happening.

Kim got Jackson's shoes on and rushed him into his coat. She had answered his questions shortly with 'we have to go' and 'I'll tell you later'. "We're ready," she finally announced.

"Okay. When I tell you to, run out to my car. Use the keyless entry button as soon as you open the cabin door. Get in and drive into town as fast as you can."

"What about you?" Kim choked, trying to keep her tears at bay.

Allen walked over and gave her a tight hug, willing her to calm down. He pulled back and looked into her eyes. "I will be right behind you. I promise."

"Okay," Kim said shakily as she tried to remember where the Sheriff's office was in Kamas; she remembered noting its location on the way up there; but she was so scared she couldn't remember the exact location..

Allen wiped away the first of her tears with his thumb. "I'll meet you at the Sheriff's office," he said before letting her go. After taking up his position at the back door he waved her to the front one. "Wait for my signal," he said, then counted in his head backward from ten. Ten, nine, eight...at zero he shouted "GO" and watched them only long enough so see them rush out the door. He pulled open his door and bolted outside. Lifting the shotgun to his shoulder, he quickly aimed at a horizontal support beam of the large porch; a beam he knew would splinter and put on a good show but wouldn't affect the integrity of the structure. Just as he was squeezing the trigger, he heard a noise directly behind him. As he turned his head to look, the piece of firewood cracked against his skull.

Kim ran, pulling Jackson behind her and pushing the unlock button on Allen's key chain to unlock the door. She pushed Jackson through the driver's side before slipping quickly behind the wheel and pulling the door shut. She pushed the key into the ignition and turned it but nothing happened. Anxiously she scanned the instrument panel as panic filled her chest; she stared at the stick shift. She had forgotten Allen's car wasn't an automatic; she hadn't driven a standard transmission in years. A small whimper of fear escaped her as she found the clutch with her left foot and pushed it to the floor. Again, she turned the key and this time the engine roared to life. Looking at the transmission pattern, she shoved the ball into reverse and tried to balance the release of the clutch while putting pressure on the gas. The engine died and she wiped furiously at the tears forming in her eyes with her left hand while pressing the clutch back down and turning the key again.

"Mom!" Jackson cried out. She looked up as a man she had never seen before streaked towards the car. Her heart nearly leapt out of her chest as she pressed and released the pedals simultaneously. The car lurched backward, spinning out on the loose gravel. She stomped on the brake when they had cleared the driveway and when she glanced up the man was running ahead of her on the road. With only a split second of thought, she shifted the car into first gear and prayed she wouldn't kill the engine again. The car lurched forward and she had to look at the pattern again to familiarize herself with the location of the higher gears. The man disappeared into the trees along the side of the road and she glanced in her rearview mirror, hoping to see Allen. There was nothing but dust behind her and she swallowed a sob as the fear became too much to keep inside.

The ride was bumpy and rough, partly due to the dirt road, but mostly due to her inexperience with driving the car. Each time she shifted gears, the car lurched and her anxiety increased. Negotiating the sharp curves and turns of the road forced her to slow the car to barely twenty miles an hour and she killed the engine again when she had to slam on the brakes to avoid a deep rut in the road. She was shaking and crying as she re-started the car and nearly screamed when she saw the small truck appear in her rearview mirror. The Camaro sped ahead again, lurching each time she shifted into a new gear, and she drove faster than she should have while screaming for Jackson to put on his seat belt.

He was bawling and Kim could barely see the road through her own frightened tears. "Jackson, put it on," she yelled but he was curled up on his seat and wouldn't move.

"Jackson!" she said with a bit more forced calmness, but he only cried harder. She attempted to reach over and grab his seat belt just as the road took a sharp turn to the left. Grabbing the wheel with both hands she pulled it hard enough to stay on the road just before the car leapt forward again. She looked at the gearshift with concern, she hadn't shifted just then. Was something wrong with the car? She was thrown against the steering wheel again and then realized that it wasn't her driving skills and it wasn't the car. The truck was hitting her from behind.

"Oh, please help me," she said out loud and pressed down the gas pedal while slamming the car into third gear. All her attention focused on keeping the car on the road, but the truck continued to hit into the back and she couldn't seem to get far enough ahead of it. Each time she gained even a few yards of distance the road would turn and she would have to slow down. The left side of the road was mostly level, dotted with cabins and thick trees, but the right side of the road ran parallel to a small river and Kim's heart pounded when she realized there was nearly twenty feet of steep gravel between the narrow road and the water. Jackson had his head in his hands and she yelled for him to put his seat belt on once more before the truck suddenly appeared next to her. She was openly crying now, but couldn't take the time to wipe the tears from her face. If she could only get out of this canyon! The truck rammed into the side of the Camaro and she screamed, increasing her speed, but it made no difference. The Camaro was thrown sideways again and she could feel the right two tires skid slightly on the incline. How much further? she screamed in her head. Where was Allen? She risked a quick glance at Jackson before returning her eyes to the road. She looked back too late to make the curve ahead and although she pulled the wheel as hard as she could, she felt the slam of the truck against the back end of the car and heard the screech of metal on metal as she tried and failed to stay on the road. The over-correction of her steering and the extra force of the truck pushed the back end of the Camaro off the right side of the road too quickly and at too difficult an angle for Kim to have any hope of correcting it, but she tried. She slammed her foot on the accelerator and kept the steering wheel locked to the left, but it only caused the back wheels to spin for a moment before the entire car slid sideways off the road. The trees went sideways first then completely upside down before she heard the busting of the glass.

"Jackson!" she screamed as she covered her face feeling pieces of glass slice at her arms. She then hugged the steering wheel fiercely, hoping it would make up for the fact that she didn't have a seat belt on either. "Jackson!" she said again, but it was part whisper, part sob. The car bounced and crunched down the river-bank before coming to rest on the driver's side door. Everything spun in her mind but she tried to focus. There was so much sound, so much movement but she couldn't hear anything from the passenger side. He should have fallen towards me, she thought. But he wasn't there. She couldn't hear a scream, not a whimper; nothing. When the car stopped she was pinned in by the steering wheel and could feel herself slipping into unconsciousness but she forced herself to look up, to find her son. At first her mind couldn't make sense of the fact that there was no tint on the gray sky that stared back at her until she realized the window was gone, so was the door; and so was Jackson.

# CHAPTER EIGHTEEN

The first thing Allen realized was that he was very cold. After blinking his eyes a few times, he tried to remember where he was. It was almost fully dark, but when he saw the cabin it all came rushing back. When he tried to rise, he moaned in pain. Raising his hand to his head he drew it back and could make out the smear of his own blood. His whole head throbbed and burned. More slowly this time, he moved to a sitting position and looked around. He could feel that his balance was out of whack but with the support of the cabin wall he was able to stand. The dizziness passed after a minute and he staggered towards Kim's car. His breathing was hard and he had to stop often to keep his balance. But he knew he had to hurry—he had to find Kim. Silently, he prayed for the strength he needed and was able to get to the car. He turned the key but nothing happened. After a few more attempts he got out and lifted the hood. He felt like he was moving in slow motion and had to stop several times to get his balance. After a brief inspection he could see that the battery cables had been disconnected. This blasted battery, Allen thought as he tightened the cables and got back into the car. It started easily enough and he pulled out of the driveway. Thank goodness he had told Kim not to take this car, he thought. What would have happened otherwise? With his heart racing, he drove as fast as he dared, wondering how long he had been unconscious.

If only it weren't so dark, he wished silently. His heart was heavy with the possibilities of what could have happened. When he negotiated the last curve out of the canyon, his stomach fell. There were three police cars stopped on the road, lights flashing. Flares illuminated the roadside and a tow truck was nearly perpendicular to the road, its back pointed down the riverbank where several flashlights could be seen moving around in the darkness. Allen pulled off the road and hurried from the car, as best he could, to the nearest police car. After knocking on the window, the officer rolled down the glass. "Can I help you?" he asked curiously.

"What happened here?" Allen said, between gasps for air.

"There was an accident," the officer said. Then seeing Allen's injury for the first time added, "What happened to you?" Allen backed up so that the officer could open the door.

"Some guy hit me with a log and took off after my uh, girl-friend's car."

The officer looked toward the tow truck. "What kind of car was she driving?"

"A black Camaro." By the look on the officer's face, he knew. He squeezed his eyes shut. No, he pleaded silently—please no. A paramedic was soon there asking Allen questions and proceeding to clean up the cut on his head. The two-inch gash was just above his left ear. He would probably need stitches, the paramedic said. Allen didn't hear him, he just kept asking questions that the para-medic had no answers for until Allen pushed him out of the way and went to find someone who could tell him what had happened.

He approached the officer he had spoken with earlier, who was now talking with another officer. "Will someone please tell me what the hell is going on," he demanded.

"Sir, do you have information concerning this accident," the second officer asked curtly.

"Tell me what happened!"

The first officer spoke up "A woman went off the road. She and a child have been taken to the University Hospital in Salt Lake."

"Are they okay?" he croaked, his emotions very close to the surface now.

Again the officers exchanged a look. "The woman was injured, but conscious and was transported by ambulance. The boy was thrown from the car when it rolled and he was life-flighted; his condition was serious."

He should never have let her drive his car. He should have listened to Kim and gone with them. Suddenly, he turned back to them "What about the other car?"

"There was no other car, apparently she just—"

"There was another car, it followed her out of the canyon." They didn't seem to believe him, so he launched into a full explanation. They said they needed verification of his story and he swore at them before demanding a cell phone. One of the officers produced a phone and after calling directory assistance he was able to contact the Evanston Police Department. It took several minutes but he finally reached Lt. Browning. Once Browning was on the line, Allen quickly explained who he was and what had happened, and then he handed the phone to the officer and folded his arms, his eyes burning with frustration. Finally, the officers hung up and looked at Allen, sufficiently humbled.

"We'll drive you to Salt Lake and take your information on the way."

"That's fine," Allen answered gruffly. "As long as we leave now."

They were on their way within five minutes. The last thing Allen wanted to do was answer all the stupid questions, but he knew it was necessary. His stomach twisted and ached as he thought about Kim and Jackson. He wanted to believe that everything would be all right, but something in him told him that things would never be the same. Staring out the window, he tried to have hope but his heart was heavy and his chest felt tight. Oh Kim, I'm sorry, he said to himself, I am so very sorry.

The night was long and painful. Allen had found Kim first but she was heavily sedated. She had been lucky, in a sense. She had a mild concussion and a serious gash on her right leg that had required several stitches. A few ribs were cracked and she had many cuts and bruises, but had escaped any serious injury that would have long-term effects. After speaking to her doctor and feeling a great deal of relief, Allen walked to Primary Children's Hospital, where Jackson was. Jackson hadn't been as lucky as his mother. Besides a severely broken leg, ruptured spleen and bruised kidney, he had suffered a massive head trauma and was in a coma. The doctor believed that Jackson had been without oxygen for several minutes, and the severe swelling of the brain stem made it impossible to fully determine the extent of the damage. Allen had graduated from medical school, and as the full spectrum of what he was told sank in, he felt the lump in his throat thicken until he could barely breathe.

"We will run tests intermittently for the next few days, but until the swelling comes down quite a bit we can make no determination. He'll be on a ventilator and feeding tube until we are sure how to proceed. You need to understand that he has sustained damage, but we don't know how much."

A heavy dread descended upon him and Allen realized then that this would not be one of those situations where everything turned out fine in the end. He stayed until Jackson was out of surgery and watched through the glass while the nurses set up the many mechanical devices that would keep him alive. Allen had never felt so empty in his life. It was nearly impossible to see Jackson through all the tubes and wires, and Allen wondered how he would tell Kim.

By morning, Allen's head had been stitched up and he was

sitting next to Kim's bed holding her hand when she first stirred. His heart started racing and the dread settled deeper within him as she tried to orient herself to where she was.

"Good morning," Allen whispered when she turned to look at him.

She stared silently for a few moments, her face blank. "What happened?"

"Don't you remember?" he asked and then wished he hadn't when her eyes suddenly filled with tears. Her face full of panic, she attempted to sit up, but winced in pain and fell back on the pillow.

"Where's Jackson?"

Allen knew he couldn't lie to her, but he so badly wanted to tell her everything would be okay. Even if it weren't true, at least it would keep her from having to deal with everything all at once. He took both of her hands in his own and looked at the floor, trying to gain control of his own emotions. Kim was crying now and he could feel her looking to him for an answer. When he looked up, he couldn't keep his tears back. Knowing he couldn't do anything but tell her the truth, he briefly explained what the doctor had said.

Kim pulled her hands free when he stopped and cupped both hands over her face. "Oh, my gosh," she mumbled into her hands. "Oh, my gosh." She started shaking and Allen moved to sit on the edge of her bed gathering her up in his arms, trying to be careful with her injuries. Clinging to him she sobbed into his shoulder and Allen stroked her hair as he rocked back and forth with her. There was nothing he could say as Kim's body shook in his arms. Eventually, he gave up trying to find a way to make this bearable and he just let his heart break with hers. Several minutes passed before Kim gained control, but she still clung to him as if afraid to let go. Without pulling away she said, "I want to go see him."

Allen swallowed and took a breath. "The doctor said that as soon as you pass the first twenty-four hours you can, but not yet."

Kim pushed away and eyed him as if he were somehow responsible. "They won't let me see my son?" she whispered; her tone menacing.

"Not yet, your leg—"

"I'm going to see my son," she said bluntly and then winced as she crossed her arms across her chest. "Go tell them that."

His first few attempts to explain met only bored looks and repeated refusal to let her go. So finally Allen told the doctor to tell her. Annoyed, the doctor entered the room and returned just a short time later.

"She can go for thirty minutes, but that's all; she has to use a wheelchair." Five minutes later they were on their way down the hall and Allen felt his heart sink lower and lower the closer they got to Jackson's room. When they arrived at the intensive care unit, the nurse informed them that only one person was allowed in the room at a time, so Allen wheeled Kim inside before closing the door. Each of the ICU rooms had a large window so Allen could see what was happening inside the room. He stood in the hall and watched. Kim simply stared at her son for a few moments as if asking herself if it was really him. His hair had been shaved off, a large bandage covered most of the right side of his face and the ventilator tube covered his mouth and chin. The paleness of his skin made the other scrapes and cuts stand out grotesquely and Allen could feel Kim's reluctance as she reached out her hand to touch his face. She rested her palm against the uncovered side of his face and then took his hand that wasn't hooked up to the IV in both of hers. He watched her talk to him haltingly until she couldn't control herself any longer and finally laid her head against his arm and sobbed. A strangled cry rose from his own throat and finally Allen had to walk away; he couldn't bear to watch anymore. He waited 45 minutes and then went into get her. She wouldn't talk as he pushed her back to her room, she just wiped at the tears that kept coming.

Once she was settled, he tried to get her to talk, but she told him she was too tired.

"I'll go make some calls. Would you like a blessing later?"

She nodded while staring blankly at the cuts on her arms. "Call Bishop Scott from my ward. He'll come."

By looking in the phone book and matching up the address, he was able to find Bishop Scott's phone number. Next, he called his parents and then left a message for Kim's folks on their answering machine. He had already made arrangements for today's appointments at work and after making all the calls he could think of he finally had nothing left to do but to call Lt. Browning. After finding the number in his pocket he dialed the number.

After the lieutenant answered, Allen briefly explained what had happened.

"Will the boy be alright?" Browning asked, feeling sick to his stomach.

"It doesn't look good, but they won't know for awhile yet."

Browning cursed under his breath as he pushed his fingers through his hair again. "Allen, are you bald?" he asked after a moment.

"Yes, I am," Allen answered, perplexed by the question.

Browning swallowed and briefly explained what had happened after he talked to Kim. He apologized and Allen assured him it couldn't be helped. They had never expected that he would be recognized and followed. If they had known . . . well, it didn't matter now. "Do you have any more information on the guy?"

"Actually, we got more information about an hour ago. He took his truck to a mechanic outside of Heber, Utah. The front was pretty smashed up and the radiator had been punctured. He drove it as far as he could and then stopped to get it fixed. He tried to pay for it with Mrs. Larksley's wedding ring."

If there was any possible thing that could make Allen feel worse, this was it. Kim had told him about the wedding ring experience and they had laughed about it. Now he knew that Robb had paid his mercenary with Kim's own ring; what a sick freak.

Browning continued. "The mechanic called the sheriff to check the license plate. The truck had been stolen in Evanston on Wednesday night. The driver is being held in Heber until we can send some guys down to pick him up. We'll probably need you as a witness, if it gets that far."

"Whatever it takes," Allen said with disgust.

"I appreciate it if you'll keep me up to date on how they're both doing."

"Yeah, sure. That's not a problem," Allen said distractedly already trying to decide what to tell Kim and what to leave out for now.

"Until then will you do me a favor?"

"Sure, what do you need?"

Allen hung up the phone a few minutes later, satisfied that at least some form of moral justice would be exercised, and leaned back in his seat closing his eyes. He was exhausted. Physically and mentally. If only it were possible to go to sleep and wake up a month from now, when everyone was more used to the situation. He didn't know how he could keep looking into Kim's face and see the sorrow in her eyes. And Jackson. How could they watch him day after day, knowing that the sweet vibrant boy he had been would never return? If there was only something he could do. But there was nothing. Nothing he could do or say could change anything that had happened. He earned his living helping people accept and conquer their challenges, but now, when it was really important, now that it affected the people he loved, he was helpless.

When he returned to Kim's room, her doctor was just leaving.

He explained that Kim would need to stay in the hospital for two more days to finish her antibiotic treatments but could leave after that. Allen nodded a thank you and let himself into Kim's room.

"I can't roll on my side," Kim said when he sat down, as if that was the worst thing she had to deal with right now.

"How do you feel?" Allen said as he slipped his hand over hers.

"I've never felt worse in my life," she said shakily and the tears welled up in her eyes again. She stared at the ceiling and tried to blink them away, but it didn't work. "I can't do this, Allen," she whispered and turned her face away.

Allen took her hand and rubbed it in his. "Oh, Kim," he whispered, but there was nothing he could say to make it better and they both knew it. Eventually, Kim drifted off to sleep. That afternoon his parents arrived. When he had called them, they asked what they could do to help. He said nothing, but now that they were here he felt a great relief to have someone to talk with. He led them to Jackson's window and they all stared silently at the painfully still form on the other side of the glass. It had only been a week since they had watched him sneaking mints from the wedding reception buffet table. They asked about Kim and he told them how withdrawn she was, how it worried him, and how helpless he felt. Just having someone listen to him and offer their support helped.

"You've been here all night, Allen. You should go home and get some sleep," his mother said.

Allen shook his head. "I can't; Kim will be waking up soon and her Bishop will be here at seven to give her a blessing: I need to be with her." His parents exchanged a look over his head.

"Kim is going to need you as much tomorrow as she does today, and if you don't take care of yourself you won't be able to help her."

Allen was silent. They were right; he knew that. But the thought of leaving Kim made his entire soul protest. "I just...can't leave her alone; what if something happens to Jackson while I'm gone?"

Tina patted his hand. "I'll stay with her until you come back."

Allen looked up, his mother barely knew Kim. "You don't have to do that," he said, reluctant to turn over his job as sentry.

She was already nodding before he finished. "Allen," was all she said, but the look on her face told him that his argument would make no headway with her. He dropped his head and tried to hold back a sob as all the emotions seemed to push through. Tina pulled him into her arms as he finally released his own pain. He couldn't remember the last time, if ever, he had felt such torment, and the smell of his mother's perfume and the comforting weight of his father's hand on his back reminded him of how important families are. The thought brought to mind that Kim, after having only recently given up on keeping her own little family together, was now losing the person she had always needed and loved the most. How on earth would she ever make peace with this?

# CHAPTER NINETEEN

As soon as Lt. Browning received Allen's overnight package, he called Detective Peart and arranged for the two of them to meet at the prison. It was time to pay a visit to Mr. Robert Larksley.

Just as the last time they met, Larksley shuffled in with the same arrogant, cocky look on his face. He recognized Browning and nodded in his direction as if they were old friends. Once he was seated Browning sat in the other chair. "How's Luke?" the lieutenant asked.

"Luke who?" Robb said with an innocent smile.

"You know a lot of Lukes, huh?"

Robb shrugged and fumbled with a cigarette. With his hands cuffed it was awkward to light up and he dropped it on the floor. He motioned for Browning to help him out. Browning didn't move. Peart remained where he was leaning against the wall. They both continued to fix Robb with a cold stare.

"This particular Luke was arrested in Utah a few days ago," Browning continued. He watched for a reaction in Robb's eyes, but saw nothing except perhaps a sick curiosity. "He was involved in an accident."

"Really," Robb said with feigned interest. "He should be more careful."

"It's interesting that he seems to know you so well. In fact, he knew an awful lot about your family." There was a flicker of something this time, but Robb still managed to stare at him with a bored expression on his face. "We also had the opportunity to chat with another friend of yours; I believe the two of you were roomies up until a few days ago." Now Robb's tension showed easily. "And I wanted to be the first to tell you that your man failed." He reached into his inner jacket pocket, took out a Polaroid photo and flipped it so that it landed in front of Robb.

Robb picked it up but couldn't seem to make out what the picture was. "Your wife is fine, Mr. Larksley. But it looks as if your son might not make it." Robb's eyes went wide and he drew the photo closer to his face, then dropped it on the table as if it had burned him. He had a frantic look on his face, but didn't say a word. "Since you're already in custody, I don't need to have a warrant, but I would like to tell you that you are charged with conspiracy to commit murder and you have the right to remain silent. You have the right to an attorney and if you cannot afford an attorney, one will be appointed for you."

"He wasn't supposed to hurt her," Robb croaked, as Browning stood after a moment of silence. "He was just going to follow her around, convince her to stop the divorce, he wasn't—" he looked down at his hands and swallowed. "Jackson," he whispered and lifted his hands to cover his face.

Browning just stared at him for a long moment before leaving the room without another word.

# CHAPTER TWENTY

Kim's doctors allowed her to go see Jackson twice a day for an hour each time. Bishop Scott and Allen gave blessings to both Kim and Jackson. Through the Spirit, Allen promised her support and the ability to cope. He also said that all things taken away would someday be restored through living righteously. She said nothing when the blessing ended, she didn't thank them. Allen knew it had angered her far more than it had helped and wished he could have given her more hope, but he couldn't deny the prompting of the Spirit. Bishop Scott was the mouthpiece for Jackson's blessing and when he finally said 'Amen' everyone present felt the heaviness of the fact that there had been no promise of recovery. In fact, the blessing taught about the plan of salvation and the restoration of family units in the next life. Kim found no comfort in it and during the days following she became very distant and depressed.

Allen had been unable to locate her parents to tell them what had happened. They finally returned home Sunday morning. They called Matt and Maddie in Jackson Hole. Allen hoped that with her family around, Kim would open up more but instead she became more withdrawn then ever.

Sunday night her room was full of people offering their support. Allen watched her from the doorway as she nodded her thanks and attempted a smile in the direction of some kind remark. But as he looked at her face and saw the pain in her eyes, he realized she was shutting down.

Since the moment he had told her about Jackson's condition and her breakdown in Jack's room, she had shown very little emotion. Her eyes found his once as he watched, but she looked quickly away and Allen finally left the room, searching his mind for some way to help her. Once again he came up with nothing.

Despite the fact that she barely spoke to him, he made sure he was at the hospital every night to take her down for her 6:00 visit with her son. Peggy came every morning to help her with her morning visit with Jackson and stayed for as long as she could but Kim didn't even seem to notice. All she seemed to think about was Jackson—no one else mattered and she all but ignored their presence.

Kim was supposed to be released on Tuesday, but she argued with everyone she could find until they let her stay another day. How could she leave him here alone? She lived in East Sandy—almost thirty minutes away; how could she be so far away from him? Peggy had come that morning and stayed until Kim told her to go home. At first Peggy refused, but when Kim yelled that she didn't need her anymore Peggy left the room and didn't come back. Couldn't people understand that she just wanted to be left alone? The sedatives and pain pills the nurses gave her were a lifeline and it was only because of them that she could sleep without being haunted by the nightmares she knew were reality. When she was awake, all she could think about was Jackson. How could this have happened? Over and over she relived what she could remember about the accident. She should have made sure he was buckled in. She should have at least put him in the back seat. She should never have listened to Allen and taken his car. This would never have happened if she hadn't taken that stupid car. Part of her knew she was being unfair, but she refused to give into it. Her son was in a coma, she had every right to be angry and she wouldn't let it go. She needed something to sustain her and anger was the easy choice.

After work on Tuesday, Allen stopped by to take her to see Jackson, as usual. Kim barely looked at him. He didn't try too hard to get her to talk until after they had returned from her visit. The nurse saw them return and had offered Kim a pain pill that she quickly swallowed with a small cup of water. She tossed the cup into the trash and waved Allen away when he tried to help her from the wheelchair to the bed.

"Kim, I have an idea," Allen said after she got into the bed by herself. Kim looked at him, obviously not enthusiastic. Allen swallowed his hurt and continued, "My house is a lot closer to the hospital than your parents' home. I want you to stay there, so you can be closer to Jackson."

"You live there."

"Yeah, I know that," he said in an attempt at humor. It didn't work. "I'm going to stay with my folks until—"

"Until what?" Kim asked bitterly; her mood swings had become frequent and severe. "Until my son dies," she spat at him, and the heat beneath her words stung them both.

"That's not fair, Kim. You know that isn't what I meant."

"Well, it's what you were going to say, isn't it?" Her eyes flashed with anger.

"No, it wasn't," he answered sharply. "I was going to say until

Jackson leaves the hospital."

Kim stared at him and felt her anger melt away. What was she doing? He was doing everything he could think of to help her; finally she shook her head. "I'm sorry, Allen. What is wrong with me?" she whispered as she tipped her head back on her bed and sighed. She felt so helpless and out of control. A week ago things had been going so well; she felt so confident in herself and her decisions. Now she had lost everything. She felt weak and lifeless, unable to control anything, and the emptiness—the emptiness was overwhelming. It seemed only a matter of time before she would be unable to feel anything. Worse yet, part of her longed for the oblivion.

"Everything's wrong, Kim," Allen said while taking her hand. The tenderness of his touch sparked her feelings for him but she pushed them away. She couldn't deal with them now. "So what do you think about the house?"

"It's really nice of you, Allen, but I can't kick you out of the house you've barely lived in."

"I wouldn't offer it if I weren't totally comfortable with the plan. There's room at my parents now and they said I can have it for as long as I need it."

Kim hated the idea. She truly didn't want to be a burden on anyone, and she knew she was currently a burden on everyone. But still, she couldn't deny how much better she would feel to be closer to Jackson. The thought of leaving Jackson at all made her insides tighten with fear, the opportunity to be twenty minutes closer eased those feeling considerably.

"Allen, I don't know, it seems so..."

"Kim, please. There is so little I can do to help you; this is something I *can* do. Please let me do this."

Kim looked at him—really looked at him for the first time in days—and saw the love in his eyes; the tenderness broke down some of the walls she had built. She had forced herself to be strong and to not let anyone see how deep her torment really was. But now, seeing her own pain reflected in his face, brought tears to her eyes. Clenching her eyes closed she tried to push the pain back down but couldn't do it; the feelings were too strong. Allen leaned toward her and stroked her hair, waiting for an invitation to comfort her even more. When she opened her eyes again she lifted a hand towards him and he gathered her into his arms.

"How can I leave him?" she whispered into his shoulder. Allen didn't answer. It wasn't a question that anyone could answer. She cried for a long time and finally let go of Allen when she hadn't the strength to stay upright. She laid back down on the pillow and looked at him. "I need him so much, Allen," she whispered as she closed her eyes with exhaustion.

Allen nodded. "I know," he said and tucked her hair behind her ear as she lapsed into sleep. "I know you do." He stood and bent down to lay a lingering kiss on her temple.

She was drifting off to the numb sleep she desperately needed but she felt the heat of his mouth against her skin, the warmth of his breath on her hair and wished she could feel the closeness they had once shared, but she couldn't find it. She felt disconnected from everything, even Jackson, and she wondered if she could survive this inner loneliness for even another day.

Peggy came in the morning to help Kim pack up, and Kim apologized for yelling at her the day before. Peggy smiled and said she understood. Kim wished that *she* did. Kim told her mom about Allen's offer and after discussing it they both agreed it would be good for her to stay in his home. Peggy called Allen's work and left a message. When he called back Peggy made sure the offer was still valid and Allen eagerly said that it was, he would meet them at the hospital at 6:00. Peggy stayed all day, and they spent almost every minute sitting outside Jackson's room, watching through the glass.

Matt and Maddie came in the late afternoon and after the uneasy conversation Kim walked away and left the three of them there together. She didn't have the energy or the desire to talk anymore. Silently, she stared through the glass, and watched as the nurse emptied Jackson's catheter and changed the dressing on his face. Kim hadn't seen the head trauma and caught her breath when the old bandage was removed. There was a sharp jagged cut that began above his eyebrow, slashed across his forehead, down the side of his face and across his cheek. It was stitched and stapled together which made her stomach churn. The entire side of his face was mottled with purple and green bruises and was so swollen she could barely see his right eye. There was also a large bump and scrape just above his temple. For the first time, Kim was grateful he was in a coma; she could only imagine how much pain he would be in otherwise.

She was still standing there when Allen arrived. He watched her, wishing she would share her thoughts. Last night she had opened up to him a little, but he could see in her face that it wasn't that way tonight. He spoke with Matt, Maddie and Peggy, convincing them all that he could see her home just fine and they eventually left. Kim barely glanced in their direction when they told her goodbye. The nurse informed Kim that she could go in and so without even saying hello to Allen she hurried into Jackson's room.

Allen had taken the day off and gone back to the cabin with his Dad early that morning. He picked up Kim and Jackson's things as well as Kim's car which he'd left at the Sheriffs office. The Camaro had been towed to a local repair shop and Allen had met an insurance adjuster there to determine the extent of the damage. It had surprised and sickened him to see the condition of the car as he walked slowly around it taking in every horrific detail. The claim adjuster pronounced it 'totaled.'

Now he was looking at the human results of the accident and after only a few minutes had to walk away. He found Jackson's nurse and asked if there had been any change in his condition. She told him that as of this morning, the swelling around the brain stem had still not gone down enough to do any further testing. Allen knew that was a bad sign; the longer Jackson stayed this way, the less hope there was for any recovery at all. They said it could take as long as six weeks before they could get conclusive test results, but as with most things of this nature, the sooner, the better.

For the full hour, Kim talked to her son. At other visits she brought a book and read it aloud, but not today. Today she would be leaving him here all alone, and she hated the fact that she wouldn't be near him. She would be far away in a strange place while he laid here connected by tubes to the machines that were keeping him alive. Several times she apologized to him, hoping he would understand, praying nothing would happen while she was away, until finally she broke down and sobbed. She was leaving him and it broke her heart. After the hour was up, she reluctantly left the room. Allen looked up at her as she walked toward him. She attempted to smile but her heart wasn't in it. Allen picked up her bag and they walked to his car in silence.

Once on their way, Allen asked Kim what she talked to Jackson about during her visits. She stared out the window and he wondered if he was going to get the silent treatment again.

"I saw a show on TV once where a husband, wife and baby all had AIDS," she said softly. "The husband got really sick and everyone knew he was dying. The wife stayed with him all that day while he came in and out of consciousness and she remembered for him."

"Remembered?" Allen questioned.

"She talked about the things they had done. Their wedding, vacations, their daughter—the happy things they had shared during their life."

"And that's what you do with Jackson?" Allen asked.

"Yes. Maybe he can hear me," she fiddled with the buttons of her sweater and sniffled. "I know some people say he can't, but I don't believe it. How do they know that? When he comes out of this I want him to know I was there, so I talk about things only I would know...I just wish I had more memories to share with him; there aren't as many as there should be."

When he gets better, Allen repeated in his head; not if. He was deeply moved by Kim's dedication, but he knew she was denying the truth and he ached for her. It was inevitable that the day would come when she would have to face reality and Allen wondered if she would be able to do that. It was obvious that for now she was trying to convince herself that everything would turn out okay, and anyone who disagreed with her was the enemy. Allen had dealt with people who never got over the denial. Silently he prayed that she would move through this phase of the grieving process quickly—for her own sake.

They pulled up in the driveway and Allen carried her things into the house for her before giving her back the keys to her car. She stared at them for a moment and then dropped them into her purse. He showed her the basics: where the towels were kept, how to work the microwave—things like that. Then he opened the door to the bedroom—his bedroom. The bag he had packed for her and had taken to the cabin was at the foot of the bed and she walked slowly over to it before stopping to stare.

Allen watched from the doorway as she hesitantly reached down and pulled the handles apart. She put her hand inside the bag, pulled out Jackson's Batman pajamas and with a little whimper lifted them to her face. For a moment, she closed her eyes, when she opened them she looked at Allen who was taken back by the anger in her face."You're doing this because you feel guilty, don't you." It wasn't a question.

Allen took a deep breath. "No," he replied with all the calmness he could muster. "I'm doing this because I care about you and your son and I . . ."

"You should never have made us go," she whispered and looked away.

Allen felt like he had just been slapped and he didn't know how to respond.

"If you hadn't told us to drive down that canyon none of this would have happened," she suddenly turned and looked at him with such coldness he felt frozen by it. "I SHOULDN'T HAVE LISTENED TO YOU!" she screamed, throwing the pajamas on the floor in front of him. "I shouldn't have taken that stupid car, Allen! It was a stick shift and I couldn't drive it. It stalled and—" her hands came up and covered her face as her shoulders started to shake. "AND IT'S ALL YOUR FAULT!" she screamed. Her fury startled him. "It's all your fault," she repeated quietly, squeezing her eyes shut and sitting on the edge of the bed before raising her hands to her face again. "It's all your fault." It was a whisper. "It's all your fault."

Part of Allen wanted to yell back at her and defend himself but the bigger part of him knew better. Instead, he sat beside her and pulled her into his chest just as he had that first day in the hospital; and just as before she clung to him desperately. She was still muttering "It's all your fault. It's all your fault." But then it changed. "It's all my fault. It's all my fault. It's all my fault." And Allen could do nothing but hold her.

She sobbed until she had barely enough energy to draw a breath. Then Allen moved off the bed and let her lie down. She rolled on her side, facing him and buried her face in the pillow as he maneuvered the blankets out from under her. He watched her for another moment, his heart heavy and his throat thick and then with one hand on the edge of the mattress and one braced on the headboard he bent to kiss her forehead before he left.

Her eyes, red and swollen from crying opened and she stared at him for a moment before she whispered, "Stay with me." Allen swallowed, but didn't speak as he attempted to stand up. She twisted quickly onto her back and reached her arms around his neck, pulling him toward her. "Allen, please stay with me."

The desperation in her voice made his protests catch in his throat, and the desire and fear in her eyes reminded him of the many times he wished he could do something to take away her pain. Then he reminded himself of the accusations she had hurled at him minutes before, hoping that the memory of her fury would help him pull away. But her lips parted and her eyes pleaded with him and despite all his reasons to leave he felt powerless. It was ironic how closely related anger and passion could be. Her hands moved from his neck down his back to his waist and he sucked in his breath as she untucked his shirt and slid her hands up and over the bare skin of his chest. *This is wrong, this is so wrong,* he chanted in his mind but he was entranced by her stare, and the desires he had been suppressing for so long became stronger than himself. In a moment of clarity, he attempted to pull back but she simply raised with him, moving her hands around to his back and pulling him against her.

"Kim," he choked, but his heart was racing and his body was responding in a way that made his verbal protests null and void. She held his eyes as she moved her face towards his and raised onto her knees. Torn between panic and a wanting he had never known, he found himself leaning into her; and then she kissed him, and he kissed her back. It began as sweet and tender, but the electricity that passed between them turned it passionate and he wrapped his arms around her back and pressed her body against his. The feel of her softness against was more than his willpower could take and he lowered her to the bed. The initial kiss spread from her mouth to her neck, to the hollow of her throat and her fingers dug into his shoulders as she arched her back and pulled him back up to her mouth. He rolled onto his back. She lifted off of his chest and touched his face softly, before lowering her lips to his cheek, his ear, his forehead. Allen closed his eyes as the burning heat of her mouth left a blazing trail upon his face and neck. Her mouth returned to meet his and he moaned with the feelings erupting within himself.

All the reasons not to do this vanished next to all the reasons to follow through with it. All the desires he would satisfy seemed to take over and he pulled her closer, frantically wanting to take all he could get. She pressed herself against him. He pressed back and the electricity ignited. Without conscious thought he ran his hands from her shoulders, down her sides to her waist and slid one hand under the back of her shirt while pulling her back to his mouth. Her skin was warm and soft beneath his hand as it made a slow ascent up her back. Then like a flash he realized that the silky fabric he felt on the back of his hand was her temple garment and his hand seemed to burn. All the thoughts he had pushed away came back in a rushing torrent. *What was happening? What were they doing?* Quickly, he turned and dumped her on the other side of the bed. Then he sat up and turned so that he was on the edge of the bed, taking several deep breaths in an attempt to gain control of himself. The severity of what they had done continued to descend like a thunderstorm and he turned to look at Kim. She was watching him with a mixed look of shock and passion, a hand on her heaving chest. Then her eyes went wide with realization. They held each other's eyes in a shared look of turmoil until in an instant they were both moving. Kim leapt off the opposite side of the bed and crossed her arms over her chest as if to cover herself. Allen stood as well, still trying to control his breathing, careful to keep his back to her for the moment. The kiss after the wedding had been just that, a kiss. They had both known it wouldn't become any more than that, and they had known even that was not right. But this; this was entirely different. Their intent had been to completely fulfill themselves this time.

"Kim, I'm sorry... I don't know what..."

"No, I started it...Oh, my gosh, what have I done." The panic in her voice made him turn, and his heart sank as he realized she was crying.

"Please don't cry, Kim," Allen pleaded. "Please don't." But she was. With a hand over her mouth and her tears spilling over, Allen moved towards her, but she backed away from him and shook her head.

"I'm so sorry, Kim. Please—" But she clenched her eyes shut and continued to shake her head, as if willing away what had happened. Allen swallowed. "Nothing happened, Kim. Nothing happened." And she nodded as if she believed him; but neither of them really did. Something had happened, and it scared them both. His mind spun as he tried to find some way to comfort her, justify what they had done but he couldn't forget that she was still married and they had been so close to... "I...I, uh, better go," he finally said when he realized the best thing he could do would be to leave her alone. Shutting the bedroom door behind him, he placed his forehead against the wall and shook his head. What had they done to themselves? He asked himself and wondered how he could have let himself fall into the trap. And how would he and Kim get past this?

After Allen left, Kim slumped to the floor, leaning against the wall, hugging her knees to her chest and noticing pain in her chest and leg that she wished she'd have noticed five minutes earlier. Was she so desperate for comfort that she was willing to destroy herself? And Allen too? Her stomach was in knots and she groaned out loud, trying to think of what to do. But her thoughts were so jumbled and disconnected. Allen had been so good to her, and yet every time she was around him she found herself angry and irritable. She reviewed her behavior toward him since the accident and wondered why he kept coming back. Then she remembered the things she had said to him tonight and her stomach sank even further; how could she possibly blame him for the accident? And even after all that she had said, he had said nothing, he just held her. Why is this happening to me? She screamed in her mind, what did I do to deserve this. The thought came to her that she should pray, ask for the Lord's help, but she couldn't—especially now.

She finally peeled herself off the floor and lay on the bed. Allen's bed, she reminded herself and buried her face in the pillow. The sheets and pillowcase smelled like laundry detergent, but by pressing the pillow hard against her face she could smell him. The slightly musky scent of his cologne brought back all the emotions of earlier and even though it was wrong to do so, she longed for him— a longing so deep and so real it was painful. She dozed, but her sleep was restless and every time she fell back to sleep, images of Allen and herself would float through her mind and she would jolt awake wishing he were there. And then there was Jackson. Over and over she watched him play and run toward her, so full of life. And suddenly, as if a TV channel was changed, she would see him in his hospital bed nearly covered with tubes and bandages. She would try desperately to flip the channel back, but she never could. And then the scene would go black and she would call out his name, which would startle her awake again. After hours and hours of the exhausting routine, she finally fell into a sound sleep just as the room began to lighten with gray light of the coming dawn.

It was almost ten o'clock when she awoke and she panicked when she realized Jackson had been alone for more than twelve hours. Her body protested when she tried to get out of bed and she wondered why she hadn't felt that way when Allen had been with her. Then she remembered the pain pill she'd taken before leaving the hospital. She took another one now and hoped it would give her the same physical relief. She took only enough time to change her clothes and brush her hair behind her ears before she hurried to the hospital. But when she got there, Jackson was the same. She stayed all day and made the nurses show her how to do the intricate details of his care. For the first time, Allen never came. At 9:00 that night she left and when she climbed into Allen's bed this time she fell into a deep sleep right away.

Friday and Saturday were spent in much the same way. Her parents came every day for several hours and although she was grateful for the support, she longed for solitude. Yet, when she was alone she longed to be with someone. Allen's absence was never out of her mind, and she felt hollow inside without him. She still couldn't make sense of her actions that night, and was unsure of what she should do now. She was still, technically, a married woman, even though admitting it to herself was bitter. Even after all Robb had done, the pain he had inflicted, she was still bound to him; the thought was infuriating.

Sure that she had driven Allen away for good, she nearly tackled him when he suddenly appeared at the window of Jackson's room on Sunday evening. She had gone to find more books and was on her way back when she looked up and saw him standing there. She was so happy to see him, that without thinking, she ran the last few steps to him and jumped up to give him a fierce hug as if it were the most natural thing in the world. That's when the burn of her healing ribs brought their last encounter rushing back and she quickly pulled away, feeling the warmth of embarrassment fill her face. "I'm sorry, Allen. I . . . uh," Kim stammered.

"Forgot?" he interjected quickly. Then he quickly looked back at Jackson, "I think we need to talk."

Kim nodded and glanced back at Jackson through the glass before following Allen to a small empty waiting room. Kim sat down first and Allen sat across from her. They were both terribly uncomfortable and Kim was greatly relieved when he finally spoke.

"I am really sorry about the other night, Kim." She opened her mouth to speak but he held up a hand. "I know you feel responsible, but it was both of us and we both know it." He sounded so tormented. "It happened and it's over with and we both have our virtue intact." She managed a weak smile before he continued "I shouldn't be spending so much time with you, it's too hard for both of us to—" but he stopped at the panic he saw in her eyes. She reached out and grabbed his arm in desperation.

"Oh, please. Allen, don't," she sputtered and willed the tears away. "I am so sorry. It will never happen again, just please don't leave me alone. I need you so much." And she did. The last few days without him had been nearly unbearable. "Please, please don't leave me now."

"I'm not leaving," he explained his voice full of compassion. "I just don't know that having me around is good for you. You're angry, and maybe spending some time alone, allowing your family to help out instead of me, will allow you to sort things out, to decide what you really want from me."

"Oh, Allen, I want everything from you," Kim said, not realizing how true it was until she said it out loud. "I didn't mean those things I said. It's not your fault. I don't know where those things came from. I just don't know how to do this. I am so, so sorry." The tears once again slid down her cheeks.

Allen stroked her hair and looked deeply into her eyes. "Kim, I don't know how to help you."

"I . . . I love you Allen. I need you."

"But you keep pushing me away."

Kim nodded slowly "I know, but please . . . please." She couldn't finish and she pulled Allen's hand to her face, closing her eyes to savor the feel of him. Allen watched her face and reached out a hand to touch her hair. At his touch she looked up with him, her eyes pleading. "Please, Allen. I need you," she whispered and the sincerity in her voice melted his heart. He pulled her face into his shoulder.

"Oh, Kim, I'm so sorry this happened," he whispered into her hair. "We've got to set some ground rules." She nodded and he continued. "I can't be in that house with you, and if I'm going to be here for you have got to let me *really* be here. It kills me to have you push me away and I can't help you if you won't let me."

Kim nodded, "So you won't leave?" He shook his head and she hugged him tightly. "Thank you," she whispered and for a brief moment all there was were the two of them.

Allen stayed for a few more minutes. They stood in the hall, holding hands but saying little. When he told her he needed to go, she nodded and went in to sit with Jackson once more. Allen stayed to watch them for a moment, then with a heavy heart he turned to leave. As he turned, he saw a man walking toward him. When the other man saw Allen, he faltered but then continued. He was in his sixties and was several inches shorter than Allen. Curious, Allen turned back to the window, determined to stay long enough to learn why the man regarded him so strangely.

"Is this Jackson Larksley's room?" the man asked quietly even before he looked through the window.

"Yes, it is," Allen said evenly. Out of the corner of his eye, he watched as the man looked through the glass and noticed how he caught his breath momentarily.

"Oh, my heavens," he murmured under his breath. After a minute or so he turned to Allen. "I'm Tom Larksley, Jackson's grandfather."

Ah, Robb's Dad. What a legacy. "Allen Jackman, a friend of Kim's." Tom nodded as if he already knew that. In the ten days since the accident, Allen hadn't even thought about Robb's parents, and now he wondered how they had found out. He was pretty sure Kim hadn't thought about calling them either.

Both men turned back to the glass. Kim had not seen Tom and

they both watched as she adjusted the sheets around Jackson's shoulders and refolded the blanket at the foot of the bed. Tom cleared his throat. "I called Kim's parents...they told me my grandson's in a coma; how is he doing?" His voice was shaky and Allen understood only too well how he felt.

"They aren't sure just yet."

"Is there—brain damage?"

Allen's heart went out to the man. Kim had told him several times how much Robb's parents loved Jackson and Allen was sure that after the pain Robb had already caused for them, this seemed overwhelming. "They don't know yet how extensive it is, but they don't doubt that there is some."

Tom took a minute to absorb what he had just been told. "What happened?" Tom asked, and to Allen it seemed as if he had shrunk an inch or two.

"I don't know that you should hear this from me," Allen said not totally comfortable with telling him that his son was responsible for this.

Tom turned to him, his eyes questioning and asked, "Why?"

"Your son is involved."

"Robb?" he choked. After a moment he looked back at Jackson. Kim had opened a book and was reading to him. Tom whispered, "What has he done?"

Allen hesitated but realized that if he didn't tell him, Kim would. "Why don't we sit," he said and Tom followed him to some chairs.

Once seated, Allen took a deep breath and in just a few sentences explained what had happened. Tom looked back at him in absolute shock. He opened his mouth to speak but no words came. Allen took the time to fill in some of the other details. Tom put his elbows on his knees and dropped his head into his hands. "I can't believe it," he whispered to himself.

"If you'd like, I can give you the number of the Lieutenant in Wyoming."

"No. I don't need to do that." Tom sat up and took a deep breath while he stared blankly at the floor. "I am sixty three years old. At my age, a man assumes that the worst of life is over." He paused, "How will I tell my wife?"

At that moment, Allen was reminded of the day he and Kim had picked Jackson up from his grandparents' house. Someone, who Kim later identified as Robb's mother, had watched him from a window while he waited in the car. A cold dread filled him as he realized the possible implications of how Robb had known about him; and how Allen had led the way to Kim. "Did you or your wife ever tell your son about me?"

Tom looked at him with fearful surprise. "I told my wife that Kim wouldn't be seeing someone, but she . . . she has been very upset about the divorce." That explained why he had hesitated as he approached Allen. "Why?"

Allen looked away from the other man, trying hard not to let his anger show. "When the police told Kim that someone was looking for her, we weren't aware that Robb knew about me. We think I was followed when I picked up some things for her and Jackson. We think that's how he found her."

Tom groaned and put a hand on Allen's arm as he absorbed what Allen had said. "I don't think I can see her right now," he whispered.

"I understand."

"Please tell her." He swallowed and his eyes filled with tears. When he spoke again, his voice was cracked and strained, "Tell her how sorry we are." With that, he stood and hurried away; Allen watched until the other man turned the corner. Taking a deep breath, he decided he had better tell Kim.

She didn't say anything when Allen told her of Tom's visit. She just stared through the glass and tried to keep from screaming. If Robb had been raised with some level of responsibility, maybe this wouldn't have happened. But it had happened and as the days went by the blame seemed to grow. She hoped Robb's parents never came back; she never wanted to see them again.

᷍

Kim's leg still throbbed and there was still some soreness in her neck, but otherwise there was little physical evidence that she had even been involved in the accident. She tired easily and didn't sleep well, but she barely noticed. Every morning she went to the hospital and stayed until night. She had learned from the nurses to provide a great deal of Jackson's care, and was grateful to be able to do something for him. It broke her heart to do some of the most private and personal things, but she was his mother and it was all she could do now. Allen was there every evening after work, and Kim's parents, as well as Matt and Maddie, visited as often as they could, offering whatever support they could. She appreciated them, and tried to show it but she felt increasingly drained and helpless. With every day, she was losing hope. Hope seemed to be all she had left, and even that was disappearing. Day after day, she watched him and it was as if she could feel his spirit slipping farther and farther away. She tried to continue to tell herself that things would work out, that the Lord wouldn't take him from her, but the words were empty. It seemed impossible that this was happening, but there he was, on life support, a feeding tube in his nose. She would sit with him and hold his hand, willing him to wake up, to show everyone how wrong they were. Miracles happened all the time, she told herself, and if anyone deserved a miracle, it was Jackson. He had just begun discovering how good life could be, how could he possibly lose that now?

Sunday night, after Allen had left, she stared through the window of Jackson's room and thought about the conversation she'd had with him about angels. "I know where people go when they die," he had said. "They stay here on earth." She had looked up some references on the Spirit World earlier that day at Allen's house and been dismayed that, according to several General Authorities and Church scholars, he was right. Just as she had wondered on the night he had told her that, she asked herself again why angels would come to a seven-year-old boy and teach him about death. She refused to answer her own question.

The next day, Kim returned to work. She had dreaded the day but knew that in order for their insurance coverage to remain intact she had no choice. Monday morning she returned to the office and watched the clock continually, waiting for the day to end. She didn't take a lunch break and left at 4:00. The heartache of being away from him for so long was almost too much to bear and she wondered how she could do it for another day. The next day followed the same pattern until she arrived at the hospital and hurried to the ICU only to find Jackson's room full of doctors she didn't recognize.

"What's going on?" she asked in alarm.

A doctor she had never met led her into the hallway and sat her down, raising her concern immensely. "Jackson has developed pneumonia."

"Pneumonia," she repeated. "How?"

"We believe that he may have had a cold or some sort of infection before his accident, but it has progressed rapidly and we—"

"How do you cure it?" Kim interrupted.

"Well, that's what we are trying to decide. If it's a bacterial infection, we can fight it with antibiotics just like as we would treat a skin infection or strep throat. But if it's been caused by a virus, there is little we can do."

Kim's heart started thumping in her chest and she looked up toward Jackson's window as if making sure he was still there. The doctor continued, "We have him on a heavy regimen of antibiotics now and should know in twenty-four hours exactly what we are dealing with."

"What if it's a virus?" Kim pleaded; surely in a hospital there was something they could do.

"If it's a virus, all we can do is wait it out. Jackson's own immune system will have to fight it."

"What if he isn't strong enough to fight it on his own?" Kim asked quickly, not sure if she wanted to hear the answer. The doctor didn't answer and she closed her eyes slowly. "You mean after everything that has happened to him, he could die of pneumonia."

"Pneumonia is greatly misunderstood by the general public, but in cases such as your son's, it can be a very serious complication."

Those words echoed through her mind long after she left the hospital and went to bed. As she lay in the darkness staring up at the ceiling a cold dread settled upon her. It seemed as if there was a presence, waiting for permission to tell her the future. But she wouldn't let it speak. She shook her head, trying to make it go away and finally got up and turned on the TV, blaring it loudly—anything to keep from learning what lay ahead. I have to have hope. I have to have hope, she told herself over and over again as she waited for the feeling to go away. Fatigue finally conquered her and she was able to sleep for a few hours before waking up and having the same thoughts continue. It was still too early for work, so she went for a walk before she showered for the first time in nearly a week and got herself dressed.

After work, she raced back to the hospital. Please let it be bacterial, she prayed silently. But when she approached Jackson's nurse for the day, she could see by the look on her face that her prayer was not to be answered. The rest of the night passed in a daze. She felt numb. She couldn't take anymore. It was too unfair. Allen came and she hoped he would give her some reassurance, something to inspire a little hope. But he didn't. He didn't say anything at all, and Kim was learning that was not a good sign. When he left, he offered to give Jackson another blessing but she refused; the last one had been too discouraging. She wouldn't put herself through such doom and gloom again. Once again, she fell asleep in front of the blaring TV, but when morning came she just didn't have the energy to get up. She called in sick to her office and went to the hospital, but she only stayed a few hours before coming home again. The phone rang several times, but she refused to pick it up. She didn't want to talk to anyone. She did the same thing on Friday. And the weekend wasn't any different as she once again drew farther and farther inside herself. Her mother had come over every day, bringing food and cleaning up. Kim said she wasn't feeling well and Peggy seemed to feel as if she had little choice but to accept her excuses.

Jackson wasn't doing well, and there was nothing Kim could do about it. Her helplessness infuriated her; as her heart was breaking, and she sank deeper and deeper into a depression. She told everyone she wasn't feeling well—maybe she was coming down with something—and although they exchanged looks, no one said anything about it.

On Monday morning, Allen realized he had forgotten to do his laundry and needed a clean shirt for work. He hadn't had much opportunity to speak with Kim the last few days since she seemed to be constantly surrounded by other people. However, during a brief conversation on Sunday, Kim had promised him she would go to work on Monday morning. He stopped by the house to grab a shirt out of his closet. He let himself in with his key and did a double take when he realized Kim was on the couch staring blankly at the television screen.

He was instantly concerned. "Kim, are you alright?" Allen asked as he turned off the TV.

"Why wouldn't I be?" she said with dry sarcasm.

"You were supposed to be at work nearly an hour ago. You promised me you would go today," Allen said coolly.

"Well, I'm sick and tired of living my life and pretending everything is okay," she snapped back at him.

"If you've been pretending that, then you've been doing a terrible job of it." The frustration in his voice was obvious. "You have to go to work today, Kim," Allen said it partly because it was true, and partly because he was fed up. He appreciated how difficult this was for her, and he ached to give her comfort, but he had been watching her for weeks and she was folding in on herself more and more every day. Her employer had been very fair with her so far, but Maddie had expressed concern for Kim keeping her job if she didn't start pulling herself together.

"Shut up and leave me alone," Kim spat; still not looking at him. She pulled the blanket up under her chin.

"I thought we decided you weren't going to talk to me that way," Allen said like a frustrated parent.

"I thought you were supposed to be supportive."

"And I am being supportive. If you don't go to work, you will lose your job and your insurance. Jackson's medical bills are over eight hundred dollars a day—can you afford that?"

Her eyes flared at him. "Don't patronize me, Allen. You have no idea what I'm going through."

"Oh, please," Allen drawled angrily. "Don't give me your crap, Kim—now get up and get ready."

"Don't tell me what to do!" she yelled at him. "It's not your son dying, Allen! You have no business telling me how to react to this."

That was it. After weeks of putting up with her, trying to let the little things slide, he was past his limit. He quickly went to the couch and lifted her up over his shoulder. She screamed and hit him but he was a lot bigger and a lot stronger then she was and he didn't even slow down. He marched right into the bathroom and dumped her into the tub. He turned on the water and lifted the shower lever. Kim swung her arms trying to keep the water from hitting her face while she screamed at Allen to turn it off. Allen crossed his arms over his chest and waited until she shut her mouth. She was crying now and Allen almost relented, but not quite.

"Kim, it's time for you to pull out of your shell and look around you. This is reality!" he yelled, spreading his arms for emphasis. "I'm sorry things are as they are, but wishing it were different doesn't change the facts. You have responsibilities that cannot be ignored any longer; the most important of which is to your son. He doesn't want you to be this way any more than you want him to be the way he is. There are many people who love you, Kim, but you are pushing us all away. If you don't get your act together you will lose everything. Do you understand?" he yelled. "Everything! And if nothing else Jackson deserves better than this. This is what you have been dealt and you need to play your hand. You have ten minutes and then I'm taking you to work." And with that he slammed the door. Outside the bathroom, he leaned against the wall and tried to calm himself down. Then he sank to the floor and spent the next ten minutes pouring out his heart to his Father in Heaven. Praying that what he had done was right.

Kim took almost a half an hour, but Allen waited without a word. He really didn't want to fight about it. He called his office, knowing that he was also pushing his own limits by telling them he would be coming in late again. Luckily, he hadn't built a large enough client base that he was booked every hour of every day; he still had some flexibility.

When she was finally ready, he could tell that she had spent the majority of her time crying. She didn't look at him as she walked past him. "I can drive myself," she said, and grabbed her purse on her way out. For some reason he hadn't thought about that option and was deflated that he wouldn't have the opportunity to soften his words. Had he done the right thing? Allen wondered as he watched her pull out of the driveway and sighed, or was he only pushing her farther away?

Allen was waiting at Jackson's window when she got to the hospital that night. She'd stayed at work late because of her morning tardiness, and, strangely, she had then found herself reluctant to leave. Losing herself in her work had its benefits. Did she really want to face life outside the office? Allen said hello when she arrived and the repentant look on his face softened her hard feelings toward him. Without meeting his eye she smiled, reluctant to drive him away or forgive him so easily. He seemed to understand and watched silently as she went to find Jackson's nurse.

They had restricted the amount of time she could stay in Jackson's room because of the risk of further infection and so she only had thirty minutes. Upon entering the room any denied reality came crashing back with painful force. Jackson's breathing had been strained before, but not too obvious due to the noises associated with the medical equipment in the room. Tonight, however, his strained breathing was obvious and each ragged breath made her wince. His small chest lifted rhythmically as oxygen was forced into his lungs. Even the fundamental task of breathing wasn't his own, and the reminder forced her to push the thought away. Instead, she busied herself with changing his gown and giving him a sponge bath. Eventually, she was told she would have to go outside, and reluctantly she kissed his forehead and left the room. For several minutes, she and Allen stood side by side without speaking until she finally told Allen she was going home, she couldn't stand just watching him through the glass. He walked her to her car and she paused before opening her door. She looked up at him and realized she couldn't hold onto her anger any longer—she needed him. "Thanks for not giving up on me yet," she said quietly.

Allen smiled sadly. "I'll never give up on you," he said and pulled her into a hug. She pressed her face against his shoulder and wished she could let go of all the heartache just for a moment in order to really enjoy his embrace. Enjoyment aside, there was a comfort she drew from him that she had been unable to find anywhere else and she tried to absorb as much of it as possible. If only she could seal it away to be opened later when she would again be in need. If only compassion could work that way.

Finally, she pulled back, his closeness reminding her that she had something to tell him and she lifted her eyes to meet his. "My attorney called today." Allen lifted his eyebrows. "Robb consented to the divorce, I can sign the papers tomorrow; I won't have to go in front of the judge."

Allen smiled, "That's great, Kim; it's about time."

She looked down at his shirt, lifting her hand to absently fidget with a button. "I can't help thinking that if I had just agreed to wait until Robb's release none of this would have happened."

Allen wanted to remind her that they wouldn't have had any chance to be with each other if she had agreed to that, but he didn't. Instead, he decided to pretend she didn't mean to imply it. She went up on her toes and kissed his cheek sweetly, allowing her lips to linger on his scruffy face for a long moment before getting into her car and driving away.

The eerie emptiness of the house made her instantly uncomfortable as soon as she walked through the door and she automatically picked up the remote. For several seconds she stood, arm pointed towards the screen, but finally she thought better of it and reluctantly returned the device to the coffee table without pushing any buttons. For several days, she had been fighting her thoughts and premonitions, drowning them out with any outside stimulus she could find but she couldn't hide anymore. *Shouldn't* hide anymore. With a sigh, she admitted to herself that she was allowing herself to be 'stuck'. She had immersed herself in hoping and wishing and being so angry, that the things she didn't want to accept couldn't show themselves. Allen's words that morning had affected her a lot more than she would have liked. "This is the hand you've been dealt," he had said, "this is reality—nothing you can do can change it." Hesitantly, she admitted how true that was.

Slowly she went about straightening the house and catching up on her laundry. All the while she made herself review the many experiences she had shared with Jackson in the short seven years she'd had with him. She also forced herself to think of how he was now. Many tears fell as she forced herself past the 'but ifs' and the 'if only's', making herself think only of the reality; the truth of what she'd had with her son. And the truth of what lay ahead.

It was nearly midnight before she sank to her knees beside the bed and, for the first time since the accident, she prayed. After the blessing she had received that first night in the hospital she had felt a definite chasm between herself and any higher power. Since then she'd simply ignored her need for that power as her own kind of protest against what had happened. This wasn't the first time she had pushed the spirit away and she wondered why she never seemed to learn. She knew now that she had felt the separation because she refused to submit herself to God's will. Even now it stung to say that she would do her best to accept it. But as she prayed she could literally feel the darkness and isolation fade away and a peace settled upon her. How could she have refused it for so long? When she had needed to feel the love of her Father in Heaven more than ever, she had shut herself off. Along with the peace came the confirmation of what she had long denied and she knew. Without a doubt, she knew that her son was truly dying; that he had only stayed this long to allow her to find this acceptance. Her sobs shattered the silence as she gave herself up to the tearing agony in her soul. She put her arms over her head and rocked back and forth on her knees as she admitted the things everyone had been telling her but she had refused to believe. All this time she had denied it, and allowed the anger to sustain her, but not anymore. It was time to accept those things that were beyond her control and not fight anymore. Her anguish echoed off the walls and seemed to build and build until it was more than her, more than Jackson—it encompassed everything. The years they should have ahead of them, the years behind them that were full of so much hurt, the grandchildren she would never have and the loneliness that lay ahead.

And on top of it all, there was Robb. The man she had loved and married, supported, cared for, created this child with, who had ultimately taken everything away—everything. Her anger and fury seemed palatable then and then in an instant, her mind cleared and her understanding was sharpened. As if the words were suddenly implanted in her mind, she realized what Robb had lost, he had given up and lost them both in this life, but beyond that he had lost Jackson forever—she had not. Despite all her imperfections, she had loved her son and lived the best she could in whatever circumstances she had found herself. Jackson would be a part of her forever. Long after Robb had faded from her memory, she and Jackson would continue. Finally, after her acknowledgment of this truth, the unquenchable heartache began to recede. Slowly, she felt some of the piercing pain drain from her and she pictured her son as he was now—his spirit trapped in a body beyond healing—and she asked herself if that was what she wanted for him. In her mind she could see his body as preventing him from his own progression.

Would a loving God want any of them to continue this way? The question was easy to answer now that she was allowing herself to listen.

Once she gained enough control of herself to do so, she closed her prayer. The assurance that Jackson still belonged to her, that he would always belong to her, seemed a tangible fact; all the questions that had haunted her seemed unimportant. Jackson's time here was finished, he had filled his measure of creation. And she was finally at peace, at least for now. She knew that tomorrow would be the most difficult day of her life, but she also knew she could face it. And she knew beyond a doubt that she would not be alone.

# CHAPTER TWENTY-ONE

As soon as she got to work Kim spoke to her supervisor. At first she avoided saying the words but when the supervisor continued to argue that Kim had missed too much work already, Kim stopped beating around the bush.

"My son is being taken off the life support today, and I need the rest of the week off to make funeral arrangements. Are you really going to stand there and tell me I have to come to work? If that's the case, I'll quit."

The supervisor blinked at her and after a long pause nodded. "Take the time off then." Kim thanked her and left. She finished up a lot of work throughout the day, consciously seeking more work to keep herself busy, still hesitant to end it too soon. At 4:00 Kim met Eric at his office and signed the papers—the divorce would be finalized in a few days—and then she drove to Allen's office and waited. While she sat in her car, she glanced at herself in the rearview mirror and did a double-take. There were circles under her eyes and her skin looked sickly pale without any make-up. She hadn't thought about the way she looked lately and was a little horrified at how far her appearance had slipped in the area of appearance.

She opened her purse and pulled out some mascara but then remembered what lay ahead and dropped it back inside. As a compromise, she pulled the elastic out of her hair releasing the ponytail that had been her signature hairdo the last few weeks and brushed her fingers through her crumpled mane. It was only a slight improvement, but it brought to mind the day of Matt and Maddie's wedding. Jackson had come into the bathroom as she was applying the finishing touches to her hair. "Mom, are you the prettiest lady in the world?" he had asked.

She had looked at him strangely for a moment, wondering where the question had come from. "Do you think I'm the prettiest woman in the world?" she countered.

"Yes."

She smiled, "Then I am. Beauty is in the eye of the beholder."

"Huh?"

"That means that if you think something is beautiful, then it is. And if you think I'm the most beautiful woman in the world then I am for you, and that's all that matters."

"Oh, okay," he said blankly making her wonder if he had understood any of what she'd said. Then he ran off leaving her to look at herself a little differently.

The incident seemed so long ago, she thought with a sigh—lifetimes ago. She looked up just then to see Allen walking toward his car. Quickly she opened her door and ran towards him. "Allen!" She called. He turned to look at her and stopped short.

"Kim?" he said to confirm it was her, then his eyes filled with worry. "What's wrong?"

"Will you take me to the hospital?" she asked, feeling suddenly foolish and weak for needing his help so badly right now. He looked at her, then her car, and then at her again with mild confusion. "I don't want to be alone," she whispered and after another moment of looking at her face he nodded his understanding.

"Should we drop your car off at the house on our way?" he asked and she agreed.

When they arrived at the hospital, they turned the corner to find several doctors talking outside Jackson's room and Kim's stomach knotted at the sight of them. The doctors spotted her and fell silent as she approached. She glanced through the glass at Jackson and her face faltered for only a moment before she turned her attention back to the group of physicians. "How is he today?" she asked calmly. Allen knew then that she was only being polite; she knew the answer better than anyone.

"Not well," one of them said. He then proceeded to tell her that they had been able to run the tests today; the swelling had finally gone down enough. After all the tests were completed, they had determined that Jackson was in fact brain-dead—there was no brain activity other than what was needed for basic cardiac functions. There was no hope that he could ever breathe by himself again or regain any measure of consciousness. Furthermore, they were losing the battle with pneumonia. The fever he'd had for days was getting worse; the fluid in his lungs was rising. Kim closed her eyes when the doctor finished and reminded herself that it would be okay. She had prepared for this, she knew it was coming. Allen came up behind her and placed his hands on her shoulders and she leaned back into him, grateful for the physical support.

"Now what happens?" she asked as she opened her eyes.

The doctors exchanged a look and a different one spoke. "It is possible to transfer him to a nursing home and continue the life support, but it is costly and . . . we would like to speak with you about organ donation."

Kim was very quiet and she stared at the floor. Could she really do this? Make the decision to end his life? Taking a deep breath she looked back up, "I'll sign whatever papers are necessary." They all nodded in unison and one of them left to get the consent form. "How long can we stay with him?"

"As long as you like."

Kim nodded and walked away to make some phone calls, giving Allen's hand a squeeze to reassure him that she was okay. Allen remained beside Jackson's window for a minute and watched her go, amazed at her strength. It was hard to believe she was the same woman he had dumped into the tub yesterday. It was even harder to believe that in a short time she would say good-bye to her son. After a few moments, he also left in search of a phone.

First he called his office and talked to Paul, his partner. When he hung up he was immensely grateful to Paul for being so understanding. Allen was well aware of the difficulties he had caused for his office staff during the last few weeks, but Paul had been very patient. Once Allen explained what was happening, his partner didn't bat an eye at Allen's request for the next day off. Allen promised to make up for it and Paul assured him that he would make certain of it.

Second he called Lt. Browning and told him the news. Browning swore and offered many colorful descriptions of exactly how he felt about Robb Larksley before informing Allen of the status of the latest charges. After Browning had confronted Robb about Jackson, Robb made a full confession to Detective Peart. His mother had told him about Kim and a bald man coming to pick Jackson up in a black car, and it had pushed him over the edge. Already furious about the divorce, dumfounded that she would give up on him now, he decided then to make sure Kim didn't get the divorce she wanted; he would not give her to another man. When his legal maneuvering didn't work, he decided to scare her into accepting his terms. Luke was his chance to regain the control he knew he had lost. Robb swore up and down that he only told Luke to scare her enough to make her change her mind. He said that he never told Luke to hurt her and he specifically told Luke not to involve Jackson at all. Browning wasn't convinced and was almost anxious to tell him that he was now an accessory to murder.

People began arriving at the hospital around seven. Kim's parents were first. Then came Matt and Maddie, Bishop Scott,

Allen's parents, Kim's brothers and some family friends. Many of them spent a few minutes with Jackson, saying their good-byes, but some just came to offer her support. For the first time in a long time, Kim could truly thank them. As opposed to her earlier need to keep herself apart, now she longed for closeness and encouragement. Before Bishop Scott left, she asked to speak with him privately.

They went to the same small waiting room that Allen and she had used not long ago. Once seated, he looked at her expectantly, his eyes full of sympathy.

She outlined the basics of what had happened between herself and Allen the night she was released from the hospital. Until now, she had blocked it out, tried not to worry about it, but now she needed to be certain she could repair the damage she had done. She was losing her son and she had to know if she had compromised her covenants to the extent of damaging the eternal bond they should have. Bishop Scott asked her some detailed questions in order to understand exactly what had happened. Once he understood, he gave his advice: "Kim, you have experienced some incredibly difficult hardships lately and I commend you for coming to me now. The Lord loves you so much, and he has no desire to add more burden to your heart at this time. But the covenants you've made are important ones, they are not to be trifled with. Why don't we kneel together."

The tears continued to fall as Bishop Scott offered a prayer in her behalf. By the time they said Amen, Kim knew she was forgiven. Her actions had been seriously wrong, but she was freed of the burden of guilt. She understood her lack of judgement when she was so very vulnerable, and she would never allow it to happen again.

"Now, as soon as you feel up to it. I would suggest that you write a letter to the first presidency of the church, requesting a sealing cancellation from your husband. I have a feeling that there may be someone else who would like the opportunity to have that honor."

Kim smiled and with a big hug thanked him for his counsel, promising to write the letter soon.

Kim's parents were the last ones to leave and she hugged them goodbye as she thanked them for everything they had done for Jackson during the last year as well as the last few weeks. Peggy, especially, had been a strong and dependable support for her; not complaining when Kim treated her unfairly; always ready to do what was necessary, but allowing Kim to call the shots. As her parents walked away, another couple rounded the corner and exchanged a few strained words with them before continuing toward Jackson's room.

Tom and Dorothy approached Kim looking pale and drawn. As they approached Kim swallowed what resentment she still held for them. She had been very angry with them, with everyone, but she was realizing that her feelings toward them were unfair. They didn't want Robb to be the way he was any more than she wanted Jackson to be the way he was; and she had finally admitted that her anger only made things worse. They were losing their grandson in a very traumatic way and she knew that she needed to be sympathetic of that. That was why she had called them, but she was relieved to know that she could look at them now and sympathize, rather than criticize. When they reached her Tom thanked Kim for calling, while Dorothy avoided her eyes. They entered Jackson's room and stayed for only a few minutes before coming out, saying a brief good-bye and hurrying away. Then Dorothy stopped and walked back. She still wasn't able to meet Kim's gaze but she touched her hand hesitantly and said, "I wrote Robb. If I'd known that he would..." she had to stop in an attempt to contain her emotions, but it didn't work. She blubbered a quick "Sorry . . . Please." Unable to continue she squeezed Kim's hand before turning into Tom's shoulder as she sobbed.

Tom gave them a teary smile. "Good luck to the two of you. I hope your happiness will make up for all the hardship you've had so far."

Together, Kim and Allen watched them walk away. "I think that's the nicest thing they have ever said to me." Kim remarked sadly. Surprisingly, she felt no anger toward them, just sympathy for the agony she had seen in there in their faces. Would they ever be able to feel peace again? She looked up at Allen and he put his arms loosely around her shoulders.

"Are you okay?" he whispered.

She smiled up at him and wrapped her arms around his waist, pulling him closer to her. "Not yet, but I will be."

As she laid her head against his chest she looked sadly through the glass.

"I guess it's your turn." Allen said quietly, stroking her hair.

Kim craned her neck to look up at him, her eyes moist and pleading. "Will you come with me?'

"If you want me to." Allen said as he leaned down to kiss her. She nodded, and they entered the room and sat in the two chairs pulled next to Jackson's bed.

"Hey buddy, it's Mom." Her voice cracked but she continued, "Allen's with me. We came to say goodbye." She had to stop and get control of herself. She found Jackson's hand and wrapped his stiff little fingers around her own. "I want you to know, Jack...that I love you very much. I wish you could stay with me but I know that you can't. I don't understand why God wants you back, but...I'm ready to let you go." She squeezed her eyes shut and swallowed. "It's okay that you go now, I'll be alright." She could barely speak and had to stop in order to get control. Allen's arm was around her shoulder and she placed her free hand on his leg. For nearly five minutes they stayed that way, silent and thoughtful until Kim could continue. "And I will be happy, Jack, just the way you hoped I would be. Even though I will miss you so very much, I know you will be okay. You are my boy, and I know that you'll always be my boy no matter what. Just like the angels said. I know you will be happier there than you are here, and I will try very hard to remember that. And I promise you, Jackson..." she paused and took a breath, "that we will be together again someday and when it's time for me to leave my body behind, I hope you will be waiting for me. I can't wait to see you again." A sob escaped her throat and she brought a hand to her face to wipe her tears away as her shoulders began to shake.

Allen cleared his throat, "I'll take good care of your Mom, Jackson. I promise."

Kim turned into his shoulder and her muffled sobs seemed to drown out all the other sounds in the small room. Finally, she leaned forward and placed her cheek next to her son's face for a minute. "I miss you, Jack," she whispered and then planted a teary kiss on his forehead. "I miss you so much."

# CHAPTER TWENTY-TWO

They drove to Allen's home in silence. After parking the car he walked Kim to the door and stopped obediently at the front steps. "You're welcome to stay as long as you like," Allen said.

Kim smiled at him and stood on the first step so that they were almost eye level with one another. She took both his hands in hers. "You've been so good to me, Allen. I don't know how I could have done this without your help."

"I'll find a way for you to make it up to me," he said with a smile. He then reached up and touched her face. "You're a strong woman, Kim."

She shook her head slightly and then lifted her face to meet his eyes. "Stay here with me tonight?" she whispered.

"Uh...I don't think that's a very good idea—remember our rules," Allen replied, vividly remembering the last time she had made the invitation.

"Nothing inappropriate will happen; I just don't want to be alone." He searched her eyes and found them to be full of fear, not desire.

"Lead the way," he said after a moment and she turned and unlocked the door. He liked watching her enter his home as if she belonged there and hoped it was a scene he would see often real soon.

"I'll take the couch," he offered when they got inside and Kim nodded. But when he emerged from the bathroom later, she had arranged an improvised bed on the floor next to the couch.

"What's this?"

"You were too far away," she said sheepishly and he shook his head with a smile.

"Okay, but I take the floor."

She nodded with relief and after offering their separate prayers they turned off the lights and laid in their respective beds. Kim rolled onto her stomach and dropped a hand over the edge of the couch. Allen wrapped his own hand around it and rested them both on his chest. "Good night, Kim," he said pointedly.

"Goodnight."

❧

"Allen, wake up!" Kim pleaded, shaking his shoulder. Allen blinked his eyes open, but it was difficult to wake himself and as he looked around he realized it wasn't even dawn.

"Wh-what is it?" he finally asked, concerned by the obvious panic in her voice.

"You have to take me to the hospital!"

He blinked a few more times in an attempt to clear the sleepy numbness from his brain. "Why?"

"Jackson needs me and I left him . . . how could I do that?"

Allen was awake now and sat up. She was on her knees beside him on the floor and he gripped her shoulders. He couldn't see her well but he could feel her torment. "Jackson isn't here any more, Kim."

"There's still time. They're going to kill him!" she shook free of his grasp and made to leave, but Allen was faster and grabbed her before she got out of reach. "Let me go!" she screamed and Allen had to wrestle her back toward him.

She fought him like a madwoman, yelling and scratching his arms until he finally pinned her down by straddling her stomach and holding her wrists to the floor. Thank goodness for high school wrestling. "Kim!" he said loudly, "Kim, stop!" After a few more seconds she stopped straining against him and started to cry softly. Releasing her hands he caressed her face in the darkness and whispered, "His time here is done. Keeping him alive will only hold him back; and hold you back, too."

Kim was sobbing now, her eyes shut tightly as if by doing so she could block out his words.

"Kim, you told him he could go. You did the right thing." Suddenly she arched her back and let out the most agonizing, heart-wrenching scream he had ever heard. And then she went limp, sobbing uncontrollably. He moved off her and pulled her to him, her sobs muffled in his chest and rolled on his back. For several minutes he held her that way, his own heart as tormented as her own, wishing her calm acceptance could have lasted a bit longer. Finally, she fell asleep in his arms. For a long time after that he just held her and wished he could help her. She was so strong, so good, and yet she didn't seem to understand that. He wished he could let her know how well she was doing. To compare the woman he had seen today to the woman he had seen the day before was a rather incredible comparison. He thought of her strength as she had bid her son farewell and he clenched his eyes shut against his own tears. Thank goodness she had let go, now he hoped she could overcome the remaining grief and agony as well.

The sun was fully up before he opened his eyes again. Kim was only a short ways a way, sitting on the floor, her eyes swollen and sad. "How can I feel such peace one day, and overwhelming torment the next?"

Allen rolled onto his side and propped himself up on an elbow. "There are seasons of grief, Kim. Denial, anger, depression, and acceptance. Every person will experience it differently and find themselves going between the various stages at different times."

Kim shook her head sadly. "I was so sure of what I was doing yesterday. Today, I feel like I failed him." The last words were strangled and choked.

Allen sat up and scooted towards her, wiping away the single tear that slid down her cheek. "And you will go back and forth many times. But hold on to the knowledge that when you made the decision to let go you knew it was the right thing to do. And remember that the worst is over, Kim, now is your season to heal."

"I wish I could believe that," Kim whispered. She looked down at her hands fidgeting with the hem of her oversized T-shirt.

Allen watched her for a few moments, and then he had an idea. "Let's go to the temple."

Kim looked at him, her brows knit together. "What?"

Allen leaned forward and placed a hand on her arm. "Let's go to the temple. Now."

"Allen, I can't."

"Why not? Do you want a reminder that Jackson is okay, and that you did the right thing? There is no better place to find peace than in the House of the Lord."

Kim still hesitated, but Allen quickly got up, went into the bedroom and started pulling clothes out of his closet. "Well, you can do what you want, but I'm going." He went into the bathroom and started the shower.

Washed, scrubbed and dried, he was straightening his tie when Kim knocked on the door. "I don't have a dress; I only have pantsuits that I wear to work."

Allen smiled at his reflection before he opened the door. "You shower and I'll take care of the dress."

Thirty minutes later, Kim was just finishing with the blow dryer when he opened the bathroom door just a crack. He covered his eyes and handed her a K-Mart bag. "It's the only place open at nine," he said apologetically, before pulling the door shut again.

Kim emerged a few minutes later, wearing the clothes he had

purchased. The yellow cardigan was a little big, but the flowered skirt fit almost perfectly even though it was a size smaller than she usually wore. Kim was momentarily struck by the irony that since the accident, she had finally managed to lose the last fifteen pounds she had fought with since her son was born. The discovery was bittersweet—heavy on the bitter. Allen had also purchased stockings and shoes, which were also a little big, but close enough.

He took her hand and led her to the car. "I'm never going to the mall again. K-Mart has everything."

Kim smiled slightly as he opened her door. When he started the engine she looked around the interior. "I've meant to tell you, this is a really nice car."

Allen just nodded, not wanting to dwell on it much and pulled out of the driveway. The insurance company had totaled the Camaro and although he had looked longingly at a few new ones he eventually had to admit he would never be able to drive another Camaro, and he was sure Kim wouldn't either. The Toyota Camry was nice and fully loaded but about as different from a Camaro as a car could be—that was the point.

The temple was better for Kim than he had hoped. Since there were fewer men than women, she was several rows behind Allen. But he didn't have to see her—he could hear her sniffling.

They sat in the celestial room for a long time and Allen wondered if she would ever leave, when she finally turned to him. "We can go now."

Kim had set up a meeting with Bishop Scott at her parents' house at 2:00 and they were only a little late after going through the Arby's drive-thru. As they drove the short distance from the Jordan River Temple to Kim's parents house, Allen asked how she felt.

"Better," she said simply. "While I was in the celestial room I was reminded that children who die before the age of eight return to their Father in Heaven and are promised Celestial glory. Jackson gets to skip all the heartache of mortality, and that brings me comfort. He'll never have to struggle with trying to understand his father." She paused thoughtfully. "I was also reminded that if I want to be with him again I have a long way to go. And the first step is having faith that God loves me. I've had a hard time believing that lately."

"So you found your peace again?"

"At least for today."

While at her parents' home, they planned Jackson's funeral service. Throughout the meeting, Kim had to keep asking herself if this was for real. She was planning her son's funeral; it seemed impossible. But she forced herself to concentrate, to get this part finished.

Kim wanted a viewing for immediate family only, sure that the injury on his face would be upsetting for most people; the services would be held at her parents' ward house. Kim wanted both Grandfathers to speak and the Grandmothers to offer the opening and closing prayers. Kim's parents offered to give Jackson one of the eight burial plots they owned. Allen and his parents wanted to pay for the casket and mortuary expenses. And when Kim's Dad called Robb's parents about speaking they said they would like to pay for the headstone after Kim picked it out. Medical bills were already arriving and although her insurance paid ninety percent, the ten-percent that was her responsibility was staggering. She needed all the financial help she could get.

When everything was finished, Allen took Kim back to his house so she could get her things; he told her again that she could stay longer but she said she was ready to go back home with her parents. Once back home, she forced herself to start going through Jackson's things. Many people might say it was too soon, but Kim felt a longing to submerge herself in the task—to find some kind of closeness. A seven-year-old boy doesn't have many valuable possessions, but now every toy; every piece of clothing, prompted memories. Kim spent the rest of that day and most of the next deciding what to keep and what to give away. In the end, she kept only one box of the most important things and sent the rest to Deseret Industries. She stopped the difficult process only long enough to go with her parents to the mortuary to choose a casket. Looking at the tiny coffins was nearly more than she could stand, but with the support of her parents, she finally made a choice for her son's finally resting place—an all white casket with brass trimmings. Then she went home and cried some more.

Friday afternoon, Allen took her out to lunch. She hadn't really wanted to go, but Peggy urged her to get out of the house. Throughout the meal, Kim sensed that something was wrong. Finally, a strained silence fell between them when they had finished eating and Allen cleared his throat.

"Kim, I need to talk to you about something." They'd talked about several *somethings* but Kim didn't mention it. Allen didn't give her the chance anyway. "I know the timing for this isn't perfect, but I . . . just think we need to discuss exactly what's ahead for us."

Until he said it, Kim hadn't realized that despite all the time they had been spending together, they had never talked about their future. His wording could have been better though, and she suddenly wondered if she had missed something he had tried to make obvious. She played it cool. "I think that's a very good idea," she said as she laid her fork down on the table next to the meal she had barely touched.

"This has been weighing very heavily on my mind and as hard as it is for me to say, I don't think we should get married."

Kim's heart plummeted; of all the possibilities, that was not what she expected to hear. "What do you mean, we shouldn't get married?" she nearly spat back at him. Her tone was more clipped than she would have liked, but his question was so startling she certainly hadn't planned her response.

"Well, not yet, anyway; I think that before we take that step you need some time to get used to everything."

"I need more time or you need more time," Kim said with irritation, trying to hide her disappointment.

Allen clasped his hands on the table and took a deep breath. "Kim, when you married Robb you went from being a daughter to being a wife to being Jackson's mother; which is good. Except that now everything in your life has changed and I think that if we married right now, you wouldn't have taken the time to learn who you are now."

"You sound like I've changed so much." The irritation had disappeared and the sadness was deep.

"In many ways you have. In the last year, you have suffered through more pain than most people have in a lifetime. Trials change us, and I feel like you need to learn what those changes are before you start another life."

Kim was looking down at the table as he said this and although part of her could understand what he was saying, she didn't want to accept that it might be true. "Having you beside me would make me stronger. I could learn those things better with you there to help me."

Allen reached across the table and took her hand. "Kim, I will still be here, which brings me to the other reason for waiting. Your marriage was lousy, Kim. You deserve so much more than what Robb ever gave you. Before making such an important decision again, I want you to know without a doubt, that it's the right one and not just the easiest way to get through this. You deserve to be courted, to be wined and dined—well, sodaed and dined—and just enjoy learning about yourself. And, when the time is right, you deserve a proper proposal. I want to give you everything you ever wanted, Kim; everything neither of us have ever had. But if we want to do what's right, we shouldn't rush this." He took a deep breath and rubbed his thumb across the back of her hand. "And you know that I want a family, but I don't believe we're ready for that yet either."

Kim absorbed all this with mixed emotions. She couldn't deny how good it felt to know that he cared about her so deeply, but she was still disappointed. From their previous experience, she knew that his longing was as deep as hers, and for him to put that on the back burner for her sake showed how important he felt this was. Yet that same longing made her want to get married—fast. Waiting was not her first choice. Still, he had a point. And about starting a family…she had yet to bury her son and the thought of beginning again made her chest tighten. She definitely didn't feel ready for that. Would it be fair to make him wait if they were married? If she wasn't fully ready for their life together, shouldn't she wait until she was?

"So how long do you think we should wait?" Kim finally asked, resisting the urge to pout just a little.

"However long it takes."

"And how long is that? A month, a year, two years; 'cause I can guarantee you I won't agree wait two years."

Allen chuckled "I don't know how long, but I agree that two years would be too long—I'll be almost forty!" he grimaced. "I think we'll both know when the time is right."

Kim pondered it a little more, and the more she thought about it the more she liked the idea of being courted. Robb was out of the picture, her marriage was all but over; then she thought about Jackson and about trying to get used to a life without him. Would jumping into marriage to Allen keep her from finding the closure with the life she's lived with her son? Would it be fair to any of them to rush this? Allen was right, despite how hard it was to admit. She couldn't deny that it felt right. Darn.

"So I guess were going steady."

"Something like that." Allen smiled gratefully and leaned towards her. "There is only one reason to do this, Kim. Believe me when I tell you that there is nothing I would rather do than marry you right now." His eyes got dark, and Kim felt that tingle she had missed these last few weeks. "But I feel strongly that this is what we need, just as strongly as I know that you are meant to be a part of me someday."

Her throat got thick as his words pierced her heart. "I like that idea," Kim said quietly.

"Me too," Allen said and he leaned across the table to seal their agreement with a kiss.

Kim's mood grew somber as the time to lay Jackson to rest got closer, and the next morning she said a fervent prayer requesting that the peace she had felt stay with her for at least one more day. The day passed slowly but time and time again, as Kim was sure she couldn't take her sorrow anymore, a wave of calmness would wash over her and she knew she could continue.

During Jackson's service, the speakers were just right and Kim was able to concentrate, without pain, on the wonderful memories people shared of her son. Robb's Dad gave an especially heartfelt and emotional description of his grandson, ending by advising parents to not love their children so much that they don't experience the consequences of their mistakes. "Love is about teaching and learning," he said. And Kim realized that she hadn't been the only one to grow in these last few months. Before all of this, Kim was sure his philosophy was more like "Love is about making them do the right thing." Kim was reminded of the saying that you can lead a horse to water but you can't make him drink. Robb's parents made him drink, but he spit it all back when he finally realized that he could.

Matt offered the dedicatory prayer at the grave and although Kim had been emotional all day long, she was able to walk away when it was over, knowing that part of Jackson would always be with her; and that his whole being would one day be fully restored. Sunday, she went to church with her parents but left soon after sacrament meeting, unable to handle the condolences offered by everyone she encountered.

She had been alone in this house many times, but the emptiness now was oppressive. She cried herself to sleep on Jackson's bed and couldn't imagine that the pain would ever go away.

When her parents returned from church, they had some envelopes and cards to give to her. There were many more that she had received the day before at the funeral and she decided this was as good a time as any to start opening them. Anticipation of having to read of everyone's sadness seemed overwhelming, but once she started opening the envelopes, she was grateful to find peace instead of pain in the heartfelt words. She was also surprised to find so much money! Nearly half of the seventy-or-so cards contained checks or cash ranging from five dollars to one check that was for one thousand. Many had brief notes like 'I hope this will help you with the financial difficulties associated with your loss' or 'when my child (spouse or parent) died there were angels of mercy that helped me cover the costs'.

All totaled, the donations added up to nearly six thousand dollars; she added them up twice before asking her dad to add them again to be sure. Never had she imagined, guessed or hoped that there would be such generosity toward her. Immediately, while the emotions were still fresh in her mind, she pulled out a stack of thank-you cards and wrote back to each and every person who had taken time to express their sympathy. It was midnight before the last envelope was sealed and, after taking twenty dollars out for stamps, she put the rest in a large envelope before falling onto the bed exhausted. Even with so much darkness and despair there were glowing candles of support all around her. Never had she been so grateful for the gospel, for the peace it had given her and the people with whom it had surrounded her with. How would she have ever survived this without them?

The next week was painfully long. She returned to her job and worked hard at catching up. At night she kept to herself, went on walks and read her scriptures. Allen came by once or twice, but there wasn't much to talk about other than the obvious and she wasn't ready yet. Getting used to life without Jackson was so hard. Everything she did reminded her of him, of how much her life had been centered around him. Trying to find a center in herself was incredibly difficult; she wondered if she ever would. She felt dazed, almost numb much of the time; as if she were on the outside, not really living this, and if she could just move on she would somehow get through this fog.

Friday evening when she got home, Allen's Camry was out front. She smiled slightly as she pulled into the driveway, anxious to see him but still feeling incapable of really enjoying it. She walked in to find Allen and Peggy talking in the living room. The way that they both stopped talking when she entered told her they were definitely talking about her. She didn't even care, just wished she could pass them by and let them pick up where they'd left off.

"Hi," Peggy said after Kim shut the door.

"Hi," Kim responded as she laid her keys on the entry table and dropped her purse to the floor. Then she looked at Allen, wishing she could feel the closeness she longed to find again. "I didn't know you were coming over."

"Actually I came to pick you up."

"I don't feel like going out."

"Nothing like that, will you come to my place for a bit?"

"What about the rules?" Kim asked dryly, forgetting for a moment that her mother was there.

"I'm going too," Peggy chimed in.

Kim looked from one to the other, trying to figure out what was going on. "I'm really tired, maybe another day."

Allen stood and came over to her. Taking her hand he looked at her with concern. "Please, just for a little while?"

Kim sighed. She really didn't want to go, but if it would make them feel better... "Okay."

Once they arrived at Allen's they went inside.

"Have you ever seen my basement?" Allen asked.

"No," Kim said with a frustrated sigh. Allen and Peggy headed down the stairs and Kim reluctantly followed. This is so dumb, I wish I could go home, she thought.

At the bottom of the stairs Kim looked around at the concrete walls. Allen had mentioned before that his basement was unfinished. She couldn't imagine how this was supposed to interest her at all. Peggy and Allen walked to the end of the room where there was one finished wall with a door. They opened the door, flipped on the light and Kim followed them in. It was a long, empty room with no windows and cement walls. It looked like some kind of storage room.

"It's very nice, Allen," Kim commented blandly. When she looked back at him he was holding a stack of what looked like dinner plates. Her brow furrowed in confusion.

"These are for you," Allen said.

"Thanks but I have plates," she said slowly.

"Not this kind you don't," he said and handed the stack to her. They were heavy and her arms dropped a little when he placed them in her hands. "These are therapy plates."

"Therapy plates?" Kim repeated. Allen was nuts.

"I'll show you," he said and took one plate off the top of the pile. As Kim and Peggy watched he flung the plate across the room like a Frisbee. It hit the concrete wall and crashed loudly. Kim jumped at the noise and then looked back at the plates in her arms.

"I don't see the point in breaking dishes, Allen."

"Don't worry about it, they cost me twenty-five cents apiece at Deseret Industries."

She attempted to give them back, "Thanks anyway."

Peggy cleared her throat, "Kim, you have to deal with your anger."

"I have dealt with the anger," she said with thick irritation.

"No, you haven't," Allen chimed in. Kim looked at him irritably. "Just humor us, okay?"

Kim sighed heavily as she thought about it for a moment. It was too much, she wasn't ready to delve into this yet and so smiling slightly just let go of the stack of plates. They clattered to the floor at her feet. Some broke, some didn't. Peggy and Allen looked at them, then Peggy left the room. "Can we go now?" Kim asked with frustration.

Allen bent down and picked up the unbroken plates. He met her eyes and held them. "No. Break the plates, Kim. Throw them for all you're worth, let go of some of your anger; release it."

"I told you I'm not angry."

"Sure you are, at the very least you're angry with me right now."

Kim looked away and folded her arms across her chest. He had a point.

"Your husband kills your son and you're not angry?" Allen prodded. Kim's jaw clenched. "He paid a man with your own wedding ring and it doesn't bother you?"

"Anger will get me nowhere," she said looking at him again. "You taught me that."

"That's why you need to let it go," he handed her one plate. She held it for a moment and thought about it some more.

"I don't feel angry, Allen, I feel empty."

"Then make yourself feel angry, Kim."

Kim looked at the plate and let out a sigh. He wouldn't let her out of this. Then she looked at the far wall, the pieces of shattered ceramic on the floor and could then feel the anger slowly trickling in. For days she hadn't felt much of anything but now as she opened up to it just a little, the emotion flooded through and she nearly couldn't contain it. She pictured Robb, in prison, talking to Luke about following her, hunting her down and convincing her to stay married to him. The image was painful and brought tears to her eyes at his betrayal and the consequence of it. Suddenly she felt the weight of the plate in her hand and she flung the plate against the wall. It shattered into shards of porcelain. She jumped at the sound again and watched as a few shards bounced back to land just a few feet in front of her. Allen handed her another plate. She pictured Robb in Evanston, sleeping with the women he told her about in his letter while she stayed up at night hoping he was safe. The second plate hit a little farther up the wall than the first one had. With a third plate in her hand, she pictured Robb as he had looked that day she had gone to the prison. "You're making a big mistake" he had said. She sent the plate flying and it was immediately replaced by a fourth. Peggy came in with another large stack of dishes and set them on the floor next to Allen. Then she slipped out of the room again.

One by one, Kim took each plate and threw it at the wall, each time connecting it to one more infuriating detail of her life thus far. She had wasted so much time on her husband, so many years. She had put her son second and now she had lost him. By the time she was halfway through, there were hot tears streaming down her face and she was connecting words to her actions, almost forgetting Allen was there at all. She was reminded of Jackson laying helpless in that hospital bed and herself being unable to do anything about it. Robb living stagnantly in prison while she worked her tail off just to get by. She was sobbing as the last plate was put into her hands and Allen pulled her into a hug as she nearly lost her balance. He released her after a moment and she looked down at the plate he had given her. It was a cream color with small pink roses around the edges. In the center was a larger rose. It was a beautiful plate except that it had obviously been broken before. There was a large crack running down the center.

For several seconds she stared at it. She turned the plate over in her hand. 'Mikasa' it said on the back; it had once been very nice. But it had been damaged and then someone had taken the time to repair it, would she be so lucky. Still staring at the plate she wiped at her eyes and tried to stop crying. Finally she looked at Allen. "I...I'm keeping this one," she stammered and Allen smiled. His eyes were moist as he put his arms around her. She buried her face in his chest and clutched him tightly. After a few moments she began to calm down and realized that she felt lighter. Some of the pain was receding, and she hadn't even noticed it was there. She could feel it now, but it was clear and not nearly as frightening as it had seemed.

"Is that some therapy they taught you in school?" she finally asked.

"Nah, Janet would get mad sometimes and toss dishes around. I could never figure it out until I suggested that a patient to do it once. I'd tried every way I knew to help him tune into the anger he felt, but nothing had worked. He came back the next week and said he had never felt such release."

Kim smiled despite herself. There was a knock at the door. "Chaperone," Peggy called and they broke apart. Kim wasn't married anymore—the divorce was final—but they all sensed the continuing need to be careful. They drove home and Kim put the plate on the shelf next to Jackson's picture. For a long time she stared at both objects. She touched the glossy finish of the photograph and thought about the dreams Jackson had about the angels. At the time she had assumed they were preparing him; now she realized they'd been for her benefit; not his. 'You'll be my mom forever—no matter what', he had said. No matter what, he was hers. It was time to heal. Glancing at the plate she finally knew and understood that she had to put the pieces of her life back together now. She couldn't wait for her feelings to just go away, she would have to process them one way or another.

A few days later she went to the bank and opened a new account. She had decided that the money she'd received in Jackson's behalf would be kept separate from her own so that she wouldn't spend it. As the medical bills came in she would use the money to pay them off, hoping that after the last bill was paid she would have enough left to be an angel of mercy to someone else someday. Feeling relieved and immensely grateful, she signed the documents and made the deposit. How would she have ever paid the hospital expenses without these generous people? On her way out of the bank, she glanced at the community bulletin board just long enough for something to catch her eye. At first she kept walking, but then hesitated and turned back. "Cozy one-bedroom basement apartment for rent. Need reliable renter that is willing to help with yard." Kim turned to walk away again after giving it a 'that's nice', but was then drawn back to the advertisement. For a moment, she stared at it trying to imagine why it should interest her. Finally, she quickly scribbled down the number before continuing to her car.

The more she thought about it the more excited she became. By the end of the day she was convinced that this was what she needed to do. She dialed the number and made an appointment to walk through it at 6:00. For a moment she thought about calling Allen to come with her, but decided that she didn't need his help. What she needed was a woman's opinion.

Maddie looked up from her desk when Kim knocked quietly on the open door. They had both had difficulty relating to each other throughout the experiences of the last while, but Kim was past holding grudges, and needed her friend. "I've got a favor to ask of you," Kim said as she took a seat.

Maddie seemed a little uncomfortable but tried hard to cover it up. "Oh, yeah. What is it?"

"I've got an appointment to look at an apartment this evening and I wonder if you'll come with me."

"An apartment. What for?"

Had she forgotten to explain that part? "Allen and I decided that we need to take our time before we get married. I had planned to just continue staying with my folks, but ever since I saw this ad, I can't think about anything else. Do you know I have never lived on my own—never—and I'm kind of excited about it."

Maddie still seemed surprised and paused for a moment, but then she smiled. "Sure, I can go. When?"

"Tonight at 6:00."

"I'll just call Matt and let him know."

They arrived for the appointment a little early, but the lady who owned the house and lived upstairs gave them a key and let them take as long as they needed. They spent half an hour looking into every cupboard and corner. The apartment was small, and perfectly square. One half of the area was a room that served as the kitchen, living room and dining room. The other half was divided into two equally-sized rooms. One room was a small bedroom, the other half was the largest bathroom Kim had ever seen in her life. It had a huge Jacuzzi tub and a separate shower. There were two sinks and a large walk-in closet that joined it to the bedroom. It was clean, cozy and quaint: Kim was in love.

When they went back upstairs they learned that the owner was named Grace. She was in her mid-sixties and had two grown sons who lived out of state. Her husband had passed away four years ago and that's when she converted part of the basement into the apartment. She had a group of friends who spent several weeks every year traveling and she needed someone to keep up her flower and vegetable gardens while she was away. Kim seemed perfect for the job—they all thought so. When Grace told Kim that the rent was only three hundred dollars a month, Maddie nearly choked on her gum. Kim said she'd take it and Grace was thrilled to have it filled so soon. It required a six-month lease, which concerned Kim, but Allen's voice echoed in her mind: 'When it's right, I think we'll know it'. Kim felt so good about the decision that she signed the contract. April started in just over a week, but Grace said she could start moving in her things as soon as Tuesday and pay a little rent for March.

Kim went home and told her parents who were supportive but concerned about so many changes so quickly. It had been just over two weeks since Jackson's funeral, but to Kim it seemed a lot longer. She explained the things Allen and she had decided, about rediscovering herself and preparing for a different kind of future and they agreed with him. This apartment was a step toward that goal. Once they understood her reasoning, they agreed the apartment would be a good change for her. Kim evaluated her finances and determined that, although it would be tight, she could make it work. Her monthly health insurance payment had gone down and, thanks to Allen, her attorney fees were paid off.

Allen was also supportive, and he and Matt helped move her larger items in on Wednesday. By the weekend, Kim was firmly implanted in her new home; her storage unit held only the things she didn't have room for here. The garage space she had occupied at her parents' was cleaned out. Several boxes of Robb's things had been ceremoniously dumped into the garbage can and rolled to the street. Everyone had helped move the last of her things in and after they left, she sat on the couch looking at her new home—that's when the loneliness hit.

She was overwhelmed with guilt. It seemed she should have been focused only on mourning Jackson's death, not on starting a whole new life without him. It all seemed too easy, that she shouldn't have been capable of feeling anything but grief. But then she reminded herself that she had mourned Jackson while he was in the hospital for all those weeks. Allen called a little later and reminded her that there would be good days and bad days, and that she had nothing to feel guilty about. 'Men are that they may have joy' and she had every right, even the responsibility, to pursue her own happiness. She tried hard to remember that and even harder to believe it.

# CHAPTER TWENTY-THREE

On Sunday, she went to her new ward, finding it hard to get over her discomfort. Throughout sacrament meeting, she felt very conspicuous sitting by herself, and even though several people introduced themselves and everyone seemed very nice, she felt out of place. Are you married? Divorced. Any children? Uh.... It felt too easy to say 'no' and she went home, overwhelmed with emptiness. Feeling like a big baby, she called Allen and explained how it had gone.

"It will get better, Kim, give it time," Allen said, and the word 'patronizing' floated through her head. For a moment she was silent, then a slow smile spread across her face. This was a new life, right? She was capable of making some of her own decisions.

"Allen, I have agreed to wait for our marriage because you feel it would be better. I'm on my own for the first time ever. I'm doing my very best to get used to this new life of mine, but I don't think I should have to go to church by myself—especially if it makes me even more uncomfortable."

"So, you're saying . . ." Allen trailed off.

"I'm going to your ward," Kim suddenly spit out, although that hadn't been her original design.

"My ward?" he repeated.

She sat up a little straighter, even though he couldn't see her. "Yes, your ward. Since we're going to be married, it makes perfect sense. Do you have a problem with that?"

For a moment he was quiet and then he roared with laughter. Kim waited patiently until he tapered off. "Well?"

"No, I don't have a problem with that," he said with a chuckle.

"Then what's so funny."

"I just wondered why you bothered to ask me in the first place."

Kim smiled, glad he liked her spunk. It was settled.

It was still too cold to plant most things, but Kim talked with Grace to learn exactly what she did want planted once it warmed up. Grace would be leaving on a six-week tour of Europe in May and it would be up to Kim to be sure the garden was planted and well tended. Kim looked forward to the project but wished she had more to do with her time right now. Nearly every evening, she found herself at Allen's, sometimes at her parents' and sometimes at his. She hated being alone and being with Allen helped her a great deal. She loved learning about him and discovering the facets of his personality she hadn't had the chance to see before. Every new discovery just confirmed that he was meant for her in every way.

Every day, Kim also thought about Jackson. She found herself picturing what they would be doing if he were with her and at times her sadness overwhelmed her. Would they have made that trip to Yellowstone they had talked about? Would Jackson have played Tee-ball in the spring? She tried to force her thoughts away from him and that seemed just as hard. Luckily she had to work and as soon as possible she started tending to the gardens and those responsibilities seemed to keep her from slipping into the depression that always seemed to be close at hand.

In addition to their nearly daily visits with one another, every Saturday she and Allen had 'day dates'. Sometimes it was as simple as shopping for groceries together, finding great satisfaction in sharing the mundane routines of life. Other times, they focused on having fun. Kim found it difficult to do the 'fun' outings, and often wished they could just do the normal things again. Life had complicated itself early for her and it had been years since she'd done anything for mere amusement. But Allen wouldn't let her avoid it and despite her excuses he forced her to experience things she found intimidating.

On one such Saturday in early May, Allen announced that the outing was a surprise. Kim hated his surprises. The last surprise had ended them up in Moab where they went four wheeling in a rented jeep. It was warm down south and they had a great time but it was still uncomfortable for Kim to embark on the adventures he planned. She couldn't help feeling guilty for enjoying herself so much.

"So when are you going to tell me what it is?"

"Never," Allen said, amused with himself.

"You're not ever going to tell me what we're doing?" she asked skeptically. He had to tell her sometime.

"You'll figure it out soon enough." Kim had a gnawing feeling in her gut that she wouldn't like this.

Just then, they turned the corner to see a tall, steel scaffolding. Kim's eyes followed it from the concrete pad to the tip-top beam and her stomach dropped. Looking from the monstrosity to Allen she hoped for a sign that this wasn't their adventure. Allen was beaming.

"I am not going bungee jumping!" she said boldly, watching in horror as they got closer and closer.

"Oh, come on. Don't be such a baby," Allen teased.

Kim looked at him as if he had just sprouted hair. "Have you any idea how many people are killed this way?"

"They're the ones jumping from bridges and airplanes. This is a safe way to bungee jump. It's got all kinds of safety features and it's only 75 feet."

"Only!" Kim echoed, craning her neck to see the top. Now that they were parked, it looked even higher. "How in the world can you use the word 'safe' to describe tying a rubber band around your waist and plummeting to the earth?"

Allen laughed and got out of the car. He went to her door, opened it and pulled her out.

"I will not do this, Allen," she repeated. Allen just took her arm and kept walking. "Allen, I mean it."

"I'll buy you one of those T-shirts that say 'I jumped'."

"Roughly translated, means: 'I'm stupid.'"

Allen laughed again; he loved doing this kind of thing to her. "I'll make you a deal. You jump, and next week I'll take you to 'Phantom of the Opera.'"

That got her attention. Salt Lake City didn't get many Broadway shows; Phantom of the Opera had only come twice before. She stared at him as the words sunk in. "It's been sold out for months. Did you buy tickets?"

"Yes, I did," Allen said proudly. "But Maddie's birthday is on Wednesday and if you don't jump I'm going to give them to her."

"You would not!" Kim exclaimed, digging in her heels to bring them to a stop. She would do anything to go; well almost anything. Allen smiled brightly and pulled her into motion again.

"I most certainly would," he said as they took their place in line at the register with only a few people ahead of them. "It's opening night," he added. "Michael Crawford is playing the Phantom and we are in the middle section about eight rows back. Well, you and me or Maddie and Matt. I paid through the nose for these tickets."

Kim couldn't believe he would do this to her. "You'll take me anyway," she said confidently. He knew how much she wanted to go; there was no way he would give the tickets away.

"Dear Maddie," Allen said, looking very thoughtful. "Happy Birthday from your wonderful brother and his chicken-livered girlfriend. You'll have to tell us all about it since it won't be back for at least another four years. Love, Allen and Kim."

Kim closed her eyes and resisted smacking him upside the head. They were at the register, and both the clerk and Allen were waiting for her answer. Throwing her hands up in the air she said "Oh, fine. I'll do it, but don't leave out the 'I'm stupid' T-shirt."

"That's our most popular one," said the clerk as he handed her the shirt. Kim spread it out; 'I jumped' was scrawled across the back. Clenching her eyes shut she berated herself for giving into Allen's manipulative tactics.

"I can't believe I'm doing this," she muttered as they put on the harnesses and made the trek to the top.

"Who's first?" the worker asked when they got to the top.

"He is!" Kim said quickly, gulping when she peered over the edge. But Allen pushed her forward and the two 'helpers' quickly got the cord fastened. "I . . . I changed my mind," she said quickly as they lifted her over the divider that separated the jumping ledge from the main platform. "I'm serious—I can't do this," she whined as tried to struggle free of their grip, but it was no use, they only exchanged knowing smiles. Apparently, they had seen this kind of behavior before.

"Okay, jump on five."

"No, no. I can't," Kim nearly screamed in panic. She looked over her shoulder at Allen, pleading. "I don't care about 'Phantom'," he just smiled and gave her a finger wave.

"One."

"Please, please, don't—"

"Two."

"Allen!" she screamed.

"Three!" And together they pushed her off. What happened to four and five?

Kim screeched as if she'd been shot. Her arms and legs flailed wildly as she screamed the entire way down. The ground came closer and closer and she squeezed her eyes shut waiting for the impact. Stretched out to its full ability the cord recoiled and she bounced back up. The trip back up was as horrifying as the fall down.

"That's the cutest scream we've heard all day!" she heard the announcer boom. Realizing for the first time that there was foam padding covering the section of cord just above her waist she wrapped her arms and legs around it and held on for dear life as she plummeted toward the concrete again. Her eyes were clenched shut and she was still screaming in spurts when she thankfully realized that she was being lowered to the ground. With her feet firmly planted, she took several breaths repeating in her head 'I'm alive, I'm alive'.

She was disconnected from the cord and, in a daze, she began walking away from the torture device until she remembered that Allen would be jumping now. Looking up just in time she shook her head as she watched him dive off the platform as if there were a swimming pool instead of bone-crushing concrete below him. She held her breath until he sprang back up and watched as he attempted to touch a green flag hanging off the ledge—he missed. As opposed to her screaming, he was laughing when he finally returned to the ground and she watched him clap the ground 'helpers' on the back. "What a rush," she heard him say and she rolled her eyes.

When Allen got to her he gave her a big hug. "That was great!"

"That was insane."

"Oh, come on, Kim. You can't tell me you didn't love it."

"I most certainly can tell you that," she said bluntly. Surprised that they were walking towards the counter instead of the car she asked him where they were going. He wasn't going to force her to jump again was he?

"To pick up the tape."

"What tape?" she asked with a sinking stomach. Please don't tell me they made a videotape.

"That will be an additional twenty bucks," the clerk said when they arrived at the counter. Kim was horrified.

"Oh, and this is for you." The clerk said as he handed her a small card.

"What's this?"

"You hit the flag, that means you get a free jump next time." What flag? She thought and then remembered the green strip of cloth Allen had swiped at. Just her luck to win a free jump, why couldn't she win free groceries or a complimentary haircut. Free jump; the very idea!

Allen laughed. "That's great, we'll—"

"Give it to Maddie for her birthday. I'm never doing this again!"

"Maddie will love it."

Despite herself, Kim chuckled as she shakily made her way back to the car. Allen opened the door for her and she went up on her toes to give him a quick kiss then punched him playfully in the stomach. "You're going to pay for this."

"I know, I'm taking you to 'Phantom' next Friday."

Kim shook her head. There were many ways to describe Allen, but boring and predictable were not among the options.

# CHAPTER TWENTY-FOUR

The next Friday, Allen picked her up at 5:00. He had made reservations at The Roof, the restaurant at the top of The Joseph Smith Memorial Building. Maddie had helped her shop for a new dress even though Kim said she had plenty of dresses.

"The dress you wear to church is very different than the dress you wear to opening night at Phantom of the Opera."

They'd spent two evenings searching through stores that carried formal dresses and finally decided on a black, slim fitting, floor length gown. It had short sleeves and black beadwork on the bodice. It was as daring as a garment-fitting dress could be and still looked incredibly elegant. The selling factor, however, was that even though it was in Kim's new size, a ten, it looked like an eight. Kim had never, in her entire life, felt so pretty.

Allen whistled under his breath the first time he saw her and spent more time looking at her than at the stage. Her hair had grown to hang a few inches below her shoulders and Maddie had twisted it up into a loose French twist that set off her facial features to perfection. They had a wonderful dinner and the performance was breathtaking—this was exactly Kim's idea of a good time. Throughout the night, they both felt the heat radiating from one another. Not since that night at the cabin had Kim felt so drawn to Allen this way; she loved it. After the production, he took her home to her apartment and walked her to the door. The May night was warm and the moon cast a blue-white sheen on everything, making it seem perfectly choreographed for a romantic interlude. Kim inhaled the spring air and turned to face her date when they arrived at the doorstep.

"You had better not invite me in tonight," Allen whispered as he lifted her hand to his lips.

The touch of his lips to her hand sent a warm shiver through her arm and down her spine, and she smiled at the sensation, so full of promise. After he released her hand she reached her arms around his neck and kissed him as she hadn't since that night at his home that seemed so long ago. They had exchanged plenty of chaste kisses and long embraces over the last several weeks, but they knew the line was thin and they dared not cross it. Allen responded quickly this time, with a passion that nearly clouded his judgement. It was all he could to do keep his hands around her waist instead of exploring the curves he had been watching all night. The feel of her in his arms, the sensation that this was right for them, stirred his soul in a way he hadn't allowed before. After a few thrilling moments, Kim finally pulled back, her eyes dark with the desire she found impossible to keep completely at bay.

"You're sure you don't want to come in?" she teased in a breathless voice. As opposed to the last time, he knew she'd never let him through the door. The chemistry was too volatile tonight. However, she liked to tease him, "I could slip into something more comfortable, and we could build a fire."

Allen groaned slightly and shook his head, but was afraid to use his voice to answer her; not sure what would come out. Reluctantly he placed one last kiss on her lips and released his grip around her waist.

"I love you, Allen," she whispered as he stepped back from her.

"Oh, Kim. I love you too." Physically, he wanted nothing but to stay and continue where they had left off the time before. Luckily, he had kept his spiritual muscles in shape too and it was them that kept him in control. "How long is your lease again?'

Kim laughed and straightened the lapels of his sports coat. "September first; if I move out earlier I have to pay the entire rent amount anyway—it's in the contract."

Allen quickly calculated the numbers. "That means that for a measly twelve hundred dollars I could drag you to the temple and take you home with me by the end of the month."

Kim thrilled at the excitement in his voice. "Don't forget your reasons for the waiting period."

Allen pulled her back to him, enjoying in the softness of her body pressed against his own. "In my opinion our goal has been reached. You have grown by leaps and bounds these last few weeks. What do you think? Are you ready?"

His mention of the past weeks brought Jackson to mind and she again questioned how she could enjoy herself so much without him. She wondered if she would ever be free from those feelings. But even as he came to her mind, she knew he was happy for her—it caused Jackson no pain to know that she could get on with her life. She silently thanked the powers above for helping her know that. Then she thought about Allen's desire to start a family, and as she concentrated on the idea, she discovered she ached for that as well. To be a mother again, to do a better job this time would be an incredible gift and she longed for it.

"I'm not only ready, I'm worried about waiting much longer."

Allen smiled knowingly; he felt the same way. "Well, we'll just have to see what we can do about that." He leaned down and started another long kiss, but she pulled away abruptly.

"I need to go in," she whispered.

"Yeah, I need you to go in too." But he watched the closed door for another minute before finally forcing himself to walk in the other direction. He had told Kim that when it's right it's right, and that they would know. He didn't think he could handle much more of this, and that was all the knowledge he needed now.

Allen's family was going to Manti the next day for a cousin's wedding and although he asked Kim if she wanted to go, she declined the offer. Having spent so much time preparing for 'Phantom' during the week, she'd neglected the gardens. Grace was returning in a few days and she knew she needed to catch up. There was corn that needed to be planted and flower beds to fill.

When she finally pulled herself out of bed, she was dismayed to realize that all the time she had spent in the dirt the last couple of weeks had taken its toll on the carpet. Remembering that Allen had a carpet cleaner, she called him quickly to see if she could borrow it for the day. He was just on his way out but said he would leave the back door open for her. It didn't take as long as she'd expected to get the planting done, so around noon Kim headed over to Allen's. After loading the machine into the back of her car she decided to surprise him by cleaning his house a little. She did the dishes that were sitting in the sink and mopped the bathroom and kitchen floors while she reviewed the evening before and all its tantalizing emotions. She wondered what his plan was and then looked around the house that had become so familiar to her. How long until she lived here with him? She glanced into the bedroom as she passed by and the responsive tingle made her smile.

After pulling a load of laundry out of the dryer, she began folding it when the phone rang. Allen had a firm opinion that answering machines are from hell, so he didn't own one. When Kim had stayed there before, she always answered the phone because people knew she was staying there. This time, she just let it ring— it rang at least ten times. She was just about to pick it up when it stopped. With a shrug, she went back to her folding and then it rang again. On the eighth ring she picked it up, more out of frustration than anything else. She had a feeling that it would just keep on ringing forever otherwise.

"Hello," Kim said making sure to show her exasperation. Silence. "Hello?" she repeated.

A few moments later a female voice asked, "Is Allen there?"

"I'm afraid he isn't, can I take a message?"

Another long pause. "Do you know when he'll be back?"

Kim couldn't be positive, but it sounded like the woman was crying. Maybe this is a patient, she thought, but realized they would have called his office, not his home. "He's in Manti for the day; I'm afraid he won't be home until late tonight."

"Is this . . . his sister?" asked the woman in a wavering voice.

Who was this woman? "No, the whole family went to a wedding for the day." She nearly added that his sister didn't live here. The woman paused again and then started sobbing. Kim didn't know what to do, so she just waited, hoping the woman would calm down. After a few moments she broke in, "Are you alright?" she asked lamely. "Is there anything I can do?" The woman kept crying and so Kim tried again "Who is this?"

"Janet. I'm Allen's ex-wife," she sputtered before going back to the inconsolable crying.

Aha. "Janet," Kim said out loud, no response. "Janet, what's wrong?" Kim asked weakly, unsure of what else to do or say.

"Who are you?" she sniffled.

"My name is Kim, I'm . . . uh . . . a friend of Allen's. What's wrong?"

"I'm sorry—I just don't know what to do." She kept crying.

"What's wrong?" Kim repeated slowly for the third time.

"I'm having this baby and I don't know what to do; I'm so scared."

Kim straightened. She could feel Janet's anxiety keenly and despite her misgivings she took a deep breath and hoped she could at least calm her down a little. "Janet, where are you?"

"I'm at University Hospital. I called my Mom and she won't come. I didn't know who else to call. I thought maybe Allen would come, just so I'm not alone." It was hard to make it all out between the sobs.

Alarms went off in her head. Allen's ex-wife is having another guy's baby and she wants Allen to be there. When did Janet come to Salt Lake? Did Allen know she was here? A little voice reminded her that Janet needed some help, and Kim could try and figure out the details later. "Janet, is there a nurse there?"

"Yeah," she sputtered, a little confused.

"Let me talk to her." She heard some muffled voices while she asked herself what she was doing and then another woman's voice came on the line.

"This is the nurse."

"Hi, my name is Kim Larksley I'm an acquaintance of Janet's, she hasn't any family and I wonder if you could tell me what's happening."

The nurse hesitated for a moment as if determining whether or not to fill Kim in, apparently she opted to go ahead with it. "Janet was just admitted a little while ago. She went into a clinic this morning with a migraine and it turned out that her blood pressure was extremely high. She has Pregnancy-Induced Hypertension. Just since she got here, her blood pressure has increased and we have put her on Pitocen to induce labor." The next part was almost a whisper. "She has received no prenatal care and doesn't seem to have a clue about what's ahead. The baby isn't due for almost a month and she is having an absolute fit. She is being very difficult. We told her that if her labor doesn't progress quickly enough we could have to do a C-section and she nearly went through the roof. I have tried to get her to have an epidural, but she's afraid of the needle and now that the pitocin is kicking in she's in pain and not doing well. If you're a friend, we could really use your help."

Kim closed her eyes and cursed Allen for not being home, Janet for calling, and herself for answering the phone. She also realized that a year ago she would have apologized and wished them luck, but the new Kim couldn't seem to do that. "I'm about fifteen minutes away; tell her I'll be there as soon as I can." Kim hung up, scribbled a note to Allen, and hurried to the car. She didn't know what she was doing—it was insane—but she remembered her own childbirth experience. No woman should have to bring a baby into the world alone. In school she had taken some classes, and between those and her own experience, Kim felt pretty well educated on the subject of childbirth. Yet beyond all the noble reasons, she couldn't deny that she was curious to meet the woman who had once been married to Allen.

When she entered Janet's room she met the chaos. Janet had her teeth clenched but was screaming anyway. Two nurses were trying to calm her but she acted as if they were trying to inflict even greater pain on her and kept slapping at their hands. When the nurses saw Kim, one of them hurried to update her, the nurse's irritation was obvious. "She isn't even dilated to a three, so she has a long way to go, but every time she has even the slightest discomfort she does this," she motioned to where Janet was trying to push the other nurse away from the bed. "Her contractions are still about ten minutes apart, but let me tell you, when she has one, she lets you know." Kim swallowed and tried to remember why she was here. What had she gotten herself into?

Kim went to the bed and touched Janet's shoulder to get her attention. Janet looked at her with confusion that quickly turned to relief. "You're Kim?" she asked desperately. Any worries of Janet not wanting her there were quickly dissolved. Kim nodded and Janet looked up at her gratefully.

Janet was probably the most beautiful woman Kim had ever seen. Even now, in her most unattractive condition, she was incredibly striking. Kim felt even more plain and dull, in her gardening attire of old jeans and a T-shirt, than she would have normally felt. Janet had long black hair that cascaded over her shoulders ending several inches down her back. She had no makeup on, but she didn't need it. She had a porcelain complexion, her cheeks bright with distress. Her eyes were large and bright blue, framed by long dark lashes. Kim formed a mental picture of Janet and Allen together, then shook away the image.

"Thank you so much for coming; I'm so scared." Her eyes were so full of fear Kim couldn't feel anything more than sympathy and concern—the envy would have to wait.

"I'm glad I can help; now how are you doing?" Kim said calmly, hoping Janet would try to do the same.

"Terrible. Everyone is telling me what to do and I don't understand a thing they're saying." She glared at the nurses who soon took the opportunity to slip out of the room, glad to leave Kim in charge.

"Have you been seeing a doctor?"

"I thought I'd just find one after I moved out here."

Janet was eight months pregnant and thought she would just start going to a doctor now? Kim was amazed that such an intelligent looking woman could be so dumb. "How long have you been in Salt Lake?"

"Only two weeks, but I figured since I'm not supposed to have this baby until sometime in June, I'd have lots of time."

"You really should have been going to a doctor on a regular basis since the beginning," Kim said, but hastened to add, "but that's okay, everything will be fine. I'm just going to explain a few things, okay."

"Okay," Janet said humbly.

"First of all, you have what's called Pregnancy-Induced Hypertension or Toxemia." Janet looked at her blankly, leading Kim to conclude that she really didn't know anything about this stuff. "It means that your body wants this baby out, and soon, so you don't get really sick. Your headaches are a symptom that it's getting worse. The medication they have given you makes you go into labor. As soon as the baby is out, you'll be better. Now, you can have an epidural." Still there was no appearance that she even knew what an epidural was. "The epidural will make it so you don't hurt so bad." Janet's eyes lit up at that tidbit. "But they have to hook it up to your spine." Eyes went dark again. "It's better than doing it on your own; the little prick will save you a lot of pain." Kim had actually delivered Jackson naturally, but since Janet was having a hard time now, Kim felt she really needed the epidural for later. "They're quite safe; women use them all the time."

"And you think it's a good idea?"

"I think it's a great idea."

"Can you stay?" Janet pleaded. The picture she created— desperate, frightened and alone—was in stark contrast to the insensitive career-driven woman she had heard about from Allen.

"If you want me to," Kim said hoping her discomfort didn't show—still she was grateful that she could help. Janet nodded fiercely. Just then Janet had another contraction and started whimpering and kicking her feet on the mattress.

"Janet, try to relax. If you're tense it will be worse. Now try to take deep breaths." Janet apparently had a very low pain threshold and didn't seem to hear a word Kim said. Untucking the sheet from the bottom of the bed, Kim massaged Janet's feet. Peggy had done the same for her when she was having Jackson and for some reason it helped immensely. As soon as the contraction passed and Janet assured her she was all right Kim went to find a nurse in order to request the epidural. She didn't need to go far—they had an anesthesiologist waiting in the hall.

They waited for the next contraction to pass before having Janet curl up on her side. She screamed when they inserted the needle and Kim saw one of the nurses roll her eyes. Janet hadn't made many friends so far. Kim talked her through it and kept her as calm as possible. Once the epidural started taking effect, Janet behaved better. Kim explained what to expect as the labor progressed and Janet thanked her over and over for coming.

Kim had arrived just a little past 3:00. By 5:30 Janet was dilated to a six. Everyone was beyond grateful that things were going so quickly; none of them could take much more. Kim tried to keep Janet calm, massaged her feet and shoulders and taught her how to breathe. But despite her help, Janet seemed constantly on the brink of breaking down completely.

The nurses were worried about reducing the pain too much for fear that she wouldn't be able to push later on. So they kept the dose just high enough to take away the bite of the contractions. For Janet, however, each contraction was still excruciatingly painful. At one point, Kim asked them to please increase the epidural—this was just too much for Janet. "If she had some kind of education and knew the basics of what to do, we would increase it. But her blood pressure is too high to risk her not being able to push when the time comes and the labor is too far progressed to do a Cesarean unless it becomes an absolute necessity."

In between contractions Janet finally asked if Kim was Allen's girlfriend.

"I guess you could say that," Kim said, giving Janet a reassuring but uncomfortable smile.

Janet looked away, but not soon enough that Kim didn't see the disappointment in her eyes. Again Kim wondered what Janet's intent with Allen really was, and her stomach tightened at the thought. In an attempt to distract herself from her thoughts she tried changing the subject.

"I guess you don't know what sex the baby is, do you?"

"They did an ultra-something test and said it's a boy," she said distractedly; her exhaustion was more than obvious. Kim wondered what Janet would have done if her labor had gone on for twenty-four hours as it did for many women. "Do you have kids?"

Her question made Kim freeze for a moment until she consciously forced herself to move again. "Yes, I have a son." Would she ever get used to that question? Would she ever know exactly how to answer it? Getting involved with this birth made it harder, somehow, to deal with his death and she just couldn't bring herself to say the whole truth out loud. She changed the subject again. "So your job transferred you out here?"

But Janet didn't answer; instead she arched her back and let out a deep-throated scream. She'd been screaming now and then all afternoon, but this one was different, and everyone felt the change. The nurse had just come back in and she hurried over to check how things were progressing.

"Whoa. Okay, we're at a nine. Janet, now try to relax." There was little hope for that. "I'm getting the doctor."

Within twenty seconds, the doctor came through the door. He was momentarily stunned by Janet's sobbing and weeping and looked towards the nurse. "I thought you said she had an epidural?"

"She did." Then she leaned towards the doctor and said quietly, "Pretend she's thirteen; it makes better sense if you deal with her that way."

Janet's face suddenly scrunched up and she stopped moaning. "Don't push yet, Janet," Kim told her sternly when she realized the reason for the change. "Listen to the doctor and do what he says, don't push until he tells you to." Janet surprised everyone by nodding her understanding.

Kim took one of Janet's hands and the nurse took the other while the doctor took his position. When the next contraction came, they both screamed themselves when Janet squeezed their hands so tightly Kim was sure she heard something crack.

The doctor guided Janet through the pushing until the contraction subsided. "On the next one, we should be home free. The baby's heart rate looks good so there is nothing to worry about, but don't push until I say so."

Janet nodded blankly and collapsed back on the bed, dazed by the hormone rush of transition. "I'm so thirsty," she whispered and Kim gave her some ice chips that the nurse had brought in earlier. The earlier fire she'd had seemed dead as Janet lay on the pillow whimpering. The next contraction came quickly and although Janet pushed for all she was worth, the baby didn't come.

"If she doesn't get it out during the next contraction, we'll do an episiotomy," the doctor said to the nurse who nodded and turned to get an instrument tray ready. Janet looked at Kim for interpretation.

"That means that if you don't get the baby out this time he's going to have to cut you."

Janet's eyes went wide and the next contraction kicked in. The fire was back now, and she pushed with every ounce of strength she had.

"Okay, we got him," the doctor announced. The nurses started zipping around the room taking care of the baby.

The wave of emotion that Kim felt was almost too much as she remembered when she had been the one in the hospital bed. The memories of the relief she'd felt when her own delivery was over, along with the joy at holding her infant son, were so vivid. She couldn't hold the tears back anymore.

"You did so well, Janet," she said as she frantically wiped her face. "And you have a son." She choked on her own words.

Janet was still holding her hand and gave her another squeeze. "Thank you so much for coming," she said gratefully and dropped back against the pillows.

Kim smiled at her. A nurse got their attention, "He's doing great. He's 5 pounds 8 ounces, 20 inches long. His temperature is a little low so we need to warm him up, but you can hold him for a few minutes."

Janet nodded but looked scared. They helped adjust the baby in her arms and she looked down at him with tears falling from her face. She seemed so uncomfortable and awkward, and Kim was reminded of what Allen told her about Janet's childhood and how difficult it had been for her. He had said that the reason Janet didn't want children is because she was afraid of repeating the same cycle. It worried Kim to think that maybe this was too much for Janet. But after a few minutes, Janet began to relax and inspect all the tiny details of her new son.

Kim watched mother and child for another minute before she finally excused herself. Just down the hall, she found an empty bathroom where she could lock the door. Once she was alone, she sat on the floor, put her hands over her face and sobbed. She missed Jackson so very much. It felt as if her heart were breaking all over again as the memories of his life seemed so real. If only she could have him back with her for only a little while. The need to touch or hold him made her burn with frustration and anger. It was so unfair.

She couldn't help comparing herself to Janet who had never wanted a child, yet she had a beautiful baby that would probably grow up and have a family of his own someday. Whereas all Kim wanted was her son, and he was gone. Since Jackson's death, Kim had several days when it was all she could do to drag herself out of bed. Even though she had been feeling better, this day had been full of tangible reminders of all she'd had, and all she had lost. The ache was as intense as it had ever been and she wanted to scream. She literally burned with envy, while at the same time willed herself to be happy for Janet. Janet was embarking on a demanding but incredible journey and Kim tried to mentally wish her luck, but the gesture soured quickly in her angry heart. All the understanding she had gained seemed to vanish and she felt empty and alone again.

Someone knocked at the door and she told them to go away,

she'd be a while. Then she simply sat there on the floor and wallowed in her loneliness. Part of her wished Allen was there to comfort her and tell her it was okay, but she knew she had cried about this on his shoulder enough times. She felt so weak and faithless to be feeling this way again, and she didn't want him to know how far backward she had slipped.

Several minutes passed before Kim was in control enough to go back to Janet. When she entered the room Janet was asleep and Kim decided to leave her alone. It was nearly 10:00 as Kim stood in front of the nursery window. There were six babies, lined up like dolls. One of the nurses recognized her from the delivery room and asked if she would like to hold the baby. Kim nodded and the nurse led her to a small room with a rocking chair. After a minute, they brought the baby in.

"His temperature is still not constant, but you can hold him for a few minutes."

"Thank you," Kim said as the tiny bundle was placed in her arms. Kim was overwhelmed with feelings of longing and something else she couldn't put words to. Babies are God's greatest gift. Consciously she had to allow herself to enjoy it, and she focused on what a blessing this baby was. She cooed and rocked him as she checked out his fingers and toes. As she did so she felt her bitterness fade and the true power of this just-born spirit warm her heart. He was so tiny, so perfect, with a full head of black hair like his mother and his face still swollen and scrunched up. Every once in a while he'd squeak or whimper and Kim would smile. How long until she could hold her own child this way, she wondered? How much longer could she stand to wait. As she thought about it, her early worries returned and she wondered again whether Allen knew Janet was in town and simply hadn't told her. Why did Janet call him? Was there something she didn't know? The thoughts were like a lead weight in her stomach.

"Now, that's a picture I'd like to see soon."

Kim looked up to see Allen leaning against the doorframe. He walked over and kneeled next to her chair to peek into the bundle of blankets. Kim wiped quickly at her cheeks, embarrassed to be found crying over a baby.

"He's so small," he whispered and looked up at Kim. He had such tenderness in his eyes that for just a moment Kim thought he looked just like a new father. The thought gave her chills and she quickly pushed the mistaken thought out of her mind.

"Only five and half pounds," she whispered.

"I've thrown back fish bigger than that." He chuckled and touched the baby's cheek. At his touch, the baby started whimpering and moved his tiny mouth in the direction of Allen's finger. Allen pulled back.

"He's hungry," she laughed. "I wonder if Janet's going to breast feed?"

"No way." Allen replied with a chuckle.

His quick reply surprised Kim. "How do you know?"

"Well, first of all I just talked to her and she said to go ahead and give him his bottle for her." A wave of disappointment washed over Kim, she didn't like that he went to Janet first; but then what did she expect? "And second, she wouldn't dare damage her new breasts."

"What?"

Allen laughed. "She got implants a couple years ago, she's afraid nursing will ruin them."

"Oh," Kim briefly glanced at her own nearly flat chest and chalked up one more point for Janet. When had she started keeping score? But why was Allen discussing Janet's breasts at all? "Janet's awake then?" Kim said softly, wondering how long Allen had stayed with her.

"Yeah," he answered while glancing up at her, confused by the tone of her voice, "but they gave her some more pain medication and she started drifting off after a few minutes. She thought maybe you had left already, but I figured you'd be here." He leaned up and kissed her cheek. "It was wonderful of you to help her this way. She has no coping methods when it comes to pain or emotion."

"I noticed," Kim said quietly. Her heart felt heavy and although she told herself it was for Jackson, something told her he was only a part of it this time. The wonder that Allen had on his face as he gazed at Janet's son made her chest burn and her eyes tear up.

"And how are you? This couldn't have been easy," Allen said looking up at her with concern.

Kim smiled shyly but didn't meet his eye. "I'm doing okay. I've never been at another person's delivery. It's a lot different from the other side."

"You getting ready for one of your own?" Allen said with a wink.

Kim didn't answer the question, leaving them both to wonder why. "It's getting late," she said as she stood and motioned for Allen to take the chair. He did so, and she carefully placed the baby in his arms. He looked as awkward as Janet had, and that realization made her feel even worse. It only took a moment for Allen to become completely absorbed with the baby. Kim leaned down to give him a quick kiss. "Tell Janet I had to leave."

"Can't you stay a little while longer?"

"I'm exhausted."

Allen nodded his understanding. "I'll call you tomorrow."

"That would be great," she said with a smile, choosing not to point out that they had church at nine, he normally picked her up; suddenly he had forgotten all about it. When she reached the door she looked back but it was almost as if she had never been there. Allen was so focused on the baby in his arms that even after she stopped to watch him for a minute he never looked up. With a heavy heart, she turned quickly and left.

Allen didn't call on Sunday. Kim waited all day long. At 5:00 they were supposed to have dinner at her parents' but when she called his house there was no answer. For a moment, she thought about calling the hospital but decided against it; it felt like an intrusion somehow. Matt and Maddie were at dinner and she tried to act as if nothing were wrong. Maddie knew about Janet's having the baby and so Kim filled in the details of exactly what had happened. When they asked where Allen was, she lied and said he had to take some things up to Janet. Everyone seemed satisfied with the answer except Maddie who gave her a *we'll-talk-about-this-later* look. Kim didn't give her the chance, however, and left as soon as she could without offending her mother. When she got home, the evening dragged until she finally went to bed at ten, taking the cordless phone with her just in case. It took a long time for her to fall asleep as she tried to define the hollow feeling in her stomach.

Monday seemed to drag as slowly as Sunday had and although Kim tried to busy herself with other things, she couldn't stop wondering why Allen hadn't contacted her. Maddie tried to corner her a few times, but Kim definitely didn't want to discuss this with her. That night she had to finish weeding the garden, but she kept the cordless phone with her so that if Allen called she wouldn't miss it. Two long-distance companies tried to recruit her business, but Allen didn't call. Surely she would go crazy if she didn't hear from him soon. As she was trying to fall asleep, she remembered the time after Christmas when he was supposed to call her and he didn't. It had been Janet that time, who had kept him detained and unable to call as he had promised. Now Janet was here, she'd had the baby, and again Allen wasn't calling her. He'd said he had made a firm decision not to return to Janet back then, but she moved to Salt Lake anyway. The baby was here now, and once again Janet had somehow taken priority. Perhaps he hadn't been as sure in his decision as she'd believed.

Tuesday, she decided she couldn't take it anymore. One way or another she had to get this taken care of—hear the words and put it to rest. After work, she stopped by his house, glad that his car was in the driveway. She knocked on the door, took a deep breath, and tried to will away the butterflies in her stomach.

"Hi, Kim."

It took a second to realize it was Janet, not Allen who answered the door. "Oh, hi. I'm just returning Allen's carpet cleaner." She motioned toward it almost as if to prove that she had, indeed, only come to return the machine. Her stomach sank even deeper and she swallowed the slight lump in her throat.

"Well, come on in. Allen's just feeding the baby."

Kim entered the house pulling the cleaner behind her. Allen looked up from holding a bottle to the baby's mouth and was unable to hide the guilty look on his face. "Hi."

"Just bringing this back," she said evenly, feeling the hurt and rage boil inside her as Janet draped herself on the couch next to Allen. Janet looked slim and figure-perfect in a pair of Levi's and a shirt that Kim knew belonged to Allen. Had she not been in the delivery room herself she would have never guessed Janet had just given birth. Looking at the three of them, it was hard to believe that they weren't a happy little family. Kim hurried to the closet without saying a word. Then she hurried out the door before she exploded.

"Kim, wait," she heard Allen say but she didn't stop and slammed the door behind her.

Kim was almost to her car when he grabbed her arm. "Kim, they were released from the hospital today and she had nowhere to go. The place where she was staying doesn't allow children and—"

"She's living here?" Kim nearly shrieked. Even her jealous mind hadn't imagined that.

"Just for a little while. She's got an apartment all set up, but she needs some help for the next month or so."

"And she's going to live here, with you, for a month!"

"Kim, she doesn't have anyone and I've got the extra room; she's having a hard time and—"

"You mean she doesn't have anyone except you," she snapped.

"Kim, please," he begged. "It isn't like that at all."

"So your ex-wife, who was begging you to return to her six months ago isn't living with you?"

"For heavens sake. We are divorced; you are making way too big a deal out of this. If you would just—"

"When I stayed here, you went to your parents' house because it wasn't appropriate for you to be here with me. But now that it's Janet, it's okay? She can't have sex for a few weeks so I guess I don't have any reason for concern until then?"

"I can't believe you just said that to me!" Allen spat angrily. "Janet is my friend—that's it. If you want to make a big deal out of it, go ahead, but it doesn't change the fact that I would have done this for anyone. Janet needs some help with—"

"You didn't do it for me," Kim yelled. "You didn't stay here when I needed help coping and had you stayed here with me I can only imagine what would have happened eventually."

Allen was furious with her accusation. "Kim, will you get it through your head I AM NOT WITH HER. Janet and I are friends— that's all we will ever be."

Suddenly Kim was very calm, but her eyes were full of fury. "Allen, look around you. She's living in your house, you're feeding her baby and she's wearing your clothes. You are very much with her." And with that, she got into her car and sped off, leaving Allen on the driveway.

Kim was feeling too angry to even cry, which surprised her. Lately, she cried so easily. She wished she could hold on to her rage forever. It was so much easier to be angry than to feel hurt. The first thing she did when she got to her place was to take the phone off the hook. Then she went back into the garden and worked as hard as she could until it was too dark to see anymore. Some people say that to have loved and lost is better than to have never loved at all, but Kim didn't agree. She wished she had never met Allen Jackman.

In the morning, the anger started to fade and the pain set in. It was all she could do to get up and go to work. Once again, she avoided Maddie, knowing that sooner or later she would have to face her. In her mind, she reviewed the argument she'd had with Allen and she tried to look at it objectively. That was impossible. Even if Allen weren't in love with Janet, no one could convince her that he wasn't *out* of love either. How many ex-husbands had their ex-wives move in with them? How could she pretend that the brief time she had shared with Allen somehow outweighed the years of marriage to Janet? Add to that this baby and the comparison seemed silly. More than once, she considered calling Allen and talking about it, but she reminded herself that it would just make it worse—he could not justify his behavior. When Jackson's doctors finally said there was no hope, she could have decided to keep him alive on the machinery, but that would only prolong the inevitable. Kim felt she was in a similar situation now.

Her luck at dodging Maddie ran out on Thursday. Maddie cornered her around noon and pestered her until Kim broke down and told her what had happened. Maddie was shocked but didn't say a word. Instead, she looked up at the clock to verify that Allen was not in any session, picked up the phone in Kim's office and punched in the number.

"This is Dr. Jackman."

"You are the stupidest man I have ever known."

"Maddie," Allen said dryly, "I wondered when I would hear from you."

"Will you please tell me what the hell is going on?"

"Since you're calling me, I would assume that you know what is going on."

"That you're living with Janet."

Allen took a breath. "I am not living with Janet the way you are implying, and I can't believe that the two of you would think for a minute that I am. I find it highly offensive that the two of you think I have any designs on her."

"What about the designs she has on you?" Maddie snapped.

That made Allen pause, but only for a moment. "Janet needs some help right now and I don't know what else I can do."

"Put her up in a motel or something; you don't bring your ex-wife into your house. Especially when you are practically engaged." Kim moaned and dropped her head on the desk; why couldn't Maddie use her own office?

"It's not just housing that Janet needs, she—"

"Exactly my point!" Maddie retorted. "She wants a daddy for that baby and you fill the bill perfectly."

Allen was seething. "You can tell Kim that if she wants to discuss this, she and I can discuss it. I will not fight about this with you. You haven't any idea what the truth of this is and I am tired of trying to explain myself since neither of you let me get a word in edgewise." He slammed down the phone.

He couldn't believe everything had blown up like this. If he had just called Kim on Sunday like he'd said he would none of this would have happened. Dropping his head into his hands, he closed his eyes; how did his life get so complicated so fast? Friday night he had spent hours planning how to propose to Kim, now everything had crashed and burned. Thank you, Janet!

Sunday morning Allen had gone to the hospital to deliver some of Janet's things. She'd thrown a fit when the baby wouldn't take his bottle and she actually threw the bottle across the room. Then she had given the baby to Allen and cried for an hour. In the past she'd become intensely angry at certain times but he had never seen her act like this and it frightened him. She had repeated over and over that she couldn't take care of the baby by herself, and Allen believed her. All day Sunday he had stayed at the hospital with Janet, going to the classes the hospital offered to the new parents. Every detail of infant care was an overwhelming task for Janet so he tried to help. It wasn't until eleven o'clock that night that he finally got home and remembered, for the first time, that he hadn't even called Kim. At work the next day, he got a call from Janet's doctor. Janet had spent the day screaming and crying and the hospital staff was concerned about sending the baby home with her. When Allen arrived at the hospital after work, Janet was surprisingly calm, but there was a distinct tension whenever the baby was around. Several times he tried to leave to call Kim, but Janet would cry about being alone, so he would stay. Again, he got home late and promised himself that he would call Kim in the morning. But he never took the time, and when he got back to the hospital Janet's doctor was waiting.

The doctor was adamantly against Janet taking the baby home and had planned a course of action. There was a program for new mothers that lasted a month. The course offered instructions and support for eight hours a day and was designed for women who struggled with caring for their babies; most of the mothers were teenagers. The course educated these new mothers in all the details of taking care of their babies as well as counseling them on issues that affected their own parenting skills. Allen thought it sounded great until the doctor explained that she needed someone with her when she wasn't at class to protect the baby from possible harm.

"You think she's capable of hurting him?"

"Dr. Jackman, I know it's hard to see when the situation is so close to you, but if you consider this objectively I'm sure that you will understand our concerns. Janet has not allowed herself to bond with her child. She is fighting it. Without that bond, and considering her emotional instability right now, I feel it is highly probable that she will strike out against the baby. Without that mother-child bond the baby becomes, in essence, just a screaming, demanding annoyance."

Allen understood the doctor's point and agreed that the course was the best option. He really couldn't picture Janet harming the baby, but on the other hand, he'd never seen her so out of control as she had been the last few days. He really couldn't imagine exactly what she would do once she was on her own.

"We've talked to Janet about this and she is willing to go along with it, but . . ." his pause made Allen very nervous. "The only person she can think of to help her is you."

"Me!"

"She said her Mother is unstable and you are the only other person she knows here."

"We are divorced."

"I know, but the only other option we feel will protect the baby is to put the baby in foster care for the time that they aren't in class. When we mentioned this, she said she would leave with the baby before she would ever let us put him in state care."

"Can she do that?" Allen asked in disbelief.

"Yes. The program is completely voluntary and the law prohibits us from taking any forcible action until something occurs."

Allen slumped back into his chair and groaned. What was he supposed to do? He sensed that Janet was attempting to manipulate him, but he didn't doubt that the doctor's suspicions were valid. Allen felt he had no choice but to help any way that he could.

They had just gotten home on Tuesday when Kim pulled up. Of course, he understood why she was angry, but she didn't give him a chance to explain. Instead, she accused him of having motives that were so far from the truth that, if it hadn't been so offensive, he would have laughed. Yes, Janet was a beautiful woman and he had once been madly in love with her. But even if Kim weren't in the picture Allen would never have considered picking things up with Janet again. He'd made that decision at Christmas time—he was only more sure of that choice now. There was nothing left between them; he had no doubt about that. Especially after the last few days.

Janet was driving him crazy. He constantly reminded himself that she couldn't improve overnight, but he was still ready to throttle her. She never wanted him to leave her alone and so he would drop her off on his way to work and pick her up on his way home. In the evenings, she would get so upset when she had to do anything for the baby that Allen just automatically started taking things over. He realized that he was enabling her, but he was at a loss to know what else to do. At night when the baby woke up, Allen fed him. In fact, Thursday night he had finally moved the bassinet into his room. Janet didn't even blink. She seemed more than content to let him take over. If the sheer lack of sleep weren't enough, not having Kim around and knowing she was hurt and angry made it almost unbearable. Now Maddie had completely ruined his day.

When he picked Janet up from class, things went from bad to worse. She didn't like going to this class with a bunch of teenagers on welfare; she was the oldest person there and she hated it. Allen had to bite his tongue to keep from exploding at her and telling her that it was her own fault she was there in the first place. Instead, he told her it would get better. Then he silently prayed that it *would* get better.

But it didn't get better. Friday was the same as Thursday had been and the weekend was worse than ever. Janet started holding conference calls for her work and spent most of Saturday on the phone, leaving the baby in Allen's capable hands. On Sunday, he refused to go to church with her; he could only imagine what rumors would start circling if he did. Furthermore, Kim might be there. How would he deal with that? Later he almost regretted not having gone because the day seemed to drag on forever.

He had been trying to get hold of Kim for days and he finally gave up trying to contact her. If she refused to let him explain, seeking her out would be pointless. He only wished that that logical determination didn't leave him feeling so awful.

By Monday night, he felt like a rubber band, pulled so tightly that the slightest pressure would surely make him snap. Work had been as harrowing as it was on every Monday, and when he picked Janet up from class she was full of all the vinegar he had come to expect. He said very little, counting the hours until he could sleep again. But by nine o'clock he was at the breaking point when the baby started fussing again. He was just finishing up the dishes and almost went to pick him up but decided to see what Janet would do. It had been a week; it was time for her to face up to her responsibilities. After three minutes of wailing he couldn't stand it any longer.

"Janet, get the baby!"

"Allen," she whined, "I was just about to get in the shower."

"I fed him the last time. It's your turn," he snapped.

"I feed him all day long, the least you can help me out in the evenings." The bathroom door shut behind her.

That did it. Allen threw the sponge in the sink and bellowed at her, "Janet get out here and pick up your son! I'm going to bed."

He felt guilty leaving the baby out there crying, but he stormed into his room anyway, intent on making the baby her problem for once. A few moments later, he heard the shower running. The baby was still screaming. He couldn't believe Janet would do this. Fuming with rage, he put the still-screaming baby in the car seat and packed a diaper bag. After loading the car, he took a minute to maliciously shut off the main water line to the house. With any luck, her hair would be full of shampoo.

He got in the car, not sure where to go. After driving around for about ten minutes, he decided to go to a motel. He pulled up outside a flashing 'vacancy' sign on State Street before realizing he'd left his wallet at home. Groaning in frustration, he pounded his hand on the dashboard; now what would he do? Maddie had told his parents and they had both taken the time to let him know their thoughts—needless to say they were not impressed—and he didn't feel up to trying to convince them again that this was the only thing he could do. What options were left? Next thing he knew, he was outside Kim's apartment.

Kim was in the middle of mopping the kitchen floor when she heard the knock. She wiped her face with the back of her hand, frustrated to leave in the middle of the job. She had never cleaned so much in her life as she had during the last week. The sheer physical effort was all that seemed to temper the churning pain in her stomach. After Allen hung up on Maddie, Kim felt that any crack in the doorway had been slammed shut. Several times she considered calling, but it was he who was wrong and her pride always stopped her. Yet, every minute was full of thoughts and worries about Allen.

Grace had come home the night before, so Kim just assumed it would be her at the door, since they hadn't had a chance to talk yet. Allen was the last person she expected to find on her doorstep. The look on his face showed his frustration and desperation. With the car seat in one hand and the diaper bag under his other arm, he looked very much the Mr. Mom but Kim found no humor in the picture they presented.

"Please don't slam the door on me, I've got to feed the baby and I don't know where else to go."

Kim didn't know how to respond to that, but just then the baby started wailing again. She couldn't just stand there and listen to him scream. "Come on in," she said, surprised by the sheer relief on Allen's face when she stepped aside so he could enter.

Before he said anything, he fixed a bottle; while holding the nipple in his teeth he gently picked up the baby. Cradling the little body in his arm, he stuck the bottle into the wailing mouth. Immediately, the room went quiet except for the sucking noises from the bottle. Allen dropped his head back against the couch, closed his eyes and took a deep breath.

"Thank you for letting me in," he sighed.

"You two have a fight?" Kim said dryly, returning to the kitchen floor.

Allen glared at her, understanding the insinuation. "Actually, yes we did and since I have become the primary caretaker, he came with me."

Kim was surprised by that, but not ready to fall at his feet and ask what he meant by it. "Does 'he' have a name yet?" She was sure that if the sweet little baby weren't there they could have had a great fight. But babies—even Janet's—had a way of neutralizing tension.

"Not officially. But Janet likes the name Joshua."

"Joshua what?" Kim said, finally taking a seat on the chair across from the couch.

"Joshua . . . Allen."

Babies can't neutralize everything. The anger sprang back and she stood up quickly and went back to taking out her anger on the floor. "That figures."

"Hey, it wasn't my idea."

"Of course not, it's never your idea," she snapped.

"You know, Kim, if you would just give me the chance to explain myself you wouldn't be so pig-headed about this."

"Oh, I see," she said and stood up to glare at him. "You're talking about marriage to me one day and four days later you're living with your ex and I'm the pig-headed one. That's good."

"See? You still won't give me a chance to explain."

"I don't think I want to hear the reasons you opened your door to some gorgeous, long legged, sexy woman with big beautiful breasts." It came out sounding very petty and trite, but it was too late to take it back.

Allen stared at her for a moment and then smiled slightly, hoping to turn the tide of the conversation he said, "Actually, I don't think implants look very natural." The humor was lost on her and if looks could kill he'd be pushing up daisies.

"I've heard enough," she said shortly, "Don't let the door hit you on your way out." She went into the bathroom and slammed the door behind her.

Sometimes a sense of humor is a dangerous thing. Joshua was drifting off so Allen pulled the bottle out of his mouth and put him over his shoulder. "Come on, Josh, burp already." Finally the baby let out a long belch that would have made any man proud. "Good job." Allen wrapped him up in the blanket and laid him on the couch. He backed up slowly to make sure Josh was going to sleep before he went directly into Kim's bedroom and entered the bathroom through the closet that connected the two rooms.

"Excuse me!" she yelled, pulling her robe tighter around herself when she saw him.

Oops. Allen hadn't considered what she was doing in there. Glad he hadn't interrupted anything really private, he said, "Sorry. But we need to talk about this."

Kim tied the belt. She was covered in dirt and cleaning products, so she decided she'd take a bath as soon as he left. Luckily, she had put on the robe before starting the bath. "I think I've heard all I can stand. So if you don't mind—"

Allen put down the toilet lid and took a seat. "Well, I'm not leaving until I get a chance to explain myself."

Kim rolled her eyes dramatically. She simply didn't see how having him try to make excuses would make her feel better. The fact that he wanted to talk about it made her even more stubborn. "Fine. Tell your take on it all, and *then* you can leave." As if to show that she didn't expect much new information she planted herself on the edge of the tub and turned on the water. After adjusting the temperature, she poured in some bubble bath.

Allen leaned back on the toilet and folded his arms across his chest, annoyed by her obstinance. "Okay, here's my take," he said belligerently. "Janet is a terrible mother and she is taking an all-day-every-day course that is supposed to teach her how to take care of this baby. Her doctor felt that all the emotional stuff she is dealing with right now puts the baby at risk. But she needs to have someone around when she's with the baby in the evenings and at night. I know I said it before but she doesn't have anywhere else to go. Janet's doctor recommended that I take on the supervision. I did not volunteer, but I couldn't say no. So she is staying with me until we all feel she can take care of the baby by herself."

Kim stared into the rising bubbles and felt sufficiently stupid. She hadn't even considered the possibility of that situation. Relief flooded through her like light streaming in a window, but she didn't give in quite so easily. Still not wanting to take all the blame, she added, "Why didn't you call me last Sunday like you said you would and tell me all of this?"

"I should have called and I'm very sorry. I didn't know all this was going to happen when I went to the hospital Sunday morning. I kept trying to get away, but Janet kept freaking out and before I knew it, it was too late to call. I meant to call you on Monday, but work was crazy all day long, and then Janet was a mess so I ran out of time again. I was going to call you Tuesday, but then you showed up and stormed off."

It would be so nice to just take it all at face value, but she couldn't. Taking a deep breath, she decided to say it now and get it over with. "It seems a little too convenient to me that your drop-dead gorgeous ex-wife has no where to go but your place. She was begging for you to go back to her in December and now you're with her again. And now she has a darling little baby that you have fallen head over heels in love with. It's hard for me to believe this is only the doctor's idea."

"So you think I came up with his?" Allen said defiantly.

"It would be a great way to test out the 'family' situation you could have if you want it."

"I don't know how to explain this any better to you," he said throwing his hands into the air, "I DO NOT LOVE JANET. I love you, and the last thing I want is to drive you away. But I don't know what to do now. As far as the baby goes, yes, I have fallen for the little guy, but no matter how I feel about him, I feel nothing for Janet. Nothing. I am not conducting some clinical trial here. I am simply doing what I feel has to be done."

"How can you feel nothing for her, Allen?" Kim shot back at him. "She was your wife for ten years. If she'd gotten pregnant when you were married, we would not be having this conversation; we would never have met. You would have been the happy daddy you always wanted to be and—"

"Kim, you are so wrong!" he cut in and stood up. He wanted so badly to go over and shake some sense into her. "Don't you get it? She didn't get pregnant then, she still wishes she hadn't. Yes, if we had kids we might still be together. But we didn't. We never will. It's not fair for you to throw the 'but if' at me, because it didn't happen. Furthermore, I'm glad it didn't. Nothing I ever shared with Janet, physically or otherwise, can even compare with what I have shared with you. I look back at the years I spent with her and they seem like wasted time; the same way your years with Robb look to you now. But she is still a good person who needs some help from me right now. I can help her, and because I can I will. She is a part of my past that I can't and won't ignore, but she plays no part in my future."

"Please don't try to tell me you're not still attracted to her, Allen, I can tell you are," Kim returned stubbornly.

"You can't tell anything," he said with frustration. "You have seen us together once when Janet was putting on a little show; that's how she is. When we were married, we would be driving to a party or something and have a ripping fight all the way there. Then as soon as we'd pull up, she'd spring out of the car and hang on to me as if we were newlyweds. Then as soon as we leave she'd start right where we left off. It drove me crazy and she did it in such a way that if I didn't play with her I looked like a jerk. That is exactly what she was doing Tuesday. She had been pouting because I wouldn't go rent a movie, but as soon as someone shows up; she plays the part of the happy little woman. Janet is an attractive woman— one of those women who always will be—but I have grown up a lot since I fell in love with her and I've changed my mind about what beauty is. I would rather have a woman who is pretty, smart, committed, and who wants a family. Janet couldn't come close to offering me all of that, that's why we got a divorce. I don't know how else to tell you that there is nothing between Janet and me."

The relief Kim felt at his words was intense and finally broke down the barriers between them. As opposed to her earlier mood, now she wanted nothing more than to run over and throw herself at him. But she resisted, still held back by her stubborn streak. "You still should have called me on Sunday," she said lamely, and looked back at the bubbles.

"Yes, I should have and I am very sorry I didn't," Allen said sincerely. "But I tried calling you several times after you took off and your line was always busy. I also waited outside your place for almost an hour on Thursday, but you never came home and Josh got fussy so I had to go. After Maddie's little advice session, I decided you apparently didn't want to talk to me anyway."

"I took the phone off the hook Tuesday. And Thursday I went to Enrichment meeting."

Allen nodded his acceptance. "So are we okay now?" he said after giving her a minute to think it all through.

"I still don't like it," Kim said stubbornly.

"YOU don't like it!" Allen repeated. "The woman is making me crazy. She doesn't do a dang thing for her baby and I'm going to lose my mind if I don't get a good night's sleep soon. I got a whole four hours last night; and that's a record." Kim chuckled. "Oh, is that pretty funny?" he said with a laugh, the amused gleam back in his eye.

Kim looked up at him and nodded, a full smile spreading across her face.

"I have gained a whole new respect for motherhood, and believe me you can have it."

Kim looked down, resisting the impulse to dwell on the fact that she *didn't* have it anymore. Allen came and sat next to her on the side of the tub. "Are we okay now?" he whispered, stroking her arm lightly, creating waves of heat with his touch.

"Almost," she said innocently and then pushed him backward into the tub. Bubble bath went flying everywhere as he sputtered and grabbed for her just as she twisted away. But he got hold of the hem of her robe and gave it a good tug in an attempt to pull her in. Had she been facing him, he'd have gotten a full view, but since he was behind her he didn't get the chance. "Allen, you nearly pulled off my robe!" Kim cried as she hurried to gather the robe back around herself. Thank goodness for double knots.

He gave her a wicked grin and wagged his eyebrows. "Cool!" Damn those double knots.

"Allen!" she laughed.

"Why did you do that anyway?" he said as he looked around for some way to get out of the tub without getting his shoes wet.

"Most new mothers think a nice hot bath would be a luxury."

"Oh, well in that case..." he crossed his ankles that were hanging over the side and put his hands behind his head as if he were extremely comfortable.

Kim laughed. "Tell you what. You take off those wet clothes and I'll wash them while you soak it off."

"Really?" Allen said—that sounded kind of nice.

"Sure. Just dump your clothes in the closet and I'll pick them up in a few minutes."

"You're not going to throw them outside or anything are you?"

"You'll just have to wait and see," Kim said coyly, amazed at how quickly she could let her anger go, once it had been faced. "I'm going to get dressed and then I'll throw the robe in here for you to use when you're done. Okay?"

"Sounds great," Allen said and reached out a hand for her to help him out.

"No way," Kim said as she closed the door behind her. "I'm not that dumb."

She shut the door just as he yelled. "You won't know when and you won't know how, but you will pay for this."

It was two in the morning and Allen was lying on the couch throwing popcorn up in the air and trying to catch it in his mouth. Kim was in the chair giving Joshua another bottle. She had washed and dried Allen's clothes and he was just about ready to go back home. They had talked about everything, or so Kim thought. It was still hard for her to dispose of her jealousy and she had to consciously remind herself of all Allen had told her. She hoped that in time she could get over it.

Ironically, it was Allen who wasn't completely satisfied with their truce. "Kim, I've got a question for you," he said, sitting up now that the popcorn was nearly gone. "I'm bothered about something."

"You're bothered?" Kim said raising an eyebrow. What on earth could he be bothered about?

"Why was it so easy for you to just discard everything we had when you found Janet at my place?"

"Well, duh. You had a swimsuit-edition cover model draped across your couch—"

"That's not what I mean. After all we have learned about each other, and after everything we have been through together, it was as if you could just walk away from it all without a fight."

Kim was stumped; she didn't quite understand what he was asking. "As far as I could tell, you had made a choice and prolonging the pain seemed to just make it harder."

"See, that's just it. If Robb suddenly answered the door at your apartment I would do whatever it took to find out what he was doing here."

"I don't understand what you're trying to say," Kim said, thoroughly confused; this wasn't making any sense to her. Robb was in prison, he couldn't come here.

"The way I see it, we both already made the choice to be with each other. We have both had the opportunity to return to our marriages and try to work things out but we chose not to. So when you see Janet, storm off, and refuse to talk to me about it I think that one of two things is going on; number one; that you think what we have isn't as powerful as I think it is or number two; that you don't think I love you as much as I really do."

Kim still didn't understand. "I still don't get it."

Allen took a deep breath; he wasn't explaining this well. "Did you think that you were wrong or I was wrong?"

"Well, you were wrong of course. Janet was living with—"

"No," Allen cut in with frustration. "This has nothing to do with Janet. Did you just suddenly realize that you didn't care enough about me to fight, or did you just think I didn't care enough about you to be truly committed?"

It took Kim a minute to sort it all out. Finally, she realized what he was asking. Before now she hadn't really thought about why she just assumed their future together had been flushed away. She hadn't considered diving any deeper because of what she had seen on the surface. The fact that Janet was there hurt her, and when she found out Janet was staying there she assumed that Allen—at least on a subconscious level—wanted to be with her. That was it. Kim didn't feel up to any kind of competition with Janet and she mentally tried to drop everything they'd had because of the simple fact that she didn't feel able to compete. "So you want to know why I didn't try to prove how I felt about you?"

"Exactly, why could you just walk away?"

"It wasn't because I loved you less than I thought I did, if that's what you're thinking. I just didn't feel that I could measure up."

"So you felt that every time I told you I loved you, I didn't mean it?" Allen asked quietly.

"No, I felt that when Janet suddenly showed up in your life you must have realized how little you really did love me when compared to what you still had with her."

"That bothers me," Allen said bluntly.

"Well, it bothered me too, it was awful to—" But she stopped talking when Allen kneeled down next to her chair and looked up at her. The tenderness she saw in his eyes nearly took her breath away.

"Kim. Just because Robb left you does not mean you can't be loved the way I love you." He paused as the tears sprang into her eyes. "Robb was incapable of appreciating what he had in you. I'm not. I am constantly overwhelmed with how deep my feelings are. I never imagined it would feel like this." Kim was holding the baby and unable to wipe the tears off of her face so Allen lifted a hand and did it for her, bringing his hands to cup her face and tilt it toward his. "When I went to Chicago for Christmas and Janet told me all of this stuff about the baby a friend of mine told me not to walk away without making sure it was the right thing to do. I spent time with her—I even kissed her once or twice." He made a face and Kim tried to look away, but he was holding her face and wouldn't allow it. "And it only made me miss you more, and want you more. I made my decision about Janet years ago and I will not change my mind. I tested it last Christmas and was only reminded of how right my decision was. If it takes me forever, I promise you that some day you will know how very much I love you. If anything like this ever happens again, try to remember that and don't give up so easily." He kissed her softly on the mouth as he stood and gently took Joshua out of her arms. She was too overcome by the emotion to respond to what he had said, and she couldn't get hold of herself to tell him that she loved him more than she could ever express and that she should have fought harder. She had assumed that if he felt badly it was out of guilt, not hurt. But he had well communicated the fact that her dismissal had hurt him a great deal. It had never seemed possible that Allen could love her as much as she loved him. It had been so easy for Robb to let her go, she hadn't believed that it would be any different with Allen.

Allen buckled the sleeping baby into the car seat and slung the diaper bag over his shoulder. "Well, I better get back, we've both got to work tomorrow," he said and kissed her once more on the forehead before he left, pulling the door shut behind him. Kim sat there thinking for several minutes. Why hadn't she confronted him days ago so that they could have solved this then and saved them both all this pain? It was as if a whole facet of understanding had suddenly been illuminated before her and she could see what she had always seen, but in a whole new light. As she pondered on this new knowledge, warmth filled her entire being and she was reminded of not only Allen's love but also the incredible love that her Savior had for her. Life is a gift, and love is a gift; and she had it all. Yet, she'd almost thrown it away. But now, she felt like the best was yet to come.

Allen walked in the door to find Janet waiting for him. She had wrapped a garbage bag around her head telling him that in fact she *did* have her hair full of something when he shut off the water. The scene gave him some minor satisfaction. Janet was probably the only woman in the world who could make a trash bag turban look like a fashion statement, but Allen was beyond caring about that.

"I cannot believe you did that to me!" she growled and her eyes burned with indignation.

"I can't believe you would leave your baby screaming, in order to wash your hair," he retorted.

"You had no right to do that Allen. I have been sitting here, covered in soap, my hair full of conditioner for five hours. FIVE HOURS!"

"It's all about you isn't it, Janet!" Allen yelled back and was taken back in time to the countless arguments they'd had during their marriage. "You don't even ask how your son is. You don't give a damn about me; it's all about Janet. What does Janet want, how has Janet been mistreated. Have you ever, in your life, thought of anyone other than yourself?" he glared at her but she didn't answer. "You are going to have to start. You have a child and if you aren't willing to care for him then you need to give him to someone who will. He needs a mother not a half-hearted caretaker—or he will turn out just like you." Janet's eyes went wide and then narrowed angrily. "You can't pretend any more; this is a child who deserves the best that life can offer him. It's your responsibility to provide that for him one way or another. If you aren't willing to do it then find someone who is."

Janet was stunned, but she finally found words and switched her approach. Dramatically calmer then she had been when he entered, she responded, "But Allen I found you; you'll help me take care of him." She walked towards him but the look in his eyes stopped her cold.

"No, Janet. I will help you learn to do it yourself. But I am not his father and I never will be."

"But, I thought that now we—"

"You thought wrong. Kim and I are getting married." He saw the tears in her eyes, but had to continue speaking. "I told you after Christmas that I wasn't interested in picking up the pieces with you. And as much as I care about Josh, I refuse to spend any more time trying to pretend you're the best I can get. I did it for ten years and I'm past it now."

"But, Allen, this is what you wanted—a family," she was openly crying now.

"There was a time when that was exactly what I wanted, and I wanted it with you. But you didn't want it, and now I have moved on. Since then, I have learned how many things we were missing and in Kim I have found them all. I still care about you, Janet, and I want you to be happy, but I don't love you anymore."

"But I can't do this alone," she sobbed as she fell dramatically to her knees on the floor and covered her face with her hands.

"Then give Josh to someone who can." It hurt him to say that to her because this child, his or not, had claimed a piece of his heart since the first time Allen saw him. But Josh deserved committed parents. And if Janet wouldn't commit, there were thousands of couples who would.

"I won't give up my baby."

"Then put your needs on the back burner like every other

mother and take care of him."

Janet's eyes flashed and even Allen was surprised by the intensity of what she said next. "You can't make me do anything, Allen. I am the one in control here. I can take care of him any way I want; you have no say in it."

"That's where you're wrong," he replied, lowering himself so that his face was only inches away from her own. "I will report you to the state in a heartbeat, Janet. After tonight, I have plenty of reason too. You will stay here and finish this course or you'll contact an adoption lawyer. You choose."

"I'll just take him and leave," she said, but Allen had scared her, he could see it in her eyes.

"I know you will never give up your *career*, and you can't hide him if you keep it. You can threaten me all you want, Janet, but you're at a crossroads here. Shape up or ship him out." Even Allen was stung by those words. He unbuckled Josh and took him into his room, slamming the door with emphasis. There were a million other things he wanted to say, but he couldn't stand to continue the argument any longer. The point had been made, it was up to Janet now. He'd give her one more night to figure it out, but starting tomorrow, things would be different.

The rest of week passed slowly for Allen. Janet barely spoke to him, but he was glad to see that she seemed to be doing much better with Josh. In the evenings, she continued having conference calls for work, but she scheduled them around Josh's feeding schedule. The only time Allen took any responsibility was when she went to a meeting the next Saturday morning. He had to admit that he enjoyed that time he got to spend with Josh, and as grateful as he was that Janet was coming around he had missed his time with the baby immensely. How he ached to have a family of his own.

Kim met him for lunch on Monday, and they spoke on the phone every night. But they had silently agreed that Kim and Janet would avoid each other. Meanwhile, Kim was getting more and more anxious to return to a normal routine. June first was next week and Kim had arranged to take a few extra days off in order to go to Lake Powell with her family. She desperately wanted Allen to go, and it frustrated them both that Janet had put his whole life on hold. As it turned out, Kim went to the lake and he stayed home.

The Saturday after Kim left, Allen's parents had a barbecue. After making sure all his siblings were well aware of the situation, he decided it would be good to join them. Grateful that his family included Janet in the event easily, Allen slipped away in order to get some well-earned peace. It had been Janet, Josh, and work all day everyday, and he was exhausted. He missed Kim so much that it was an actual ache in his stomach; he survived by telling himself it was only another week until Janet left. What a relief it was that he and Kim had been able to get past the initial difficulties. He didn't know how he would have managed without her. He also found it interesting that throughout Jackson's ordeal he had been doing the same thing for her. Now they had switched roles; she was teaching him things he wouldn't have been able to figure out otherwise. It was yet one more growing experience for the two of them.

Janet was making progress but it seemed that the bond he had hoped would develop between her and her son still wasn't there. It had irritated him when they had arrived at his parents and everyone had cooed and clucked about the baby; Janet automatically acted out the role of a merry mother; everything was wonderful, Josh was a great baby, and she was so thrilled. It reminded Allen of the games she had played when they were married and it frustrated him that even though she seemed to be getting better, she still tried to be someone else when there were people around.

Earlier in the week, he had called the supervisor of the course Janet was taking and she had raved about the progress Janet had made. It nagged at Allen, and he had to wonder if she really was up to the challenge of motherhood on a long-term basis. At lunch the day before Kim left for Lake Powell, he had voiced his concerns to her.

"I just don't know what I can do. She seems to be going through the motions, but without really committing herself to the job. I'm afraid it won't last, and where does that leave Josh?" Kim had no advice to give. "I look at Josh and see Janet playing the role half heartedly, and I just can't stand it."

"Maybe Janet has to learn this though. This could be her chance to truly better herself," Kim offered.

"I just hate seeing her learn those lessons at Josh's expense."

And that is exactly how he felt. It seemed unfair that Josh had to suffer because of his mother's selfishness.

# CHAPTER TWENTY-FIVE

Kim came home earlier than the rest of the family from Powell. Jackson's birthday was on that Saturday and she had been dreading it for weeks. That morning she woke up and took a long lonely walk along the rock strewn shoreline, remembering the last time she'd been here. Jackson had chased rabbits and tried to get up on water-skis for the first time. It had been so much fun last summer, but now, being here was too painful. When she reached camp, breakfast was in full swing. No one seemed to remember the significance of the day and although she tried to convince herself that it was okay, it made the whole experience that much more painful. It wasn't that she had wanted to dwell on it or anything, but as the day had been approaching she had been more and more anxious about it and perhaps it wouldn't have been so bad if someone else had remembered—if someone would have understood what it was like to get through his birthday without him. After breakfast was cleaned up she decided to go home. The family protested, but eventually seemed to believe it was not having Jackson that made it so hard to be there. By noon she was on her way home, glad she'd brought her own car. She wondered when they would realize her true reason for leaving. It was so hard to accept that Jackson wasn't a part of her life, this experience seemed to make that very stark reality; no one else even remembered the day they used to celebrate his birth.

Kim awoke early the next morning and lay in bed until her back was so sore that she had to get up. Sacrament meeting was all she could take, keenly aware of her single status as she sat where she and Allen usually sat together, and she slipped out as soon as possible. Eventually she found herself at a park—a park where she had taken Jackson several times last summer. She sat under an elm tree and remembered, with as much detail as possible, every birthday they had shared. At first, she could smile at the memories, even though they only seemed to increase the ache in her heart, but eventually the feelings of anger and self pity oozed through.

It was discouraging that the anger was still coloring her memories of Jack, and she wondered if she would ever be free of the need to blame someone. Her anger towards Robb was still very intense so she tried not to think about him at all. He had been sentenced to 8 to 12 more years for conspiracy to commit murder after Luke admitted that Robb had not given him instructions to take things as far as they had gone. Luke was sentenced to 20 years. At first, Kim had been furious with both sentences. These men had taken away Jackson's entire lifetime, and the quality of hers as well—but in time, she decided to just try and block it out because her own frustration would accomplish nothing. Robb had written to her three times since Jackson's funeral but she had sent each letter back unopened; she had no desire to hear his excuses. There had come a point when she realized that although she would have to forgive him someday, she wasn't ready yet. She was still too angry—her wounds were still too fresh.

The most difficult issue she faced now was her lingering anger toward God. Although she knew it was wrong to be angry, her faith in His omnipotence was so strong that she truly believed He could have prevented the accident—yet He didn't. Kim knew that life is a trial of faith, and she could understand that. But wasn't everything she had gone through with Robb enough? Hadn't she already taken her lumps of adversity by having such a terrible marriage to him? Was it truly necessary for Jackson to be taken from her too? It made no sense to her and she felt as angry about it as she felt guilty for thinking it.

She closed her eyes and leaned her head back against the tree, weeping silent tears and wondering just how many times her heart could be broken. All she wanted was peace—a peace that wouldn't fade in and out. She knew Jackson wasn't coming back; of course she knew that. But couldn't she at least have her memories of him without all the bitterness? She wanted memories of him to be a part of her life, to live within her. However, she'd already noticed that since thoughts of him brought pain she thought of him less. That isn't what Kim wanted. She wanted to remember him with joy and happiness, and think of him everyday that way. Without that joy, she feared he would become an unhappy part of her past—that she would rather forget than remember. It made her heart ache to imagine living her life that way.

Kim spent hours at the park that day, finally returning home in the late afternoon. She had found little solace, and emotionally she felt drained. Allen called her and she was relieved to have an excuse to interrupt her thoughts. But she was irritated that he too had forgotten the significance of this day. They talked about trivialities of the day, church, Josh; the usual. They had run out of topics when Allen finally started probing.

"Why are you so melancholy today?" Kim said nothing, not wanting to seem as if she needed sympathy. "Is it Jackson?"

"Isn't it always Jackson?"

"Sometimes it's Janet," Allen said lightly, but she didn't laugh as he had hoped. "Tell me what's going on."

Kim sighed, "I'm sure you're tired of hearing about this, Allen. Never mind."

"Will you just tell me, please, I've told you before that grief has a way of drifting away until you think it isn't there anymore and suddenly it appears before you and you wonder if it ever left. Things happen that trigger all the pain to come shooting back: a toy; a friend, an event . . ." he paused and Kim knew he had remembered now. "Oh Kim, I'm sorry; I forgot."

"Join the crowd."

Allen pictured her alone all day thinking about the way things should have been and wished that he could be there with her. "Why don't I come over," he offered.

"No thanks. It's okay, Allen. I'm not mad at anyone—especially you; I just can't seem to find the peace I need in order to get through this. But I need to learn how to handle it."

"I'll come over and we'll talk about it."

"And what—bring Janet along? I know you can't just take Josh any more; so don't feel obligated. I'll be okay. I just need the day to pass," she said quietly. It actually surprised her that she truly wanted to be alone. She didn't feel up to supporting anyone else's sorrow but she had to wonder if perhaps she was getting a little better. At least she was facing her loss today, and not running away. "I just wish so much that I could remember him without the hurt. I want to, but it seems to only get worse, the harder I try."

"It's only been three months, Kim, it'll take more time."

"How long? I don't know if I can survive all this pain every time a memory can't be ignored. I want to get on with things and some days I feel like I'm doing better, and then I slam back against the ground and have to start all over again."

They were both silent for an uncomfortable length of time and Kim was just about to start the good-byes when Allen suddenly spoke again. "What are some things Jackson loved; songs, sports, anything."

Kim thought for a minute. "He loved 'Give Said The Little Stream'," and she could actually smile at the memory of singing that song with him every night before he went to sleep. She searched her memory some more. "He loved to watch basketball with his Grandpas. He loved dogs, and I promised him that when he got as big as Matt he could have one. I figured it would be a good long time before he got as big as Matt."

"See? Now, doesn't it help to remember him with the things he loved about life, rather than focusing on the bad parts? Focus on remembering the good things, but not in the sense that you lost it all but rather in the sense that you had so much. Many people never get what you had, Kim, and you have something with Jackson that no one can take away now. You have some incredible promises to cling to; you don't have to worry about him going astray or being hurt by someone he loves. Think about how lucky you are to keep the memory of him in his innocence; unsoiled, free of the pain that this world can so easily inflict." He paused, "Maybe that will help."

Kim was silent, taking it all in. "Yes, I think that will help. Thanks, Allen, I need to go now."

As soon as she hung up she found a notebook and, as fast as she could, she wrote all the memories she had of Jackson. She wrote them almost as if she were giving a speech. She wrote nothing about his death, only the good things about his life. At ten o'clock she finally ran out of memories and she sat back with satisfaction. She couldn't say the bitterness was gone, but there enough joy to ease its bite. Carefully, she put the notebook next to her journal, resolving to focus on those things instead of the negative thoughts. Relieved that the day was over she went to bed, a little lighter than she had been when she had awakened.

Monday morning, Janet informed Allen that she would be moving into her apartment when she graduated on Friday. The week was long and painful for Allen. The relief of finally having Janet out of his life was tempered by the knowledge that Josh would go with her. Janet seemed to almost gloat about it as if to say 'you had your chance'. On Friday, Allen went to the short graduation exercises and left with a knot in his stomach the size of a basketball. He had watched Janet smile and glow as she received all the attention and praise she could have possibly desired; all the time holding Josh close to her. She appeared so different from what he saw at home. He tried to explain his concerns to the supervisor again but she completely blew him off and seemed irritated that Allen wouldn't be more supportive.

Saturday, Allen planned to help move Janet and Josh into the apartment but while he was at his parents' house borrowing boxes, Janet left without him. He returned to an empty house, devoid of any baby-related items. There was no note, no thank-you—just silence announcing that they had truly left. He slumped onto the couch and felt empty himself. After wallowing for nearly an hour, he finally called Kim.

"I'm sorry Allen."

"I just didn't think I'd miss him so much."

Kim's heart went out to him; she knew very well how he felt and also knew that nothing she did could make it easier. She realized that Allen must have felt this same way when he had supported her through Jackson's death; that he must have suffered then too.

"And I just can't shake the feeling that Janet isn't capable of caring for him. I'm so scared that something terrible will happen."

And he was. The fear stayed with him the next week until he got a letter from Janet. She thanked him for all his help and apologized for all the trouble she caused him. Josh was doing well, and she said she'd chosen a wonderful daycare that seemed to take good care of him while she worked. The letter seemed sincere. It calmed his fears considerably. However, although he was relieved, he still didn't feel completely at ease.

Kim had kept her distance the week following Janet's departure, partially due to the fact that Allen spent several evenings at his office catching up on paperwork he had put off during the previous weeks. She could sense how hard this was for him, but didn't ask for more explanation then he offered. On Sunday, she went home with him after church and they went for a walk holding hands, saying little but enjoying the companionship immensely.

Just a few days before, Kim had received a letter from the First Presidency of the Church informing her that her sealing to Robb had been cancelled. She hadn't expected their response so soon, she'd heard it sometimes took a full year for the sealing to be cancelled, but apparently due to Robb's excommunication and the circumstances of their situation there had been a rush put on it. The house had been put up for sale when she moved into her apartment and she'd accepted an offer last week. She was finally free to go on with her life. Kim felt there was a lot they should be talking about but Allen kept to himself and so she didn't push. She knew as well as anyone that sometimes you just needed the silence. When they got home she began rummaging through the fridge.

"What are you looking for?" Allen asked from his seat at the table.

"I don't know yet," Kim said over her shoulder as she pulled open the fridge. "Aha," she exclaimed triumphantly and dropped a package of chicken breasts on the counter. The chicken was soon joined by mushrooms, mozzarella cheese, bottled garlic and butter. Spreading her hands across the items she turned to him and said, "Mushroom Mozzarella Chicken."

"I didn't think you knew how to cook," Allen said. More often than not, they put together sandwiches or ordered pizza.

"I've still got a few tricks you don't know about," she said innocently and continued pilfering the cupboards for pans, dishes and other items she needed.

Allen watched her bustle around his kitchen and smiled when he realized that someday she would truly belong here. But when? The night of the opera had been magical, romantic and full of promise, but Janet had successfully broken the spell. The times he and Kim had spent together during Janet's stay were always in public and somewhat formal, he hadn't had many opportunities to try and recapture the spark they'd had before then. As he watched her prepare dinner he looked back on all they had shared over the past months and was amazed at how much had happened— amazed at how much they had grown. Kim turned on the stove and put some olive oil in a pan to heat while she sliced the mound of mushrooms on a cutting board. She is so beautiful, he thought to himself; so good and the waiting was over. The thought made him smile. The waiting was done; there were no more excuses. Having Janet come back, despite its difficulties, had shown both of them how deep his own commitments were and he pondered, for a moment, if he would have ever really convinced Kim of that otherwise. 'Mysterious ways', he thought to himself.

Meanwhile, Kim was also deep in thought. The pile of whole mushrooms and the pile of sliced mushrooms were almost the same size as Kim continued her slicing, hoping to hide her worry. For a man skilled in getting people to talk, Allen was strangely silent. Perhaps she *should* give him some more space, let him work things out on his own; but the very thought made her stomach tighten. There had been so much space lately she didn't know if she could stand any more. The space hadn't been all bad; she had been forced to face being alone again, in a whole new way; and she could see that she'd grown because of it. Dealing with her jealousy towards Janet hadn't been easy but at some point, Allen's encouragement aside, she had to just trust him. It wasn't easy to do but as she forced herself to do it she realized how truly hurt she had been by Robb's unfaithfulness. His was an exaggerated betrayal, and after learning all the things she had overlooked it seemed to be just a matter of time, but it was still very painful. How easy it would have been for Allen to show the same disregard—but Allen was different. Her heart swelled at the knowledge that he was so very different from her first husband, and she was different too. Would she have been able to discover those differences, to fully trust Allen if Janet hadn't returned? Probably in time she would have learned how steadfast and dedicated he is, but certainly not quickly. She longed to get on with things, to start their life together. But now it was Allen who needed time to heal.

Allen's hands around her waist made her catch her breath and when his lips touched her neck she exhaled slowly and closed her eyes to better savor the moment. It had been so long and she had missed this. His arms wrapped around her, pulling her back against his chest and the warmth of his breath on her neck filled her entire body with fire. He rested his chin on her shoulder and sighed, "I really miss him, Kim."

A lump formed in her throat, "I know you do," she whispered back. They stood that way for a long time, getting used to being so close again until the olive oil started to smoke and Allen released her. He leaned his back against the cupboard and watched as she cooked the mushrooms, browned the chicken and put it all together in a casserole dish. The oven was preheated and she quickly put the dish inside before returning to him. She put her arms around his neck and slowly drew closer. Their foreheads met and then she turned her head and kissed him on the mouth, loving the way her whole body seemed to live the sensation of it. "I won't push you, Allen," she said after pulling away.

He looked at her for a moment and then smiled slightly. "You kiss me like that and then tell me you won't push?"

She laughed lightly and ran her hands over his smooth head. "I won't hold you back either; you told me once I needed time, I won't deny you yours."

Allen regarded her thoughtfully and then leaned forward and kissed her softly. "Thank you." Then he pulled her into a tight embrace. She clung to him tightly but berated herself for being fair. She was so tired of waiting.

The next Thursday morning Kim got up and got ready for work as usual. She and Allen had spent a lot of time together this week and she was meeting him for lunch today as well. She liked the casual normalcy that had returned to their lives since Janet had left but continued to mentally kick herself for giving him time. The physical tension seemed to grow stronger every time they were together—but she reminded herself that she would wait as long as necessary.

While she was fixing her hair in the bathroom she heard a knock at the door. For a moment she paused, wondering who was knocking at 8:00 in the morning. When she opened the door, a single pink rose rested on the doorstep. She looked around for someone but when she didn't see anyone, she smiled, picked it up, and went into the kitchen. It took a moment to find a vase, which she filled with water before putting it in the window above the sink. What is this all about? She wondered with a little thrill of excitement. Allen must have dropped it off on his way to work. How sweet.

There was another knock, but this time she hurried to the door. When she opened it again she was surprised to find another rose lying in the same place—but Allen was no where to be seen. She picked it up and walked outside.

"Allen," she called, expecting him to step out from behind a bush or something, but he didn't. She spent a few minutes looking for him, but he wasn't there. Smiling to herself she decided to let him show himself rather than hunt him out and went back into the kitchen. She left the door to the apartment open and put the rose in the vase. When she returned to shut the door there was another rose and she laughed out loud before looking again.

"Allen, I know you're here," she said, but still the search was fruitless; she even checked the street to find his car but it wasn't there. She returned to her apartment only to find another rose on the doorstep, she bent down, cast another look over her shoulder, and went inside. She left the door open again, just in case. When she turned around from putting the roses in the vase there was yet another rose waiting for her. This time she took the vase of roses with her to pick it up and made a thorough search of the yard. Five minutes later she looked at her watch and hurried back into the apartment. She was going to be late for work if she didn't hurry. When she reached the doorstep a sixth rose was waiting for her. Realizing she couldn't win and having no idea how he was doing it she went into the kitchen added the rose, hurried into the bathroom and checked the front step to find another one. Again she put it in the vase turned and there was number eight. Pick up rose, put in vase, turn, walk to the door, pick up new rose, put in vase. When she turned after the ninth rose the doormat was empty. She shook her head and decided to forgo mascara in exchange for one more turn around the house to make sure he wasn't there. If he were still there, he was determined not to be found and she finally left for work after setting the vase on the kitchen counter, where she'd be sure to see it first thing when she got home that night.

Throughout the morning Kim expected Allen to call her, as he often did between sessions—but she didn't hear from him. At 12:30 she skipped down the stairs and smiled when she saw Allen's Camry waiting for her in the parking lot. After opening the door and sliding into the passenger seat, Kim slid over and sat on his lap, quite a feat in the sedan, and wrapped her arms loosely around his neck. "Thanks for the roses," she said before giving him a long hello-kiss.

"Well, hello to you too." Allen said when she finally pulled back. "If you thank me like that every time I give you roses, get ready to purchase a lot of vases."

Kim laughed and slid back into her seat, glad he fessed up. "So how did you do it?"

"Do what?"

Kim gave him a hello-dummy look. "The roses. How did you get the roses on my porch all morning?"

"Oh, that," he said as if it were something he did everyday. "I'll tell you someday, until then it's my secret."

Kim punched him in the arm playfully. "No, really how did you do it? I looked and looked but you weren't there."

"Once you figure me out I'll be boring, so I'm going to make you wait."

"You're a nerd." Kim said in defeat, arguing would get her nowhere.

Allen smiled. After another minute he said, "Did you know we've known each other for nine months?"

Kim had to chuckle, "Hence nine roses."

Allen looked at her and winked but didn't say a word.

"So where are we going?" she asked a few minutes later.

"The Joseph Smith Memorial Building."

"For lunch?" Kim asked.

"That too."

Kim looked at him strangely. "What's going on?"

Allen turned to her with a surprised look. "Whatever do you mean?" He looked back to the road with a smile on his face and Kim shook her head. Her toes were tingling.

Several minutes later they parked underneath the Joseph Smith Memorial Building. Kim was old enough to remember the huge white structure when it had been the Hotel Utah. The renovation was breathtaking, but she wondered why they were here. Allen took her hand and led her to a set of double doors on the main floor. He opened one and showed her in. She shook her head as she passed him. Just inside the door she stopped and looked around, further confused by the events Allen had likely gone through great expense and work to orchestrate.

In the center of the large reception room was one table covered in a white linen tablecloth and set for two. A slim crystal vase was placed in the center holding a single pink rose, identical to the ones she'd gathered from her doorstep that morning. She turned to look at Allen. "What is this?"

"Why don't you sit down first."

She considered arguing, but resisted. Obviously this was connected to something very important; she didn't feel like defeating that in any way. Allen pulled out her chair and then helped her slide up to the table. Then he sat opposite her. There was a napkin folded in a fan pattern in the center of her place setting. After Allen was seated, he set about unfolding his napkin and she decided to follow suit. When she lifted her napkin her breath caught in her throat. In front of her, under the napkin, lay a small black velvet box. She looked up at Allen and wondered if she were still breathing. Even anticipating this moment, she could never have truly prepared herself.

"There's been something I've been wanting to ask you," Allen suddenly whispered at her side. When had he moved? Kim nodded as she continued to stare at the box she had yet to open, suddenly overcome with the emotional intensity of it. Don't cry, don't cry, don't cry she thought, but the tears had a mind of their own.

Allen moved to face her, and bent down on one knee. Part of her wanted to tell him to stand, but then again, the fairytale quality of his proposal seemed to fit just right. "Kim, I love you more than I could have believed I was capable of, and more than anything I want you to be my wife now and for eternity. Will you marry me?"

Kim lifted a hand to touch his face and for several moments remained lost in his eyes; when she spoke it was soft, but powerful. "When I found out what Robb had done I thought my life was over. I looked at Jackson and decided I would do anything I needed to do to take care of him; but my time for happiness had passed." She looked deeply into his face and attempted to smile through her tears. "I've learned a lot since then." Allen smiled back. "I never expected this . . . happiness, and wholeness and . . . I love you, Allen;

more than words can say."

Allen's eyes were moist. "So you were able to love again?"

It took Kim a moment to remember where those words were from. She remembered the conference, her greatest fear and smiled. "And I am loved, deeper than I ever imagined I could be."

"Now it's my turn," he said and she knew exactly what he meant.

Kim smiled broadly. "I refuse to have your baby until you marry me."

Allen smiled and his whole body tingled. He flipped open the lid to the box he still held and revealed two rings. They were nearly identical. Thick bands of gold—one with a diamond solitaire and one without. Taking out the smaller one, he held it toward her. "I had these made so they match, I hope that's alright."

"I love it," Kim whispered.

"They're gold because gold, of course, it is the most valuable of all metals, but it's also soft and therefore requires the support of another metal to make it strong. I think that's a pretty good representation of you and me." Kim nodded and wiped at her eyes. "They are circles because our love is endless and continuous. The diamond represents 'Forever' and the glorious transformation that trials have on each of us." He put the ring on her finger—it was a little big. "If you look closely you will notice that there is a pattern of oak leaves weaving around the band. The oak tree is a legendary symbol of eternity; it is strong and sturdy and when hardships or droughts come and other trees die, the oak tree remains standing." He looked into Kim's eyes. "Kim, I have no doubt that there will be times ahead when we will face more struggles and hardships. I hope that this will remain a symbol of how much strength we really have and when the tough times come we'll remember that we have already weathered so much."

Kim tried to choke back her tears as she stared at the glittering diamond on her finger. When she looked up, she could see all her own feelings reflected in his eyes with equal intensity. She smiled and leaned forward to seal it all with a kiss.

After a few moments, Kim pulled back and said a little breathlessly, "I don't think we should wait very much longer."

"How long do you need to plan the perfect wedding?"

Kim considered it a minute. "Three days." Allen raised an eyebrow. "The perfect wedding consists of you, me, a temple, a marriage certificate, our families and a heck of a honeymoon."

"I kind of thought you might say that," he said as he stood and walked to the door on one end of the room. He knocked on the door and then returned to their table where he sat down across from her. The door opened and several waiters and waitresses began filing in holding pans of different food items. A plate was set down in front of her and samples of the various treats were placed on her plate. She laughed and wiped at her eyes one last time. "We're sampling foods today," Allen said. "And Maddie's already arranged for you to take the rest of the week off to get ready."

Kim's mouth dropped open, she wondered when he would run out of surprises. "The rest of this week?".

"We have meetings with the bishop and stake president tonight, and a sealing appointment on Saturday—although the only time they had left was 6:40 in the morning."

"You arranged everything?"

"Our moms helped. They arranged for all our siblings to fly in on Friday night and it was only through your dad's connections that we got a sealing time in the Salt Lake Temple at all," he said with a grin. "Are you mad? Cause we can put everything off if you want to do it yourself."

"Did you get me a dress too?" she asked, still reeling from the shock of everything.

"I thought you might be better at that than me, and you can choose the food too—I tried to keep it fair."

"No you didn't," she said as she cut herself a bite of decadent chocolate cheese cake. She looked up and smiled, "You did all the hard parts."

"Are you kidding?" Allen retorted. "You have to go *shopping!*"

Kim laughed and started tasting desserts as the waiters left. Once the two of them were alone again she stood, came to his chair and slid onto his lap for the second time that day. "Wedding plans, engagement rings and cheesecake—you really know how to treat a girl."

Allen smiled and kissed her sweetly. "Give me the chance and I promise to treat you like a Queen."

"You already do," she whispered as she kissed him again. "You always have."

# CHAPTER TWENTY-SIX

Kim didn't want an elaborate dress—just something simple and elegant. However, by Thursday afternoon, after searching three shops, she realized that she didn't have time to be picky. No one could make alterations by Saturday—when she asked she thought the saleswoman would have a stroke. The dress that fit consisted of a snug fitting, short sleeved satin bodice with a large poof skirt. To Kim, it looked like a Nutcracker ballet dress and she made a show of peeking under it to find all the little children. Her mother thought it was perfect and Kim had to admit that it was kind of fun to wear, so she bought it—you only get married once, right? Well, maybe twice—but only once to the right guy.

Family started arriving Friday afternoon as Kim and her mother bustled from one detail to the next. She didn't get to bed till almost midnight and all night long she reviewed what the next day would hold. Sealing at 6:40, wedding breakfast at the Joseph Smith Memorial building at ten, pictures till noon. It seemed so incredible that this was happening this way, and she almost felt guilty that life looked so good to her right now. As it often did, her mind wandered to Jackson and she ached for him to be a part of this. It seemed that by marrying Allen she was leaving him even further behind, and it hurt her to know that he would only be part of her 'before-Allen-and-I-were-married' life. She and Allen would have children who would grow up in a loving home, and Jackson would not be a part of that. Someday, someone would see his picture and ask 'Who is that?' and someone would answer 'Oh that's Kim's son from her first marriage, he died'. Oh how she wished it were different—how she wished that Jackson would share her new life with her. But she also knew that the longing would get her nowhere and she reminded herself that these thoughts would not do anyone any good. She focused again on tomorrow, resolving that she wouldn't let herself ruin the day by feeling sorry about anything. She knew that Jackson was happy for her, and she would honor him by allowing herself to be happy for her too.

# CHAPTER TWENTY-SEVEN

The next morning everything went smoothly and just as they had planned. Kim decided that the reason everything went so well was probably because she and Allen simply didn't care if there were all kinds of mistakes—there was only that one moment that they needed and they knew that nothing would affect them there.

After all their waiting and anticipation, they were finally in the sealing room surrounded by the important people in their lives. Once in the room the sealer reminded them of the sacred nature of marriage and spoke of the eternal commitment they were making. He was aware that this was a second marriage for them both and he instructed them to leave their past marriages behind them and not allow the pain from them to affect their marriage to each other. Kim sat next to Allen, overwhelmed with the experience. She was getting married—again—only this time she had no doubt that her husband understood clearly how serious their commitment was. There was no fear or anxiety about what lay ahead, only excitement and anticipation. They were finally here, together, and when they left the temple they would always be together from this day forward—forever.

They knelt across the altar from each other and watched their infinite reflections in the mirrors behind them. They savored every word and when the actual ceremony was finished, Allen and Kim took their places at the small sofa against the wall. Expecting the sealer to now invite their family and friends to offer their congratulations, they were surprised when he began speaking again.

"I'm sorry," he said, as he seemed to be sorting through his thoughts. "I feel impressed to share something more with you." He looked from Allen to Kim. "There has been something fluttering around in my brain since I met the two of you, and I feel that I need to express these thoughts. In almost all temple ceremonies, there are presences that are felt around the couple. But today, I feel a presence that is nearly as strong and powerful as your own." Kim's breath caught in her throat as she was suddenly aware of a powerful sensation that there was indeed someone here, and it wasn't difficult for her to imagine who it was. Just behind her shoulder she could feel energy radiating like heat waves. "Jackson," she whispered too quietly for anyone but Allen to hear. At the sound of his name on her lips, came the assurance that he was indeed here—how could he miss this occasion. She resisted turning to look for him, because she knew she would be disappointed. But the 'knowing' was as certain as any image could have been.

The sealer continued, "You have both overcome incredible challenges that, in the eyes of many, were adequate reason to deny your faith. You are commended for conquering them so completely that you are here today. There was a time and place before our earthly life that we made the choice to come here and obtain our earthly bodies. At that time, we knew the trials and tribulations that lay ahead, and we all came in confidence that we had what was necessary to not only survive these obstacles but to flourish because of them. The fact that you are both here, together, shows that you have overcome great odds and have proven yourselves worthy of the incredible blessings of eternal marriage; eternal families. You are both to be honored for your faith, and you are to know that your Father in Heaven is very pleased with you. He anxiously awaits the day that he can welcome you home and thank you for the good lives you have lived, the eternal contributions you have made. You are to know that today, in the presence of all your loved ones, mortal and immortal, you have shown your fortitude, your commitment to truth. This day was foreordained to be just as it has been, and you are reminded that in this life, it is not for us to know all things; it is for us to have faith in all things and live our lives to the fullest. A time will come when you will both fully understand why you are together today, and why you were also meant to be apart for so long." He stopped, looking surprised by his own words, as he stared somewhat blankly at the two of them. Finally he gave himself a mental shake and smiled, "I would now like to invite you all to congratulate Mr. and Mrs. Jackman."

Everyone in the room seemed frozen. Allen and Kim, still staring at the sealer, blinked, trying to re-orient themselves to their earthly existence. Kim closed her eyes and took a deep breath. The sensation of Jackson's presence was so strong, so tangible. Everything felt different. The room, the air, even Allen's hand in hers seemed changed somehow and in that instant her mind's eye saw Jackson. Not as the child he had been but as a man. He looked at her with such love and joy that she could barely breathe. At that moment, the bitterness and anger she had struggled with continually, melted away and she held in her heart only the joy she had known with her son. And the joy that lay ahead for them. It had been the supreme desire of her heart to let go of the pain, and finally she could do so. There was no lingering doubt of his happiness or of his purpose here on earth. Yet, at the same time she knew he had an even greater mission apart from her, and she could accept that. She would always miss him—but he would always be a part of her. And now the heaviness was gone.

The feeling was so powerful, so full of joy, she wished she could keep it with her always. At the same time, she knew that to hold onto it would be to lose the deep appreciation she had to have received it at all. The remarkable is no longer remarkable when it becomes constant. As the feeling faded, she didn't fight to keep it, because she knew that by letting go it would always be a part of her. Finally after what seemed to be a long time, but was actually only moments, she opened her eyes and took in all the people surrounding her. She looked at her family, her parents, and then turned to her husband to give him a smile that she hoped would convey what had just happened for her. Maybe it was her imagination, but it seemed to her that he had felt it too—perhaps not all of it, but enough that he could understand. Kim then stood and pulled Allen up with her. He put an arm around her shoulder and gave her a squeeze as their families, after savoring the sacred words and experience, came to offer their congratulations and best wishes.

After pictures and food, they cut the cake and made a mess of each other while trying to give each other a bite. They laughed as if this were the highlight of their day while continually sharing a look that spoke volumes of what lay ahead. After all the laughter and cleanup they said good bye to their guests and Allen led Kim to the front of the building, where a limousine was waiting for them.

"So where are we headed?" Kim asked a minute later, her insides quivering with anticipation as she looked around the elegant interior of the car—she'd never ridden in a limo before. It was real, they were joined for forever. Finally she was living the joy she had always dreamed about.

Allen looked at her briefly his eyes reflecting her own thoughts and lifted an eyebrow. "Does it matter?"

Kim smiled back and leaned to kiss him sweetly on the cheek. The limo turned a corner and was soon pulling into the parking lot of the Red Lion Hotel just a block or so away from the Joseph Smith Memorial building. As the driver pulled up to the front door Allen pulled her onto his lap. Layers of fluffiness from the full skirt of her dress encompassed them like a cloud and they smiled at one another knowingly. "It's the closest Hotel," he said as he lifted his face to kiss her.

"Tomorrow we have reservations at a little place up Logan Canyon." She chuckled and he continued. "I spent a weekend with this woman there awhile back, and I'd love to *fully* enjoy it this time."

Kim kissed him again and then pulled back slightly. "I've got just two things to say," Kim said as she used one finger to undo his bow tie. "First of all I don't care where we go." She pulled the black tie out of his collar and began undoing buttons on his shirt. "And secondly..." She looked into his eyes and he smiled expectantly. "What are we waiting for?"

# EPILOGUE

It was the same place, same date, same room even—but there were many differences. The first difference was that it was now a year past their wedding day. The second difference was that this time Kim was very much pregnant. In fact, she was only two weeks away from her due date. She had tried to convince Allen that reliving their wedding day wasn't necessary and that she had delivered quickly with Jackson and ought to stay at home, but he wouldn't hear of it.

The ultrasound had confirmed that the baby was a girl and they had chosen the name Alexis Kimberly. Lexie couldn't have wished for more excited parents than the two whom she would soon have.

As far as Kim was concerned, she was feeling as unromantic as a woman could feel. Her face was only slightly less swollen than her ankles and she wondered how she would ever make it through the next couple of weeks. Pregnancy in late June is a miserable experience and Kim was very grateful for the air-conditioned room. It seemed she could never feel cool enough. She lay on the bed, greatly relieved that making love was not on the agenda for the night. Allen laid his head on her chest, also swollen in readiness for the baby, and pulled her shirt back to reveal her large round belly. He rubbed her stomach in a circular motion and after a moment Kim rubbed his bald head in much the same way. They both laughed, and when her belly jiggled because of it they both laughed harder.

"If you're not careful, you're going to send me into labor," Kim managed to get out.

"Wouldn't that be funny if our baby were born on our first anniversary," Allen said, still rubbing her tummy. "I wonder if that's ever happened before?"

Kim chuckled. "There are millions of babies born every year, I'm sure some of them are born on their parents' first anniversary. In fact I worked with a lady that…"

Allen lifted his head to look at her, wondering why she had trailed off, when something else got his immediate attention. He hopped off the bed but all he could do was stare at her.

Kim moaned. "My water just broke," she finally said when it

became obvious Allen was completely perplexed.

Allen's eyes went wide and he looked around the room wildly as if looking for something to stop it with. "What should I do?" he squeaked.

"Stand there looking stupid and do nothing," she said in an attempt to calm him down. He just stood there looking stupid and doing nothing. Perhaps humor wasn't such a good idea right now.

"Call 911," she said calmly, "and don't forget to give them the room number."

Kim's calmness heightened Allen's anxiety but he nodded and quickly punched in the number. He barked orders into the phone and hung up quickly before returning to Kim's side. She was already in the middle of a contraction and she clenched his hand tightly before it finally subsided.

"Now what?" Allen said, trying hard to control his panic.

"You'd better pray they get here soon. Jackson was born less than forty minutes after my water broke."

Allen swallowed and tried desperately to remember all the stuff he had learned in the childbirth classes; his mind was blank. Three contractions and eight minutes later, there was a knock at the door. Allen scurried to open it, almost bowing to the paramedics as he let them in. An anxious desk clerk followed them in and then turned quickly away as the paramedic went about checking how close to delivery Kim was.

"Whoa," the paramedic said under his breath, then immediately they went into action. They placed her on the stretcher, secured her and covered her up while taking her vital signs. Allen watched, frantically waiting for someone to tell him what was happening. Whenever Kim had a contraction she would breathe deep and loud, but in between she looked calm and almost asleep.

"So, what's going on?" Allen finally demanded.

"Your wife is dilated to a five, and she is progressing quickly; we're going to transport her to LDS hospital." The paramedic yelled over his shoulder, as they wheeled the stretcher into the hall. Allen ran along with them; scared out of his mind. Once at the ambulance, he was told he would have to follow in his own car so that the paramedic could stay in the back with Kim. He kissed her good-bye and ran for his car as fast as he could. It was the longest drive of his life.

Once at the ambulance bay of the emergency room, white coats swarmed and hurried Kim into a birthing room. Allen left his car out front and only paused when a stern desk clerk promised to have it towed if he didn't find a proper space. Didn't she realize his child was about to be born!? He ran right past her. She yelled at him and picked up the phone threateningly, but he paid no heed. Let them blow up the car for all he cared—his little girl was on her way.

He ran through the doors and rushed to Kim's side to take her hand. She was in the middle of another contraction and surrounded by hospital personnel, but she managed to look up at him and give him a quick grateful smile. The contraction subsided and someone said that on the next one she could push.

"Did you hear that, Kim, you can push on this next one," Allen said as if that were a completely wonderful thing. Kim didn't respond much. She had her eyes closed and was trying to take deep breaths. Allen knew the next contraction was building when she looked up at him rather frantically. What was she so worried about? She'd done this before. Tears filled her eyes and she started shaking her head. A nurse told her sternly to push but she clenched her teeth and groaned. "She's fighting it," someone said and then someone else said to Allen, "She's in transition—get her to focus on you—make her understand she just has to push a few times and it will all be over." Me! Allen thought to himself, why me! He looked around and everyone was watching him, waiting for him to do something.

Allen swallowed and brought his mouth down to her ear. "Kim, it's almost over. All you have to do is push at the next contraction. Lexie's ready for us—she waiting."

Kim kept shaking her head. "I can't," she whined.

"Sure you can," Allen said sweetly but bluntly. "You're a pro; you've done this before. Buck up." He saw a nurse try to hide a smile. Well, what was he supposed to say? Kim kept shaking her head until the next contraction kicked in and a nurse nodded at him. "Come on, Kim, push," he said but she shook her head even harder. "I'll burn the bungee tape, but only if you push Now!" And then she pushed. Her whole face went red and she groaned loudly, reminding Allen once again of why it is wonderful to be a man.

"Slick little bugger," he heard someone say and then the doctor held up a wet, wailing and wiggling baby. Allen's breath caught in his throat. His baby—his daughter—he was a father! Someone handed him a pair of scissors for cutting the cord and he took them in a daze. The doctor held the baby and Allen watched her as he cut the cord. The baby was then whisked to a little bed where the nurses did their thing and Allen returned to Kim's side. She was a mess. Her hair was sweaty and stuck to her face, her cheeks were flushed but she was smiling now and her eyes glowed. He had never seen her so beautiful.

"Did you see her?" she whispered.

Allen nodded and bent to kiss his wife, the mother of his child, and felt sure he would burst with the overwhelming love and joy that churned within him. "She's beautiful."

Kim smiled, "And she's alright?"

"Everything is perfect. You did great."

Kim closed her eyes, dropped her head against the pillow and smiled contentedly. "You are going to burn that tape, right?"

Allen chuckled, "As soon as I get home."

Just then a nurse came over to them holding a wad of blankets. "She is perfectly healthy and doing just fine."

Kim took a deep breath as the baby was placed in her arms. They both looked in awe at the wide liquid eyes that looked up at them. Allen touched the baby's cheek softly, in absolute awe that this little person was a part of him. Lexie looked directly at her mother and blinked, making Allen's heart skip a beat. A living breathing person, created by the two of them. Could anyone doubt the Lord's plan when it delivered such miraculous gifts?

"Allen," Kim said after a minute to get his attention.

"Hmm," he said distractedly, but then he looked at Kim, his eyes so full of love that it made her want to cry.

Tears came to her eyes and she held his rapturous gaze for a moment and then she whispered, "Happy Anniversary."

# ABOUT THE AUTHOR

Josi S. Kilpack was raised in Salt Lake City, the third of nine children. She graduated from Olympus High School and attended Salt Lake Community College. In 1993, she married Lee Kilpack in the Salt Lake Temple and they are the parents of four children; Breanna, Madison, Christopher and Kylee Jo. They currently reside in Willard, Utah.

In addition to being a full-time mom and home maker, Josi participates in her ward, community and her husband's multiple business interests. In addition to writing, Josi also enjoys reading, baking, scrap-booking and traveling.

*Earning Eternity* is her first novel. She is also the author of *Surrounded by Strangers,* published in 2003. Josi enjoys hearing from her readers. She can be reached at:

**kilpack@favorites.com**
or
**PO Box 483**
**Willard, Utah 84340**

9 26575 74736 5